The Ice Lens

Paul West

Onager Editions
Ithaca, New York

Onager Editions
PO Box 849
Ithaca, New York 14851-0849

The Ice Lens
Paul West

Copyright © 2014 by Paul West
ALL RIGHTS RESERVED

First Printing – August 2014
ISBN: 978-1-60047-957-1
Library of Congress Control Number: 2014936685

This book is a work of fiction. Any references to historical events, real people or real locales, names, characters, descriptions, places, and incidents are either the product of the author's imagination or are used fictitiously. Any resemblance to actual events or locales or persons, living or dead, is unintended and entirely coincidental.

No part of this book may be reproduced in any form, by photocopying or any electronic or mechanical means, including information storage or retrieval systems, without permission in writing from the copyright owner, except in the case of brief quotations embodied in critical articles and reviews.

Cover artwork Copyright © 2014 by Paul West

Printed and bound in the United States of America

First Edition

0 1 2 3 4 5 6

About Paul West

He now lives in Ithaca, New York. ("I'm a country boy, born and bred," he says, "I like trees and lawns, animals and huge silence.") West has been the recipient of numerous prizes and awards, including the Aga Khan Prize in 1974, a National Endowment for the Arts Fellowship in 1979 and 1985, the Hazlett Award for Excellence in the Arts in 1981, the Literature Award from the American Academy and Institute of Arts and Letters in 1985, a 1993 Lannan Prize for Fiction, and the Grand-Prix Halpèrine-Kaminsky for the Best Foreign Book in 1993. In 1994, the Graduate Schools of the Northeast gave West their Distinguished Teaching Award. He has also been named a Literary Lion by the New York Public Library and a Chevalier of the Order of Arts and Letters by the French Government. *The Tent of Orange Mist* was runner-up for the 1996 National Book Critics Circle Fiction Prize and the Nobel Prize for Literature. He's working on his fifty-second book.

BOOKS BY PAUL WEST

FICTION

The Invisible Riviera
The Shadow Factory
The Immensity of the Here and Now
Cheops
A Fifth of November
O.K.
The Dry Danube
Life with Swan
Terrestrials
Sporting with Amaryllis
The Tent of Orange Mist
Love's Mansion
The Women of Whitechapel and Jack the Ripper
Lord Byron's Doctor
The Place in Flowers Where Pollen Rests
The Universe, and Other Fictions
Rat Man of Paris
The Very Rich Hours of Count von Stauffenberg
Gala
Colonel Mint
Caliban's Filibuster
Bela Lugosi's White Christmas
I'm Expecting to Live Quite Soon
Alley Jaggers
Tenement of Clay

NONFICTION

The Left Hand is the Dreamer
My Father's War
Tea with Osiris
Oxford Days
Master Class
New Portable People
The Secret Lives of Words
My Mother's Music
A Stroke of Genius
Sheer Fiction-Volumes I, II, III, IV
Portable People
Out of My Depths: A Swimmer in the Universe
Words for a Deaf Daughter
I, Said the Sparrow
The Wine of Absurdity
The Snow Leopard
The Modern Novel
Byron and the Spoiler's Art
James Ensor

The Ice Lens
A Heathen Romance

In 1949 some friends and I came upon a noteworthy news item in *Nature*, a magazine of the Academy of Sciences. It reported in tiny type that in the course of excavations on the Kolyma River a subterranean ice lens had been discovered which was actually a frozen stream—and in it were found frozen specimens of prehistoric fauna some tens of thousands of years old. Whether fish or salamander, these were preserved in so fresh a state, the scientific correspondent reported, that those present immediately broke open the ice encasing the specimens and devoured them *with relish* on the spot.

-Aleksandr Solzhenitsyn, *The Gulag Archipelago*: 1918-1956 [Author's Note]

Cannot we deceive the eyes
Of a few poor household spies?
-Ben Jonson

We Russians do not need to eat; we eat one another and it satisfies us.
-Victim of Ivan the Terrible

Table of Contents

1-3. New York, 1981 1
4. A Romantic in Central Park 14
5. Care Packages to the Gulag 31
6. A Guest 45
7. Nimet 54
8. Krivoshchekovo No. 27 62
9. Bimini 67
10. The Toad of Disgust 81
11. Great To Be Alive 85
12. A Cell in Sukhanokvka 97
13. Contraseptics 101
14. Vridlo 113
15. A Snow Gazelle 116
16. A Wheel 127
17. A Saint of Suet 145
18. Nimet of the Airwaves 149
19. Rat Man of Paris 166
20. The Moscow Stations 176
21. A Big Radar Spider 179
22. Calendars Be Damned 190
23. A New Race of Hermaphroditic Fish 207
24. Vot A Day 211
25. Ere 226
26. Camps Become Colonies 247
27. The Kohlui Box 250
28. Certain Adverbs 269

29. Last Night's Wound	272
30. Smiling's Cousin	293
31. Mutilé de	296
32. Flatlander	315
33. Leiothrix, Omaos, Elepaios	318
34. My Own Chain of Lovely Islands	340
35. The Great Velvet Negative of Sleep	351
36. The Sweetness of Epicurus	368
37. Russia 1982	375
38. Why So Large a Vagina?	380
39. So	384

1-3. New York, 1981

Once you know what you're doing you can start all the way up at the Arctic Circle. I did once. Then, as the season changes, you work your way downriver and, as it gets warmer and warmer, even in that time of year, you keep your nose and head clear by chewing a strong mint. One of those that burn. I always ask my employers for a long scoop with plenty of flex in it so that, when I bend over the pool to scoop up the frogs, I can get the right amount of traction, if that's what it's called. The moment arm is long enough, anyway, between where you apply the force and the place you hold the pole at. Then in one graceful lunge you can fling the frog high into the trees, out of the pool into the greenery. Yes, my beauty, there's an art even to that. I see them now as they soar, catching the sunlight on their backs, and I sometimes hear the birdlike flutter they make as they fall through the branches and the little plop as they land, wondering what the hell happened. They're not tree frogs after all, they know that.

  The trouble is, they keep on coming back. It must be the same frogs. How many frogs can you have in the area of one pool? And it took me a while to figure it out. Then I saw. They weren't coming back for the pale blue water, ever more lucid than I was, which might rank as bubbly in the kingdom of the frogs, but for the flight. They really liked flying, sweetheart, but what bit of them registers anything at all told them it was grand to sail through the air like that, not having to swim or to try. So, all down the Hudson, there have been frogs starting little flying clubs, soaring clubs, until of course winter closes everything down. Not that they have clubhouses or lapel pins. These are frogs after all, with proud and trivial imaginations. It may take them a day to get back to the water, only to be fished out again and launched; but it's worth the long haul after the concussion of landing, then the tussle through long grass or bracken, and the night march up the lawn until, plop, there they all are, ready to be sent into space. The chlorine water can't be that nice, can it? You can tell the old hands from the beginners. The old hands try to get on to the mesh of the scoop before you've landed them whereas the others dive away, not having known the joys of flight. If the word can get around among frogs, it never seems to. Only the old stagers know what's coming, and all the others must think they're pure wacko, heading for the pool only to be thrown out of it. Time and again. I guess their landing gear is good, from long practice. Kind of rubbery anyway: that's what they are. They bounce and they look quite streamlined whereas your toad makes more friction in the air. It is mainly frogs, anyway.

So you see, precious, as I work my way back south from late August on, there's lots of frogs for company, and I sometimes feel like the president of All American Airlines as I go about my chores, getting some of them up to two hundred feet. The wait for the little dry splash of their landing can be really long, and you sometimes wonder if they're coming down at all. I like this better than the movement northward, when I have to leave at the beginning of the season as all the pools open up their hearts and begin to twinkle. Heading *north* with a cold heart is a wild thing to have to do each year. Or it was. I never worked on indoor pools. And outdoor are hardly worth it, only for the frogs, I suppose, although there are certain effects of light, I mean light-effects, I might give an arm and a leg for on a temporary basis. When big lozenges of skyblue float on the bottom as if they were breeding or just jostling one another. When toward evening the water surface looks violet and you could go lick it and get a purple taste. That kind of thing. Maybe that's what the frogs come for first of all, until they get to fly. North or south, it's confusing.

Sometimes I've seen half a dozen of them waiting by the pool wall for me to net them and hurl them skyward. Six in one go? You may well ask. I have never done it, maybe because being a bit simple-minded or at least single-minded, I can attend to only one frog at a time, although a group launch isn't out of the question, honey, if I could only get those already in the scoop to sit still while I catch the rest.

Those frogs amaze me. They wait all night for an airlift the next day. The pool owners amaze me more though. They ask if they can use the skimmer after me, but most of them don't have the knack, the timing, the muscle coordination, that sweep of the pole I have developed over the years like a fisherman casting far out over the waters. Then, of course, you have kids and they want to stand under the trees to catch the frogs when they fall. But how would they do that? A frog will pitter and patter from branch to branch, going this way and that, before it reaches the ground, and you can't tell them apart from the leaves, except when the year is well on its way. If I was going to stay in the job, precious, I'd buy my own skimmer and then I'd always get it right instead of being at the mercy of whatever pool things you find from home to home. When there are no frogs, I move on fast. When there are a lot, I tend to linger, overcleaning the pool, fussing with baskets and the pH.

I go *up*river slowly, but, rejoicing, I come home fast, back to the city, which is always a winter place to me, whereas I associate the river with summer. I open their pools, I find the leaks, I fire the boilers, I trim the filters, I fold up the covers and stow them away, I clean up the ladders and the floats. I hardly have time, in May and September, to write my sweetheart saying I am overcome with work; but you never bug me, do you, you leave me to my job. You are hardly likely to unstick yourself to come and help. That'd be too much, you'd be too much of a honey if you ever did that. I like being alone with the frogs.

Year to year, they have come to know me too, I suppose. Maybe I am disrupting their whole life style, their life cycle, but it was they themselves who first headed for the chlorine, not it for them, like alcoholics who end up skydiving. Maybe they see me as some kind of infernal gondolier, stalking the landscape with my long pole, casting my shadow on the lawns and the glinty azure water, my mind all the time on my precious, my sweet-dreaming aloof one with the severe face at which those around her guess and guess. How many of them would ever know she has her mind set on an odd-job pool cleaner making his way up and down the valley for one third of the year? Rather than write, I *will* my longing to her; it works, I learned how to do it long ago. I think. The thought flies. She receives it. She sends one back. High above the heads of all. I never have to wait for the dilatory rural mailman, not that he could find me. I am never in one place more than a few days at a time. Oh, she has other men, I know, and I never feel at ease phoning. I used to try, but her number was always busy. Around late September time, when only the swimming maniacs are still in their water, in hats and wetsuits, paddling around in a cloud of expensive steam, I feel the urge to go home, to the city, where it is not only warmer than in the valley, but where I have someone whose arms are always open. I set down the skimmer pole for the last time, collect my wages, and rattle home on the old-fashioned train.

Almost a perfect life, sweetheart, or it would be if only certain things didn't chase after me, spoiling my mood. What, I wonder, about the frogs who hop into the pools after I have gone my way southward? What about the frogs who find the pools sealed off after I have gone? The first of these wait and wait until, if they're lucky, one of the owners gives them an amateurish fling up into the trees. They probably fall short, they no doubt don't go high enough. In a word, they have been thrown, not launched. As for the second group, they can fend for themselves in the water on top of the cover until it freezes over, but no one is going to launch them. In that season, eyes are no longer on the pool, its little Siberia, and the skimmer has already vanished into the garage or the outhouse for spiders to build upon and sowbugs to prowl. I wonder how many waiting frogs freeze to death during my months off.

Why should I worry, though? I am not a building, I am not an insurance company. I am not Uncle Sam. I am the Martin Heidegger of pools, who "throws" frogs into the fray, much as he does people.

    Hello, honey. Tuning in again. Thank providence for the music I hear as I move back toward you, piped into my ears through little plugs like acorns: black cup, see-through plastic nut, so to speak. I stalk down the valley with a lengthening stride, maybe even skimping a pool here and there, and having to argue with those who say: "It's still warm weather. We'd like to keep it open a week or two more. Can you come back then?" They are never ready for my grand declaration. It throws them every year. "Sir, my loved one awaits me to the south. Close it now or deal with it yourself." They can never see I've worked up a momentum, a rhythm, loping into their midst and then away from them like a migrating animal aimed at the heart of warmth. They usually, being lazy folk, let me close it for them, but they complain and kvetch the whole time especially if the sun turns hot and the leaves persist in sticking to the boughs. They have no fellow-feeling for their frogs, these folk. Frogs to them are as irrelevant as birds or worms. They don't like them in their pools, so they don't mind the way I seem to punish each individual frog flyer as I sling him, her, up toward the trees. Where there are no trees, I aim for the next door lawn. "Off home to my honey," I tell them, "whom I have not seen these several months." I talk funny, don't I, precious, but that's just my way of being formal with those I have nothing in common with, except money.

Here I come, my precious.

Here he comes.

There he is, at work on the approach, his hands sore from yard work, his shoulders beginning to ache as he closes the last pool and begins to miss the exercise, especially as he boards the train.

I go up fatter, I come home thinner.

I know it's only my umpteenth homecoming along the valley, with the jets high above me following the same track, but I like to think I am crossing Tartary, on one of those old maps they used to have in the proofreading room, propped up against a broken window: down from Bulgar and Cham past the Caspian on my right (Mar de Bachu, once *Mar Caspium*), through Turkestan to the tent of the Great Cham. I don't even know if such names were ever places, dear heart, but I used to see myself curled up on the legend of the map, one hand groping for a green bird perched on one limb of a cross, the other hand holding that of a naked woman with stiff nipples who is riding a chunk of maroon scrollwork without the least discomfort. Those were the days, when you got pornography amid the title.

Anyway, thinking of Tartary and the Caspian of old feels somehow more epic than reciting the real names of the places on my route: Whitehall, Comstock, Fort Ann, Glen Falls, Troy, Rensselaer, Coxsackie, and so on. If they had resonance once, they have none now. After Ossining, White Plains heaves into view like the underside of a disease-stricken spaceship.

I too was once something else. Once upon a time I was somebody else. The punishment is that they age you. They take you away for ten or fifteen years and they age you twenty or thirty. You can be young at heart but next door to being quite worn out. You come all that distance from there to here only to get bitten by beloved family dogs romping around while you fix the pools. What else can you expect if you leave your shins and calves unguarded? I bear the scars of crouching at my trade, most of all from the nearly static moment after the arms have achieved their maximum traverse and the skimmer is way over your shoulder, the frog on his way up. When you are frozen. That's when they come for your ankles and nip you hard to remind you, well, of dogness. What else could they remind me of, my pigeon?

Each year I journey southward, hoping this is going to be the year of years, when I am singled out for something new and unadulterated. I'll know it from a vibration in the reek of the atmosphere and you'll understand, my sweet. You won't ever mind that I am sometimes not quite happy enough with happiness. I want something more, something with more bite to it, like the frogs wanting to fly. Shall this be the year? Will I enter politics or high finance? Is there a low finance it's easier to get into? Or will I be the lucky winner of the lottery, electing not to change my life style one jot, never having needed that much money, but only the presence of it just out of range of my eye? No, dearest, I am not ambitious or greedy, I sometimes want that knife-blade of eminence trailed across my throat, and this is not to be won by plastering my face atop all the taxi cabs in Manhattan. Not that way. The gesture has to come from outside my orbit: something I'll have no knowledge of. Like death, like stroke, like a speeding truck.

You scream, my heart's boon.

I scream back in buoyant baritone.

It's okay. We know it will never happen. I have had an underhand career of sorts, nothing to boast about, nothing to be much ashamed of. I am the battleship rusting in dry dock long after they abolished champagne. There is only love left, God's greatest gift, my pretty. It will have to do.

Between one bridge and the other, in that little stretch between the Hudson and the Harlem Rivers, I see a boat with oarsmen stroking. Aren't they cold? Row hard, I tell them: I have just come from the warming-up room of winter and this year it means business. Its horny thumbnail touched the back of my neck.

Like the La Marqueta outdoor market, your face has not changed, sweetie. The main ravages have not yet begun. All is taut and trim. An afterglow of summer persists as if brownstone has been shone through with dry persistence. The damp has gone. You turn your face away. I clutch at your ear lobe and turn you back to face me in all my suntan, with my red-streaked eyes, my hands wattled with hard labor from some sentence served. I have kept ends together for another season. I offer my wares. I arrange the bills in the rough shape of your body, making avenues and streets of twenties, keeping the fifties for the river. You are unimpressed. I die repeatedly during this. I come back to life. You are unimpressed. You smell of busted beets that have been scorched: your late-summer smell, and it does something to me intimate and sly. I give you my all, my chin to chuck. And here you are, your lips in that dour clamp as always, your chin having a tiny plateau facing forward as if you had scrunched it up a lot with one hand and it never regained its proper contour. Your eyes as ever aim upward as if summoning something ethereal, as if you have a radar that both tracks things and steers them, making them behave from an enormous distance even at night as they overfly the vast barricade of lights. Your eyebrows are too big for your eyes, your sockets are cavernous bolt-holes for a purblind giant. For two. Your nostrils hold their shadowed flare. You do not breathe except when I return: one of your most winning tributes. But now you do, and your exhalation has in it something mellowly sulfuric. This could be the very knife I need across my throat. And out you look, sublimely infatuated, at a country dead and gone, at the real Tartary, beyond an ocean a fit playground for icebergs. This is home. You are supercilioussweet. I am sibilant, groveling a bit, eager to please, to get my welcome kiss from, oh, how many fathoms beneath your big triangular brow, your comb-ploughed fringe, your spiky crown filched from one of those old maps: an image of the sun. Here I am, darling, take me in again, there's thousands wouldn't.

Take me in again, I say, you harsh medieval mistress. Merciless one with the seven-rayed diadem representing the seven seas, the seven continents. Through any one of your twenty-five windows I will jump like a bridegroom into his bedchamber. I could climb home through your yard-wide mouth. "Take me back," I yell. "I've been away too long. I am yours." I used to be someone else's, but that's ancient history. Have me back. Hear me whine and slaver, grovel and plead. I have not come all this way for nothing. I am one of those you are famous for taking in, with a heavy-featured static nod that tells of your self-preoccupation. I have been away too long, dreaming of another long-lost love. Making do with frogs. But the frenzy mounts after a few months. You can tell. You can tell anybody if you want. I no longer hear you, but you uplift me in your arms as if I am welcome home again and still worth showing to the sun.

4. A Romantic in Central Park

After a short trip down to Battery Park to say hello to my lady, I head back for that other more famous park, aiming not for my mother's house across the road from its lower west side but for what I sometimes call Tree Fourteen. When I'm being prosaic, that is. When I'm feeling more fanciful I call it The Great Nebula in Orion. Not that I expect to find much left, and in the dusk of early fall who can tell you what he's looking at? Anyway, precious, I haven't forgotten you, I look up hard into the greenery, feeling for the rope. Now usually when I get back, the rope has gone, the whole thing has vanished, hauled out of the tree in a downward crescendo, and then I have to start again. It's one of the chores of fall. This time, however, the rope is still in place, carefully braided to the trunk with other ropes, yet looser than I left it. I look around me, noting a couple of dogs, one with ague, the other with dropsy, maybe like their owners, and then I give the rope a shake to get it loose after removing the cords that held it. It holds firm. Up I go, towards cloud and yellow leaf, half-wondering if the lady down off Battery Park is telling them to shove it with her upraised arm or, rather better, with all five fingers uplifted, telling them to treat the family.

Now I am coming home, to what is left of it.

Up and up I go, lithe as a panther, knowing that, if I am lucky, my head will soon be near the trapdoor in the green-painted bottom floor. It is. The trap is open. The floor is there, beloved. For once, it seems, they have not smashed it all to bits. I am lucky one year in five, so this far I have been sacked four times. My head ascends. I am like a diver arriving back from a ruptured submarine. And the sigh I have ready vents itself in a cough of pain. Something has just cracked me on the head, not a bough, and not a bird, but something hand-held, a kind of leathery slam.

That does it. I haul myself up and in. No more bangs on the head. I can smell the wood of the floor. On goes my flashlight, sweetheart, and all I can hear is breathing. Maybe the frogs have gathered here to exact a homecoming vengeance. Thousands of them are going to nibble me to death up here high above the traffic and the muggings. It isn't my own breathing, though, not so deep, not so slow. I reach around, near the table, the chair, then toward the window with its butcher's muslin screen, and there it is, in faint dusk outline: a big round face like an Eskimo's wrapped in a woolen cap. It could be a bomb, I decided, but this bomb heaves and breathes. One touch tells me it is made of skin. A she, but not my lady. Not a word. My wheelhouse is more or less intact and I have a squatter on the premises. We are forty feet high and there are two of us, neither speaking to the other, but each sniffing right there in the twilight. I am usually in green, even if only a couple of garbage bags to keep the rain way, but in the dark all colors are the same.

"Who's there?" I say, aware of a tremor in my voice. "You got a name?"

No answer save the wind gently soughing through the rattling leaves. That window lets in a lot of noise; all else is closed off, what with four walls, a roof, and a second floor. Now the flashlight, hooded red like those of pilots and astronomers. Face like pudding, kind of stunned, its expression frozen, mouth open as if to speak, but not a sound comes. I ask again, but the face does not move although, off in the cone of darkness beyond the light, I see an arm or a hand move as if gesturing. "You live here?" it finally says, the face with the red wand touching it.

"Who *are* you?" I say. "And where from?"

"Who you?"

"Well, this year," I say, being sociable, "I am going to call myself White. Never before, never again. But this year yes. What the hell are you doing here?"

"Yours," I hear. It's a statement.

"Oh yes," I tell myself. If it's intact when I return. "How long you been here?"

"Ever since," the voice resumes in its thick, impeded way, "they was going to cut the babies out of me. They put me to sleep just to look at me and they said they was going to cut me open and cut them all loose."

I believe it. They do things like that all the time, just like that Russian interrogator who used to do a scissors kick at the dangling testicles of those under his care. In his galoshes, from the ground, flat on his back. They do it all the time, being men, then they do it again.

"Tree-house," the voice says. "Tree-house made of trees."

"Not always," I say. It sure isn't the police or the Mafia. "You sometimes call them that 'cause they're up in the trees, but you can build them of anything at hand. This happens to be timber, this one. Lumber. Bit by bit. I know folks who swear a treehouse isn't proper unless it's boughs and branches, leaves and bark. I'm not that much of a purist, though. Who're you?"

All I hear is a wasp or a bee, but this is the wrong season. There it goes again, coming from that wide-open face. Is this a creature that eats wasps and bees?

Buzz-buzz, I hear it again and can tell it is coming from that mouth. A helicopter goes over low, blotting out everything, and the big waft of the rotors makes the treehouse tremble. You get used to that, but not to buzzing.

"Who?" I say.

Buzz-buzz.

I listen harder, then ask again, my hand beginning to stray forward to the source of that sound, "Dz" or "tz." I am not dealing with your average intruder. She can climb ropes up trees and swing through trapdoors all right, even manage to survive up here for who knows how long during the good weather. Her hands are cold, her feet are bare, rustling a whole crop of paper wrappers as she moves around. She must have lived on chocolate and other goodies, sprinkling her waste through the trap: a dead giveaway of course. You have to use a plastic bag, then throw it far away during the night, surprising the occasional two-backed beast making it on the grass. I tell her. She doesn't even laugh or argue. She nods in the light of the lamp, and I rummage for one of those fat old candles of my Aunt Tasha's, whom I think of as my mother. Matches I have. I strike. I light. I look. It burns bright as if gaining hope from somewhere and I see this elegant but somehow ruptured face, cheerful but blasted. About sixteen, I guess, and shaking with fright. No, her body is shaking, but what's on her face is a twitch, a convulsion.

"You sure," I say, "made yourself at home while I was gone." No popsicle-sticks, though. Maybe she eats grass as roughage, like Ivan Denisovitch.

"You here long?" I say and she answers, after a hectic pause, "Since I remember. I brought myself. I got thirsty to begin with, till I learned. Once you've learned you're all right. It takes a while. I'm skurd."

I am already tired of this conversation, loved one, when I could be perusing the stars, admiring the lights, the traffic watching the city fidget and twinkle. Instead of a night to myself, one of the cozy ones known as home-coming to treehouse night, I am getting the equivalent of arriving back to find they have pulled the whole thing down and I have to go spend the night with my mother in semi-automated luxury on the Park, yet no nearer a park than a typewriter is to the Tower of Babel. I didn't want company, dear heart, I wanted only me and the funny churr in my head that tells me I'm alive. Unsociable, that's me, apart from frogs and my beloved.

"You got some nerve," I tell her.

Not a sound.

"*Some* nerve," I say.

"What?"

Now I don't want to talk again. By flashlight she looks like a mongol, not a Mongolian, but one of those Down syndrome people. In a treehouse yet, at night, with all her defenses down. Babbling about having something cut out of her. Maybe my mother would like to take her in. No, mother is too busy, she would be afraid of the insurance costs, the medical costs, the aroma of incontinent dog.

"You can stay a while," I say. "It's dark."

We are in a little garden shed I brought here bit by bit and assembled without so much as hammer and nails. I know joints, the dovetail, the mortise and tenon. I saw in my mother's box room. I thong things together with cord dipped in glue. I bore holes and then shove in a glued dowel to hold things tight. In winter, all you need is plenty of padding to keep your body heat in. I always slept in a cylinder lined with newspaper, but she won't have found that, she won't have needed it. She seems to have thrown nothing down.

Now I haul up the rope behind me, coiling it tightly in a corner as I gesture at the world outside through the meshed window. "New York," I say. "Manhattan."

"You got a date down there?"

"Tonight," I say. I sure have, with my honey.

"On the town," she says as if pronouncing the number of a Bach fugue. "On-the-town." The way she says it, the phrase has no human content at all. She learned it in some talking exercise.

"I call it the Orion Nebula when I'm in a hurry," I say. "I name all my treehouses after my favorite stars. I'll never run out of names, I'll never have enough treehouses to go around. Just imagine."

"I like the dark," she says, "my face is all wrong. That's why I like the dark."

"Me too," I say, "and *my* face is all right."

Why she starts to weep I do not know. Maybe some passing jet has jarred her nerves, but it comes over her real fast and passes like a summer shower. She has the one chair, the one cushion, the one hassock. If there were a spittoon aboard she'd have it. Or a Morse tapper. A bullhorn. A xylophone. I do not like having my possessions being taken over in this way. I say so. She does not move or speak, but begins to hum, not a tune or a song, but something more like a transmission to another species, and I half expect them to come swarming up the trunk of the tree, big red balloons of blood wobbling where their mouths should be. When they kiss you, you drown in it. Nothing happens. She gasps, sighs, does a burp, and seems to shiver into some place deep inside herself, in the one chair, et cetera, as if I were not there, as if she were cozy by some fire somewhere. We must be the two best camouflaged people in the world, apart from most of the spies, snipers, and big-game hunters awaiting tigers in their blinds. I hear it now, the jungle, the animals and people howling in the 840-acre wilderness below, and I am the skipper of an airship again, ready to cast off, crew of two. Oh, the humanity!

I had been looking forward to a good night's sleep, at my mother's or in the treehouse if they had let it be. The easy thing, my angel, would be to leave the squatter to it; she knows how, this not being her first night up here, and

The Ice Lens

I can tell with my flashlight how she's done it in the warm nights of summer. There are sacks on the floor, an old comforter, a couple of plastic bags blown up for pillows. She hasn't done that badly for someone, you can tell, who wasn't cut out for treehouse living in the first place. I ask her all kinds of questions, but she is through with answering for the night. I let her settle down to sleep, then I take my place in the chair, my transistor radio gently playing WQXR into my earphones. She has to go tomorrow, honey. I'll tell her early so she can get a good start. I wonder if I should drop her off at my mother's place, but can see it's not such a good idea. Here we are, we two, cut off, severed from the human race, while my Aunt Tasha over there, not far from here, in her four-bedroom apartment, lives on connected to the planet by pipes, tubes, drains, manholes, conduits and wires. If I can't budge this funny person out, I'll have to leave her be and go build myself my sixth in some other part of the park, whereas this is one of my best ones, maybe my favorite, like the first and a couple of others. Who she really is, I have no idea. Her movements are quick and bouncy, but there is something wrong with them, something not quite coordinated, sweetheart, my delicate one, my peppermint gazelle. Unlike yourself, this twitchy one seems to blunder about, but never quite blunders, leaving the ghost of a blunder in the air around her, as if she just managed to collect herself in time.

The wind has quit, the park has emptied of its routine users, the lights of Park South are on in all their glory. Time past, I've had friends up in my treehouse with me, playing bongo drums and making those below us nervous enough to think a new breed of arboreal savages had taken roost. Then I've had to hush my friends, telling them not to capsize my little craft which really is a star. Having her up here is different, though, asleep, awake. She's one of the uninvited, and, although she seems to have managed well during the time she's been up here, she can't have learned the whole thing. It takes years, treehouse savior faire. Lights more than anything give you away as well as raw-cut wood, which you have to paint green or brown as soon as done.

I find the hibachi, a bit damp-feeling and encrusted with soft-feeling sticky stuff, but the charcoal I have brought with me lights first time. I make the toast, I set the little non-whistling kettle on the embers and prepare my cup of tea. Taken at this height, food has something ambrosial about it. You need less of it because up here it's more mysterious, more impossible. Tomorrow I'll begin to stock up with canned goods, batteries, bulbs, the usual. I read my mail by rosy flashlight and make a note to get in touch with some friends down in the Village. We have things to do. I join them for their early winter frolic, eager after all those months involved with the righteous and their antiseptic water to do something public again. My thoughts wander to my uninvited visitor, who has fallen into a steady quivering snore, undeterred by my resentful acceptance. I still feel like one of those astronauts who go outside the spaceship to fix something and have a long umbilical to keep them from floating away. I have no umbilical, my precious, I have the sense, though, of almost floating off into space, of being beyond the main zone of attraction. My neighbor snores even louder, clogged as if she has a cold, and I notice that she's spurned or just not noticed the torpedo-tube-like cylinder stuffed with newspaper I designed as a bunk. If you slide in there, with several wads of the best insulation in the world around you, you get through most nights if you manage to keep your head inside the contours. The bedcap helps, stuffed with newspaper as well; it is, in fact, three balaclava helmets stuffed together with two linings of newspaper. Only your face gets cold, but not if you pull the helmet all the way down, which is when you wake with tiny thready icicles on your nose and mouth from your breath.

Now I know who she really is, she who has come from afar, my honeybunch, to win us over. She must be the chubby-faced Anna Skripnikova whom they sent from a warm climate to a much colder one, the Solovetsky Islands, in a summer dress and a straw hat, the first part of her punishment for not being the woman she was supposed to be having been that unholy shivering all the way from Moscow to the White Sea. It was to those monasteries that they sent misbehaving priests in the Middle Ages. She had no permission to get her winter clothes and no one had permission to get them for her; her room had been sealed up. So off she went on the transport, denied even a sheepskin coat until she got there and, in part, became the beginning of the woman they wanted her to be. Why? Because she was there, like those monks of old in their rough habits. Nowadays, I suppose the good old bad old train still awaits its prisoners at five in the evening at Moscow North on odd-numbered days. I see long trains of red cattle cars or baggage cars into which in a flash they bundle you like flax or dead beef. You never see that station and it never sees you. Maybe she is one of those, waiting to be shoved into place. At least she's not wearing a summer hat and a straw dress. No, the other way around. She must have done something or she wouldn't be on the run. They have funny ideas about what you ought to be. They think they can put it right and they try brutally hard. I look around the floor for what she might have had on the journey: half a herring or Sea of Azov anchovies coated with rough salt, both best kept rolled up in your handkerchief if you still have one. If

The Ice Lens

they give you dried carp they dump it on the floor. As often as not the only water you get is from the locomotive itself, with oil floating on it and making it a dusky yellow. Those with syphilis drink last, please. Then those with T.B. Let the healthy ones begin. She must have drunk after the healthy ones, but before those with T.B.

My broodings must have awakened her. She cries out, something indeterminate, but I leave her be, I do not want her to think she is being attacked. I do, however, remove a "liberated" red and blue airline blanket from my rucksack and lay it over her gently as a dew. She quietens and must have been restless from the chill. Now she is on the way back from those frigid islands to Moscow, that land-locked paradise.

Are you there, my sweet?

Are you waiting for me to arrive? Bless you, my miracle, I am home again.

How much of me is left? Hard to know if the travelling I do in my mind wears out my feet.

If you can, get yourself arrested in the winter. It is easier to take clothes off that you have on than to put on clothes you do not have and will not get.

Best to travel alone or the thieves they bundle you in with will help themselves to all you have: your coat, your bag, the roubles sewn into the lining.

My lover, you forgive me when I slither back from what I'm in to what I came from, either the infamous factory at Taishet where they creosote railroad ties and the vapor streams through your skin and bones and rots your lungs—I cannot remember the alternative. It must have been so awful I have blocked it out, or I was never there at all. When was it, beloved, I did as they all said you must? I wanted to let you know where I was and was going. I gave away my piece of carp for a stub of pencil, I found some paper (an old label snagged on a tiny stanchion spike), and I made sure my feet were not facing the corridor of the train. Then I began, writing the few words, then folding the paper into something like a triangle and carried it to the toilet, there flushing it down to freedom as we were coming into a station. So, beloved, a love letter comes to you soiled and sodden, retrieved from the embankment slope, that glacis. Snowed on for months, but found, stuck in an envelope with a clean address, and sent on to you postage due. I imagine the day it arrived and you almost tossed it aside, it looked so unworthy of human reception, and all you could think of was how Max Reger, having had a bad review, wrote to the newspaper that published it: Sir, I am sitting in the smallest room in my house. Your review is before me. It will soon be behind me.

It's behind *me*, ah what a place. Things that belong there keep on swooping back over me, blotting out the North American sun, my beloved's face, and all I can think about for hours on end is that shit-soiled billet-doux, no more than a rough whereabouts enclosed in an address, tossed through a drain on to the landscape. Just so long as the guards didn't see you doing it, the writing or the flushing, and yell at you: *Get a move on there, don't you dare touch that, get about your business. Come on. Come on.* Once a one-legged man got stuck in it and they refused to let us use it for two days because of the time wasted on getting him loose. It was later on that I saw them cut the straps that held some other poor devil's artificial limb to his shank, so we had to help him along while he carried his leg. It is those days, fifteen times 365 plus some, that keep on coming back like a stench and making me wonder at the species homo sapiens that spends so much of its time proving how savage it can be. Not out of anger or pique, but as if to make an artifact of horror. The thinkable is doable, so do it. Anything unthinkable is thinkable, isn't it? If so, it's doable. Every nation needs its whipping boys. It's as simple as that: somebody destined to eat from the bowl he voids in, and vice versa. That sums it up for the last five thousand years or so, my dearest, expert at unfolding and drying out and construing the most faded scribble, as if it were the Domesday Book, Magna Carta, or the Bill of Rights. Clack the train wheels go and with each breath I am several yards farther from you, my sweet, en route for fifteen years of starch.

With what delicate aversion you research the paper that has come your way, perhaps only six months later. You eye it lovingly and murmur *He has the runs again.* You can see it. Or: *They have stopped him up.* What with carp and oil and salted anchovies, my long lost dearest one, whom I long ago transformed into that lady who waits down by the Battery, I was no more loose than I was clogged. I had no need of a bowel at all. They tutor you in that, in the end coaxing you to some grand plateau of heedlessness where you admit that you would be better off without a mind. Well, they say, if you have half a mind to lose yours, we have some excellent devices in this little room. We have an acid bath and we'll develop you like a photographic plate. Or we'll put you in an airtight cork-lined cell and cook you until your brain boils, like Nikolai Klyuyev the peasant poet and Berta Gandal. You choose. We'll oblige. But get this, you dirty-mouthed adulterer. We are obliged by law *to do something to you.* We can't just let you sail along scot-free. You do appreciate that, don't you. You see the problem. We might not even let you sleep, we want your full attention.

Yes, my lovely, they talked like that, and they were not interviewing me in a suite at the Plaza or the Hotel Algonquin where the novelist

Faulkner once scalded his back when a pipe burst. Oh to be Faulkner, scalded there in such a place. Or even to be an American and assassinated. Any American fate would have been better, dearest, and it is in the main your memory and the frogs that save me.

5. Care Packages to the Gulag

Since my release, not that long before the collapse of the regime, messages have come to Aunt Tasha, explaining how my sweetheart is and what punishments are being meted out to her. After all, for adultery with an agency spy, the penalty would have to be severe, she the wife of a commissar. How come we did not manage to cheat those household spies? Cold soup again. Deprived of sleep. Brutally searched several times a day by pussy-hungry guards. But otherwise she is all right. She survives, and I have earmarked for her on Forty-Second Street a little job as receptionist in a tattoo parlor, ideal for a woman of her paralyzing education. Will she get asylum? Of course, after all she has put up with, not to mention things they might dream up in future as the rift with the commissar gets ever wider.

In the old days, medieval, some duke trapped two lovers in separate towers a mile apart, and they howled for each other daylong. Emily and Arcite, if I remember well. *We* howl at each other across the oceanic wastes in between. But one day soon... long after they have finished filling her mouth with marbles. Half the time, Aunt Tasha does not know whether to give me the news or not, and sometimes says she had a phone call from the Soviet Embassy saying she was all right, which meant no

The Ice Lens

better than usual. In English slang this is known as giving someone "what for."

Again and again I rehearse the pattern of it: getting away with it for close on six months, then noticing signs of being watched, followed one gloomy Thursday by two barred vans and a small force of soldiery catching us in flagrante in the classy dacha where beetles roamed free and the upstairs rooms stank of greens cooked months ago. We took our pleasure with constant sudden smacks at whatever crawled on our naked limbs while we held our breath. The room of the centipedes, we called it.

Was *he* there on that occasion? No, outside in his heavy-built Soviet car. He did not want to see, but he saw us brought out in handcuffs and bathrobes. They could have shot us right away, defenseless winter sophisticates, asked to follow a guard who without warning would about-face and shoot us in the head, or following another guard to a moldy little shower room where he told us not to look behind. Such tricks of the trade. *He* could be seen, I was later told, raging in his car, while his hands gently manipulated a slide rule, no doubt planning our sentences. No one to back us up, not even my own people. "You've dipped it," I heard, "now suck on it." Had the Salvation Army been on the scene, we might have enjoyed more succor, or the Alaskan Libido Club, or the Ninety-Nines who have coupled at high, preferably anoxic altitude. After the Gulag, coming home to the States was like going to Harvard from the zoo. And she, she will just weep for a year to have a bottle of scent and a lipstick again.

As if in a postwar situation, I wander the supermarkets, those increasingly enigmatic bazaars in which the price no longer appears on anything, and amass cans of fruit, asparagus, ham and chicken within the prison grilles of my squeaky cart. I add to these and ship off to her the food and some little Russian-to-English phrasebooks, ever in hope that she will actually receive any such care parcel rather than having the contents rammed into her body cavities on the strength of an Extra Degradation order from our old friend the commissar. Potentates coming to an end of their regime go either soft or savage. Indeed, when all the other slimes are taking it easy in hopes of reprieve, a man like "our" commissar will go to unusual extremes. When, if ever, she arrives, she will be in poor shape, ready for the best hospitals, no special agent being welcomed back, but a mere *Dúshenka* who will have to take pot luck and ever after say her thankyous for asylum. Monthly I send the packages, with never a word in reply, indeed with never a word in all this time. I am forbidden to go over, and what could I do if I went?

"Forget her," some say who know.

I'd rather shoot myself, I tell them.

The Ice Lens

"You should have done that years ago." They wear their hearts on their sleeves, these old agents.

How do those parcels go? To where the milk is brought home in slabs, not frozen home in pail as in those jovial poems of the Elizabethan era. Through the zone of radiation. Through countless blizzards on swaying, chilly trains. Then by lend-lease truck, its tarps frozen stiff as linoleum. All of a sudden I cannot connect spasmodic utterances with verbs. My brain stammers. The Siberian cold has paralyzed my vagus nerve. The guards in fur hats and light-colored greatcoats take over, opening the parcels by a roaring fire, jerking off in glee into the seething coals so that their semen bubbles up while they smoke Luckies and Camels, trough on fruit cake, arrange an artificial vagina from peach halves in heavy syrup and perform again, making consummated noises. They go outside, shoot eavesdroppers at the window, then return to the protein phase of their endeavor. Whatever parcels get through have a broken, invaded look, filled with snow or turds, though neatly tied up again. A prisoner is lucky to receive anything at all, and to complain invites a bullet; two, one in the groin, the second in the head. You stumble out into the blizzard and walk unsteadily past the cesspool, unable to spit into it in derision. I have heard stories of those who, in farcical extremis, have jumped into the six-foot wen, but never saw it.

I suspected a benign myth to give the inmates hope.

I may have discovered a new algebra, a calculus of gangrene even, in which, however you calculate, things *will* go wrong:

She will never return.

She will be freed but never leave Russia.

She will die in the Gulag.

She will die soon after arriving.

She will kill herself after being freed.

She will be commanded to return to the commissar.

With her sentence over, she will get ten more years.

It is not worth going on with, hypothesizing such pain. It could have been so free, so sweet, granted a few escapes, even if *he* somehow came after her. As he yet might. It is plain that, were he to die, shot by some envious rival for power, she would have been let go, her punishment dismissed as a besotted geezer's halitotic last bellow for power. Geezer Gulag, as we used to say. Last blast. Final finial. But it never happened that way, and while he lived he scared the pants off them all with flamethrowers and acid drips. Why on earth had I gone after her, then? Lack of imagination, like all those colleagues posted to the Middle East who never learned Arabic and those posted to Pakistan who dreamed the only lingo spoken there was English. There were any number of willing in those days, as long as you weren't political.

When being unpolitical I was nosing around those often deserted unmown plinths of grass peculiar to Russia, on which obsolete airplanes were put to rest, much as planes of our own end up in the Mojave Desert, there to be cannibalized and not much else. The Soviets, being a punitive society, put their jets out to grass with a firm sense of rebuke: these planes had failed. I was there, in the guise of a small inquisitive boy in England writing down the numbers of trains, a hobbyist, a maven. Supposedly, I was to keep track of new designs, the theory being that the canny Russians would "hide" here the very latest models, just to put us off the scent. So I spent many a day writing down the tail-feather numbers and specifics of golden oldies. Sometimes, at the less strictly guarded airfields, I was the cheerful NCO who bicycled along the runway, one hand holding the wingtip of a plane that crept forward to its parking place: a reckless pose, of course. The planes were unpainted.

On one occasion, a guard who was on foot, also escorting the jet, asked me something about what I was doing. I didn't quite get it, but responded in my uncouth Russian worthy of routine NCO.

"Trying to get the smell of last night off my hand. You know how it gets."

"Man or woman?" he scoffed. "They get to boil down to the same stink in the end. You gotta watch out for fish, though." The plane minutely advanced ahead of him, its wingtip towing me with it, leaving him behind, changing him from escort into follower. That exchange, I told myself, had entered into the mythology of Russian aviation. Half the questions they put to me they asked without even looking at me. So long as you were part of the retinue, all was well, and the bikes leaned against the walls of various outhouses, available to whoever wanted them, rather like the bikes marooned in alleyways at famous universities; you rode whichever one came to hand, and you just left one propped up in the last place you went before you went away for ever. A freemasonry of bikes, as at the outskirts of Russian military airfields.

Ars celare artem, as they say in the non-communist countries. How strange it was to observe up close the lines of these assorted warbirds, marveling at their simple construction, the occasional use of a pragmatic periscope that gave the man in the rear seat a better view, the derivativeness of certain designs, and the exact angles of those with swing wings. It was almost as if they were people with chins, eyebrows, noses, and stances, while failing to recall in comparable detail the chamber in which she and I disported ourselves, our general impression amounting to lumpish polished wood, huge obtuse clocks ticking and chiming and wrong by ten or twelve minutes, dead and dusty fireplaces equipped with cumbersome andirons, rugs in whose nap various insects snoozed by day and crept out at night to patrol (exact duplicate of the rugs in Tucson's Arizona Inn villas). True, the arid turmeric aroma of inside was missing in the vicinity of the planes, but the nervous tension attending our escapades must have been more forceful than what I felt as I perused the planes for aerodynamics getting beyond or above itself. Fear or favor made us nervous amid the massive tables, the layers of sullen dust, the creaky disintegrated light that came from untended windows. The commissar believed in decay, having always out of prudence tried to look older than he really was. She had believed him and then strayed.

Strangely, I remembered her best for her emotions, not for her face and physique, as if she had somehow been factorized and recombined as an abstraction. Details, yes: eyelashes and untinted polished nails, but the whole array of tender or apprehensive looks floated off into Russian infinity, of which that cumbersome country had a plentiful supply, leaking into everything, the bedding, the rancid kitchens, the chain-driven, constantly dribbling toilets. In Russia, where memory has so vast a drooling body, it is hard to remember anything at all. You try, but too many gongs, chimes, balalaikas, bells, loudspeakers, and snowplows obtrude, forcing you back into memories of some other place, where you felt less pestered. Hence that recollection of Arizona, superimposed on the rugs of his *dacha*, the one gushily named "Vesnyvolna," "Surge of Spring" to us.

So, you might say, it was *not* her with whom you dangerously frolicked not that long ago. It was some other woman, cross-eyed, club-footed, afflicted with a phlegmy cough that got worse whenever she tried to kiss? You remember so poorly, it might have been anyone at all. No, I disremember her because she is penned up in the Gulag, and my recollection shies away from her imprisoned face and body, can't stomach it. When she is released, memory will become normal after being itself jailed and punished. I find that explanation too winning to be true, too glib. Have I no photographs? No: everything they took away to file in some cabinet, as Russians do. It is a country that thrives on secrecy, so much so that nobody seems to know anyone else, neither Biblically nor casually. Ye shall know one another by your papers, which of course we have sealed away among mouse droppings and hidden, stale vodka glasses. So she has become a cipher, then, unfaithful to the man and to Russia too, to whom her labia upper and lower should have been dedicated without thought. It is like remembering a Mayday parade without a single participant's demeanor, still less an accidentally thrown-off disloyal smile.

Do I then remember the hot rooms? I remember only the whitewash fug of the stairs.

Do I recall the arrival of his official car on the gravel outside? No, but I remember his arrival on pine needles as we fled.

Now my mind is grappling with the old problem: they grabbed her with the ivory Isis-headed dildo still inside her, potentially embarrassing, the only thing she was allowed to take away apart from her bathrobe, as they promised her sacking and cheesecloth up in the snows. Rudely forced apart, we at least had our thoughts to contend with, I wondering if she would get all the way to Lubianka or Gulag with that tool embedded in her, a keepsake, or if, somewhere on the rattletrap train between Uchta and Chosedachard, she would release it through the gloryhole into the between-tracks snow along with whatever else, and there it would sit for ever, a tinpot godling, waiting for Osiris to come and collect it. The clickety-clack of that shabby train goes from one ear to the other and back, not my train, but hers, merging now and then with the puzzled, self-absorbed whine of jets as the derelicts of the airfield take over from the dreaded trains of the tundra, heading farther and farther north on the line to an encampment so dark its lights remain on for years.

Do you remember the last cries you exchanged as, first she, then you were frog-marched down the fan-shaped stairs?

"Don't worry, you'll be all right." I had rarely yelled anything so vapid. What she called out I remember only as "Forever" because there was an outburst of coarse cursing, then a series of bumps on the stairs. I had yelled in English, she in Russian, but silence stoical and severe might have been better. Were we going to trial or not? If so, should we grovel and plead? I never heard what they did with her; no doubt his excellency the commissar trumped up his own kind of court, no doubt held in a toilet with a cattle-prod. No trial for me, but straight to the ice-palace of Siberia, that inferno of barbed wire and mutant guards. Straight there, with no holds barred, a slam in the chops greeting every effort at conversation. Speak to a fellow-captive and you got one in the face. Speak to a guard and you got two. The system had its zany consistency. I guessed I was the only political adulterer on board, among thieves and rebels, dissidents and namecallers. Headed for the *vita nuova*, not of Dante but of Comrade Brezhnev, we spent the time observing one another glassily and wondering what on earth had got *him* into a mess like this.

At this point I had no inkling of my future as a pool-cleaner or a treehouse dweller, but more a sense of having no future at all beyond paralyzing headaches and heartaches, to be followed by the bullet without warning. No passport, no ID card, no pass or ticket, no St. Christopher. Just an indelible quietus such as predeceasing mothers worry about.

Striving to make sense of what had been created, I was sure, *not* to make sense, I said *Our sweetest songs tell of saddest thoughts, so do our saddest songs tell of sweetest thoughts?* I didn't think so. There were sweet songs all right, but only sadness for them to be about. We lived lamentably. If we could not disentangle the mare's nest attending sweetness and sadness, had we any right to pose as thinkers at all? All I could come up with was that what scared us about monsters was their implacability, whether ogre or tornado, despot or disease, sadist or dragon. Who cared what thought came next? Who cared if politics was a morbid form of statecraft or a special way of making marmalade? Was there any appreciable difference between the Gulag and life in Central Park? Some shamefaced drivelmeister says a reluctant yes: anything for a comfortable life, with a view of the Plaza and the other hotels.

The hard thing, as ever, is to decide if all along I have been a serious employee doing important and even dangerous things, or the mere annotator of a charade. If the former, I *should* have been shot for deserting my post, and shot by my own team. If the latter, then I deserved all I got, and I at least got into some serious business, quite an authority on the Gulag, about which I could warn anyone spying in earnest.

Too, of course, I also in my skewed way became something of an authority on Central Park (Down and Out In), fancying the whole place as my very own "Imagine Garden" (phrase of Yoko Ono's), happy to live close to the model boathouse and the Conservatory Water Pond where the Hans Christian Anderson statue is, where the storytellers gather (including myself), I the meistersinger of sailboat and gondola, the whisper of ice skates (or is it a mellow skirl?), the semi-automatic struts of puppets and marionettes, the spruced-up toilets *chez* the *Dana Discovery Center*, in November the inflating of giant balloons along Central Park West. Long enough ago, I met and rejoiced in my bower, fighting off the cold as any Gulagian would, taking special pleasure in weekends when the traffic virtually ceased, the birds arrived in greater numbers, perhaps (November) to mop up after the huge Winter Festival, feasting on the Giant Lawn as if it were some huge iced cake in a Nazi conference room in '42. Call up *Bite of the Apple Tours* and they might just tell you that, contrary to law, some renegade ragamuffin had been seen scooting about in the high trees, a curved saw thrust through his belt, perhaps a sasquatch come south for the winter. He had even been seen with a fishing pole intended for use as what? A TV antenna? A spear? A flying trapeze? Oh, Hans Christian Andersen, come back, all is forgiven.

6. A Guest

Not least among life's privileges is that of imposing a bedtime story on someone already asleep, telling them about the three-month train journey from one lockup to another, surely the one farthest away, farthest north, in the course of which you acquire an extra sentence for misbehaving en route.

"Anyway," I vaguely tell the huddled form that has wafted into my harum-scarum life, "I am glad to say that eventually I arrived after crouching for days with the others under a tarpaulin rigged over an open flat car. You disembark by the light of bonfires and line up for counting. It is twenty or thirty below zero Celsius. Know what that is? You aren't allowed to warm yourself at the fires. They are illumination. You almost expect the yelping dogs to be wearing sheepskin coats like the guards. You bathe, run naked across the yard, and get ready to be assigned to what—a tent? There is no room in there so they march you all the way back to the train only to be marched back again on the next day to your reward: hot food if you were lucky, scrabbling with half a dozen others for a handful from a tin basin. If you were unlucky, some armed goon went up to a fir tree and nailed to it a sign that announced the site of a new camp. Start from scratch in the deep snow with a wad of dried fish in your frozen fist whereas, in the other more established camp they mixed all courses together into a sludge. It saved time as well. All courses at once."

She does not stir. I am not really addressing her, but I am saying it aloud, like some tactless misfit monkey who, having come down from the trees, decides it's time to go back up. I am addressing all the available sweethearts in the world, all the available squatters, all the willing ears. As if I am still on a barge or a flat car somewhere near the Arctic Circle, I hand her the jelly jar to make water in, then I realize where I am and understand that she will have already found her own way of solving this problem. She might have been here weeks. At least there is no lavatory barrel to spill over on to her from the motion of the treehouse in the wind. A treehouse is not a train or a barge, not quite. She does not hear the local orchestra at Magadan, those feisty marches and flirty waltzes. Trapped in the ice, the barges are useless, so we have to march the rest of the way. There is never a destination. Oh there is, we are told. You will mine gold once you arrive, for fifteen years. You will lead brisk and vital lives, pure as snowballs in your tents. Those of you unfit to mine will have no buttocks, which fact a medical examiner will determine. Now who does not have buttocks? I will always be boarding a train to nowhere, then transferring to a flat car or a barge, after which I march for weeks to a destination more abhorrent than hell. If I can't sleep, I relive part of that march, and I am soon out, my dearest, I am out like a light. The Northern lights play and fizz overhead like an ice carnival of the longlost dead.

I try again. Am I trying to wake her so that I can lull her off again with my dreadful tales?

No, I want her to wake up and know what the next word will be before I utter it.

The fortune cookie has always intrigued me, mainly because it gives me a chance to live recklessly. I eat the cookie whole, I never crush or split it open to see what the future holds. You are supposed to devour your fate, not peek at it. After all, what if it told me I would die by falling from a tree? Who died years ago in the wastes of the Kolyma River, in pigskin shoes and pocketless quilted coat. Who was it? Was it me? Who ripped a lung out of his chest and used it as a fishing net? It was the pants, of course, but the pain of getting them off and then the double affliction of cold, it was almost as rough as doing it with the lung.

I exaggerate, but I have lived an exaggerated life.

"Yes, whoever you are," I resume, "I now believe that, if humans did not die, they wouldn't be so keen to bump one another off. The habit would lose its allure. Or would it? Death by then would be a real novelty. No, there'd be no death, that's right. If there wasn't any, you couldn't have it as a novelty. That's logic. That's sense."

"What had you done?" She's awake and talking, asking.

"Laughed in the wrong place," I say. "They don't like that."

"Oh," she says. "I thought you'd been messing around with boys. Well, girls. That's why they say they're going to cut the babies to come out of you. They don't like you messing around and being felt at."

"For fifteen years," I inform her, "that particular thought never crossed my mind. You miss the ones you love, but you do not miss the secret places of their bodies. You need a hug, but you don't think about babies, or what makes them."

She begins to mumble, as her way is, as if she is thinking in one language and wanting to speak another but can't translate. I talk instead.

"I was there longer than you are old. I bet."

She says nineteen, so I subtract three. She wins.

Asleep again, she snores on, and this time I decide to say nothing to her. For all I know, she has a baby with her now and they will come after me for molestation. She may have had several already, making up for everyone lost en route, in the deliberately sunk barges, or left behind in the frigid wastes after being clubbed in the head. She would have to breed from now until Doomsday to make up for all those thousands whom at last the lice left. They too laughed in the wrong place at the wrong time and the dogs ripped their rags off them where they fell. It was allowed. It was preferred. Always, fewer was better. When you are going to die, those who care about you, if they get chance, make you comfy on the snow, then wrap the peasant cloths you have around your shoes *around your face*, to keep the wind out, the last few warm breaths in, so you end with your hands up along your cheeks if you can move your arms. If only they had more facilities. But stunned snowmen are not nurses.

"I'm going to stay here," she says, having heard some of it.

"Oh yes."

"Wherever it was, I'm not going there. Where was it?"

"The country of snow," I tell her. "Where, when they want to drive you out of your mind, they give you the picture of a flower, or a real leaf. Or they take you at gunpoint to a small shack you think is an execution shed but turns out to be an actual toilet you can squat in. They stand outside laughing and making vulgar noises until you come out. You never come out. They have to drag you. You want to remain on the toilet for the rest of your days. You want to freeze in that position so that anyone else coming to use it has to squat on your legs."

The Ice Lens

"You're nasty," she says.

"You haven't been where I've been," I tell her.

"I wouldn't go anywhere with you," she says.

"Already are," I say. "See how good my English is."

"What is English," she asks. "I never heard of it."

This is good. If this is really the Orion Nebula, then she is my first Nebulist, talking in unruly blurts of electricity, awake when she's asleep, asleep when she's awake, guiltless no doubt but doomed to have that entire star nursery cut out of her, all the baby stars snipped out. I want to call them starlings, but that's a bird. I am coming to it slowly, though, dearest one. I soon won't know a star from a bird. Why bother? Up here in the big wash of wind, the distinctions between things matter less. That was one country. This is another. They overlap though. They do have their penal colonies. They have their snow, their barges, their flatbed railroad cars. They give somebody two life sentences to run concurrently, adding a fifty-thousand-rouble fine, after which they tell him to behave himself or else. Is that worse than what they did to Vasily V., going so far as to bring him a typewriter after ten years in nearly total darkness. Trouble is, the key caps keep coming off the spikes beneath. They bring him some flour paste to stick them back on with. He persists anyway, typing his life story on to the paperless cylinder while the spikes make his fingers bleed with every letter. A year later he has worn the letters and the cylinder quite out and his fingers are festering. He was once a novelist. I wonder whose treehouse *he* is sleeping in now. Were there a treehouse to each tree in Central Park there wouldn't be enough for us, those who need some other place to come home to. They cut the babies out of us too.

First night back, I can never sleep. It's like the first night out, which I distinctly remember as the kind of thing usually induced by chloroform: drinking soup all night, borsht and sliced cucumber, black bread and weepy guffaws. The main fear, dear heart, is that the shock of becoming free will drive you off your rocker, or stop dead the excited heart. It is too much to bear, especially with the rest of life to live.

I could make her my prisoner, of course. I'd know how. But who needs a specimen such as she is? She took her chances when she climbed up here. Easily strangled, lowered, then carted off to some other part of the park to join the usual human leftovers. But the one thing I do not need in my quotient of a life is another death, another someone to be responsible for. Not I, the prisoner of the vocative, endlessly talking to whoever isn't there. Talking to her cramps my style some. She is too real, almost like one of those mutant fishermen after that atomic explosion: burned and sapped of life. Where was it? Bimini, the atoll of. How strange the mind is, holding on to scraps inedible and useless, not because you're that interested in the onward plunge of the century, but because for once the name is easy to say. Bimini. The music lover in me calls it Francesca da Rimini. We'll see. Bimini. Why not? Francesca da Bimini? Oh no. Bimini, then, pure and simple.

Then who am I? Are names that easily come by?

The name White appeals to me. No harm in trying it. But it doesn't overwhelm me with sheer rightness. It would do in a bureaucratic pinch. Scratch White. Try again. She would never be able to pronounce my real name any more than I wish to say it. To say it is like saying syllable-slow the name of some dreadful disease. Then what? Who? I rather like Andy, Phil, Mike, Dan, Jim, Bled, good solid American blurts all of them. Not quite right, though. How about Basil, name of an old friend? King it meant. Then what about Rex? It too means king. I am a relative of the renowned Kong, king of the upper trees and the skyscrapers too. What is weird is that I am here, in the country, legally, although they never offer you a tree as temporary accommodation until you come up with something more permanent. Rex meets Bimini. Now there's an opera for someone to score. All the way from being under somebody's heel to being on top of things. Subway. Street. And tree. Siberia had no dimensions at all. Let White play first.

7. Nimet

Wonderful, being in a park, Central or otherwise. Everything is a park to me, and I never know if the squirrels I see doing high-speed runs across the grass or burying nuts against the coming winter are from where my treehouse is or from the river valley at large, which is certainly where I hear hickory nuts falling to concrete with a crack like a shattered two by four. Edible but bitter, some of them anyway, whereas other hickory nuts are sweet. Now things are falling upward as well. Waifs and strays and runaways have found out my most secret lair when all I wanted, my sweet, was to be left alone to ponder your glory. She sleeps quietly compared with some, neither pleading not to be taken out to be shot with a towel in her mouth nor babbling for a hot meal to be poured over her belly. Some I've heard, my loveliest one, pleading to be shot to get it over with, and others pleading to be transferred to one of the gentler camps, where you are allowed to walk in a garden and actually watch the chickens being fed. Less of the hardship without in any way less of the abominable hurt. The easiest way out, if only they'd get along, is what in slang we refer to as nine grams, meaning one bullet, but that ultimate boon remains subject to much paperwork and unceasing delays. If they issued us with pistols, one bullet only, half of us would shoot ourselves for the kind of relief you can't know you've got once you've got it. There's faith for you, sweetheart.

Operetta, then. This is the land of the musical, where you wash that man, Stalin, right out of your hair, or any one of his successors. It is the land of the pajama game on the West Side with, somehow, the ghost of Marc Chagall flying above them elongated and primitive, asking the way to Des Moines. No, not for me, not now. I have gone beyond all that, honeybunch. I have lived for years in the trees, my ears full of WQXR and the wisplike oral rectitude of another night creature: Nimet, who murmurs with delicate mouthwashed precision as if gently rehearsing all the life sentences handed out in the kingdom of the snowball, the kingdom of nine grams of lead, the kingdom of the icy march. Truth told, I have too many sweethearts. Not sure I can cope. Bear with me, dearest. Now I have three, you included. I am, as they say, going places.

Item: I have the ghost of living ghosts, your lovely interminable unextinguished self.

Item: I have Nimet of the airwaves, playing specially for me, the night owl, the music of the spheres, unheard for a decade and a half, so I therefore link it helplessly with the sound of my blood rushing through my skull. Rushing? Limping, then.

Item: I have my guest, my cuckoo, my Bimini, my Francesca da Bimini. A hearty mumbler, good-natured and maybe not quite right in the head. Good climber, though, and determined to breed. If only this were a stud farm instead of a treehouse. A studhouse, say. It is not. I do not do things like that. Like some ancient animal on the tundra, the veldt, the desert, the steppes, I breed on the run. Just think of all the names they have for empty places.

Item: That's a lot of womanhood for one. Not really. One is the overghost. Two is the electric overghost. Three is to be reckoned with, the unknown. Best sent back to her ovary-slicing parents in a squad car. Those who have been through the mill have an aversion to flour.

I marvel at the speed of the mind when it has nothing to do. Give it a chore and it seizes up and stops. It clams up. Tight. Four a.m. and only WQXR stirs, apart from the wandering drunks, the slow-gait taxis, the endless corona of lights mutating as someone here goes to the bathroom, someone there answers the phone, someone over there gets murdered in bed and the murderer now flicks on the light to erase his fingerprints by, and far away over on Staten Island which I can't see, someone has put on the light to go after a huge rat, bust in through the thin plaster of the wall while the lens-grinder wakes. I say it random: there's bound to be a lens-grinder somewhere on Staten Island plagued by a rat. Maybe my mother, meaning my Aunt Tasha, is my fourth sweetheart, just for leaving me alone, to my own devices, as if I were a wandering moss, a fungus in transit. She knows when to leave well alone, except for well-to-do relatives, to whose bosom we charged like fleeing muskrats.

Nimet is playing the music of Erich Korngold, an underrated composer, sweetheart: his Opus Ten Sextet has moments of august loveliness, the whole thing surges neatly upon an emotion you think he found in the act of composing and not beforehand, demanding expression later. Before that she played Brahms. I have never phoned in a request, or written one on a card. Does she work amid flames at this hour? Is this the hell-bent shift? Or does she purr to us in that essentially non-American English from a velvet sofa with albino cats fawning on her every vowel? It is high time to phone her and ask for Francesca da Rimini, in honor of my guest.

Down I go. The number I have, scrawled on the back of a taxicab card. I dial. The call goes through. They take the message. It will take a week because of the backlog. Are they serious? Or was I just connected to the Lubianka prison courtesy of some unpublished international pact? At least I gave my name as Rex. That should stop them for a week or so. How many

The Ice Lens

Rexes call asking for Francesca da Rimini? Now it comes. I know who composed it. I always did. My mental blocks move into place as if oiled. I even know what Peter Ilytch Tchaikovsky wrote in his diary in 1891, in between harsh bouts of weeping. Homesick, he wrote, "American customs, American manners, and habits generally are attractive to me, but I enjoy all this like a person sitting at a table set with marvels of gastronomy, devoid of appetite. Only the prospect of returning to Russia can awaken an appetite within me." And the Russia he wanted to return to was still there. Large as life. Or nine grams.

I take it back. *I* am not that keen to return. But, precious one, your mind can play you funny nasty tricks. When they let me go, let me out, not out of the country but out of the camp, the only emotion I felt was an overflowing love for Mother Russia, as if she were a hospital that had saved my life. That's how screwed up you can get. There must be a logic to it. Runs like this: only for those who can end your days do you ever feel real passionate affection. We make love to our own executioners, do we not. Except for you, the one already gone, particle by particle, to where all the dearly beloveds go, into the heads of those who love them. Yes. And the tears come out, to make room for you.

This America, which you can only understand if you have learned English at an early age, is full of other English that you only pick up once you have landed. Like a code. I used to go around saying *a whole bunch of* because I had never heard it before and I wanted to prove how American I was. In front of a parking lot, I would march businesslike fashion toward a car, swinging my apartment keys (Aunt Tasha's, actually), as if I were on my way to drive somewhere. If you don't, you become a suspect, a displaced person, all over again. And the names are like some incurably exotic zoo, names like Urban and Kittenplan and Selvarajah: little poems for the tongue's tip, with actual people behind them who think the name's normal.

What's normal, my angel, is what happens when I go to the dry cleaner with one of my two pairs of summer shorts—walking shorts, as we say. I come back holding the thin round hook of the hanger against the top of my shoulder while the shorts float behind and sometimes above me like a kite, and everyone knows that is a citizen going home with his dry cleaning. The aerodynamics of it amazes me. I could almost lift off in a high wind. Nobody comes up to me and asks what I'm doing. They all know. It is even more normal, I suppose, to toss the shorts into the back of my car, but having no car I walk them home, to my mother's, and rejoice in the understanding looks I get on the way. I love to walk toward a parked and locked car with my kite. Surely that suggests the acute degree of belonging. He can't be a spy or an undesirable, not if he conducts himself like that. He's a whole bunch of regular. Not one of those approving of me has the faintest chance of being transported to Siberia for anything at all. They have no idea. They greet a ghost.

"Nor," I tell the sleeping form across the planked floor, "do you. You don't not, ever, mess with the wife of a high party functionary, neither for love nor for lust. And you certainly don't do it for the sake of doodling, something empty-headed to occupy you while you wait for a true disaster to come your way." She does not stir. God loves his own tonight. No rain. No pitapat. Only a semi-summer wind losing heart as a hump of warm air comes in from the south to keep us toasty aloft.

No good to talk of disaster when you look at her. She has had her own disaster already: one chromosome too many. That's all, but it has blighted her looks, her brain, as my red-hooded flashlight makes clear. An innocent face all right, an American face to be sure, but already heavy with emphasis in the wrong places, painted with too thick and hasty a brush. Lumpish and vacant, neither male nor female, neither virginal nor used, it's the sort of face I used to see scrunched into the hood of a quote inadequate parka, the nose an outsize red blob, the eyes almost sealed with frost, the mouth pale as a moth's wing and tautened into a suck so as to expose as little of the lips as possible to the lethal air. Now my astronomy tells me I am looking at the human version of the Eskimo Nebula in the constellation Gemini. Maybe I should change the name of my treehouse, if she stays. She is bound to want to move on.

    Sleep tugs at me from a thousand different places. I begin to lose all coordination. I drop the flashlight. She grunts and does an athletic sudden turn in sleep. I decide which bedtime story to tell myself and chose the one in which, after only a few minutes' flight, I am vertically at the same appalling temperature as I got to after weeks en route to Siberia across the horizontal wastes. Every time I get up to thirty thousand feet I look out and recognize invisible Siberia where, when people walk, a habitation fog surrounds them.

8. Krivoshchekovo No. 27

Among the ironies of life in a place where guards shot inmates merely for making the obscene bent-arm-fist gesture, was the death and burial of a guard, maybe once a year. Certain of them, rather than being shipped to hospital and warmth, elected to stay in the camp to die, especially those few with no family. In both these and any other unlucky guard, we took a perverse, sadistic interest, glad of a moment's satisfaction multiplied a million fold by something as simple as the drop in temperature each night while the defunct "shooter" as we sometimes called him lay in the brittle tundra, pieces of his jaw and hands snapping off in the night like ivories from a baby's teething ring. Once they were dead, we should have been allowed to shoot them, just for the gladness of it, but of course no such thing took place. What we saw instead, and rejoiced about as much as we could, was some guards actually setting fire to the permafrost on the gravesite and then hurriedly digging a few inches down into the melt. Now they had a shallow trench, which they then refired, digging again. This procedure went on and on until they had reached the correct depth for the casket. Those of use who had been there longest knew that, such were the churnings of the permafrost, eventually all kinds of headstones, photographs, and

Christ figurines would work their way to the surface, much as others, from the surface, would begin to sink. There were elevator shafts, we used to joke, in the cryogenics of Dante's hell. Thus departed, only at length to arise again on the upward tectonic, a few of our pale-furred tormentors, innocent boobies if seen at a distance, but baby-faced killers close up. Out there, flowers cracked off like artificials on a wedding cake, and tears, if any, bounced off the frost. The idea had circulated that, if you could get your hands on a guard's greatcoat and busby, you might have a chance of getting away, but the walk would kill you and the pursuit helicopters were too fast. No, we took what joy we could in their undoing by the Destroyer of Delight, half-fancying that the only guards permitted to watch us wane and die should be those already granted a terminal illness, like old Genet in his jail wishing only murderers became judges. Lightheaded on grass soup and cabbage water, we got our analogies wrong, but soothed ourselves all the same with such willful rhetoric, making the Gulag world do our bidding in our own blurred court of miracles.

Marooned in Manhattan, I worried about what happened to a woman in such an abominable place, especially one marked down for extra grief by some high muck-a-muck. Would she be safe from lust in the bushes or, worse, the high-pitched spiritual love that flared in

Krivoshchekovo, triggered by a casual smile, this from some feeble, impotent scarecrow, a former politician, to a female travesty whose pellagra-stained face distracts you from the uterus that hard labor has made dangle, not to mention the fatless frame, the pouch-flat breasts and the steam-rollered buttocks. As for rampant VD, a mythic thing transformed into a slavering lion, you took pot luck, knowing that fifty per cent of the camp was infected and only someone such as a medical orderly, privy to charts and slides, could plan his own promiscuity; if you were not lucky enough to get him, you were doomed. The barbaric vision of my beloved, standing there like a mahogany grandfather clock with fingerless vacant face and womb swinging between her emaciated legs like a pendulum, was not one to linger on. Would either of us want the other when the time came? It might be possible that we would each die of shock on witnessing the ravaged quiddity of the other, but in that brief moment subscribe to a token treaty of those who have been pushed too far for further human contact.

I could not ponder the future any more, nor the present, the past. They were all the same, leaking and prefiguring, overlapping and fusing to make up a triple compost through which one was supposed to soldier, imagining heroism and nibbling on it like holy wafer.

I could not ponder the past either, embellishing it as I at first had on being posted to Russia, with effigies barbaric enough to make Elizabethan London seem a nursery charade. Bells, boyars, brawls, five-letter words, stark-naked women in front of the public baths or drunk in the gutters, vodka swindles, public torture of felons (their heels broken), floggings, hangings, breakings on the wheel, impalings, burials to the neck in earth, burnings in iron cages, counterfeiters forcefed molten lead, the sacrilegious torn asunder with hooks, heedless corpses littering Red Square for months on end: such was my image of the place to come, the place that was, with the same old mix of whores, bailiffs, peddlers, musketeers, comedians, acrobats, bears and touting priests swarming the squares and streets. *Pirogi* (meat pies). *Sbeeten'* (hot mead). *Kvas.* Tanks of live fish down by the river, where women did laundry in the shallows. Red Square, I told myself, having boned up on the subject, was a democratic club for idlers and the unemployed. People dined at noon and took a siesta. The police were helpless since so many retainers, unable to survive on what they were paid, had turned to criminality. By the end of the eighteenth century, the *skomorokhi* (buffoons or wandering minstrels) had disappeared as the city tried to be staid.

Recovering my old academic self, I told myself that Moscow was a traditional story originating in a preliterate society, dealing with ancestors, heroes, villains, and supernatural beings that served as primordial types active in a primitive view of the world. A bit much, *hein*? Worked at, as for a term paper, it would get worse, and I would be peddling a notion of myth (what I was really after) as the conjectural extrapolation of a non-teleological norm, expressing through both concord and counterpoint—here my first Russian cough saved me, as well as the resultant spit and snite—an ostensibly full image of coincidence as it widens into mystery (ah!) and awakens us to the incalculable twists of contingency. I had arrived, loaded for bear, just another of the Ivans, the Romanovs, not one of the glumly purposeful millions who worked in factories and under the sky. My Russia was going to be different. No twisted gold wire picked out with enamel, flat gold nimbuses becoming haloes and then crowns.

If, as they say in boxing circles, you have good speed, you're tempted to reach in from too far away, and that's when they get you for not being fast enough. My only reprieve for being a bit of a slowcoach goes back to that spit and snite: nose or sinus trouble, what I called my Russian clarification. After sucking a Polar Bear mint, it was as if an express train had gone through my nostrils, spitting cinders of mint.

9. Bimini

She doesn't mind tea, but she scowls at the early morning fume that rises from the grass and hovers at treehouse level. Asking if I was in some kind of mental home, she shows her wit, calling such places the best places for people with brains. No, I tell her, it was different: more like a camp. A summer camp? No, a permanent winter camp. Who'd want to camp in winter, she says. I tell her it had nothing to do with choice. I suppose it had, in the beginning. If I'd behaved myself, sweetheart, and if you had too, then we'd be closer together, each reading the same book. Taboos are not toothbrushes, dearest.

"I was sent," I say. "A long time."

"Jail," she says, twigging it. "To make you change your ways. Nobody changes their ways they don't, not in places like that. I *know*."

She has already shot a brief copper-colored arc of water over the side as if this were a lifeboat. She has no modesty whatever, no shyness. She asks why I don't relieve myself in the same way, but I tell her I've beaten her to it. I was up most of the night anyway, listening to Nimet, so my bladder is thoroughly seen to.

"Nice tea," she says. "The fresh air makes it stronger."

"Sometimes," I say, remembering, "it makes you a lot weaker than you were. Depends on

The Ice Lens

snow, ice, and the number of degrees below zero."

"You're cozy here," she says. "Can I stay? A while?"

"They'll be looking for you, a pretty girl like you."

"You know I look horrible. The prettiest thing about me is between my legs. The boys think so too. The doctors want to cut—"

"You've already told me," I say. "They always want to cut something. It's what they do best."

"Nobody's looking for me," she says. "They'd be glad if I never came back. I'm from Queens."

"You're from Queens. How long have you been up here?"

She doesn't remember, but it's been a week or two. The hue and cry has died down. Now she turns raucous, vehement, thinking I am going to turf her out rather than expose myself to heaven knows what charges. She stamps and pounds, but also does a miserable little grin through all the grime and salt. "You won't?"

"I'll think," I say, as if I have said, "I'll give you a day or two." She fist-mops her eyes and makes them sore. In the light her face has that same porridge color, that same jowly out-of-true bloat. She has spunk, though, and she knows how to talk. A virgin? I very much doubt it. "Show you mine if you'll show me yours," she laughs, as if she has been reading my mind. "They're all the same. Only two kinds. Did you ever wish there was three? I used to wish that tits would get long and hard like doies, but I stopped hoping. You can feel me up for another cup of tea."

"You," I tell her, "can have the tea for free."

Between us we devour a can of ham, half a loaf, and a whole bag of Danish. I am glad I arrived so well supplied. I take my vitamin, offer one to her, which she tries to chew. She spits it out in a big spitty commotion. Yes, I muse, Bimini will do. It's just about right. She's a hunk of tender wreckage. She's been burned. She has no place to go. She has some restitution coming. After burping, she motions me to do likewise. We hold a burping contest she wins. Now she has squatted over a paper bag I provide in the nick of time. Life in the punishment barges was as nothing to this. She daubs herself with last night's radio schedule, asks to try the earphones, scowls at the classical music (some Haydn), but is only trying to distract me. She curls her body, arcs her back, to sling the bag overboard, but I grab it just in time. "It waits for dark," I say. I remember, darling, slithering around in the vomit of the hold, the slop from the latrine barrel, with the tarpaulin over us to keep the smell down rather than the water out. Then, one day, it was like going to heaven. "You can go and look at the town," the guard says. "I'll collect you in the morning." He meant, of course, that I would spend the night in the local jail. So what? I walked so slowly that someone twenty yards away would have seen no movement. One foot in front of the other, heel to toe, and so on, over the width of the road. No one shot or yelled. They were laughing, though. "Look, he's forgotten how to walk. That's university for you. Give him a cow to milk and he'll ask which end." I did not care, beloved, I was the man walking the plank that never ended. A carpenter's nightmare. "Know what he'll want next? He'll want to be sent to the tropical islands." I did. I had heard about them, dismissing them as wet dreams. They met you with a small silver tray on which they'd piled fresh underwear, new shoes, a thin linen business suit, clean shirt, a silk necktie, and gold cuff links, a tie pin, and some collar studs. Then they fed you the same apology breakfast, as they called it, whatever the time of day. Toast smothered in cream. Sausages embedded in a paste made of hot mashed potato and not so hot scrambled egg. There was one condition, however. You had to agree to serve an extra five years if they asked it of you, and you had no idea if they would. You had to sign. Otherwise they sent you right back to rave and dream and go insane for having stuck one toe into the oasis of delight. It was the old figure-ground problem restated with bitter severity. I signed, gave my profession as proof-reader-linguist-translator-interpreter, and hoped.

I had done all that before I realized I had given in to that insidious, destructive dream. Some, you heard, sweetheart, actually got the breakfast, the new job, and the authorities did not claim the other five years. But it was all mirage to me, a bubble of pink champagne. I was utterly where I was, buriable only when the ground was soft. How was I to know I would one day come to a treehouse?

"Miles away," she says. "Treehouse man."

"Another country," I tell her. "The farthest one. The one farthest away, thank God."

"*Dzz*," she says. *Her* buzz. I had forgotten. To me she is Bimini. The noise she makes is the sound of radiation burning its way through the hull of her boat. I explain that I have to go downtown to see some people. She wants to come. She begins to howl again. Maybe I can lose her in the crowd and maybe she will never find her way back to the treehouse. Or I can vacate it and build another in about a month. She can hardly inspect all the trees in Central Park. Off we go, she humming, I wondering what kind of thing awaits me. After all, this is my vacation time. In winter I don't work, I regale myself with the overheard prattle of the workaday world. *She won't work Sundays, she always said so. Now he takes it outside to smoke it. They unhooked the water meter with some kind of bypass, and then an inspector....* Lives in life's hive buzzing. I love it. I am an ex-snowman from the kingdom of the dead. I

The Ice Lens

played hard for love and lost. I lost so much that the word *lose* is no longer in my vocabulary, and sits off the board, a pawn in permanent exile, mutilated by cold.

Treehouse yearnings began, my sweet, in the yearning for a room with a big window through which the morning sun will pour, even though the night has been cold and the morning is chilly. I will hunch at my table (lucky me with a table) and read or write, sensing with every bit of me the big pummeling golden thaw. Is that a Siberian nightmare? Is that a hothouse fruit on some deadly vine in Snowman's Land? There were, according to different accounts, twelve or twenty million of us cooped up there, all the way from peasants who had taken a bit extra from their land to saboteurs, one of whom had spent his life snipping almost through the cords of parachutes. Most of us had what we called a "quarter," but we never said the other part of it as being too formidable, too devastating: a quarter of a century was unthinkable. For all of that, unless you got lucky, you were going to be contained, curbed, denied, and then you were supposed to pick up where you left off, chastened and enlightened, edified even, and you were a walking example of how the system worked. It was successful, that system, but so few of its pent-up offenders had done something sexual, something adulterous. The crime of the heart I call it, crime of the groin. Usually you get away with that, unless you happen to be unwise enough to meddle with someone else's spouse. It happens in America. There it is almost normal, almost required as a mark of sexual ebullience; but in my country it could take you to Snowman's Land, a peccadillo, nothing more. So you would have plenty of time in which to recall each ecstasy, each instant of passion. You spread it out like jam for all those years, go-slow snowman with genitals of ice. What you were arrested in you stayed in, irrespective of season; the main thing was not to get arrested in a season of the year, or in any kind of clothing whatever. Dressed for summer, you had to soldier through the long autumn of transportation. And vice versa. It was only much later on in the game that they actually got around to dressing you for the part. Yes, dearest mine, we paid for it, you in your camp and me in mine. What a shame you were not strong enough. He would have done as well to cut your throat back in civilization, but he wanted you to feel the gradual burden of the system, he wanted you crushed bit by bit while you reflected on your lascivious ways. We were not lovers for long, but it was enough. We learned how small the mills of bureaucratic hatred can grind, sending us thousands or hundreds of miles apart (what did it matter?) to be fed on herring and locomotive water, dried carp or cattle feed or something made from dolphin meat. The desperate but lucky ones were able to do a deal for human livers filched from the dissecting rooms in the major jails, but we never got into the big league of cannibalism. I say we, but it is all imagined. We never, my swan, communicated with each other again.

One fellow I knew actually swallowed the pieces from a chess set he had groveled and pleaded for months. That ended chess for the rest of us. They were mad enough to suspect the very flies that settled on our face during sleep, which is why we set spit-moistened handkerchiefs in place before we nodded off. If you ate enough flies you could choke yourself to death. If you ate enough flies you could get enough protein to get by. Or not. Or not. The worst thing was watching those who received parcels, such as Mother Tasha was from time to time able to get through. They poured everything out of its can into whatever you had to receive it, so you witnessed the fatuous and tragic act of someone's trying to receive condensed milk or jam into his cupped hands, or the folds of his jacket, or a pocket, or a plate. It came through the slop hole in the wall and it all came at once. To come back with seconds after your plate, or your cupped hand, your jacket fold, or your pocket, was empty, would have been too generous, too evocative of good behavior. There we sat or stood, trying to master our misery, and you did not even get chance, as in Japanese prisoner of war camps, to be beheaded for trying to meet with a woman in the other camp on the other side of the barbed wire. No risk of that here, which to them meant they were saving you from making a fool of yourself, yet condemning you to a fate worse than making any kind of fool of yourself. I have seen men put their wide open mouths to the swill slot in the door to be, as it appeared, force-fed honey or condensed milk from the container on the other side, with no let-up, no time allowed for swallowing or getting a gulp of air. Imagine.

"You're very quiet," Bimini says.

"Sometimes my mind goes far away like a kite that's broken its string. That's what happens, Bimini."

"Don't walk in traffic," she commands. "*That* isn't my name."

"Up here it is. We don't need your name, your real name. The less we know, the better, as with spies."

She does not understand this at all, nor would she buy the concept of us prisoners being like mincemeat fed to ourselves, but that is what it amounted to. You devoured yourself day after day since there was nothing else to use your energy upon. One man called himself the Galactic Tourist, pour soul. Another said his name was Worm Captain. We had bedbug marshals and flea maestros, lice leaders and roach commissars. It was all a matter of adjustment. I might just as well have told her all this. I can tell now that telling her things is one of the forms of sheerest privacy. She comes from a zone in which the norms go bad. Certain elemental things occupy her, but not much else. Bodily functions and the words derived from them. Like some innocent version of the Gulag, she asks me "Don't you like your shit? We got lots to occupy ourselves with. All kinds of stuff comes out. Spit. *You* know." I know. Most of the time, however, she seems rapt, entranced by the vision of herself as a converter of this into that, no doubt at the far horizon of her wonderings aware that one squirt of sperm can turn her into a mother, unless. She asks, in her idiom, if I have big balls, and I am shaking my head before I've even thought about it.

"Then," she says, as after some complex feat of Socratic elenchus, "you must have a whopper to make up for it. Let me see." I fight off her exploring hands, amazed at how muscular they are, I shudder to think from what uninhibited manual chore. Let this one loose in the camps and she would turn hell into chaos in an hour. "Look," she shouts, and I see the furred pleat of her sex. She has no underwear. I think I must either lose her or wear her out with little invented tasks, such as counting the trees in the park, or collecting up the leaves that have fallen on our makeshift balcony. She has to be calmed. No wonder they want to sterilize her, darling. She is Mother

Courage with fangs. Her dress drops, thank goodness, but now she shows me her boobies, full and ripe. Maybe she is hoping they will erect horizontally under the impress of my stare. She belongs to somebody for sure. I am surprised at how shocked I am, dearest, I who have soldiered through the worst of the camps. I conclude that it is life that horrifies me, not death, or pain, or denial. It's the lunging life force that makes me quiver. I recognize how it fuels just about anything, is oblivious. No, you can't even say that because oblivious suggests an agent, a subject, capable of oblivion's opposite. No, it's the mindless energy behind everything, the flukey powerhouse behind a cosmic freak. Things might so easily have been otherwise, and, while I don't think I could ever get to the point of wishing you and I had never been, I sometimes toy with the notion of how much pain we'd save by never having been eligible for happiness in the first place.

"Never having been eligible for it," I say aloud, "in the first place," as she tweaks my tummy, feeling for the navel. "What a ghastly thought."

"You don't have one."

"It's little," I tell her. "They should be so."

"It's really your mother," she says. "It's a bit of you that's her."

She warms to paradox, I can see. Did her mother look down, see what she'd produced, and shove it back to be baked some more? You wonder. The short basin cut doesn't suit her hair, which seems almost wavy. They have cut across the wave, so she has little bits sticking out at all angles. She looks like a badly combed turnip, today at least, but I can just about see her in a party dress and with long hair, guiding one's attention from the face to the shoulder, the back, the bosom. It would help. Seems to me they have tried to mongolize everything else about her, getting the whole of her in tune with the bit that's odd. Oh well, she has a perky thunderbolt smile, and she keeps a keen look-out through the branches, now and then motioning me to look downward at this or that casual passerby. They never look up. They can't see the rope and the floor's underside is stippled in camouflage colors. A sniper could fire away from here for days and be found only by the puffs of smoke. How far from Russia I feel, as if I too have come across intergalactic space, mapless and idealess, determined to find a roost, that's all. A plank. A kennel. A nest. The camps disqualified me for ordinary living in ordinary rooms. After a while you get to need the danger, the sense of being on the edge. You crave not being fed for a week on end, the chance of being taken out at night to be questioned or beaten, the chance of suffocating in a room with no window, too many bodies, and intense summer heat. I call it the penal itch. I do not miss the smells, but I miss the spells. Yes. Beside the point that men in close company seem to reek of creosote, whether they have been working with it or not. What counts is the edge, the fear, the night-stalking guard who tumbles you out, as if for nine grams, and then just tells you to tidy things up in there. Clear that windowsill. You obey. If you have dysentery they will bring you a dentist, or rather a dental hygienist. If you have a heart attack, they will pass you magic powders through the bars. Programmed irrelevance, that's the style.

So, my pigeon, it works like this. I prefer talking to you, wherever you are. I could tell all this to the lusty young wench presently aboard my treehouse, but she needs memoirs of a different salt. So, as I said, they will sometimes, as you know, allow one book to circulate among several hundred prisoners, and you can sign up in advance for it. Maybe five months from now you will be allowed to have it for a while. They never let anyone finish his book. Or hers, I guess. And it is usually something innocuous, such as a handbook on lathe repair, but you have to read it with entranced little skips, imagining your way through, making it into a million and one Arabian nights as the bushings wear and the metals fray. It's not so much that it's a book. It's print. That's the magic. Ideas made flesh. The daydream of the human mind chiseled out and made portable. The book symbolizes an almost random freedom to send something out into the world without much idea of where your ideas will end up. Lucky-dip readership is almost god-like, is it not, my precious? A painter may lose charge of his work, but a book writer loses charge of it a thousand times over. There is a diaspora of the book having nothing to do with libraries or museums. The Mona Lisa is a known thing whereas a book is not; it goes out, sinks in, and remains in that *unknown* place. Such as a prison, a transfer jail, a camp.

10. The Toad of Disgust

Some genially disposed prisoner once told me that trying to cope with Gulag conditions was like trying to cut a gem on horseback: a mild account of a dreadful situation that began with the trains, not even cleansed of what they might have carried before—quicklime, coal, or corpses. That was bad enough, but the convoys (escorts) being equipped with long-handled wooden mallets was worse: with these the guards tested the woodwork of the train, but also battered the prisoners while ridding them of all private possessions such as wallets, money, cigarettes, keys, photographs, letters, all tossed into a barrel, then of such materials likely to be used for escape or to blind or otherwise incapacitate the guards: belts, suspenders, bandages, twine, cord, straps, soap, sugar, salt and pepper.

All this fiendish abuse of the passive, awestruck human aghast at the *taiga* outside, where he already envisioned himself gnawing on snow and dried fish, was deliberately contrived not so much to move prisoners from A to Z as to terrorize them from the first, thus introducing into the savage transportation system something metaphysical. Sheer discomfort left you shitless, of course, but abject terror installed in you a lethal part of the universe that was always going to get worse as the journey continued or ended. "All out to unload a rail car of corpses!" The cry came from no human throat, and out into the crackly cold you would toss yourself, groveling to help and not be noticed, thankful to detect the stench waning as the chore wore on and your hands went numb. It was always better to get to your camp as fast as possible. Your mind played abstruse, hopeless games, wondering if a year of the train was worse than a year in camp, and (this helplessly) if one might not work out some kind of exchange, agreeing (!) to remain on the trains for ten years. Of course, those arriving by train knew the camps only by repute, so the trains, the devil you *did* know, seemed more benign. You soon, but too late, realized you had been right: the camps were worse, even for women unless they somehow (guess how) ascended to the golden order of trusties. In Moscow, women had arrived at the departure station in high heels, revealing furs, lipsticked and coiffed, flashing silk and jewels, as if they were assembling for a lecher's treat, only to be divested of everything amid a tumult of screams, yet no doubt giving the guards or convoys a taste or glimpse of the erotic life that in some cases lingered in those primitive imaginations, awakening yokels to new possibilities for wooden mallets, broken glass, and rusty railroad nails. After all, the main purpose of all this entraining and confining was to refine the calculus of horror for those who, in their indefatigable stupidity, had transgressed. In one sense, this was a waste of time because, if you just got too much en route of what Zola called the toad of disgust, by the time you arrived at, say, the Sukhobezvodnaya Station, you could not be shocked further, or thought so. There was that lingering sublime immunity that held on to you for a day or two before the extremes of the catastrophic grotesque set in.

These were the wretched thoughts I shuffled through my anesthetized mind as I fretted endlessly about her and her ghastly situation. In the end, if lucky, we would come together at long last, perhaps at some commonplace rail terminus in Norway, salt herring greeting smoked Caspian carp, each bearing a feces bucket just in case, determined to keep at least that part of our beings separate and private. We would not smile or weep, or even remember, but like two dolmens of ice sag towards each other, neither strong enough to support the other, and breath into each other's lungs for the first time in years.

So, you see, no matter how sordid Manhattan had become, or on the other hand how dazzlingly exquisite, it had no bearing on the gruesome years, which of course were not over. Manhattan, I stagily told myself, was a reverse discourse, but one I could approach only through portals both uncouth and crude (the Park so far, and the pools along the Hudson). Of that fabulous Rialto—theaters, restaurants, libraries, department stores, taxis and landaus—I had no part, any more than a Blackfeller could glean the beginnings of English from his own aborigine tongue. I could cut a gem in an ice palace, but not on horseback. I stank of herring and oak leaves. I was an optional human being, part fowl, part the bleached wolf of the woods that Villon envisions, daunted by too many sharp-cornered snowflakes.

For sheer dislocation, though, apart from all the graver traumas, there is nothing like tuning in your favorite classical station at the usual hour and hearing, through some variant of sideband splash or aerial bungling, not the suave cadences of the Composer of the Week but the metal voice of the U.S. Naval Observatory Master Clock: "At the tone, Eastern Daylight Time, Two hours forty minutes exactly. Universal Time...." Again and again. Surfeit of accuracy in the wrong place, both unnerving and crude.

11. Great To Be Alive

I ask her if she wants to stay behind. No, she is going to come. So I pull her woolen cap down low over her brow, give her my sunglasses, and tell her to stay close. She doesn't mind any of this, almost as if she is accustomed to mutation, to taking on a different shape or hue. Her repertoire of adjustments is bigger than mine, and in any case she has this doomed air. She knows that anyone looking for her will find her. That will be part of the adventure. You could hide a loon in a sackcloth and zebra skin, but, if the bright blood clot of its eye showed, that would be that.

She carries her bag of droppings, into which I have tossed the tea bags, and I put on my backpack to bring things home in. Down we go, gently and with a sense of tender mysteriousness: two strangers out on a mission together. I do declare it feels different down below. There is an actual change in air pressure and the air feels more stable. She half grins, her look one of crushed expectancy, and I suddenly realize that for her this is an outing. She looks at me as if she is going to exclaim something or shout for help, but nothing comes out of that bald face with its pelt of heavy down, and I move along from base of tree to nearest trash can with an abiding sense of how mobile her face can be within its limited range. To fathom her, you have to tune in to the sub-conversation that lingers in her cheeks. Not that she couldn't say things, as she's shown. It's more that wonder claims her before she's gone too far. Amazed to be able to begin to speak, to consider speaking, she draws back from it as from an ecstasy she would rather postpone. She thrives on expectation, then, and I wonder if she isn't right and hers isn't the better way to go. What on earth will I do with her in November?

"Warmer down here," she says, glad to be rid of her shiver. She lifts the front of her cap and I firmly tug it back down.

"Spoilsport," she says.

I ask her if she would rather be caught, taken back, and put into hospital for whatever they want to do to her. I know the answer. I sympathize with all people on the run, in the shadows, hiding out, lying low. They seem to be the ones who have really tested the nature of our civilization, looked into its innards and found it cruel. Not that I am confusing bums and layabouts with true devotees of the contemplative life: I just feel that, to plumb the goings-on in any society you have to have spent a certain amount of time, preferably a long time, away from it all, out of sight, out of touch, in tune with grass, mice, and weather, or the wheeling flickering constellations, and then you are qualified. Anyone whose link with society is firm and solid has no means of taking stock. Most ex-prisoners rationalize thus, I suppose, but this ex-prisoner has paid infernal dues and roams the hide of his planet, doesn't he, precious one?, a postgraduate in loss and hurt. Not that he is looking for anyone, anything, to heal him up again, sweetheart; he is keenly aware of the is-ness that sits and festers behind all the *howdydo*s, the *Fine, thanks*es, the *beg your pardon*s, and the *till death us do part*s. I can sense the growing and withering behind the tweeds, the silks, the denims, and I have come to look upon people, as I learned to look upon fellow prisoners— from the man actually eating his beard to the man writing a novel about Berlioz, from the man who had memorized *War and Peace* to the man who had made a paper glider from the linings of his shoes, shaping it with snot and spit—as samples of growth, test tubes in which chemistry can conduct itself. If I look into someone's eyes it is as if I am looking into the eye of the hurricane that person is. Before I know you, I know your chemistry, the chain-link fence of cells that make you up. It comes from living so long with men at close quarters that, instead of seeing them as they are, you see into them, and have accurate notions of their bloodstream, their pepsis, their muscles. Locked up, in interrogation jails or labor camps, you learn to savor human fabric, the stuff from which all are cut. You become impersonal, my dearest one, you dote on highest common factors and lowest common denominators. And that is part of your punishment. They stunt you because they would rather have you deformed than as you were. It's easy, it's not creative. All they have to do is give the energy within you nowhere to go, and that is that. Aunt Tasha's in November. *Alone.*

We take the bus, I thanking heaven for the unfeigned indifference of New Yorkers, as if they have been reared in a funhouse and have achieved that acme of sophistication nothing fazes them, or interests them either. In no time at all we are burning trash on the corner of Bowery and Houston, washing windshields for a quarter, and smiling at the big crude cardboard sign that reads ITS GREAT TO BE ALIVE, a message that has come all the way from northern Siberia, scrawled not in blood (it looks that way) but in lipstick, something found and ripe for use. You would think it is like going from being apes to being Neanderthals, but it's nothing of the kind. You can actually make a dollar or two, keep your hands warm, and be part of the gang. I do it most of every year. Nobody asks questions. They know that, if you're willing to stand and hustle by that sign, you have been somewhere lethal, never mind how long. *It would be better to be dead* is perhaps the other side of the ad, but only a logical head would think so. There is no obverse to this al fresco slogan; it just flowered out of what surrounds it. We have to move on, anyway, just in time to take part in a show on the Fourteenth Street subway platform that requires both Bimini and me to put on Hefty bags then to crouch and keep still while several others put the grandmother of all plastic bags over and around us and then pretend to drag us away, a bag of bagged human garbage. Of course we cooperate by shuffling on our feet as the hauling group advances, wailing their untidy cry: "There is somebody in control, O Lord. Bags spilling greed. Bodies of bags. Bags of bodies. There comes a threatening stillness." Awful, of course, darling, and meriting a full nine grams in the base of the head, but adequate when you need something to do and have in tow a houseguest of uncertain temper. Bimini likes the frolic of it all, in seconds losing the last five years of her fifteen, returning herself to the perfect age of ten, when all is mellow and secure. At least that's how *I* remember it. A couple of dozen others are involved in this escapade, and some of them have taken the time to daub things on their bags, from outsize eyes to crescent moons, from swastikas to Stars of David, from undoable crossword puzzles to words that won't fit into them, like SOW and BIGFOOT. All in all, it's busy but banal, and we have to move on to bigger things, taking our bags with us. We ride the train as if wearing improvised raincoats, an idea not alien to those who live here and not in the trees. We pass muster and begin to sweat mightily when we clamber out on to the 50th Street platform. We help to lift a long shiny banner that is really a two-dimensional model of a subway car. As it floats and wobbles along, the real thing comes roaring past it and makes it buckle with a temporary wind, so we have to pull it taut again by moving ourselves, and the sticks we hold, farther apart.

"Fun," Bimini says with a gurgle.

"Surprise," I say. "You'd no idea."

"I was never down here before. What is it?"

Down below, I tell her, it's all trains. "Down here you go fast. In all directions."

"Let's do it," she says, and we board an express with some members of our troupe, after some trouble managing to align our plastic subway car down the center of the real thing, like a line with plastic washing hung on it, and its tenders or attendants like hunched gnomes in shiny black fisherman's oilskins. I am no longer homesick for the frogs, my treehouse, or Mother Russia; I am part of the ongoing human pageant again, yelling "This train will not stop again. Do not board this train. It is going on to the very edge of the universe. So beware." Now an exploded nuclear family joins us at Columbus Circle. They can hardly move around, so wide are their atomic fright wigs, shaped like mushroom clouds, five feet wide, three high. Styrofoam, I know, but the effect is pure Alamogordo. One look at them and you know they're doomed, have no red corpuscles left.

Any moment their faces are going to melt down on to their chests. Next thing Bimini is wearing one too as the grateful former wearer finger-washes his brow and ears. Now she looks the part, she really does, like a wasted human being ready bagged. Her awkward face fits in, and you can tell because people are looking at her as if she's the real thing, although they're sure she's wearing some kind of face prosthesis, dentist's wings and all. What better disguise, dearest, than an apparent disguise? Or is this the icebound logic of the camps? I can never be sure; but who cares? I am one of the walking wounded, a real wacko among the pretend ones, and if they asked me I could give them a few hints and tips. I prefer, though, to go along with what's already in motion. Bimini looks as if a pale blue cliff has fallen on her head and stayed put, or an electric haystack that doesn't weigh half enough. The trouble is her laugh. She is having too good a time to stand for anything so serious as holocaust, so she might be read as an ad for its advantages: Then you too can look like me. That she's a mongol doesn't matter. They wouldn't care if she was a coelacanth or a poltergeist. Whatever she is, it fits. Even the gusty, erratic laugh. As we head for 116th Street, we seem more numerous because others of the troupe have come into this car from others, some with flashy trinkets pinned to the insides of their coats, some in outsize pajamas bearing ancient-looking chamber pots.

And all of a sudden I do one of my shriek-outs, one of my whimpers. I wish it were winter because winter is all snow and then I can savor the voluptuous pageant of the city's blacks walking at freedom through it like ghosts. Whites don't count because whites do not show, any more than we did, doing our fifteen years, but blacks, they have shadows of obsidian, they would be blatant in Siberia where there are none at all.

Black sausage in a wasteland of cocaine.

I wish I had had them with me during that siege.

They would have sung me to sleep, the once-upon-a-time slaves singing the new slaves to sleep. Packed in their holds, crammed into tiny, hot, houses in the South, they knew long ago what the camps were like.

I tell her, my newcomer, but she gives her choked, prematurely exploding laugh and says something about how they scare her death. They look right into her eyes and she knows she looks funny.

"Black as night," I say. "Consoling."

"They come after you," she says, "and want to do things to you. *Things.*"

"The men," I say. "Like all men."

"I don't mind," she says. "I wouldn't. It's what I'm for, isn't it? I'm good for nothing else except whitening a step here and there, wiping a window, unstopping a john."

Amid the clamor of trains, we might almost be said to be talking at a shout, but we are shouting at a bellow. No, there isn't much beyond a shout that a human can rise to. How about a roar? We are shouting at a roar. Then we are roaring at a whatever it is, but we can't really hear each other. "Eez," she keeps saying, "*eez*." That's what she said before. "Eez me up," she screams. "They want to get next to me in this roach coach, then I be getting outside children." Her English has changed all of a sudden and I have to ask her again and again.

"They want to run my gates," she yells. "Don't you know what it is when you run a girl's gates?"

I can only guess. Is it within the camp or outside?

I guess wrong. "Fuck," she yells. "That's what it means. Really sloppy hard-on squirt-it-out fuck, like."

I ask her where she got such words, such turns of phrase, and she mutters something about a maid from, no not the South, but the South Sea, which must be her word for the Caribbean. The louder the noise around her, the more carnal she gets, the racier in speech. The saltier. Thank the Czar I have a translation background. I can cope.

"You iggrunt," she says. "You hurt my head."

Then bug off out of my treehouse, I think, but I do not mean it, do I, my distant darling, my *ulubiony*, as they say in Polish. My own language I do not do any more. I do not do it. It does not spring to my lips. It is among the dead languages. It is the language of the dead. I do not tell her this, but I am tempted. Come November, I will.

"You look like you had your chocklits," she says. "Like you ate 'em up."

This I understand, as I do when she says I belong in a horspittle, or that I am getting on her wick, but not when, as our train grinds down, stops, and a huge whore with vast breasts walks in, wobbling like epileptic lard, she giggles "Married by ten parsons." I ask, but she sniffles and pulls her face into a point with both hands. A Bimini pout.

"Big titties, iggrunt." She laughs again, then flashes her own at the mob, who are beyond caring about human physique.

"But," she says, "you don't always have to say the F word. You can say Fat."

"As in Fat Off," I ask.

"Fat Off is good," she says. "You learning."

"And Eff Off," I say.

"That," she pronounces, "is too dickty."

A long way off, far and away and unretrievable as a spent blizzard, my sweetheart hears me and with tears in her mouth says to stay away from this fresh trouble with an antique dictionary in its mouth. They'll give you another fifteen years, she warns. They always will. *Ulubiony*, I will, I will. Better, she goes on, to fix on the stone lady in the harbor there, the one with the bad-tempered bleb of a lower lip.

I promise, I say. I promise her. It is like trying to kiss the wind, to hug the fog. My heart is full of rhapsody, but my hands are full of Bimini on a crowded subway station with a riot beginning. Sleek in our plastic bags, we try to move away, but the mob shoves us toward the trains. It is like milking a cow with one hand while kneeling before the enthroned queen to propose marriage. Something as devastatingly uncouth. Sometimes someone will see his sweetheart from far off and try to aim his smile at her all through his approach, as she aims hers, and you have to be a third person, a watcher, to realize how hard it is for them both to keep the same smile as they near each other, their smiles flickering and altering from delight to fixed-grin delight, from that to self-conscious smiling at their facial predicament, with all the while the gap narrowing although they are not close enough to say anything, they are saving it up. They meet and they fuse their mouths. They no longer have any expression, but they remember all the shades of approaching love, each smile changing as it heeds the other's eloquent but awkward shifts. It is fun to do that through snow or rain or in the strong sunlight that makes even war veterans squint, or even lifetime pilots who have scrunched their eyes up against the avalanche of cloud-top light. Now, blindfold those two lovers approaching one another, and watch their expressions change before they are shot at the very same instant. So my mind goes, as it fails.

12. A Cell in Sukhanokvka

Eager for the tidy, the reciprocal, we cling to a miscellany—a four-leafed clover, a burnished medal from a foreign war, a sprig of edelweiss or a bluebell—that reveals an end in the beginning. We abhor the chaotic, as did the ancient Egyptians, insisting if we can on pattern, symmetry, design, yet rarely getting it. For instance, I could never catch myself saying, Well, I have seen the worst, the Gulags, dare I find the best in Central Park, that haven of luxuriant growth and spasmodic mayhem? I do not know from complementary opposites. There was the almost long-forgotten marriage, when I was a young agent sent away on taxing errands, and the wife who trained a big dog to attack me on my infrequent returns. Do I then find a genial hound of the Baskervilles in the Park, grovelling and fawning on my return from the pools? Not a bit of it. Life is messy, discontinuous, haphazard, and this I am almost accustomed to, ever ready for what comes next, which sounds to me like an old definition of sophisticated (the person who is never surprised). The Gulags make a useful testing-ground to see how sophisticated you really are. Or, in a quite different way, Central Park, of which in a way this is a story. Maybe, then, I am wrong; I should have seen what the

The Ice Lens

taiga park of the Gulags has in common with Central: the malefic and the benign.

A subtler point follows. The parallel exists in the mind, but not in actuality. What I presume to call open spacefulness reminds me not of bleakness and comfort, the vile and the accomodating, but of the open zone against which we figure, cavort and pose, forgetting how the end creeps toward us like a toxic fume from the sky, slotting the loathsome word "never" into our euphoric chandeliers. We will never come this way again. If King Lear, that touchy old fogey had extended his famous pentameter from "Never, never, never, never, never" to a billion nevers, he would not have exhausted the concept *never*, the infinite neverness of never. Had he, for a prank or to make a serious point no doubt backed by some holy reprieve, inserted a "just once" or even a hedging "usually," into the space occupied by the 1,000,000,000th "never," we might have taken heart. But, dead, you will never see your sweetheart again, nor, alive, will she see you. Nor, *dead*, will she see you. If this bears thinking about, or analogizing in terms of Gulag sentences and being shut away from each other for Stalin knows how long, then I am not the man for you. I find this paralyzing bleakness of the human interim too much to endure. Is this why some people wish they had never been born? One can see the point.

Even if you have not found your honey, the same will hold. You would like to have a further encounter to look forward to in half a million years, say. And the goodbyes, if somehow managed, have a basalt savagery, an unutterable bite that can transform the human, the moribund or the mourner, into a devastated mess of syrup. It is a misery we have not been trained for, unless by some resurrectionist faith, and even that cannot be trusted. Not by the likes of me, anyway, knowing in life what death will be like, and not even knowing how long her sentence is, what her condition, what her yearning says.

What sustains me then?

Opportune chance of falling out of my tree to my death.

Word from the Soviet Embassy that she has died or been released. Or is it the same?

Her voice on the oh-so-clear New York line.

Thoughts of going back to Russia to find her, but not being allowed in. Awful.

You can tell what kind of hero I have become, wailing from my tower, peering into my pools, finding her everywhere.

Or I would plead for a cell in Sukhanovka, the worst jail of all, converted monastery that it was. Please, a black-painted cell in which one can only stand.

Far from having confessed everything, I will make you an offer, a bargain: if you promise to read on, I will tell you how, up in my tree, I sang, and what I sang, with celibate gusto. Most of the agents I knew had been rebuked for not having schooled themselves sufficiently in languages. It was not enough to spout and savvy a little French or Spanish, not even Cypriot Greek or Turkish. No, we were never enough into Arabic, say, or Pashto. So, having applied myself, having had far too much time on my hands, I studied my big dictionary up in my tree and ended with a salient song:

O deu— per spacious skewja—
  Per anbar wegh agp gre-no—,
Per purple men-meg
  Upo to— brugh pele!
Amerigo! Amerigo!

Patriotic and not so furtive, really, it was there in readiness for any visit to an Indo-European country, to which none of my colleagues in the force were certain to have never traveled.

13. Contraseptics

When the show is over and we have handed back our plastic and banners, our sticks and wigs, it is as if the sun has gone out. Glum, we head back for Central Park and walk to our tree, watched by a couple of dogs. "You first," I say, "and be quick." She is more agile than she looks. Up I go after her, marveling at how people vanish into foliage. Maybe half the trees have houses built into them, and I wonder if this would increase the odds of our discovery. If there are enough tree dwellers to draw attention to the trees, then we're likely to be found. But, if there are hundreds of us, it will take the authorities a while to get around to us. I'd rather we were the only ones, though, like the last Neanderthals, or the first.

"You had an outing," I say.

She nods, but she seems abstracted; maybe she's forgotten about it already. There she sits in the rocker with her legs drawn up beneath her, posing, and I recall how I brought the rocker up here bit by bit, reassembling it with glue and a fanatic's care. You could bring half the world up here, I tell myself, if you had the patience to take it all to bits and climb the tree with it, like somebody smuggling Spain into Andorra. It's harder this way. Andorra into Spain is a mug's game, of course, isn't it, my darling? We did our bit under the very gaze of household spies. We met and we unmet, in garages, attics, cupboards, closed cars and open parks. Always with our blood pressure up high, so I came to link happiness with that old pounding in the chest, that tight headachy feeling, either of these as nothing compared to how I felt after they had slammed my genitals with heavy-duty plastic shopping bags full of sand, leaving not a mark behind but lowering one's spirits a great deal. Those were the days, when danger sharpened bliss.

She seems to come-to now, to return from whatever drab reverie has drawn her. "You look like you had your chocklits," I say, trying to be friendly in an idiom she likes. "You don't have to talk like that," she says, piqued. "I'm not a child, you know. What I say is one thing. You don't have to talk like it at all just to suit me." I see it now: she will have to go, either shoved off the platform during the night or manhandled away and tied to the nearest hydrant. As a street wacko she will pass muster, but as a live-in graft she won't do at all. She is too tricky, especially for somebody whose own pains occupy him to the exclusion of others' pains. A diversion, yes. An accompaniment, yes. A reminder of how badly mother nature can behave, yes. Yet there is this bloom on her blasted-looking face, this almost demure agitation to her limbs. She has a ruined charm. So perhaps the way to deal with her is to harness her, to arrange her in such a way that she'll do no mischief. I don't mean gagging and blindfolding her, although such things have figured in my past so much that I think of them as natural (like blowing your nose or picking your teeth). I mean harnessing her energy, curbing her reckless side, and I begin to think of the prosthesis windows of certain drug stores, where steel shines and rubber in its matte way collects up the light, and invalid chairs sit in frozen splendor and bedpans await their first mire. If only she could be catered to, she'd be no trouble at all but a marvelous and malleable plaything, a cross between a dog and an inflatable, yet able to talk her fancy pidgin when she fancies to.

"Bimini," I say, "do you want to stay?"

"So that's my name," she says. "For you."

"Why not? It's pretty enough."

"Pretty enough for a cow polly like me."

I do not ask. If I ask, she bridles, whereas, if I pretend to understand whatever she comes up with, she relaxes, comes out with something else every bit as bizarre. It is like watching a glacier calve.

"You just chopsin," she says, "like talking through your doie."

"If only I knew how," I say.

"I told them," she says, "before I lit out, they could always feed me some of their old contraseptics in case I was misbehaving, with so many trying to get past my gates, but they said that wasn't the way to go. That was not the way to go. It might go wrong. I might forget. That's how you get a squad of living outside children."

"Where did you learn?" I ask.

She barges on, heedless of questions. "I never had a chyle up in my life, not yet, but they always fuss about me that I will, see, and that is their main concern. They don't give me no credit for common sense. You put yours in before they put theirs in. It's that simple. Or theirs on them. You've heard about these things wherever you come from. Who are you anyway? What's your name?"

"Where," I ask her, "did you learn to talk?"

At home, she tells me witheringly. "I suppose you, being so smart, learned to talk from talking to fishes." I feel like the taxi driver who, instead of a radio has only a beeper, and cannot call in, receives only, is an hour behind, and whose meter is broken.

"Well, champ," she says. "You didn't say."

"So I'm champ today."

"Don't you get no wrong ideas," she says. "I was only talking."

Actually, I rather like to be called champ, as if I have acquitted myself with distinction on the track, in the arena, or the ring. The name appeals to the vainglorious side of me, the quiet longing for glory without ever taking my shoes off or exerting myself for more than thirty seconds. I used to be a champ at not getting nine grams of lead in the back of the neck. A lost skill. I did as I was told always.

"I'll let you stay," I say impulsively, "if you'll do as you're told. If not, there's no point. The only way to get on up here is not to attract attention. The champ has spoken."

"Crucial," she answers. "That's just crucial. You don't know what that means, do you, champ?"

Champ confesses, but he guesses too. "You don't like the idea," I say. I see us now as squirrels fattening themselves for winter, growing gray tails and punching nuts into the ground with that riveter-like motion, then scurrying back up to their drays, whose once-green leaves have turned gold and yellow and weightless enough to blow away. Onto, indeed, the covered pools.

"Maybe I do," she says. "Plenty much. Better than being cut open with them dickty knives."

Then, I tell her, I will work on things to make sure she lasts the course. I want to watch, I want to learn how to talk like that, I want to see what it feels like to have someone in your care. You see, darling, it has been so long since I had this sense of calling.

"Slong as I don't get no pumpkin in the oven," she says with a burly leer. "You better watch your ways. I got a nice purr and a fine easement, but they not for you. This is strictly room and board."

"Room," I say. "Unless you want to eat birds."

"You not even," she says, "going to put the munch on me."

Deciphering a mile or two behind her, I translate that she has a nice pair and a fine doie, and that I am not even allowed to kiss her, though. As if, my treasure, I would want to. After all the pageantry of bliss over the illicit years, I have to listen to this mutant talk about what she calls formication. I could put her on a special diet of grass porridge and nut salad. She would rebel. I have to find some way of calming her down, making her stay put, and shut up. I am a snowman turned anthropologist, I suppose, looking for exotic beings in the strict spirit of someone scouring the surface of Mars or any planet going around Proxima Centauri. What have we here? The youngest old bag in the universe? The oldest young one? If I am Champ, then she is going to stay Bimini. We can't have a lot of shuffling around, or names dropping off people like water from a dog. It takes courage, does it not, to live up to the name casually assigned you, just like the number they led you to Siberia with. When she yawns, I see bad teeth, which is amazing in someone whose family has a Caribbean maid, who probably has no teeth at all, but good gums trained on the mashing up of bananas. When she smiles, I see her other self, someone who without the language to express it has discerned the gap between the mind that yearns and the world that lets you down. On her bold bumpy she sits, as loath to go as to stay, not quite knowing how to make sure the champ doesn't shove her overboard while she sleeps.

Partly to counter her own brand of English with almost anything of mine, I begin to tell her the worst of it, the atrocious years as a snowman who learned to stare at a splotch on the wall, or even on his own hand, and see in there whole legions of the damned, regiments of infantry, hordes of weeping women, not to mention circuses, parades, pageants, weddings, birthdays, reconciliations, dances, airshows, surgical operations, show of painting and sculpture, and enormous ocean liners docking. The world. All you needed was the energy, and your mind's eye filled with rivers, trees, rocks, valleys, plains: the landscape amid which some miracle, miraculous because in the world outside, could come to pass.

"All you needed," I tell her, "was energy."

No response. She seems to have subsided into body language, her prerogative to be sure, but almost a parody of the energy I'm blathering about. For all the commotion of her fingers, wrists, knees, jaw and bumpy, precious little comes through that means anything. She seems to be writhing to an unknown tune, or to a metronome only jays or robins can fathom. Is she listening? No worse than the dead listen, at any rate. I resume, telling her, as if she were the representative from the United Nations, about the sixty million wiped out for one political reason or another, as if the whole of Mother Russia had become a gigantic mincemeat factory making a sludge or paste for all the cats and dogs in the universe. Worked to death, then ground or chopped up, left to wither like fish scales in the appalling winter of their graves, or simply "put away" with nine grams into the skull: that's what they were, and I sometimes marvel at the attention given to, the vogue for, other atrocities on a smaller scale. Sixty million is the entire population of some country such as Britain, isn't it? I imagine England, Wales, Scotland, and the northern part of Ireland devoid of people, completely empty for thirty years. Just damp echoes. No more. Just the wind.

More body language from her, a decelerated St. Vitus's dance, I suppose, with her eyes fixed on something far beyond the trees, and a minute strand of slaver running down the front of her chin as if exuberance has sprung a leak. On I go, reciting, for I have done it before in my mind's ear.

"Urinating into your hand, if you could, or into the hood of your jacket, or, if you had a bowl, using your ration of water to wash it out with. These were the jollies. We all got a daub of medicinal tar slammed between our legs, and you haven't lived until you've walked barefoot naked through the snow with that burning your groin like something invented for ribald counterpoint. What were the others there for? Not for fornication, to be sure, not for formication as you like to call it. One did a faulty analysis of some corn. Another allowed a spark from an engine to set a field on fire. Not much, when you come right down to it. The main point of such punishment was to show you how tight the range of good behavior was. They were so finicky. There was very little you did as a human being that was judged acceptable, and you only found out about it afterward. Oh, if we had only known what massive penalties attended such trivial things as not knowing when to stop applauding, or when to start, or when to utter one syllable less rather than one syllable more. The difference got you plucked away, sometimes with affable finesse. You could never tell if they were being nice to lure you in, or just being nice to tease you with how they'd be when they really came to get you. You listening, Bimini? One man, more determined than some, attempted a dry hunger strike (no water) until he reached the point at which he could see daylight through his hand. His hand had become translucent, Bimini, a bit like the man at Alamogordo who turned away from the blast and nonetheless saw the bones in his hand as if he'd been X-rayed."

None of this raises her, but it chastens me, I who of all things have cut my tongue on a mint with a hole in it, same shape as the Ring Nebula in Lyra. So whatever I say seems to come out lisped, and will for a day or two until the wet split heals. Such are the privileges of freedom: to speak with forked tongue cut on a candy.

"Yes, darling," I resume, addressing Bimini no longer but someone dearer by far and long ago ground up. "We took the kicks in the groin, the pummeling with sandbags, the heavy boots treading on the balls just a bit harder each time. And the rents in the intestinal wall. Being uplifted by the hair on jumbo-sized pliers. (Or, in some cases, by the mustache, like a certain engine-driver.) Or the cheese-grater on your back followed by a splash of turpentine or urine. Bedbugs and eczema. This is the kind of thing we should be enacting in the streets, on the subway platforms, outside the magic slab of the United Nations Building, not to protest, it is too late for that, but to warn, to say, darlings everywhere, this happens to be the main occupation, hobby, and career of mankind. Imagine that. Not books, symphonies, paintings, sculptures, dance, and sex, but mincing meat. The living flourish as a figure against the background of those chopped up. Not a pretty image, but one worth wearing in the buttonhole or any other hole for that matter. Never mind having to sit erect on a stool for three days without the slightest wobble, or being constantly hauled off to an interrogation, sweetheart, that never happens, or the feather up the nose, the hot iron up the backside, as if a sadistic blacksmith were the Lord of Hosts. The worst is when they tell you your sweetheart, your dear heart, is in the next cell. *Just listen, dear fellow.* And being raped by a bunch of syphilitic psychopaths. Hear those screams, Champ. They're all for you. Now, why not sign and get it over with? You never knew if it was playacting or what. And then they let you see a muffled female body walking away, limping away down the corridor, leaving a trail of bloodspots, maybe from a little bag of red ink, but maybe not."

I hear a voice from, where? Archangel? Magadan, or Omsk? No, it is the voice of Central Park saying "You look like you ate your chocklits." Thank heaven for levity. I can almost persuade myself that things weren't so bad for those fifteen years. Tempted to look on the bright side, I argue with myself. If there's a bright side, why not look on it? That's what a bright side is for. Choke to death on the silver lining. After how many years was it, you were allowed to have a few sheets of paper, which they numbered when they handed it over, and then you filled both sides, after which they took it away. You could not smoke it or eat it even if, later on, even later still, you had that Aladdin's lamp of a library request sheet on which you listed the books you had chosen from the catalog. That was a whole year's reading at one go. Fifty books ordered ahead of time for a year you knew you were going to survive because you'd ordered your reading already. It's all in the mind. I tell her this, the fidgety Bimini whose paw has now strayed into a grocery bag in search of cookies, instead of which she unearths a cheese snack. Wolfs it crumbs and all even while twitching in the incommoded slow writhe of hers. I too try to do it, as if we were dancing apart from one another, but visibly a couple who have come to the dance together. She whispers something. I do not ask. She whispers again. I ask. She wants something else:

"Humpday on the shank," she says. "How-sabout it?"

14. Vridlo

Time the vulture has no feathers on its neck. A sentence of seven years, plus an extra one for insolence, might well be construed as twenty years of life in the outside world, where, unless I am wrong, we do not live with the same frenetic intensity, the same locked-in misery. Unless we do. So, if you enter the Gulag at forty, you emerge, if you are lucky, at sixty, at least by that reckoning. And there, where you should be eating a meal with protracted slowness in order to use up the time, say a second breakfast of double mastication, you have to gobble. And so, while forced to live in defiant intensity, half-wishing you were not alive, you have to rush things. No wonder they trap you in colliding equations, opposing miserable depravity to fateful speed, turning the inmate into a dawdling lightning bolt, turning him inside out with contrary motions. You listen to your fellow-prisoners and can tell they have no idea what speed to imagine their lives at, beginning a sentence slow but ending it fast lest the knout fall, or starting fast, just to get a word in, but ending in slow meander out of sheer relief as the knout has passed by unaimed. What has got them there? Wit, nerve, luck and lewdness, dogged smarts and stealthy grandeur, mayhem and melody, the bread of paradise and the nettles of hell, minds like tadpoles or outboard motors, misunderstanding, slander, plagiarism, libel, treason, envy, myth, mummery and the blithe indifference of the eupeptic citizen, making of his life a grateful album.

You see, I know how to sentimentalize both cause and effect. A well-suited man climbs into a train, sheds his pelf and cufflinks, and emerges at the other end your perfect hobo, wincing and breathing fast. Conceivably, in certain camps, you could spend the entire fifteen years being tattooed, or changing sex back and forth, or scribbling on bits of paper shoved into a secret hidey-hole. Or you could go into a state-of-being called accidie *durée*, the apathy of timelessness. Now and then you hear tales of prisoners who got away, to tramp the snows until they reached Finland or Finland swooped out to grab them, having arranged in one rail car a false partition with just enough space behind it to accommodate three men and their bread. When the train is completely unloaded, the guards inspect for emptiness, and the cars move off. The rest is up to initiative or imagination, the final count at the camp gate having been fouled up by some commotion over a fox. In one version, they took a guard with them and, using knives, cut him to bits which they dropped onto the tracks at regular intervals, first the eyes, then the ears, the tongue, the penis, the balls, the fingers, the toes, then the internal organs in a kind of reverse paper chase across the drifts. I think this modified myth has a cannibalistic basis, since, it's said, two of the escapees ate up the dead third, raw and cold, for weeks. Who were these men? Former commissars? Had they no names? Increasingly, thanks to conjectural misapprehension and blurred naming, the escapees amounted to seven—Zhuk, Rapporport, Kogan, Yagoda, Berman and Frenkel—notorious assassins and killers, now escaping with their own lives from their own camps. One poor bastard, smelling smoke while on some drab assignment in the Church of the Beheading on Sekirnaya Hill, peed on the fire all the way from the belfry to the pews, and was hanged in the belltower for his cheek. Or so it was said, as the corrosive magnifications gathered impetus, aimed at history, and the believers began to wilt, thinking myth rather than truth would save them. Why myth? Not, *I* say, because Aristotle could never define it (had they even heard of Aristotle?), but because myth had the human touch of meddling and interference, a scar carved on the universe, an invented life ever more prevalent than a real one.

 This must be why, having survived, I cherish a diminished response to truth or fact, inspired years ago, perhaps, by the camp acronym, *vridlo*, meaning Man Temporarily Replacing Horse. Such were the dream-teeth of the put-upon.

15. A Snow Gazelle

Half-inclined to dandle her on my lap, to feel her up as she'd like, fingering and measuring this hole or that, I lose interest before I've even begun to signal her across the homemade tree room to come and get it, come and be cuddled grown-up fashion. My mind is on the Angels of Mons, who flew above the battle in the trenches, the Madonna of the Sleeping-Cars, the gorgeous phantom of the *wagons-lit*, and then at last the female figure, buxom and lithe, who used to come and stride along a distant ridge in the wind, her skirts blowing, her hair awry. Each of us thought she was his own, come to hearten him before she plunged down into the airless valley, to the iron-bound gates of the camp, there to plead for us, give her body for us, volunteer to take our place. The syphilitics could have her for a day if only she could have us. She was an apparition, I suppose, unless hired by the camp commander from among the local whores to come and drive us mad with longing. For a year she came and went, at least for me, a snow gazelle, a wind temptress, a pain maiden. Then one day she vanished and it was as if she too had been gathered up, confined, questioned, broken, sentenced, and transported according to the good old recipe for making good citizens.

Hello there, you on the ridge.

Give us a flash, darling, sister, mamma.

Come on down and let us sink our remaining teeth into your succulent hams.

That idyll dies, though, as Bimini heads across the floor to me, having played stinkfinger with herself for the length of an old prisoner's reverie, accosting me with an almost murderous imperious whisper such as some of us were obliged to speak in for years. She would have been a terror in the camps, not so much a camp follower as a camp hollower. Nothing moved. We stayed put. I stay put right now while she paws my broken genitals as if prospecting for a crocus in early spring. I shove her off. She bites my thigh. I give her a token slap. She spits on my hand and licks it off. It cannot go on like this. She is not striding along a Siberian ridge in the gale, she's tampering with a garden, with a potpourri best left dead and buried in my pants. Too late to be my sweetheart now, I tell her. All that is over, though it was a fine lusty thoroughfare for a year or two, until we were found out on that terrible day: the club-foot commissar with his revolver, raving away in a language only a zoo could love, shoving the barrels and sight up her nostrils, into her places, tapping my teeth out, one, two, three, with insane precision as he wondered what to do: shoot us there and then or save us up for the spit, the treadmill, the ducking stool, the zweibacked fire made with gasoline and handcuffs.

And it was she who yelled at him, calling him lout, sadist, ogre, goon, psychopath, cocksman, half-wit, beast. As if *she* had caught *him* in some unspeakable act and not he us among the ferns and the dahlias, as plugged into each other as two summer flies. Stay like that, I thought I heard, and then he charged us like some football player, to barge us apart. Next, he pounded back, limping grossly, to the other wall and ran at us again, growling wetly, either to knock us apart (which by then we were of course) or to knock something loose from us, from out of us. Off came his jacket with the shoulderboards, and then his pants, and in no time he was charging us naked, missing each time as we moved out of the line of fire. How he bellowed, how he smelled and sweated, the revolver in his hand all the time. I was amazed it didn't go off from sheer percussion as he thundered into the wall again and again, vowing feats of vengeance so awful I expected the blood to come out on his brow like ectoplasm. What he proposed would require only a few tools: a frying pan, a knife, some wire, a chisel, a pair of pincers, a flame thrower, a liter of acid, a big darning needle and some fuse wire, lard, cement, and a hammer and nails. After that a sack with a wide neck.

And none of it happened. The hand in the front of my jeans can find nothing to fondle. I let it happen. I go up, I come down. She jabs me hard in the anesthetized zone, then yells something right into my face about easement, one of her most-used words. All right. She starts again. I rise, and oh how she works on me. A quick flash later she is squatting right by me with my seed on a cheese cracker, humming to herself as if this is all she wants out of life, so long as I can provide. No madonna of the sleeping car, she, but the vestal of poontang. *Bimini Quiminy*, I murmur, but she reaches up and taps my mouth. I have interrupted a spell. She is eating the host. It has been a long time although, I, not to put too fine a gloss on it, have never spurned the advances of the ladies who own the pools I tend. On the average, one in five has let me skim her, drain her level, empty her basket of leaves, always in the abstracted way I reserve for predominant human activities. I hump with what is left. They marvel and coo at the scars, the weals, and then they busy themselves mightily to prove to me that I am still a man. Once a man, always a victim, I say, but never aloud, as they toil with whatever skill they have. I am like some ethereal plumber.

What I have just allowed to happen, no doubt of it with a minor, can get me jailed in this state, so clearly something has to be done, not about the ladies who own pools, the chlorine tribe, but about this ragamuffin amateur masseuse who's moved up into the trees with me, her mind an aviary, her body a defeat, her tendency voracious. All lick and flick, she belongs anywhere but in a tree. For fun, but also to shut her out while I think, I slip a garbage bag over her head and shoulders and she leaves it there, contentedly munching or savoring inside, just visible behind the brown-green film.

What she needs is the commissar to charge her with revolver in hand. That would curb her, send her to the other side of the treehouse floor.

What I need is the right means of restraint for both me and her. I can see it now, how I will get used to her delicate handling, start sipping and tupping when I should leave well alone, and end up with a bad case of taboo, as addicted to her snotty-milky smell (the urchin and the baby both in one) as the jailer to his keys. She even has the contraseptics with her, as she says, brandishing them like so many foreign coins. What I really ought to do is send her down among those who can appreciate her most, not so much sexually as, say, the feline-faced novelist who *does* the wretched of New York, or the Salvation Army who will give her a bugle and a headband and let her march. She does not have to end her days inspiring a semi-castrato from Mother Russia, adding his ammonia smell to the ones she already has. I can just see the headline about the massage parlor in the treehouse, the giveaway having been the endless line of clients going up the rope-ladder for what she calls easement: Bimini's Brothel.

Still under the see-through plastic, she looks as she did in the subway earlier in the day, as if what's going on here is an encore performance but private, kinked for special tastes in a special kind of bind, and no holes barred.

If I were superstitious I would think she'd been sent to me for special treatment. I'd feel I'd been singled out: a unique man for a unique case. Neither of us is unique, however, and unlikely to be so. Two passing samples of the majority, that's us: I merely one in sixty million, she—well, I don't know the odds of being like her, having that sort of Japanese-Korean face, the swollen dumpiness, together with the levitating smile that comes right out of her condition and flies away after a brief good-nature ground reconnaissance. Two sherpas that pass in the night. That's us. Either leading the other astray, with no more sense of responsibility than those ghouls in Russia, picking up each Friday a payslip for destroying other people's lives. What, I always wondered, did it say on the slip? Did it spell things out?

> Two nine-grams, in cellar.
> One nine-gram in yard.
> Unphysical interrogations: three.
> Physical interrogations (part of team): four.

The Ice Lens

One house arrest. Woman and man. Resisted.

What might they pay for a random lot such as that? Do you know that, my dearest, wherever you are? In whatever lending library of the soul you have landed up in, my *ukochana*, my bed of roses, my garden of delight, my sundial, my celery root, my hothouse. You too learned that one overcoat is worth how many onions, I suppose, in whatever loathsome cowshed they assigned you to, where they read you fake letters from me, urging you to confess. They urging you, I urging you. Strange: they urge you to confess so that you, as distinct from they, know what you are being punished for, rather than at someone's whim. It kind of clears the decks, appeals to their sense of neatness, lets them get on with somebody else just as innocent, at any rate not meaning any public harm.

Here comes Bimini full tilt now, up out of the garbage bag, her eyes streaming, but all she wants this time is a cuddle, and I do believe she has wet herself, not in the dank faciliatory way of all women as they grease the chute, but as a child would. A flood out of excitement and maybe even happiness.

"Sea pud," she says. Is she hungry?

"Got to daub yourself," I say, groping for kleenex a year or two old, and as frayed and old-leafy as the stuff in the branches around us.

"Just an old sea pud," she says. "See what I did."

Acrid, picric. That's how she smells. All words ending in -id or -ic fit her. She's a normal soul for all her wanderings, all her lusts. Wiping and blotting, I feel more female than I have in years and curiously pleased at so humble a role at this altitude in this day and age, like someone called to service after long disuse.

Ever since my release and my discharge from the DFI, I have pondered what some call the problem of evil, to my mind a problem of blighted balance: six million Jews versus what? Armies of millions or just a few psychopathic zealots? Sixty million Russians versus the NKVD? It is hard to know how many have actually done the evil deed, instancing various war crimes trials in Germany and Japan, whereas the ancient Greeks make a better job of it, calling the whole depravity *deinosis*, things at their worst, almost implying that the evil has done this to itself. Evil has made itself be evil, and whom do you punish then? The Russian way, it seems, is to let sleeping dogs lie, bad history to be abandoned in a secretive mist, which is no doubt why the camps lingered on, even after Chernenko. The newest category becomes "bad luck." Round-ups take place, of war and peace criminals, but how they drag. The ever effervescent world spins on, twice faster than sound. We never catch up with the evil done us, even if we manage to live out a normal span. And I end up mooning in a tree, a comparatively liberated, unemployed man, well aware that, for me, the whole racket has whirled away too fast in a changing world even while, for my loved one, it endures, a ghost present at its own imminent absence. To be stretched back in time while going forward in a treehouse, because my sweetheart is lost in my own past, is brutal, and to worry about her (grotesque understatement, considering her conditions) is an act of deliberate anachronism. She is lost in a political jungle and will come out, if at all, warped and stunted, a doyley of a woman.

My problem is that, once you get past the sadic lusts of the guards and convoys, there is the political structure to reckon with, and how much of what it ends up doing it intends. The awful thought is that its viciousness, so routine, becomes unintentional, like the famed punctual walking of the philosopher Immanuel Kant. Horrors dreamed up in Moscow translate themselves in the Gulag into primitive behavior, which seems to be the only artform of the goon. If there is a straight, vile line from HQ to the razor wire surrounding the *zek*, it is hard to find, even harder to reveal. The only thing harder to reveal is a good deed. My only guess is that, if there were no death, there would be less hatred. Oh there would be some, but it would not have behind it the fatidic disappointment verging on madness that afflicts us all and drives some of us into savage, near-mathematical reprisals, not on death, but on its other victims. To take death or its siblings into one's own hands is to commit a sibling chivalry, is it not?

Our Department of Foreign Intervention has not taught this, but it has taught us intervention, which is what crimes against humanity are. Alas that, instead of getting on with our formal jobs, we intervened, as it were, with each other. Love always finds a way, but our chances were limited, with the weight of our governments pulling us back. We would have done better to stay apart and read *Romeo and Juliet*, wishing we too had started being star-struck in our teens.

Yet, if you ignore the psychological component in all this grief, is our predicament as bad as that of the poor devils who have actually perished amid an oily fug that smells of apples and garlic, leaving a yellow fume behind it? Of course not. We still have a chance of rebeginning life as two *mutilés de la paix*. They will watch us as we shuffle together from greasy spoon to some rare public toilet, pausing to share a hotdog from a street vendor, accepting the guidance of a blind man and his expert dog at a Manhattan intersection, our mouths grotesquely crinkled by an attempt at crypto-conversation in German:

She: "*Sitzenpoppenbangtuben?*" ("Car exhaust?")

I: "*Donaudampfshifffahrtsgesellschaftskapitaen.*" ("Ferry on the river.")

Oh better far, we think, the lilac foliage of jacaranda trees in Harare. We trudge across, inhaling rank dog and car exhaust, a bit farther eastward. Then halt, not liking it. We decide to go back, once guided.

16. A Wheel

Familiar night sounds begin, but I tell myself this is more than the onset of night, it is the beginning of winter. Of all the gifts I have, most of them so minor as to have no name, my strongest is the drive toward hibernation, to slow heartbeat and brainbeat, hunker down and let it all happen without paying the slightest heed to it. I am also strongly tempted to hibernate in spring and fall too, but I never do. Now with another mouth to feed, so to speak, depending on how long I can stand her, I need to broaden my range of interests. Maybe we will slink into a movie theater some day, muffled up as if celebrities afraid of being identified, I the long shank with the brylcreemed shock of gray, she the incipient sumo wrestler with hands as broad and hard as tortoise shells. At least she is dry now or at least untackily damp. The fit is over. Sleep steals across her brow even as she sags from my clutch to the floor. Now I can listen to Nimet of the airwaves. Had I enough initiative, I would have the cable in by now, tapped from some inconspicuous spot at the park's edge, and be watching the night porno shows with the sound turned off and the grand ovations of Richard Strauss or Villa Lobos pouring in a lovely chromatic swill into my earphones. All this noise in silence. I do declare that, around three in the morning, I can pick up the city's pulse. A tree is a stethoscope, my beloved faraway one in your shallow ice-rimmed grave, could you but hear it with me. Would you approve of my afternoon's escapade with this hoyden or would you curse me for being a hapless Onan?

The midnight music soothes, the manicured tones of the announcer strengthen its effect, and in my hands I have an old lacquer box supposedly painted in the village of Kholui. I know the picture by heart, dearest one: a rather glowering ruddy-faced sun looks sharp right as the young crowned prince with flowing scarlet cloak holds a quite zaftig princess tight aboard his over-muscled charger, trapped by the painter in mid-leap above a motley though gaudy parade. Beneath its right hoof glows the *de rigueur* minareted castle, while behind the galloping prince and the hefty princess in green silk there puffs an ancient North Wind, his face haloed in a ruff of pale gray fish scales. A piece of my childhood, this, it conveys not merely the notions of capture and escape, but also the joys of flying, although the horse with long billowing orange tail seems to have no wings. It flies through sheer exertion of leaping. The whole background has filled with whorls, which look like snails of varying purple tints. I run my fingers in the dark over the surface and re-touch that fabled ground on which I too romped and jumped, flew and disobeyed. His feet in crimson boots dangle down at the same level as the horse's hooves, but the horse is not being ridden, it is going its way under its own steam, while her feet encased in pink slippers dangle flimsily beneath the horse's belly. They are headed for the castle, precious mine, they have a rendezvous with fate or some wicked uncle or benevolent sire. It doesn't matter. What matters is that they are on the move, and the castle, which I now recognize as a chunk of proto-Disney, could be a somewhat elaborated treehouse lodged in branches of the sky, amid the arms of almost any galaxy. The foreground is all boiling seaweed, so no wonder the horse has taken to the air, its coiffed mane gleaming for being that much nearer the sun. How many lives all right and awry went into the smelting of this myth, this fairytale? Did it come out of the painter's head as it were out of nothing? It couldn't, surely. There had to be antecedent examples even if he lied about them, as with the sixty million without whom we'd have no myth of the nation chopped up for dog meat, would we now? You can't just blow the bubble of such an atrocity and get people to take it on trust. No, it has to happen to the sixty million first so that the Gulag will become as real, as dismally powerful, as Troy, say, or Babylon. Similarly with treehouses: there have to have been enough actually built and lashed in place for there to be any respectable lore about them. It

The Ice Lens

has to have been. How I wish, though, it were possible to live among things predicated on nothing at all: whim, fancy, doodle, uninspectable, and then my long lost one and I, having soared out of the framework of a fairy tale, could soar back into it. We were never real.

Out of Cloud Cuckoo Land into the Gulag and then back out of it into Cockaigne or wherever else we had imaginary visas for. Then they could not have killed either of us or driven either mad. How does that conversation go?

"A mistake has been made, Comrade."

"In this society mistakes are not made. We may not know much but we know that, and I do not mean to imply, in saying we don't know much, that we are inadequate judges of how wonderful our polity truly is."

"Nonetheless, a mistake. You are not of Earth."

"No?"

"Your sentence has been adjusted, from fifteen to minus three."

"Minus three?"

"Correct. You have our ideological apologies, lady and gentleman."

"You are deferring to our princely status. How, though, does a minus sentence come into effect?"

"It is a gift of years, to be used as you think fit."

"But how do we get our hands on the years given?"

"Live twice as happily. For three years, Comrade, think about the thirty not handed out."

Now there's a fairy story for you. What gall. What callow high-handedness. I wonder what his wages slip said for that week. Restitution of pipedream rights? My love and I are made of paint laid gently to rest on the lid of a box, and then lacquered to make us immortal. If only it worked like that. Then you could abide opening up the box and finding a Bimini inside, herself a legend inasmuch as nobody thought such beings as she could be until the first one appeared. And even then.

No doubt she's wondering who or what the hell *I* am too. What ails me. What keeps me going. Which doctors I am in flight from. (Those who inject sulfur into your knuckles, darling.) She is not real to me because I am not real to her. Something dubious there. Finders keepers. So it would seem. Except that finding her is hazardous. There are laws. There are no laws in Russia against bumping off sixty million through attrition or with nine grams, but there are laws in the United States against tampering with the groin of someone fifteen. It's all relative. By no stretch of imagination can I be her prince galloping off with her to the Disney castle, but I seem to be doing something akin. I have passively kidnapped her, or she me. We have come together under the branches, not to discuss poetry or politics, but for nothing at all. We amount to a collision of atoms as ephemeral as butter smearing bread. Her snuffling snore reminds me that I have become responsible for each and every gram of her, flawed as she is. I could not sell her or give her away. Or donate her. Make her into a celebrity, yes, granted the means. Or I could just tie her up, gag her, and leave her here in a Gulag all of her own, to fate and the chance of a park attendant finding her.

The thought dies, if ever alive, as something lands with a crash, not a squirrel, no doubt a crow, on the frail roof over us. They are bombarding, invading. We are theirs. "Was that thunder," she asks. "No, a crow, I bet. Go back to sleep." Surely there isn't another treehouse built above us, dumping its garbage after hours? Even a crow dropping as dead weight wouldn't make a bang like that. In the gloom with my astronomer's redhooded flashlight I begin to look. Whatever it was must have come right through the roof and what I heard was its hitting the floor. It could have brained either of us. By feel and fidget I try to find it, touching only a bucket, the rockers of the rocking chair, and the paper bag for garbage. Then I feel the round hardness of it, the thing that does not belong: smooth at the center, about eight inches across, and round, rubbery, with a bit of give in it. A wheel. A *wheel* has fallen from the sky into our treehouse, from a not very big airplane. How will it land now and where? This is a minor wheel, I guess, a nosewheel or a tailwheel, but by any standards it now belongs to *us*: a footrest, a paperweight, a podium on which to make speeches. Two things have arrived unbidden: she and it, the princess and the charger, which is an odd way of looking at it. What will be third? Will it be soon? Will it kill one of us off? It will either solve my problem for me or make a new one for her, although she did rather well before I arrived. Tree-living is rather easy to pick up, I suppose, provided you don't go for sudden walks.

"Can't sleep." She says. "Humpday's come again."

No, not while I am listening to music: Bach at his most pounding. She is already upon me, sour-breathed and urgent. She grabs. There is almost nothing. Now there is more. It doesn't feel so bad in the dark, almost like wetting yourself in a dream. Our fingers fly in unspoken consent. And now I am waiting for the jailer to appear with his sandbag, the usual glob of tar in his hand, and then the twin stools on which we must sit erect in the corridor for three days, beaten if we wobble. Is that why she wets herself again? It is like sitting in the middle of Holland, howling for a ton of blotting paper. In her, too many things have linked themselves together: to become hot is to have to wee, and who knows what else goes with it. Maybe a tendency to throttle her lover and feed on him high in the trees, chattering like a squirrel. Dropping the shreds of me to the ground like nut shrapnel.

"Off to sleep again," I say, yearning for Bach or even Sousa. "You're nothing but an old sea-pud." She agrees and takes the few steps to the other wall where the partly inflated pool inflatable has become her bed. She knows nothing of the wheel. I almost said of wheels, but she is nowhere near that primitive unless she wants to be, in a fit of backtracking barbarism.

Now I have to find the lacquer box so that I can stroke it again while listening to the vulnerable delicacy of Nimet's voice and whatever she happens to be making spin. All operas merge for me, opuses into opera of my own casual making. When I flick the switch I tap the dimension called music rather than taking in the confines of any one specific work. It's rather like Bimini's approach to sex: an endless bolt of fabric rather than any specific garment.

Soft-pawed rain now, fostering coziness, helps me drift among the sirens and the music as I fondle the lacquer and rest one foot on the wheel almost in the pose of the shot down genius pilot who flew the wheel down safely after being jumped by a Red in the sun. Blasé, at rest, but suffering little twinges of post-coital sadness, I half-long for the camps again in an outburst of sadistic self-derision, as if I have not fulfilled my promise. Having to make one's mind up from scratch about everything fatigues the man whose every move for fifteen years was laid out for him beforehand, so that instead of a man he became (didn't he, dearest one?) a bundle of reflexes, a post-Pavlovian puppy. From pools to treehouses, that was fine. It met my needs, like WQXR, and pretending to be wacko in the subways. But now, the holy design on the lacquer box has broken up, the lacquer no longer embalms me, the box is open, it has a wheel and a girl in it, the inside of my shorts is wet and sticky, the sentence has been canceled, I have been awarded minus three years in which to savor the delights of being still alive, and I wonder: Do people actually make this up as they go? This life, I mean. Off the cuff, on the spur of the moment, sight unseen? The very word reminds me of what I used to be. I *translated*, which meant, strictly speaking, I carried things across, from one language to another, with only the torrent of incomprehension in between. Yet what I liked most of all is what I did as a child in school, confronted time and again with something called Unseen Translation. They'd hit you with it, out of the blue, and you had to do the best with it you could. No help. No dictionary. No clue as to where it came from or by whom it was. I thrived on that, better then than now. I have become so sedate, an ex-prisoner whose essence has become the seen, the familiar, the known. Why, even then, in the days of our cavorting adulterous passion, I would go to a strange city, seize the map and draw the dia-

The Ice Lens

gram of the addresses I was to call at, and then become so engrossed in drawing it, embellishing it, adding curlicues and minarets to the plan of my doings, that I never even went outside to use it. It remained on the bed, cartography of the might-have-been. When I got back, you chided me. "You never went?" I drew the map, I used to say, and that was enough, by which I meant to tell you that the symmetry or asymmetry of my street plan was a better treat, for me, than actually mounting the steps and ringing the bell for Howdydos. Sometimes I would have to go north, then retrace my steps to go east, after which I went north again. You can see the pattern developing, and the various options that presented themselves thereafter. Years of this gave me a wad of little street plans, crumpled and frayed, not from being jammed into my pocket, pored over in snow and rain, but from being fondled indoors until put away into the lacquered box. Constellations I called them, dear heart, as you know, yet not so much, in later years, in the position of the amateur astronomer trying to make a recognizable shape by connecting up the dots as trying to find the dots within the pattern. I was a universe trying to find its signature carved into this or that pine tree in the orchards of space.

From all those light years away you chide me now, again, saying not your old refrain (*Dear heart, how you like this,* your mouth uncupping the glans, then cupping it again), but something vaguer, about my not being much of an explorer.

Imagine me, then, while she was at her devotions, explaining to her, even if somewhat breathlessly, that I was at best a fondler of lacquered boxes, a throwback to a Russia hardly anybody could remember: not just an aristocrat of the soul (having a mere translator's salary), but a Tartar of taste, a Boyard of style. And a luster after other men's wives, never mind the risks, but mainly a luster after one in particular, enmeshed in a marriage virtually arranged, beauty made to wed the beast in his rough tunic with the fancy shoulderboards which, for all their pomp and sheen, looked almost homemade, poor-looking stars on poor-looking material to make an austerity epaulet. I sometimes, during my vists, donned his spare tunic to make her laugh, strutting with naked loins as a pseudo-commissar. Actually he was only a deputy commissar, but had enough clout to send sixty million away if he had wanted to, to empty the country out even if only for the weekend, so's he could get a better view of the landscape, the city streets, the Black Sea coast. I arrived disguised and left in different disguise, sometimes done up as a woman in wig and everything. How she laughed when I appeared or got ready to go, unless she was weeping, which she often was until ardor consumed us, fanned us on, on the rug or under the bed or in the wardrobe or out in the greenhouse swathed in plant and bloom. We lasted longer than I thought we would, but nothing goes unrevealed for long, not even outright happiness.

My, what a restless sleeper she is. Now I have to show her the wheel by pink light. She tripped over it on the way over and, give her credit, knew it wasn't there before. I do not tell her it fell from the sky, I let her think it somehow rolled there, all ten pounds of it, from some other part of the platform, stirred to motion by a train passing far underneath us. She likes it, I can tell, fondling the treads of the tire, the hubcap (if such wheels have them), and smiling that self-satisfied mysterious smile of hers as if, later on, she is going to do something to me with this wheel, something I am not much going to like. For now, though, she seems content to pick it up once, heft it knowingly, then set it down with her foot on it. She must have fielded wheels before, in some playground of the night. "Well, you don't like it much," she says.

I know what she means.

"Now and then already," I say.

"Nothing regular," she says, saying it as *redlar*.

Hearing nothing, she goes on. "It isn't right. You got to have your jollies, you need to get your greens."

I sure as hell do, but the past—how can I tell her, my ultramontane darling in the camps, about the past, not so much a past as the simple absence of time. I am not going to start up now, all over again, not with this one; and yet, only someone this outrageous can quicken me now. I am far gone. The ruined man needs the scourge. The moth yearns to be lit by the passing butane lighter. Tell her something, then, anything, or she will bash my head with the wheel.

"It comes and goes," I say, "with me."

"What I said," she says. "Nothing redlar."

She scoffs at the music I have left playing, hands me back my earphones with a surly whisper. "Old stuff, that. You need some life in your life, champ."

Now I dislike being called champ or Champ. Five minutes ago, I didn't mind, but now it offends, it makes me want to be called almost anything else: Chaffinch or Catherine, Gulag or Aloysius. A number would be better. Or a stuff. Cotton or Sacking. I have it. I tell her to call me Snow. She ignores me, doesn't want to call me anything. She has trapped herself up here with a dud. She was better off before, when she was alone and had the whole of Central Park to chop at, slipping down the tree of life to affright the rapists, the muggers, steering right toward them with her terrible intense frown and those not quite coordinated limbs beneath which, for some reason, you expect to see tank treads. That was her golden age, so I guess this is her Enlightenment. I try again. Call me *White*, I say, and this seems to please her a bit more. "I'll be White for a day," I say, "to see if you get used to it. It doesn't sound bad. Mister White." Comrade White. Prisoner White. I am the white elephant who can't forget. Call me up by any random number and I will answer to it. I have been trained to be nameless. I know the one syllable of my name, much as a dog does, but its texture eludes me, and trying to get to know myself by name is like trying to munch a tunnel through the Siberian snows with my entire body become a conduit for tepid water, briefly mulled before it squirts back out of me to mark my track with watered-down saffron blobs, easy meat for helicopters or dogs. They let you munch your way almost to the border, then haul you back in and forcefeed you with scalding soup that has no food value. You can't serve your sentence if you're dead and gone.

None of this is for her. She'd never believe it, but I do begin to see the first glimmerings of something she might like, something more ambitious than doing mime and drama in the subway stations, though she would have to be trained. She would have to restrain herself and, yes, go partly in disguise. How about a red face with a white mouth? In sunglasses. With her hair trussed up in the flag of some half-decent country. I will take her out in society, not to show her off but to show it off to her, much more richly and persuasively than today, with far finer props and much more demanding company. If only she will behave, we might have a going-on of sorts. Until we tire of each other. It might be 1905 and a dove-gray electric car has just pulled up, the chauffeur in his peaked cap perched high in the open air at the wheel, his gaze aimed downward as Bimini in fluffy evening wrap faced with fox prepares to step up, quite high, to the running board between the two glowing pale blue wheels. This is an electric vehicle. I, for my part, suave with a bow that exposes the deep central part in my larded-down hair, hold the door lest a soft breeze make it bang against her. She soars like an aerial blossom up alongside the lantern, then ducks into the car as I straighten, the buttons on my vest catching the lamplight of the street, and prepare to move around to the other door, having sealed Bimini in place, careful not to trap her train. Except that, when I get there, she has vanished. She has walked in and through. The chauffeur is no longer looking. His eye is on the boulevard that is his destination. Not a sound save the slight creak of the magneto inside the hood somewhere. As with electrical cars, so perhaps with treehouses: she will walk in and through, off and down. That is the point. The scene fades. I will never again, my dearest one, be the sleek servitor of any sumptuously attired passenger, never again be escort and gallant. The car drives away and ends up on some Italian rubbish heap. The chauffeur dies piloting a carelessly flown bomber in Ethiopia. All I can recall now is the deputy commissar on the telephone, his face the red of raw beef, summoning men in raincoats to escort us to our new resting place where we will wait until he decides what to do with us. Coming in, he slams her face with the nearest thing, a lamp, and gives her a deep cut from ear to eye, and it is still bleeding when they frogmarch her away while she lets out one slight high-pitched scream as if the steam of her life is coming out. I never saw her face again although I may have seen the back of her head.

"I've seen some terrible things," I murmur to Nimet.

"I am a terrible thing," Bimini says. "To some."

I am lost in another world, of samovars and blood, of torture and romance: political, whereas, I presume, she comes direct from the Almighty. "Not so bad," I say. "You'll do. You do."

Oh not again. "Sea pud" she says. "Aren't I a one?"

At least she has kept her distance this time, but I know I am already beginning to smell picric and cupric, tannic and acidic. All those things. She inundates on cue. I have only to speak and away she goes, provoked by some delicate osmosis I should wonder at. I don't. I all of a sudden feel invaded, looked in upon, my bolthole turned into an asylum.

"Go to sleep," I say harshly. "It's beddy-bye time."

"You've got your music," she says. "What about me?"

"Hug your wheel," I say, unthinkingly, as if she has it over there with her. She does. She has. She's got it in bed with her, so to speak, but she still wants music, although not WQXR. Next thing I am humming somebody's Quartet in G Major, tracking the tune as best I can, and five minutes later the long even breaths begin to sound as of a tide coming in, and the wheel goes bump from her clasp, and the night sky clears and begins to wheel its brilliance for me to admire. It is the harmony of a jigsaw puzzle whose black spaces you get to love, lower by one eighth of an inch than the surrounding curly fretwork. Oh, she's not so bad, *White*, I tell myself, actually lapsing into using a name. She has her moments after all. Maybe there is a reward from her shipping magnate father. He more probably wholesales celery and beets. I stop humming the tune. No, I lost the tune ages ago, it was too complex for whistling. Now I can listen to it at my ease, wondering when it was I first put music in sleep's place, back there in snowman's land trying to play entire symphonies in my head, drowning out the berserk wind that had nothing to halt it. Our bed, or rather his bed and ours, was a conventional double, with an unswept rhomb of dust beneath, the furniture ordinary pale boxwood, and the walls bare except for one photographic mural of a Mayday parade over the bed's head, as if a whole procession were there to scare adulterers away. The curtains were of thick velour, dark blue, over each of the three windows; Svalocin liked to sleep late, and his rank entitled him to do it. He was hypersensitive to light, perhaps from having been a wartime child habituated to the blackout, much as, some of us later, got habituated to actual blacking-out ourselves from too little food, no sleep, and far too little love.

17. A Saint of Suet

Once upon a time, as a lonely single virus eager to freeload and travel light, I—or at least a prototype of me—felt impelled to make contact with other viruses, which after an eon it managed to do, amassing millions of itself also yearning to make contact. Thus, in a primeval slop, all those viruses made a real fizzler of themselves, a sparkler, in fact a penis that, however rudimentary, yearned again, to shove home somewhere, toward other viruses similarly amassing. Thus sex *was*, *golúbchik*, my little dove, *moyá dushá*, my soul, *dúshenka*, my soul again, and the whole sorry saga of our affair was started. It is hard to believe that so ghastly, crucial an outcome had such teeny beginnings, so long ago, from the ache to reach out to the moment of mutual spasm. Moments plural. To put it so baldly sounds foolish, naive, but love *is* foolish and naive, blundering about, heedless of the rules of engagement. And so this, beginning with a tiny microdot urge that was all ego, Oliver Twist-like asking for more and more. Is this a case of rearview mirror blindness, with neither of us aware that the strong wide angle curvature makes the threat behind us, the hunters trying to overtake us, look smaller than they are? Somewhere in the universe there should be a school for coaching imminent lovers in the etiquette of

The Ice Lens

the surreptitious, as in the olden days when the British, well coached, spurned the predictable thing and so watched foreign diners talk and listened to them eat.

That sort of savvy rebellion.

I must be a mystic, I always think I am getting through, infatuated with my wavelength, construing your silence as your complacency at having got through too. Out of nothing, make all: that kind of vainglory, *dúshenka* mine, excluding all save us, marginalizing all impediments and traps. Can it really be true that we can tune in to each other at will, like those pesky old viruses, and transcend all circumstance? We wanted what we were not getting. It was as simple as that, as with millions of others destined for the red trains that never stopped or the other trains that did.

So we do not say where do we go from here?

We say how do we stand while here, how do you stand while there, how do I stand while up in a tree? No knowledge is being exchanged. As you leave at the end of your sentence, a highly-strung old crow with ruined eyes, will they hand you a hefty package containing all my letters over the years, all in dimity, chronological order lest you get mixed up when you try to read them in series by the feeble shade of a paltry lamp, to the reek of moldy porridge and undumped chrysanthemums? If you are lucky. If they have saved them. If they want you to have them. If, indeed, they had not been burned on arrival. Why, they could have handed them to you, for good behavior, at the rate of one a year. I have no idea. I hear nothing of merit. I have to invent the act of inventing, with whatever company I can muster in the arboretum of my skull. Are we any good to each other? Is either of us a sufficient other to recognize where either other ends and the other other begins? Do far-apart stars talk? Have they books? May they share a pillow? Do they warm each other's feet? Do they from time to time share a toothbrush, an apple, a loofah? I have heard of something called the transmigration of souls, but outside of Boethius and Hildegard of Bingen, I have not heard much of its practitioners, and I would like to go to school with them, cadging a little favor now and then, say a kind word once a year, an ability once every five years to go in a straight line to where hurtless souls toil with a whirlwind, knowing they will get there if they try hard enough, my *golúbchik.*

It is done with music, they say.
Utmost of refinement, pernambuco with catgut.
Yearning cast as the spirit ditty of no tone.
Love as the legendary amber room no longer visible.
A tree will do if you have not angered it.
Or a cobweb rendered unto lightning.

Of all the remedies there are, there has to be this.

Electric, wordless, heartfelt.

Heavy lidded eyes set wide apart in an abnormally peaceful face on which tamed buoyancy and strict ebullience mingle to produce an effect of earned repose. That at least, is how I used to see her, not one of the most animated faces around, but a touch sultry, a grace longing uppermost. She must be far beyond that now, after all the grades of privation, no longer the tall sleek matron, sweet meat for commissars, more likely a face driven inward, on the outside a penitent's mask, a saint of suet. What on earth shall we say when at last we see? Or is it just a matter of looking deep and, at long last, deciding that the surviving dominant expression is one of composed ruefulness, all adjustment and repose? To dream of that final mask is to acquire some of her calm, and much of what she'd had to bottle up for sheer survival's sake. It is as if her open eyes know that her eyes are really closed, having already seen too much, willing to populate her remaining days with such melodic musings as have not been stifled. Tunes of tact, formulated by the dormant memory in its few forays.

18. Nimet of the Airwaves

Imagine that lady, Nimet of the airwaves, after sharing serious music with us from midnight to dawn, at last being helped from her chair, revived with orange juice and fresh hot pastries, then escorted away at the semi-faint by two burly music lovers in guard uniform, she who actually thanks you for listening to a Mozart Mass with her. With equal graciousness she does the commercials too, touting Russian food (I could tell her otherwise), listing the movies, and even going so far at times as to argue with herself in what I envision as the black-velvet morgue of music where she sits: "Did we do the operas? No, perhaps we didn't," and then she runs through a list of the operas on in town. Does she, at what she calls the halfway point, meaning three in the morning, get the urge to scream into the microphone? No, she is too demure for that, too well-bred sounding, but she must begin to flag sooner or later unless she manages to nod off during the longer movements, and I cannot see that; she sounds too engrossed, too thrilled.

To loaf through the night with her, she being part guide, part Aladdin, is surely a ritual. Only believers tune in. It has something to do with music, of course, but it also has to do with being shepherded blindly through the massed aural furrows of dark, with only harmony to sustain you, and only the clock to thwart. Temptress, siren, expert, she coos and whispers, winning you back to Shostakovich, making you wonder if you aren't hearing too much Mozart (someone obliged to die only once isn't required to hear that much Mozart), and, now and then, going afield to play the first symphony of a long time Carnegie Hall usherette who, like someone crouched beneath Niagara, at last begins to pour something out of herself in a veritable hemorrhage of emulation. I lament the coming of dawn, but not now as, with rosy light in hand, I inspect my guest, wondering which light, the one on the horizon or the one in my fist, makes her skin seem for the first time healthy.

Her features all look sharply sliced, cut from a minimum of skin and flesh, as if the keenest female mind in the world has found a physiognomy to match. The forehead looks frail, but bulges forward, outward, flanked by strands growing close to its front. A small forehead, it could be that of a poet, shrinking thoughts even as they bloom, and the keen deep eyes rest beneath it like tiny curved swords. The green-blue of them has closed off of course, but the nose is straight and rather thick, its two side lobes cutting deep into her face, as if some highly strung volubility has tugged at them year in, year out. Or because she flexes her nostrils nonstop. The-once-every-two-seconds tic continues through her sleep, convulsing the entire left side of her face, massing the flesh over her cheekbone, pulling the mouth and eye askew. The other side stays put, more or less, but she certainly seems to be fished for with a hook within her face. Again and again she flinches in response to it, and her sleeping face assumes expressions appropriate to this or that dream, but almost always one or other of these: incredulity at last losing faith in itself and accepting something at face value after all; pain at a hot cinder blown into the eye, then relief as it cools; or recoil from a sudden bad smell right under the nostrils, the face wrinkling and twisting to get away from it. When she is awake, the twitch is faster, the commotion more blatant, and then I find it hard to look, whereas at night, or by dawn, I can stand it, blaming dreams or the peculiar air currents that thrive at treehouse height.

She stirs and at once begins to question me, her tic or twitch now mounting to a fierce rhythm that she tries to still with even bigger screwings-up of her left-side face, so that she seems to be trying to vomit or not to, to shake her crossed eyes back to true sight, to line up the one side of her mouth with the other. Terrible elastics drag her good looks this way and that, and she begins to fondle and toss her hair out of sheer agitation. In repose, if you can catch them at it, her features have a look of the imperious Germanic princess capable of

The Ice Lens

swift and severe response, never joking or making asides.

"I look funny enough," she says.

"No, not funny, I was just feeling curious."

She does a tremendous slithering leer quite without meaning to, as if all her features have been electrified at random, or (and I stir mildly at the thought) as if some mighty orgasm has coursed through her from her feet upward, in zig-zag thrills, making her long self-loathingly for more. Does she ever not do it? She does it all the time, amounting to (in the daylight) some sixty twitches an hour. The math of it appalls me, and I suddenly realize that here is a face you have to learn to know in motion, not repose; her passport picture will have to be a movie. I confess that, over the past few days, the twitch has begun to endear itself to me, suggesting some unprecedented degree of attunement or of sly ecstasy. If we were as highly coordinated as she, we too would twitch like this, and be glad of it, and we would scorn those whose faces, inert and sluggish, evince a mind in the doldrums and a pack of senses with batteries burned out. She has this preternatural flicker to her, as if wolves are on her trail, as if she is seeing elaborate beings invisible to everyone else. Her very brain is trying to squint.

"Sea pud," she says, and I begin to wipe again, a dutiful retainer cut down to size. In her sleep, the tic will sometimes appear to drag her entire body about, making her thrash and hunch, not dangerous if as now she is sleeping on the floor, but surely a hazard on a bed. I make a mental note to arrange things better lest, indeed, she go whizzing clean off the platform, wheel and all. "Now you're dry," I say. "Drier, anyway. It's the morning chill."

"You were watching my face jump around."

"There's nothing dull about you," I say.

"You were spying on me in my sleep."

"During mine, rather. I was more asleep than you. Listening to music most of the night. I thought something was happening I didn't like the look of. As if you'd been frozen and were—well, thawing out too fast. Where *I* come from, we often did."

She asks and I tell her the name of Mother Russia.

"Me," she says, "I come from Bar-muda."

Bermuda? Balmuda? Bahamamuda? She's making it up.

"Oh yes," I say. "Oh yeah. *Queens* more like."

"Well," she says, "Queens too."

She comes from folk who once had a Bermudian maid, hence the funny talk she sometimes does. Bimini from Bermuda, I think. I say it aloud. She laughs. "Who're you?"

"White," I say without a second's thought. "I'm White."

"Not a name, that."

"Kiwi White, then. You can say it like Hee-Wee. Or like Kee-Wee. Take your choice. It's only a name."

"Fucking hell," she says mildly, "you call me Bimini and yourself Kiwi White. We don't sound like human beings at all. Not like people."

Call me what you like, I tell her. "I'm not proud."

"You should be, then," she says earnestly. "Of anything you have."

"Then I am." I urge her to get up, drink some tea. I once had a samovar up here. No, up another tree, but somebody stole it, I never having had the prudence to take things back to my mother's place when leaving my tree, for winter or my northward trek in spring.

"Drink," I say. It scalds, but she sips it anyway, and I do declare that for a moment her twitching stops.

"We're going out tonight," I say. "Maybe a movie. Maybe a play. Something to take us out of ourselves. And I'll have some shopping to do. You'll see." Now she is smoking grass, bold as day, but I decline, leave her to it, wondering how she got it. It was never mine; all smoke evokes burnt sacking for me, and burnt sacking means death. I ask, but she waves me and my question away from deep within her trance. The twitch has slowed almost to mastication rhythm and, all of a sudden, her face looks less highly strung, less keen, more than of a young girl with a date at the movies, a home of her own, a name not filched from some atomic detonation. Kiwi White had better get his act together before she gets us both arrested.

The very word is like a bell, taking me back to an old thought of mine, spawned in atrocious circumstances, yet logical in its nature. The whole of Russia has been misbehaving, so those who run our fates have decided to teach us a lesson. For years, half the population slaves away converting old monasteries and castles into prisons and camps. They should. The powers have decided that the entire population has to go to jail, not of course beyond the national borders, but essentially relocated within them, with just a skeleton staff of guards and warders, who in turn will spend their own five, ten, or fifteen years away. After twenty years the whole nation will have purged its misbehaving ways, although the birth rate will have sagged, which means the country is going to become emptier. There will be room for more camps. Amazing to consider the size of Mother Russia: huge enough to imprison the entire population without coming apart at the seams. Imagine the shift of population centers. Imagine the capacity for masochism of a people who, in the interests of some abstruse national rightness, are willing to deny themselves life, liberty, the pursuit of happiness, and warmth, not to mention sleep, privacy, daylight, food, and love. If Bimini had any inkling of this, her rictus would speed up to half a dozen a minute and envelope her entire face. It's as if, to mend her tic, they beheaded her. Yes, my distant beloved one, she is now the woman in the case, hardly one of your most illustrious successors, yet one deserving tenderness and tact: another one of the walking wounded I supposed you'd call her, on the run from who knows what surgical marvel, what grieving family. One of these days they will catch up with her. The dragnet will hoist her down like an errant fish, and I will enter the Tombs, for the first time in an American jail, rather like escaping from Dante's Inferno only to stand in a corner with a dunce's cap on. The main thing, sweetheart, is to do what's left in style, with a bit of the old Cossack flourish: Kiwi White and his neighbor Bimini Engstrom going down for the count, graciously bowing while drowning, with goodbye music from Nimet. They will have to arrest us by night or there won't be the right somber locked-in kind of music to climb down by.

Leaving her at home, assigned to clear the deck of nutshells and the floor of mold, I saunter forth on a Monday morning with what I fondly call the pendant card to my mother's credit card account: I sign and she pays, so far anyway. I can hardly have things delivered, of course, can hardly tell them to write on the invoice the fourteenth tree on the right. So I end up making several trips, arriving treetopside with three different parcels, one so heavy I have to haul it up after me while Bimini hovers and feints, cooing and lurching, twitching and asking, asking, asking, "Wait," I say, "you'll see soon enough." Then away again for water, cans, charcoal, some fresh fish, toilet rolls, a Lysol spray, a large plastic bottle of mouthwash, and a bottle of cognac. Only for the fish and the cognac do I pay cash, from my hoarded-up supply of summertime bills in my Kohlui box.

"All on your own," she says.

"That's how we do the big things," I say, gasping from the effort and wishing I didn't have to unwrap things and set them up. "You know that."

"Like you was starting up a ly-berry." she says.

"A--? Oh, I see," I say. "That's right. Hundreds of books. How are you for reading?"

"Try me," she says.

"Books to come later," I tell her as I slit the cord and delve into the brownwrap and tissue. "Here, blow into this." Over the next hour, as we punish our lungs, a urethane-coated nylon wonder of the world takes shape. At first she calls it a bed, but then it firms up and she sees what it really is: a bath, requiring only a good night's rain aqueducted, Bermuda-style, from above. All it needs, out here on the deck, is a deluge, and it can fill, cleanse, and polish itself without help from us.

The next item pleases her less, however, but as soon as I have it assembled she sits to test it, stamping her feet on the twin footrests and rolling her shoulders and neck against the padded sides. Her legs are rather too long, though, since I had to buy the child's model, and she hardly needs the cutaway table designed to fit snugly at the waist.

"An open space," said the merchant, all avidity and zeal, "in the seatfront is good, so girls can wipe themselves."

"Yes, girls are messy," I told him.

"If it's a particularly bony child," he said, "you might want a seat with extra padding. The footrest is good because a child cannot really work at a bowel movement, a *motion*, with its legs dangling."

"Gotcha," I said, "and those with wheels on can always be wheeled up to the bath, or anywhere else. No wheels."

"Or casters?"

"No wheels," I told him. "We aren't going to travel far. Not horizontally anyway."

"You want it for a plane." He meant an *airplane*.

No, I told him, it wasn't a travelling commode but a static one, intended for use in the trees, which remark got me much faster service.

Now she tests it without using it and finds it comfy: a better chair than anything in the entire treehouse with the added advantage of safety when she happens to have to go. It is very difficult, as the merchant said, to urinate uphill or to get the child off the pan without spilling the contents. But at least I will know where she is, even if she doesn't like sitting still, and in no time she'll think of the thing as hers, her station, her plinth, her base.

Bit by bit, I am getting my world together again, dearest farthest, while patience mellows into helpfulness. I am making the best of a bad job and, within my limited resources, making a treehouse life the best there is. On red letter days, as in the dim hives of Lubianka, I will serve both lunch and dinner at the same time, but we will never smoke manure, dearest, or shape papier-mâché-like cakes from potato skins. As in the bad old days. I am already planning for the snow, worrying about our tracks to and from the tree, and I say again, as I said about you and me, cannot we evade the eyes of a few stalkers and spies? Here at least they will never smear red lead over the tiny window glass so as to weaken your ration of God's good light.

I myself am too big to sit in it, but Bimini doesn't want to yield it up anyway, whereas the bath, dry as in the store, makes a quite good chaise lounge, and I can easily persuade myself I am floating about on the silken surface of a pale blue pool, my day's work done, my shoulders and back sore from constant flexing, my mind on the owner's lady and wondering if this evening will be one of those magically romantic ones in the aromatic tool shed or the big open amphitheater of the king size bed alongside the forty-eight-inch television screen (one could almost lie on the latter to watch things on the former). Ever the amateur carpenter, I toy with the idea of making for Bimini a Bradford frame, one of those wooden platforms with a buttock cutout in the middle, used mainly for children in body casts, but also useful, I'd imagine, for instant access to bedridden nymphomaniacs. You never know what impediments are going to arise, my lovely. You and I, in our time, circumvented many, did we not? They had us on tape, on paper, and in person, but they never quite got all the evidence they wanted. There were, oh, some hundred hours of unmitigated bliss they never knew about, for all their microphones and cameras, their gumshoes and snoops.

"Like a queen," she is saying, "on her throne."

"Don't whatever you do abdicate," I say all in one breath as if afraid that the idea will break up as one syllable after another leaves my mouth.

"Queen of the roach coach," she says. "Queen of *Queens*."

"Never," I tell her. "Up here all you get is spiders and caterpillars. And all these damned nutshells, at least in the fall you do. Go barefoot and they'll cut you up."

She is not going to move, she says. She will sit there forever, waited on hand and foot. "Like piggly-wiggly," she says. "I roll myself up into a ball and fall through the hold underneath."

"I'll catch," I say. "Never fear." I get the hibachi going and grill the franks, wondering how much of a mess the fish is going to make later on. Last time I had to scrape with my knife for going on an hour to get the fish-soot off the iron frame. "It's getting on for lunch time. Brunch. Whatever you want it to be. Served to you right royal in your chamber." No anchovies and no dried carp.

"On my t'rone," she says, omitting the *h*.

"On your whatever," I say, intent on getting the charcoal to glow. A slight wind helps, oddly aromatic with hops and I wonder where they are brewing beer today. The wind must be coming from the west, New Jersey way. My first ten books are already here, brought with me from the Hudson Valley, but I dream of building shelves and lining the walls with books, maybe so many that my tree develops a list, or just my house within its tree, and I rejoice that the itinerant sap is not in the end going to rust and break my nails; my nails are all of wood, tapped home with a mallet. All I have to fear is termites, or rather, as the owners of wooden airplanes say, the time when the termites stop holding hands.

The Ice Lens

Now I arrange myself in the plastic bath to have my daily snooze. You can't stay up all hours without sooner or later being unable to lift your eyelid for another billionth of a second.

"Keep watch," I say unnecessarily, "I'm off."

"Off," she says. "Off out."

"Off flat out," I say. "G'bye."

"Seapud again," she says, eager for company at any cost.

But I relax and begin to swoon away, knowing she sits ass-naked where she sits, free as a bird to savor the air, the squirrels, the withering leaves, the keening sirens of midtown, the snuffle of traffic, the jets nibbling their way across the severe blue traditional this season. It is as if a whole assembly of the commonplace has become a magical frieze for Bimini and me, a command performance of light acids and combusting gas while Nimet sleeps, maybe in one of those illustrious towers. All I can imagine before I fade away is the uplifted arm of the local Lady, assembled in sections as it is, with quite discernible rings at the elbow, the mid-arm, and the wrist, a touch of Frankenstein just for a nation made of leftovers, brought back to life by their zombie lady with her uplifted ice cream cone.

One way of getting bile out of your system is to barhop, confiding in all and sundry, as if they cared, or even at the zoo standing in front of tigers and ostriches, telling them or their spectators. Unreasonably, perhaps, you might expect your bosses to take pity on you and bail you out, as if you were Gary Francis Powers, who had bad luck. You, however, you hear, *you* made your own luck bad, and get no sympathy from us. Do your Russian time and, next time, pick an American woman, certainly not a Russian. Were you hoping to become a commissar or what? Commissars rarely hire their cuckolders. You are lucky not to have been shot in a leaky, smelly shower and buried in a manure heap. Don't, please, embarrass us by coming to ask for your old job back.

Their response is as homogeneously raw as Miro's painting of a man and woman in front of an excrement pile. In fact, after umpteen years of punitive sameness, you learn to take delight in trivial, ordinary things such as dust, insects, mucus, sores, nail clippings, dandruff, smells, the sky. Indeed, if you have had any kind of education, the brand that boasts of equipping you with internal resources that will stand you in good stead in later life, you find yourself leaning back to it, culling images and trumped-up events that might just see you through: Samson shorn; Bunyan's pilgrim treading onward; the red badge of courage or adultery; Oedipus porking his mother; Boethius being beheaded. A bit stagey, all this, but a passable procession of substitutes, at last identified like a camel caravan passing in the night, with the spot of the flashlight ranging from one to another as they waddle on from classical times to forever. Did I forget *Romeo and Juliet?* Of course not, nor *Antony and Cleopatra.* Not that, years ago, I cottoned that much to either play; it's just that, suddenly, it became relevant, as if Shakespeare had read my future. What an eerie feeling when the motifs and predicaments of classical literature, always presumed to be irrelevant, an aimless impediment or an examiner's Iron Maiden, suddenly encircle you like a Polish firing squad and squeeze in on you, murmuring we knew this ages ago. Now take heed, American cocksman, and suck on your self-imposed jungle. It's like being haunted, not least by the fact that, although you worked at a couple languages, in my case Spanish and Modern Greek, you never paid much heed to the literature composed in those words. Pore over any paperback dictionary, noting the taste and temper of the words therein assembled, and you have no idea of the literature expressed in those very words, or even of the Spanish or Greek way of using them casually. It was the same with Russian, on which too few of us spent any official time. *Cabezas muertas in todos los lugares*, I could rattle off as if it were some contribution to knowledge (*deadheads everywhere*), or *pou einai o leoforio?* (*where is the bus?*). Our Russian came from sheer fanatical ignorance, boned up on in the small hours or getting red-eyed from vodka. Not that difficult, my *dúshenka*, as we both know, since you already knew some English, slewed and picky, fault of you know who: "I don't know from gonifs" or "I'd love to come and visit with you (wid youse)." It went on, my conferring on her eager semi-immigranted intellect the kind of English that would have got her snubbed on the Main Line or in Greenwich, but which endeared her to some in the Gulags and provided the wrong kind of intro.

Just imagine. I was undoing her while I was doing her.

I was her multiple undoing.

She was not my Trojan horse unless....

I was her finest nightmare.

Oh, we could have been set free, deported into asylum, ushered into Finland or Norway if only Svalocin could have banished us from his prurient mind, all lips and nipples, oestrus and jissom.

And so we were made to come full circle, and the best I can hope for is that she will be banished when her time comes. 'Night now.

19. Rat Man of Paris

After a day spent mostly dozing, or attempting responses to her argot at its most uncouth, I rush her through a hastily cooked meal of fish, and, with the hibachi left soaking in the inflatable bath, off to the movies. Muffled in scarves and woolen hoods, we skulk at the back as if to neck, but all that happens is that she plants a heavy fist on my groin, which refuses to tauten, while we watch a weird-looking character walking the boulevards of Paris with a live rat in his coat. He rears up in front of people sipping their pernods and pops his rat at them. They pay him to go away and off he shuffles to scare somebody else. After a while he stops using a real rat, rats being hard to manage, and uses a rubber one instead, but gets just as much money. Now we learn that it isn't really a fake rat, even, but a fox fur, the only thing he has left of his mother's, who died when the Nazis way back in the Forties burned his native village and killed everyone in it but him and some old biddy who brought him up, mainly by tapping his penis with a cane. You can see how it's going to go. He has to find a friend. He does. Shelly, they call her, and she's a lot younger. She takes to him, I'm not quite sure why, and begins to clean him up, gets him to consider other ways of earning a living. She is doing quite well at civilizing him until he reads in the newspaper that the war criminal who murdered his, the Rat Man's, parents, has just been deported from Bolivia to face trial in France. At once the Rat Man goes bonkers and offers his services to the authorities: he would like to work the guillotine or at least fit the neck into the lunette. This goes on for a while and he tours the streets with placards, a baby carriage, balloons, and a lifelike effigy of the war criminal, name Klaus Barbie, which is all very well until he, Rat Man, finds out he's got the wrong Nazi, which more or less arrests his belated growth. He ends up cleaning fountains in the South of France while Shelly goes about the business of having a baby that may or may not be his. I doubt if it's his, but the movie doesn't show her with anyone else, although, if it were up to me, I would make it the war criminal's just to confuse the issue. She could visit him in jail, or visit his jail, yes. He could smuggle some sperm out somehow. No, no hope of that. So it might be somebody else's, maybe that bullfighter-like character who keeps following them all over Paris and who may, just may, be the fellow who shot Rat Man through the cheeks while he was yawning one night in a public square. It is very much that kind of film: you have to guess because it doesn't exactly flood you with information, so you have to deal with it as you deal with everyday life: making irrevocable decisions on the

The Ice Lens

basis of insufficient evidence. In other words, you gamble on a guess.

Bimini likes the rat stuff, I can tell. She breathes hard whenever Rat Man unveils it, real or fake or fox-fur, inhaling deep, holding it in, then letting it out like a hemorrhage against the neck of the poor devil sitting in front of her. The baby makes her laugh out loud as if at something gruesomely inappropriate to the human couple, and the image of Barbie, disheveled and unshaven, seems to disturb her profoundly, as if she has just seen her own father on the screen. After the Rat Man gives up his trade for vengeance, she gets rather bored, hoping he will get back to real business, but he never does, and she keeps asking me in a stage whisper "Where's the rat gone to?" She adores the scenes in which Rat Man puts his rat to bed in a doll's house fitted with tiny furniture and soft little beds. Off comes the roof, as in the old Spanish novel, and in goes the rat, sometimes called Zvicka, sometimes Vendl, while Rat Man fills the little feeding tray with corn that tends to spill all over the floor, and, of course, attract mice into his hovel that he enters beneath a vertically opening door.

"Why doesn't she clean up?" says Bimini. "She's the mother."

"She isn't the rat's mother."

"She's the mother all the same."

"And she isn't *his* mother either," I say, as consternated faces turn around to shush me. "It's not her fault and it isn't where *she* lives anyway."

I can tell it, they are going to throw us out. Now there is nothing but yelling. Bimini has started to yell at me about the corn, about the nutshells on the treehouse porch, and we are getting too much attention. They can just about see her and I don't want them to hear about the treehouse. So out we go, having missed about ten minutes. There's nothing more they could do with that plot anyway, even if somebody threatened them with nine grams of lead.

Outside is no picnic either. We walk into the middle of a procession, a parade, bang next to a man in a pink leotard festooned with women's shoes, on his head a cellophane wig that gleams like torn aluminum foil. He is Imelda Marcos, his sign says. It is as if the dead have come above ground. Here is someone made up as a radio tube, someone else clad as an erect penis. They all seem to be men. I wish we were in our garbage bags, just to show willing. Here come some people who have been beheaded, with papier mâché shoulders carefully built up over their heads. The stump of the neck streams with blood, for all the world like a bit of wishful thinking from the movie we just abandoned. What seems to be a woman dressed as a rat has a mechanical mouse in its mouth advancing and receding like a big taxidermied tongue with a head. Maybe this is some publicity stunt for the movie, but no, I can see all kinds of folk: rhinos and giraffes, heads planted inside see-through pigs that fit as neatly as tea cozies some heads buried in enormous pies made of corrugated cardboard, some impaled by gigantic arrows with testicles instead of feathers.

It is Halloween, a festival little regarded by tree dwellers: the best disguise in the world for the Biminis of this world. I suddenly realize that I do not need to cringe. I am not on the run anymore. I am no longer condemned, hunted, found, jailed. I am free to be as outrageous as any of these people in the street or even those in the movie. Deep within the human tide, we laugh and jabber, she in her Bermudian lingo, I in my best frog-slinging gibberish, neither addressing the other, but addressing ourselves outward to the parade as it fidgets and accelerates, and polished hysteria splits the night as this or that group of fans spots the next attraction heaving rottenly into view, all sequins and candy floss, face make-up and satin wraps. This is the circus version of the serious act we put on in the subways in our Hefty bags, like spring hard on the heels of winter, yet another frenzied agitation against the hard walls of cement, against the ungivingness of the sidewalks and the cars. Yes, all that was rehearsal in daily dress, but this is the real thing: a gala full of delicate, refined emotions, punctuated by the antics of doomed male cheerleaders with soaring batons and lovingly scoured thighs. Men again, not exactly Rat Men, but Baton Men, yes, and Beheaded Men, and Snow Men, and Rhino Men and Giraffe Men, with not an elephant man in sight, although I count over a dozen with diseases: boils the size of apples, mouths hanging like suckers on the tip of a proboscis, eyes congregated on the brow like mammoth frogspawn, and unspeakable black and green growths sprouting from the ears, cascading onto the shoulders like ectoplasmic gangrene awaiting only its first lyric poet to achieve the same repute as roses, clouds, and golden hay. All goes here, anything goes.

Yet none of them, sweetheart, have a treehouse, or a long gone dearest one to tell about it as, even beyond the grave, they squeeze her nipples with pliers to make her confess. She does. She confesses to everything. To our lewd, uncivil crime in the deputy commissar's bed. Now confess to the others, they tell her. But there were no others. Still they squeeze. She confesses to adultery with ghost after ghost, to acts of intimate spontaneous originality with them, acts we made our own. Yet there are no commissars in this parade, and no Gulag lovers either. Libido is its premise and alias its method. It interests me because, like the universe, it is always the last place to go, the last enterprise to identify with. It is where the Rat Man of the movie belongs, he and his rat, maybe for only one night a year, but something to remember; its image burns into my mind like some stained glass window on the move, no, a series of windows walked past the human race on high-heeled legs.

In this uproar you can say anything, even to the beloved dead. And I do. Raving and ranting my tenderness, I seize Bimini's hand, aiming my mouth away from her, and pelt the muggy evening with all the pent-up endearments within me, from dearests to darlings, from beloveds to dearhearts, building my ovation into howls that tell the world your nipples were like wild strawberries, your arms as firm as peaches, your loins like freshly risen aromatic dough, and I recognize that I am in the role of the Biblical love poet, the Hebraic pornographer, trumpeting the splendor of an eternal female in the very teeth of those, the majority, who get their jollies by licking the glans of the so-called gift of death: mortal themselves and therefore involuntary killers. It makes you retch. The logic does. The human passion to join the enemy, to be on the side of the strongest artillery, even if it means doing in the loveliest mortals on all the Earth. I can see this Rat Man's point when he raves away about the dominance of the death cult when we are surrounded by the beauty of butterflies and hibiscuses, birds and trees, but surely he goes mad for blood. He too joins the death squad, he whose nearest and dearest were cut down and set afire. That's what bothers me in the heart of a parade devoted, surely, to life on earth, even if it is mainly men who wish to be women or, at least, men who don't want to be standard men. Would I, if I could, like to wring the neck of our deputy commissar? Yes, I would do it easy as farting, but I wouldn't make a crusade up out of it, I wouldn't let it run my life.

I would, though, I'd go right off the edge if I ever got near to it, just the chance of it. I'd only fry his balls for half an hour, not the full afternoon, in the olive oil, and then the machine oil, and then the butter, and then the oil of cloves, the oil of vitriol. Drink this, Svalocin, old friend, sup it up like a good boy, it will put hair on your chest. And on your eyeballs too. And on the eyes of your parents as well. You will sprout the fuse-wire of agony even as you melt. There, that's the true Rat Man stuff, and all I saw was a movie just before re-entering the parade of life. He too knew.

Have to be careful or I'll end up howling from the tree and being taken down to Bellevue.

Curb it, Kiwi White, whoever you are.

They have no Gulags here, but padded cells aplenty.

Take her home before she starts to enjoy it too much.

The Ice Lens

Everyone loves a parade. A Mayday parade?

Well, you don't have to go overboard, she says.

No, she didn't say it: a faraway, lost, doomed, disfigured, utterly sequestered one said it into an ear that picks up echoes only.

I don't know much, but I am going to have to change my daytime music before she shoves me off the platform. Nimet for nights, but, by day, some music more in keeping with my Bimini, my other lady, the one with the torch.

All that would be awful if only another awful thing had not just happened. I could feel it beginning to happen, right in the core of me. The crowd is noisy and they shove like mad. My hand is light and free. Bimini has gone like one of those old mail bags snatched up by a passing train. She will soon be in Siberia at this rate. Perhaps she went back to see the end of the movie. Perhaps she was swept away. Can she already have found her way to the treehouse? How to begin to ask? You do not ask a mob, only a bit of it, but which bit? How do you look? Where? You do not enlist the aid of the police, who do not seem to be here anyway. Men in blue, they had them in the other country as well as here. Why blue? Why that color, so fated? I could let her go, find her own level, be picked up and taken home for the operation on her ovaries. Or not. If not, then how to set about beginning to begin to start looking for her? I am a man used to being told when to whisper, when to walk, when to sleep, when to keep my hands above the top of the blanket. I am not used to searches done by me, only to those done upon me. Here I am, far from the camps, my head an unbeheaded elegy, my domain that of the monkey, my main concern to search for someone I hardly know and am not even sure I wish to find. Sometimes the nine grams has an almost flawless appeal.

20. The Moscow Stations

Here I sit on my bed of branches, brooding on turgor, the elasticity or springiness of skin, gone alas like our youth too soon. So, then, fasten on fixity, as some folk do on certain churches, museums, galleries, airports. I have known Londoners who leak a tear at the very mention of St. Pancras, Paddington, Euston, Victoria or Waterloo, perhaps because of where those London train stations lead you to: Derby, Oxford, Liverpool, Dover and Southampton, stirring you with dreams fulfilled yet never relinquished, or other dreams never realized. Perhaps for no good reason at all save hatred of Moscow North, I settle on the other stations of Moscow, wondering at the literalness of Yaroslavski (to Yaroslavi), Kievski (to Kiev), Leningradski (to Leningrad), and Riga (to Riga). Anyone peering at these immoveable terminuses would never credit the imaginativeness of much in Russian literature. Had they not enough time to name these places after eminent Russian authors, or was the Muscovite populace too dense to heed any but the most obvious of pointers? Leningrad evinces the same tendency: Finlandski just across the Neva from Moskovski, and Baltiski (to Riga). Only Vitebski, conducting you to Varshavski, shows much initiative. Berlin, on the other hand, shows off with its Spandau, Wannsee, Baumschulenweg, and Zoo, while Paris regales you with Nord, Est, Orsay, Invalides, St. Lazare, and Austerlitz, only the first two lumpishly matter-of-fact, for the dopes who show up in just about any human population.

That these places stay still is reassuring, though, as all else seems to be on the move. Myself, I tremble at any mention of the Russian stations; trains are daunting, ever since... well, I have explained all that, though in the old days I lit up my mind with exquisite stories about Irish trains, aboard which you could request a three-minute boiled egg and get it, with a side order of bread-and-butter heavy on the butter, just for being a traveler and in need. In India you could rent a mailbox at the rail station and pick up your post on the way to somewhere else, the only snag being that, as you thrust your hand into the opened box, a rat might bite it. It is such tales that enliven me as I sag into and out of a near-perfect delirium. I long for Istanbul (one station only, Haydarpasa) and Basel, where the French maintain a separate station within: the S.N.C.F. within the good old S.B.B. of the Swiss. One could make an affectionate, stationary lifetime touring from station to station, reposing in those that boast acceptable, stern hotels, lurking in greasy waiting rooms sometimes with pothering coal fires when there was no hotel. You could get used to such penury in no time, obediently bowing to local laws, actually changing money like a fakir at those overlit windows where notes and bills flutter about as if they had a soul, like *putti*. Imagine someone who has been sequestered in the Gulag next being given the "freedom" of all the railway stations in the world, just as certain celebs get the freedom of a particular city, or the key to the place. Imagine an unreal city full of dreams, in which the various rail stations have quickly identifiable famous names. So, if you have had enough of stinkfinger romance, you take the express from Byron to Bunyan, which will guarantee you a stricter ride, then change at Malraux, a station the French S.N.C.F. maintain in the bowels of the S.B.B.'s station Ramuz, which will take you to the region of most avalanches. Failing these, you can head for Jünger if you crave a zone devoted to botany, Pavese if you have suicide in mind, Silone for the breadbasket of Italy, or Cervantes if you are of a horsey disposition, need a servant or two and fancy living in a windmill.

There. Such are the mind games one is driven to, the one problem being that you need Baedekers and timetables to spur memory while in captivity. Memory, as a willing servant to intellect, tends to blubber at times, especially if the food is bad. You need an aide. When you are "over there," to borrow an old wartime term, you need your aides de camp.

21. A Big Radar Spider

What happens next is predictable, except to me. I am not in the habit of thinking about what to do next; I have not been trained in the Navy Seal mode of decision-making, preferring to float with the tide, having over a decade and a half learned to do nothing else. Having some faint trust in machines rather than in crowds, I do not go about asking if they have seen a strange-looking girl, I do not go into the little shabby stores. Nor do I shout. A shout would be wasted. Instead, coin in hand, I head for the nearest phone, contact the operator, and begin to tell her the story, as if she has an all-seeing eye, a big radar-spider at her disposal. It is as if I am playing an instrument, growling into my trumpet or trombone, even as the metal melts at its other end. A girl has vanished into a crowd, I tell her, and there is no way of finding her. What does she recommend? *Rat Man* would know what to do, wouldn't he? She has never heard of Rat Man and tells me, buddy, if this is a crank call you better hang up right now, but I don't, I tell her it's an emergency, and she connects me to the police, whom, because at a distance, I tell, lying about Bimini's appearance (I don't really want *them* to find her) at the same time as ventilating the idea of her being adrift. I think they understand, but I decline to say who I am, although I am tempted to say Deputy Commissar Svalocin.

Long after the police have hung up on me, I go on prating into the mouthpiece, telling the world at large I am sorry to have lost her, let her come loose, promising to devote every effort to the chase, the recovery; I even tell my long long-lost sweetheart, in her grave, about my fecklessness and think I hear her answering "Steady now, don't try to do it all yourself." You know how other voices come toward you at an angle from the other phones. Well, here there are two, and here I am thundering my misery and frustration into the mouthpiece while somebody, really loud, is doing something of the kind into the one only a yard away, although I cannot see the person's face. Then I do, by delicate cranking of my head, and I see a tallish fellow, swarthy, genial, perhaps unshaven, in a tweed jacket, his hair somewhat greased down and, most conspicuous of all, a patch over one eye. The face seems almost animated as if, wherever it went, it always managed to entertain itself with whatever spectacle offered itself. He is looking at me hard, and, I suppose, so am I at him, at the dropped forelock that almost reaches the eyebrow of the visible eyes, the decisive, rather fleshy mouth, the tough chin, the laugh lines fanning out from the side of his nose like skinflush antennae. He has the look of someone who at last has found what he always wanted, but how can that be me? He sees me talking into the mouthpiece. Perhaps he can decipher my words, but he doesn't seem to be listening to me; he is quietly smoking his cigarette and, just perhaps, trying to hypnotize me with his right eye, lord help him, while I babble away. He intends to mastermind me into silence and he has no idea of how good a start he already has; I need little persuading to lapse into silence. I have been trained. But, whatever he wants that devouring eye to do to me, it doesn't happen, although I can see from its very intensity that it's the sort of eye which writes things down, into the memory, with nothing skimped. It's a recording type of eye, a human camera, and all he needs is a blue uniform, security police shade, and he'll be well away. I know he is going to arrest me the instant I hang up. Do American police arrest people while the people are on the phone, umbilically trapped, as it were? Ah, I see a wedding ring peep out just over the rim of his corduroy pocket. He wears a tie and his shirt has one of those semi-stiff collars, maybe a little too tight, and the buckle of his belt is as big as a gate, the belt itself is almost as deep as a cummerbund. He still does not move or speak.

    Then I realize that he is not attending to me at all. That look in his eye was one of utter abstractedness. His ear is on the person at the other phone. Again I crank my neck and there, clutching the phone like someone with a life-belt, is Bimini herself, babbling in Bermuda talk or whatever it is, all kinds of stuff from seapud to humpday, stinky to Vot a day. If he understands, you would never know. She does not see me at first, but maybe she is actually talking to an operator willing to give her the time of day because she, Bimini, is a woman in distress, and talking an unknown lingo. Now I hear how Bimini has eaten all her chocklits and I shove my face round and forward, almost dislocating my neck. I am still reluctant to let go of the empty phone, but there you are, dearest angel of mine, I used to hold on to a bit of dried carp as if it was the lord of hosts, feeling not so much that it was mine to hold as that I was its. It seemed solider than I, more dependable, something to believe in, handed down from above.

"You," she cries, not into the phone.

"Here I am. I found you on the phone."

She begins to weep big boiling tears and the man in the eyepatch retreats a foot or two, but still observing hard, and I think: I know that expression of his, it's just about the one you'd have if you lived in a treehouse and all the noise came toward you at a slant from the ground. You look down and you see nothing directly underneath you, so your whole world comes to you at an angle.

"Thank you," I say to him while Bimini bawls. "I am Kiwi White, late of the Gulag. I thought she was a goner."

He shakes his head, and, out of sheer relief, I begin to think: When he takes a nap, he has twenty winks. My English is good enough for that, and I wonder if he'd mind my saying something like that. Bimini dries her eyes, expediently ripping out some pages of the phone book, softening them up with a few seconds' rough manual twisting about, and refinds her smile. The long sharp eyes resume their shallow curve and the twitch slows to half speed, except that her entire face has surrendered to it. She looks as if she is doing facial exercises to tighten the muscles, and her eyes actually seem to change position on her face, now up, now down, too restless to settle. She doesn't need a cup of coffee to tighten her nerves still further, but I do, and I steer her toward the nearest place, half-expecting the man in the eyepatch to follow, maybe even join us. He's police after all, I muse: maybe he'll just wait for us to come out, and then he'll follow us all the way home, and, by five tomorrow morning, they'll have sawn our house down. But he is nowhere in sight, as if he just dissolved. The parade is still going by, so maybe he got caught up in it, hauled off to some place he never meant to go, against his will disguised as five poodles, all five heads nodding and bouncing about on their slinky-coils from the thing he wears on his, like an updated and fancified version of some dog in Greek myth. He's gone, anyway, so we drink our coffee in peace.

Bimini's twitch speeds up for a while, then settles back into a more usual rhythm, although, because when it goes fast she becomes keenly aware of it, she from time to time screws her entire face up in a vicious-looking grimace to shake things loose, perhaps, to use up all the spare electricity in one go. I try it myself and it feels as if my face is coming loose like a mask, so that is how it must feel to her. She might have daubed her face with one of those oatmeal masks that women use in sophisticated countries. Then it dried and hardened, and that's how it feels when she twitches, only she can never get it to come off, never mind how much she tugs the muscles in contrary directions. She's a marionette who pulls her own strings. No, Kiwi, her strings pull the marionette they make her into. Get things right, and, next time you use the phone in an emergency, know what to say. You were lucky this time, but next time will be different. It's bound to be.

Now the true emotions of us both come to the surface. I, who didn't know her a week or so ago, now want to strap her into the commode and chain the commode to the tree. She, I can tell from her face and the pressure of her hand, wants to head for the treehouse and never come down again. Not only might she have been picked up by police; she might have been raped or killed. She gets around all right, but there is a piece of her so gullible, so helpless, she should have a permanent escort. She has wet herself, of course, so I escort her to the Ladies. I do not dab her off in public. When she comes back, still doing a mild twitch, she looks more cheerful, shall I say afflicted with a buoyant fatality or fatalism, and we go outside to watch the tail end of the parade, after which, on a whim more hers than mine, we go into a club after paying twenty dollars. Anything to distract her, so goes my reasoning, and I hold her hand as tight as I can. The music in there is not exactly conducive to thought. We have arrived in the middle of a piece the sheer massiveness of whose shrieks and screams makes the head bones ache. Until you begin to listen to it. She likes the noise, but I have to listen to things as carefully as if I have tuned in to Nimet, and I begin to see what is going on. The whole aim of it is to push each instrument beyond its acknowledged limits in such a way that, if the experiment works, something pure and unprecedented will arrive among us. The pitch goes up and up, the speed of the notes played becomes frenzied, the whole band—strings behind the brass and the woodwinds is having a convulsion; but, in the end, a couple of them, a sax and a trumpet, get where they want to go, almost fusing their respective high speed squeals: truly a sound I have never heard before, and I think of how Liszt punished the piano and the pianist. You have some twenty soloists all playing in total disregard of the others, so that whatever counterpoint there is comes as an accident. They want cacophony rich and brutal, and they get it, reminding you of all the impossible dreams humankind has had, from the stealing of fire to the decipherment of God. This is the musical version of making stones speak, timber dance, and butterflies hold seminars. Pushing the givens until they bust, the band or the group reminds me of stampeding unicorns, and I am astonished to feel any sympathy; but they are trying to do the impossible, like the saxophone player who pushed and pushed for that never heard note, sure that when he hit it a door would open for him into an unknown world, maybe one of harmony, but certainly one forbidden until then. He never hit it and he split his lip in the attempt.

Well, I, who have spent much of my life at the naked extreme of things, know how that feels, and I guess I did the equivalent of cutting my lip, but the door did open, as for my fellow prisoner who memorized one whole book in two days, just before they took it off him, and it kept him going for all the bookless years afterward. A warder had given him the book by mistake, and I thought they were going to come with the big mallets they tested the railroad cars with to see if anyone had sawn through any of the boards. Bang bang on his chest they would go, to see if there were any books concealed within his ribcage, or if he had sawn through some ribs to make a hiding place between his lungs and his heart.

A jam they call it, I think. All things come together and collide as if in some nuclear accelerator. The banging and squealing is that of fallen beings wanting to be gods or of gods wanting to be apes. The title of the number is mild, something like *Eddie's Ladder*, but the effect on Bimini is weird. She loses her twitch, maybe because she can transfer it to them, and a new smile, one of natural refinement and civilized ease, dawns on her face. She might have swum naked in tranquilizer, guzzling what she cavorted in, to get this effect. She becomes the Pallas Athene of their pandemonium, cooing with delight, gesturing without the least trace of jerkiness, talking inaudibly with what looks like cleansed precision and demure pauses. So: to get this girl calm you find bedlam, and I recall that she smiled the same way down in the subway as the expresses howled through, their steel plates grinding. She seems none the worse for her brief foray into lostness, and I begin to think she is a big-city girl after all, her heart open only to the air hammers, the sirens, the muddled thunder of trucks and buses. A treehouse is the last place you would expect her to find peace, although it makes a good way station if you, or she, intend to regain your hearing.

We listen to all the numbers, or rather we let them ambush us, determined as the instrumentalists are to drown out any city, all of it done with uncommon finesse and evident training. These are the ace players of the string quartets, the maestros of the old-style jazz bands, having a nervous breakdown in the presence of music's muse, already as mad as Caligula. *Swazz* they call it, from swing and jazz combined, and I can see that you need a couple of dozen players to produce that exact effect of non-coordination, poly rhythm, and sheer unbridled striving for the moon. The whole band is in a paddy, and I let them blast all over me, happy that she has found some kind of aural turf to be happy on, my mind on some old thoughts, unthought since leaving my cell and the camps, about how harmony is a state in which everything has a place and how the old word *symbol* had to do with throwing the sundered parts of a broken world back together. Prisoner's thoughts, these, they make less sense in the world outside, but they do have a cobwebby allure to them as if you could amass all the candles you ruined your eyes by and lit up an altar whose place is the retinas of your eyes. When the mind's ashamed it's the eyes that hurt. All of a sudden they begin to play what they announce as an old Duke Ellington number, "I let a song get out of my heart," and we are back in the Middle Ages again, or so it sounds: no more bedlam, but mellow sketching, a music of palpable insinuation designed for the intimate ear. I am at home again, back beside the lettuce patch after spending time in the foundry of the sun.

Ready to go, she says, just as I am settling into a milder mood.

"Don't you like it?"

She can't hear it, she can't hear me; the bedlam jam of swazz has done its deadly work. So how come I can still hear? Is it that my lip reading is better, after all those years of hush?

I make her wait, though, as a smaller combo from within the assault band begins to cruise through golden oldies as if the preceding tumult has never been.

22. Calendars Be Damned

Just as potent in the realm of makeshift ikons, lurking there in terse self-sufficiency, the shorthand symbols of a Sheraton directory tug at the mind and the most footloose yearnings. *Camino Real*, it says in bold, then ducks into parentheses (Oceanside). Behold a holiday inn, the candyfloss of heart's desire. "At the beach. Dwtn. 1 mi. Palm Beach Airpt, 20 mi. Shopping 100 ft. *Features*: Ambrosia Rest. Rooftop Rest. Lounge. Beach. Whirlpool. Showtime. In-room Movies. ESPN. Atrium Lobby. Gift Shop. 150 rms. 5 flrs. Rates: Tax 7%. XP $6. Teens Free. RB $6. Suites avail. Std. $79-140; King L. $84-175. 1 per." They reserve the right to abbreviate whatever and however they fancy, but what wouldn't I, late of the Gulag Inn, do for that rooftop, those twin "Rest"s, in-room movies, the gift shop denied me all those years! I would even take on an extra P. for six dollars or a free teen, a six-dollar RB (whatever that is). Slavering and pleading to take A1A and exit at Atlantic Avenue, I envision the raucous, technicolor beach, and, look, they even show little wavy lines for the surf, more wavy lines for the coastal wall, though it's made of concrete. Imagine being haunted by that, during Gulag and after, as if it were some afterlife rigmarole designed for those the French, with their keen nose for the unkempt and poxed, call the *maladif.* Imagine, if you will, the purgative, erotic effect of a Camino Real, or even a Holidome, for only five minutes, on one of the punished. When you had such things, they were never much, but Gulagged you subscribe again to the whole idyll of calm sea and prosperous voyage. Imagine having a choice of rooms and a bedder to clean up after you, a *golúbchik* of the Inn.

Fabulous pipedream, haunting you because, at first, you remember it, and then because you had almost forgotten it, and ever afterward because it figures among the hundred thousand things denied you. Oh to be Oceanside instead of Snowside, Cesspool Side, Razorwire Side, all those golfless acres leading to Finland or Norway.

She, of course, no stranger to the Black Sea resorts, could always remember something better, classier, snazzier, more glamorous, except that to visit the Black Sea with her commissar was like lugging the Kremlin after you, and she felt like the neurasthenic, snubbed composer in Mann's *Death in Venice*, making *that* journey too by train, actually (after things I told her while our sweat mutated) craving boardwalk, gift shop, Sea World, deep-sea fishing, sailing and scuba diving, in other words the resplendent panoply of humdrum Americana.

"And," she would say, "you can go wherever you want, unstalked?"

"All day in the toilet and no questions asked."

"Nirvana."

"We take it for granted."

"No one peeping."

"Only Toms."

"You always make fun."

I bitterly regret ever having seemed to make fun, taunting or ribbing an angel with all that's jocular. My *dúshenka*, my soul, I hereby forgive you all your complaints about "bifshtek," *kipyatok* (hot water), *narzan* (bottled water), lousy dry cleaning, the insistent proddiness of the commissar (she takes a supply of red ink and rather coarse sanitary napkins whenever they head for the Black Sea, calendars be damned).

Did the brutish facts dog her mind as they did mine? Both "in" in 1961, I for fifteen, she for twenty, I "out" in '76, she theoretically in '81, both entering in the time of Krushchev, she released (one supposed), as hindsight tells us, in the queasy period between the enfeebled and therefore *laissez faire* Brezhnev and the already enfeeble Andropov ('82-'84 only). Such was the period of the phoney pardons and the impromptu extensions: "But, Comrade Karavansky, your sentence was twenty-five. You were released after sixteen and got married, began a university course. *You still owe us nine.* Did you think we would forget? You were wrong." He finally got out again in '74, long before the shy dawning of the tentative, doomed Andropov.

Now I recall something odd about that one-eyed man: his sideburns had been reduced to narrow, eighth-of-an-inch width single lines straying down his face, not so much tapers of hair as, recalled again from the movie of *Death in Venice*, the cheap dye-job of the Dirk Bogarde character's hair leaking a boot-black tendril down either cheek, whose ultimate curl, seeking a fresh direction, gave the face something mediocre and satanic. The composer had sought to become younger, but ended up ridiculous, a personage the buoyant boys on the lido would merely scoff at. I the self-abusing outcast merely wanted to stay alive, disgraced or not, and I felt something in common with clinical Aschenbach. Sometimes, listening to a shell's interior for voices, of children, aliens, the mere sea, and not finding them, a human being will make do by licking the flesh tint of the shell itself, in furtive, iridescent linctus.

We are no sooner back in the treehouse than she wants to dance, and off we go, in semi-darkness, treading lightfoot on the nutshell-strewn platform, not exactly musicless as she has tuned my radio to some syncopated beat right next door to WQXR. We stumble and collect ourselves again and I think that I have come all the way from Siberia to a treehouse in

Central Park, there to dance with an almost complete stranger given to seismic twitches. And wetting herself. All of it. Would it feel weirder to go from here to Siberia, with no warning, where the bones from the uncollected bodies of prisoners wait all winter and then, with summer, somehow get mixed into the concrete along with shingle and heaven knew what else? I am no judge of what's appropriate to a human life. Far gone, I am not quite as far gone as Deputy Commissar Svalocin, reputed to have observed that most of the people who had failed to be respectful with him died sooner or later, as if laying claim to cosmic fiat.

"Watch it," I have to tell her, "or you'll be over the edge. Move more steadily. Move back in."

She doesn't care. Her evening out has perked her up. She has lived what I presume is the normal life of a runaway, but I can't get the image of the eyepatch witness out of my head. Who was he? Why so interested? A social worker who has now identified her? Never: he wouldn't have let her out of his sight, would he? I have the strangest sense that, one of these days, with much panting and good-natured self-reproach, he is going to clamber up our tree and ask for bed and board. Or else. When these things come to mind, my most angelic one, I begin to remember what I have really learned in the country: that criminality has its place in the spectrum of life, liberty, and the pursuit of happiness, otherwise why should the country idolize its gangsters? I have learned too, my long lost pet, that the animal I would like to be if reincarnated in some other camp, with another fifteen years to do, is the good old lungfish, on the planet for three hundred and fifty million years already, never in a hurry about anything, and therefore able to hibernate for ten years at a stretch, no water, no food, no air. Maybe they should fill the camps with lungfish, who would lift their heads only after the first ten years, then go back to cold storage for the next five. That kind of prudence I have learned from nature, or at least from nature at second hand. A third thing I have picked up, but cannot tell Bimini, who has no need of such recondite knowledge, is that the zip of a body bag makes the same sound as a snarling terrier. Try it sometime, you who overhear, only one of you my beloved, the rest: well, you are welcome, it isn't every day you hear the arboreally raised voice of a genuine horny-handed survivor.

 Let's face it, Bim has just too much energy to be kept pent-up in the trees. If she were an animal, a squirrel or a raccoon, I'd have to tether her lest she fall off or give us away. Falling off would be one means of giving us away, of course. Best secure her during sleep, then leave her secured until we leave for the day, on our rounds like mailmen, on the trot like salesmen, on the go like brokers.

The Ice Lens

Now she tapers off, has spent whatever kind of energy she has. I am in good training, from all those months of heaving frogs and poling pools, so I can more or less keep up with her abandoned antics. She doesn't so much dance as wrestle you fast, chattering something not at home in words, and she has this incredible sense of balance as if her feet had suckers that worked in spite of the nutshells.

By now the inflatable bath is hers (noblesse oblige), so I can't really tie her down to that. It will have to be done during the day. She isn't at risk during the night anyway, is she, and by day I can see her coming, but I do believe she will one day work up such a spinning rhythm she will whisk off the edge and maybe fly all the way to Staten Island. A touch of witch, that's what she has, *cara mia*, not that *she* is *cara mia*, of course not. Sometimes the headlong vocative gets tangled with another thought, as it should not, seeing that what I wanted to say to you, long loved one, was that I do not agree with those who claim that it is not an alive person who does the dying. By the time you are at death's door, hand on the latch with foot poised to enter, they say, you aren't really anybody at all because the approach to death is gradual and entails a slight reduction of vitality each day. So: when you are close to it, you are, as we say, moribund. A feather would knock you off at that point, so death isn't quite so bad, they claim, it's not as if it cut you off in full flower, in the grandest flush of blood and sweat. Oh no, it merely rubberstamps what's already pretty far gone. Not true, I say, as many who have undergone treatment by nine grams would testify. Or is it that the mind, given half a chance, dies beforehand? How was it, fondest distant one, to exchange one state for another, to hear your cells give out their final gasp? Why will you never say? Sad in this universe to think that there are knowables for which no knower exists. Or that there are tellable knowns for which no teller shall ever be. I used to read to you a piece of a Latin poem, my sweet, in which the poet used the word *infandum* pertaining to grief, and the word meant unsayable, it sounded so dead and numb, so final and remote, that eventually I could not bear to utter it, but would skip over it, taking it as said. And you'd smile, saying the word for me each time I came to it, telling me not to be so timid. The complete line read something like this: *Do not ask me to renew unspeakable grief,* and I thought it one of the saddest, even if grandest, lines in literature. That's what you get for reading: a pain in the neck and a bad case of the bleats. We were tougher than that, were we not, outwitting just a few private dicks, the men in cheap thick raincoats in the alleyways and on the street corners, the phone taps and the little cameramen with telescopes. Master and mistress of disguise, of wrong-footing the enemy, we kept his face before us: that brooding, scrunched-up truculence of his, the way he blew papirosi smoke into the mouthpiece of the phone while talking (as if to get it into the eyes of the person at the other end), the devout and kindly look that came upon him when he was truly dangerous and had gotten some poor devil to the point of signing a confession. Not that he did such things often, only now and then to keep his hand in, fondly remembering the old days when he advised the man who advised Stalin on how to set up the camps and get hard labor out of soft hands. He wasn't your run of the mill sadist at all, just one who, having seen the furnace, liked to strike an occasional match under a comrade's chin. The lethal worrier, I called him. The ghost of acid and rainbows. He was a myth, but by no lunge of the imagination was he as much a myth to us as we to him.

Oh no, we two fair weather lovers were harnessing the sun, we were blinding the Cyclops, with just a few cuddles and some juicy protracted hugs. And, if he could smell me on you, or I could smell him on you, he never got to smell me until much later, at which point my aroma had changed. By then I stank of fish, an almost womanly smell, and in any event he always had trouble picking up the scent of anyone or anything, what with the air from his feet being so strong. How he scrubbed and sprayed. The stench was within him, waiting to come out, if not through his toes, then through his eyes, his teeth, his ears. As if Mother Russia had been lodged with him, dead, ages ago, and were rotting away, festering and swelling with pleas and screams. He even had to sleep with his feet wrapped in towels, one for each, secured with pajama cords, and then sad peasants press ganged to the city had to launder the towels and no doubt died in that service after receiving arduous duty allowance for only a year or two. They were dragged howling from their crops to the rail siding, then bundled aboard the train to Moscow, pleading to be shot or blinded, but, please, not to have to wash those dreadful towels.

You and Nimet, neither of whom he hears, I can tell you both about it all while serving as guardian to Bimini, for all the world as if I were one of the more considerate apes alive. Down from the trees he comes. Back up he goes, quoting Latin poetry and the music of Tchaikovsky. WQXR is playing Nielsen the Dane just now, a lonely toot if I ever heard one, full of cold winds and ice floes, not so much butter and eggs. It takes all kinds to make up a night's music, as if you were setting out to populate a planet. I like those twirly woodwinds, though, as they come spinning out of the mainstream dirge.

Now the rain soon to be snow taps and enters. We are not quite watertight, but only as much enters as would make a small cloud of steam. So let it. We are not going to get wet, we are only going to get a fraction damp. We will always be drier than wet. We will be in more danger from crocodiles up here than from getting soaked. Always leave something wrong in whatever you make or build: that was the word in the camps, and then there will always be something for you to fix later on. I saw young peasant lads, powerful as bulls, work themselves to death, never having entertained the notion of the safe minimum. After all, they were hardly being fed. When on the edge you do things small and as slowly as your overseer will permit. Does Nimet, I wonder, go and lie in her grave in between announcements? I would like to think of her listening to every single note, breath held, her finger tapping out the rhythm, but they rarely do that: they go out and eat, they visit hospitals, they go and ride stationary exercise bicycles. So, in a sense, the listeners are alone with one another, in an anonymous trance, each wondering how many others there are, ravished insomniacs or daysleepers lonely for music of real class. Three hellos, then: to you, whose atoms feed the Galaxy; to Nimet, whose manicured tones calm the night-fretters; and to Bimini the flawed otter (she has that kind of heedless energy). One perfect *andante* is worth a full night's sleep, or so I am trying to believe as I press the earphones tighter than ever.

The richer your life becomes, the more you begin to miss things you never thought you'd miss, such as, upriver, the bang of cake tins hung out on trees to scare deer away from roses. Not tin, I mean aluminum that shines and flies, spinning around in the faintest breeze, so much so that any half-imaginative deer would think it had run into a wind-chime from Betelgeuse, or, if not that, then an autogiro from the White Sea. That might scare *me* off, never mind a deer. It just might dazzle them to death if the sun was just right and I wonder if it does something the same to frogs, raccoons, and squirrels. If I rigged up something similar in my tree, maybe I could keep the gray squirrels off us. It's a toss-up between nutshells and bird muck, at least in this season, when we have no airborne caterpillars to keep us alert, little aerialists of canny chlorophyll hitching a ride on the faintest puff of air. Snakes, no, thank my stars, and now the bees, the wasps, have quit and lie all around underneath us like the dead and dying from some famous Russian battle with the snow in the wings, the last wet nurse, in starched whites, ready to come and clean things up.

Ah me, ah thou. How antique to say *thou*, not being a Quaker or an ancient poet, but I enjoy its lisping roundness, as if it isn't really a word at all but an exhalation, a tongue into the reluctant ear to get the gonads going. My Bimini now, if anyone can be said to own a Bimini, which must surely include all the moods and electrical discharges passing through her, she seems at times to have a lisp of sorts. Her teeth don't quite come together. That's the source of the sexy little slither in her talk. There I go again, farthest darling, and there is no need for you to understand. I still have needs, but vastly cut down, somewhere between those of a lungfish and the century plant, although you have to watch the makes of names, those nomenclators of old. The century plant blooms once in ten or twenty years, so what did they do with the other eighty or ninety? Get it straight, Kiwi White, or give up on the whole comparison. Let's see: anyone whose needs are equidistant between lungfish and century plant has those needs, if we attend to averages, every fifteenth year. Or, with your short-lived century plant, never at all, in the sense that between a ten-year hibernation and a ten-year flowerlessness, there is no room at all. I'll take the first, remembering wanly how, after my decade and a half among the entombed living mad, I had my first coming, all alone, in a toilet, just to see if body still connected to soul. The poor little tiddlers only got halfway up the phallus and then fell back exhausted, if they ever left their hutch at all. Or perhaps one, a pearl among swine, reached the top and toppled over the edge, a goner you could tell from its drained smile.

O life. O vigilant guardhouse of the brain stem, topped by those dynamic halls of drives and emotions under the big roof of the cortex, why do you do us as you do? Why don't you leave us alone, brain, life, love? All these years lived and nothing to show for them save a few of what I call my Kiwi-fruits, as follows:

The universe is run by a demented grandmother, with a cold, in a wheelchair never oiled.

Senility is nature's anesthesiologist.

Dare I go on?

One man's excrement is another man's *Critique of Pure Reason.*

A little better?

It is not the vastness of space that terrifies us, nor its vacuum silence, but the off-chance that it was *thought* into being.

You see: some of them work.

A man of imagination among scholars is like a sodomite at a convention of proctologists.

When they ripen and fall, they last me for a full year, even two, then I let them rot. I have control.

Christmas, Mother's Day, Halloween, perpetuate themselves because people prefer the dictatorship of the calendar to the subjectivity of dominating time casually.

And, if these are not fruit, they are hyenas that crawl up around me during the night, then have to decide which one will jump me first.

A dead genius is better than a living Yahoo.

I have known both.

Better a neighbor who is dumb than a nephew incessantly phoning from Russia collect.

Words are the outpatients of a mind diseased.

Enough. Nimet has finally eased Nielsen back into the Scandinavian shadows and I applaud her timing. Cesar Franck has arrived and I should take that as a hint, go to sleep, if I can, snoring like Bimini. It is the same as being in a zoo, one near Lubianka jail. Up here we are animals, not to be seen, but reverting, going back to nature and beyond that to unplumbable simplicities.

Good night, Nimet.

Good night, Mother Russia.

Good night, Statue of Liberty.

Good night, twitchy Bimini.

Good night, you long-lost dismembered dissolved powdery dearheart of the dunes from whom it is as if the planet has ceased to be and you do not know that it has never ceased to be although I am certain that, when I join you, it will cease to be for ever and ever. Yes. There are just one or two small matters to take care of, doodles in the smaller categories of chaos, and then I'll be ready, not to talk, or to meet, but with a sour smile to melt lovingly.

Do you know what keeps me straight? No, not the street plans of New York, and the outlines of differently shaped pools, in my lacquered Kholui box, but some such token of the innate tendentiousness of humankind as this: the history of one word, just the kind of thing I was always good at, little realizing back then how useful something this bookish might eventually be.

First you write *quartz*, silicon dioxide, begat by Middle High German *quarz*. Easy going, so far. But that *quarz* was begat by West Slavic *kwardy*, whose parents you can find only in the Indo-European dictionary, under *twer-2*. There you begin to ease up the lid of this commotional treasure trove. It was to hold, to grasp, to hold hard: it was the hardness of the held from the hardness of the holding, see. It almost looked like *turd*, but it really was more like *tvrd*, which came way back when from *twer-y-en*, said *twerryain*, meaning "she who grasps, or binds, or enthralls," and now it is only one move to checkmate, beloved angel. In Greek that word is *siren*. Fancy going up hill and down dale, all around the houses, to prove that quartz is a siren. The words we use are better and older than we are. Just imagine: someone in those only faintly vocabularic mists was dreaming of how hard his sweetheart held him, and then there were ten, a hundred, a thousand, a million. On and on. Tender huggings galore. All across the eons.

The Ice Lens

My Siren holds me hard as I drift off.

Spring came around. With the first warm weather, when the pear trees elsewhere began to blossom, she suffered from dyspnea. When it came around again, warming into summer, when the pear trees in other places were in blossom, she had moments of suffocation. During the next spring with not a pear tree in sight she began to suffer breathlessness. By fourth spring, with the blossom all over the upper globe save here, she had spasms of being unable to breathe. The fifth spring, she found breathing impossible, just when pear trees were bursting with blooms everywhere else. After that, during the time of blossom, with the first intimation of summer's heat, she began to have fainting spells. I was a heartbroken aeronaut in a country where the truth ripened and fell like blossoms with each season.

Goodbye, then.

No *au revoir.*

23. A New Race of Hermaphroditic Fish

When was it exactly that we decided on being refrigerated (as if we were not to be treated thus in the Gulags)? Each, unable to face life without the other, each as it were the other's child, opted for cryogenics, little as we trusted it. But surely, we argued when reason reasserted itself, why would I opt for the deep freeze if she had not? She would not be revived ever. Similarly, why should she, if I had succumbed to an event out of the blue? No, to contrive a complementary, exact match, the one freeze would be responding to the other. Hard to arrange, most of all if one or both ended up in a Gulag. The Gulags are not that helpful anyway, although, in punitive terms, they have no objection to freezing anybody.

So, she said, "it would be the frozen one warming up in a hundred years to no welcome at all, no happy reunion. A poor homecoming."

"Bleak," I said. "Better off just staying frozen."

"Or just dead," she said at her bleakest.

Then, over-rehearsed, we went into our 5-nevers riff, ending in tears. Scratchy and untidy as our union was, illicit and dangerous, we had fallen into that same sucking, clinging need, kissy and joyful, though you might say that I wouldn't have been susceptible to a Russian woman if I hadn't been on the premises for years, guised as an airplane historian. Moyá Dushá and I had hit it off only too well, and when we reached the grand climacteric of our mutual infatuation, the point at which we might have called it a day and gone elsewhere, we blundered back into each other's arms, bewitched by something stronger than before. We had found we could not do without each other, although, even after marrying or otherwise uniting after that salient phrase only to part company years later, many people realize they have to go through passionate addiction first. Who knew where we were going, or how soon? As things turned out, we barely had time to adjust to this new, intense phase of our jubilant relationship before we were found out, grabbed, not even tried, and shipped away separately, with love left to die on the vine, which it did not, although a more refined, circumspect version of that old saw would read: we kept it alive without any information from the other side, which amounts to a declaration, I suppose, of solipsistic tenderness. *Tend and water this rose, my dearest: I will be back.* We hardly had chance to say even that, but the message was read. The declaration of dependence flashed between us and went into the cold abeyant abstinence of the polar bears.

Consider then, in the light of such findings, such successive reports as the following, phoned to Aunt Tasha over the years, by God knows whom. Who could be blamed for, in face of these, whining and whinging, wishing to learn how to pray, ogling a revolver or trying to swallow one's tongue (I cite only my own responses):

Faring well.
Unusually obtuse (over a year later).
Not at this location (after a further month).
Aging.
Uncooperative.
Ill-tempered.
An ornery old witch.
Bitch.
A cow.
Once charming no doubt.
Not her husband's sweetie now.
Infamous.
A disgrace.
Fat.
Old gassy.
Ready for the snows.

I choked. Aunt Tasha stopped relaying messages, finding that the Star-69 method retrieval (what number called) did not work, producing merely a buzz. I did not miss the bad news, grieving that there was none of me, yet wondering what any news of me good or bad, in my own labor camp, would have done to her, yet unable to pursue that speculation to the end of the line, shrinking from it to a story I had heard from a recent arrival, an Englishman with what seemed a permanent stye: millions of contraceptive pills washed annually from London's toilets into the River Thames had started a new race of hermaphroditic fish. Somehow I felt like one of those fish, helpless in the grip of nature's tonnage.

24. Vot A Day

Only several centuries later Bimini is watching me shave with cold water, not so much amused as appalled. Has she never witnessed this dismal ritual before? "Your father," I begin to ask, but she shakes her head with some violence and begins to speed up here twitch; I say this as if she has control over these things, but I may be wrong. I cut myself, of course, and curse. A vampire could not be more pleased than she as the blood courses down my cheek and chin. Tissue fails to stanch it, but the bloody tissues look impressive on the planked floor. I remember another one who watched me shave and with her tongue dabbed the cut until it swooned. Oh yes, my far-off blood stancher. You exerted the pressure until the flow knew better. Then they exerted a pressure on us, widening the wound in between until a bison could have been born through it. In a fit of pique or savage nostalgia I put the razor back in the cut, as near as possible, and make it worse, no doubt as the textbooks say wishing to hurt myself. I don't think so: I wanted to see what would happen, if it would hurt (not much), how much extra blood would pour (a lot), and what effect this little show would have on Bimini. She points at it, makes no effort to stop the flow, and then lets out a weird high-pitched coo as I use my little bevel-edged mir-

The Ice Lens

ror to examine the wound. A flake of skin dangles, then I have it between finger and thumb. I have really eaten all my chocklits now.

"Look at you," she says.

"I *am* looking at me."

She comes up close to see the bit of skin. "A poor thing but mine," I am going to say, but don't; she is nodding in her wild, impetuous way, having just realized that here is a bit of the real living me, at least until a minute or two ago. Just like the umbilical cord. I can see it dawning in her face; in her primitive way she is just about to embark on some hair-splitting distinction between life and death, between the flake of skin attached and unquestionably alive and the flake reposing on my finger, down for the count. I think the umbilical is altogether different and am just going to say so when I realize that she hasn't said a word but has the razor in her hand, applying it hard to her palm as if it will cut like that. It does not, of course, but she will soon discover the slash and the slice, so I dispossess her.

"Mine," she bellows.

"Not to keep," I say. "Don't be silly."

"I most always am," she says with carefully managed poignancy, and I am almost ready to hand it back to her when I get another impulse and nick my ear, just for effect, my darling distant stancher. Now I am really bleeding and I get this silly thought: because, never mind to how small a degree, my blood pressure is lower because of the blood already gone, is it actually lower or has the excitement of cutting myself boosted it anyway? How much can a human being get away with? The vision of an entirely new career swims into the slimy space behind my eyes, a career so unspeakable that even I, connoisseur of horrors and shocks, wince at the thought and its attendant scenes. Bloodletting? NO, something less violent, but Bimini is after the razor again and perhaps intends to preempt those who want to remove her ovaries.

"No, you don't," I say, magistral, curt.

"This once," she pleads.

"No way," I tell her. "You don't want to look like me."

"I won't," she says.

"Not like that," I say. "Bleeding."

"I promise," she says.

"No."

Seapud time again, I see it coming, but the answer is still going to be no. Down with piddling blackmail.

She threatens. I refuse. She streams. I allow it. The razor goes into my pocket, her hand goes after it, I twist my pelvis to tighten the pocket's mouth, she gives up, I decide to shave in the dark in future, by flashlight, some wacky humanoid inspecting himself like a dentist for signs of cosmic diseases. Somehow I have the feeling that today is going to be more troublesome than yesterday was. She has energy to burn. I will not be its fireplace. I have had an idea and I am not going to discuss it with her.

Variable cemetery, I say to myself without even mouthing it. It used to be my idea of Mother Russia, when I thought about Russia at all, and came originally from my response to the Soviet Encyclopedia as worthies mentioned in one issue vanished from the next and, occasionally, those who'd vanished showed up again, no doubt with cleansed conscience and freshly painted to plant the new dead. They just flung the old dead on the snow and the new dead into the compost at the bottom of the trench. *That* was my variable cemetery: tomb of the unknown soldier, civilian version. Musical graves. After a while you could not bear to think of your loved one at all, above ground or below it, on the ground or in the act of lifting a piece of it heavier than she would be if pregnant. She never lifted it, of course, and so won herself a punishment, time and again. No, I do not *know*. I never did. I imagined and almost died of my imaginings. The White Sea, I was convinced of it, was not a sea at all but an avalanche of space amid which invisible white planets twirled and neutral aliens invigilated us with gradual and ultimately definitive loathing. Out there in the center of that so-called sea the Magellanic Clouds hovering like divine froth, waiting to see how Russian sweethearts fared under a system as bald and brutal as that of our own Sun. They ate axle grease and moss. The skin fell off her hands, then again, and again, and that was the end of skin; she was lifting rock with the bare meat of her palms by now. Imagine the gasps she made with each attempt to lift.

Now I know why I am playing with my razor.

What did I hear? Blood is a tissue and skin is an organ. No doubt Leonard knew that, Vesalius too.

Hence my preoccupation. I could first skin my hands, then my feet, then my genitals, my face, my belly, at long last reaching her because we were in the same condition. If I needed help, Bimini with a free hand would pitch in.

What do you think of that, my dearest exquisite, marooned in an eternal bathroom with shelves from floor to ceiling, each one stocked with cold cream for your hands, oils and balms of almost intolerable fragrance, able to slither in between the epidermal cells and calm the heart? As they say in God's Own Country, how do you like them apples, honey? Too late. That must be why I am in a treehouse with, not a dimwit, but a person who finds life insufficiently ceremonious, too slapdash with her innards. I can feel something valuable slipping away. I have felt it before. It must be something unique to our species. I am losing it, for certain. Does it go from you out between your legs? Or might it simply evaporate from a tiny temporary vent in your shoulder blades? No matter. Perhaps it is just an idea and goes from you like an image on film exposed to the sun. In lieu of a god. That must be it. The notion of a god is falling away from me like a theological hemorrhage, and with it all fond dreams of love in the universe, all hope of a jolly uncle like Santa with a weakness for folks. Good bye.

"The thing that really matters," I say to Bimini for simple lack of an audience to lodge the thought with, "is to say this. If all of us who have been through it, so to speak, are the crazy ones, and our tormentors, our jailers too, and all the rest of the world is sane for the simple reason that they never entered the Gulag, or Dachau, then surely by sheer contamination of the mind the whole race is crazy too, just for being on the same planet. To be aware of these things is surely to be driven partly crazy by them too. No?"

She is having a quiet laugh because I am using the long words again. How could she know? She is closer to the gods than to the bereaved.

I try again.

But not to Bimini.

Is it fair to go on being one hundred per cent sane, sweetheart, when millions are being ploughed under? It comes to this: the vision of the human animal as maladaptive fertilizer must surely drive the gardeners batty. No? She noes that no. She will say anything, my sweetheart will. Anything I put into her mind she will say. Anything I put in her mouth will end up in her mind. She agrees. She happens to be part of the subject matter. My vision, or my local private horror peepshow included another thought as well: in a world that has its fair share of Biminis, is there an acceptable reason for the nonstop killing at home or abroad?

"Good morning," I say to Aunt Tasha, who is not my mother although I call her that. Aunt Tasha was an unusual case, garnering up all her energies to get herself and her disgraced nephew out of Russia, then firming up her connections here, after which she seems to have lost heart altogether. All hope, all joy. Today as ever, she sits in her living room, a well-to-do woman come to think of it, surrounded by books and photographs having to do with the Holocaust (nothing Russian in view of course), over which she pores with tender mania. Her main occupation, though, is to tie together hundreds of feathers with little wire twists such as you use on garbage bags. The resulting chain goes around the room some hundred times already and will, in a year or two, begin to work its way close to her as the available space diminishes. Weekly there is a delivery of assorted feathers from some depot in Brooklyn. I had always thought feathers were taboo, not only of the endangered species, but she seems to have no trouble buying them: they don't smell, they come in all colors and sizes, and I must say they have begun to add up to a festive-looking bracelet in the same shape as others have contoured barbed wire. She might be creating an antenna for some as yet undetermined "television," though I know that the ends of the wire twists do not connect, so the girdle or wreath has no chance of picking anything up. It's a thought, though, if only she'd go back and link them.

It would take an extra month or two. She doesn't rush. She abolishes time with patience, listening mainly to the music of Ernest Bloch, and taking her meals on paper or plastic plates even though she has a cupboard full of bone china. She hands over the money as if it is so much lard; I am spending what she doesn't spend on fun. Feathers is all, for her. She says the phone rings always.

Her hands are sore from the twists, she says.

Use scotch tape, I tell her.

No, she doesn't like the way it sticks to fingers.

Then peel-off labels, I tell her. "You only have to roll them around the root of the feathers. I mean, the root of one and the tip of the other." All along she has been looking for a way to combine two feathers without ever having to stick something to the exquisite point or curl of a given feather; but, as I tell her, it is in the nature of feathers to have two ends. "How'd you like a feather with two roots?"

She ignores this callow even if quite practical suggestion, and she is into monstrous wide yearning, rage at the nature of thing, wanting evolution to go back over itself with a blue pencil. "Mother Tasha," I say, "let go. We're here. We're installed. You have your place, and a proper palace it is if you ask me. I have my own version of it. Let go. Don't push."

As well plead with the White Sea in winter. She gives me that look of righteous introversion, shoves her glasses higher on her nose, and goes back to feathers. The whole room is beginning to look like a birds' Christmas, and one day, I imagine, she will have birds flitting around it, hopping from one festoon to the next, her heart entombed in an aviary of the supremest delicacy.

"Time to go," I say. "Don't you ever get tired of Bloch?"

"Does the tape it's on? It drowns out the phone."

So, she is like a tape. It doesn't help to hold these mundane conversations with her; they agitate her and unfit her for feathering, and they certainly don't inspire me to make the best of my tree. The tape does not tire of the music recorded on it. The tree does not tire of the squirrels that prance about its limbs. The snow does not tire of the dead endlessly shoved into its face. Maybe she has a point. I pick up the garbage and take it with me since she refuses to use the dumb waiter; indeed has had it sealed shut lest some uninvited SS doctor ride up to her to share her vigil over the black and whites of bone, ash, sludge, hair, rings, ovens and pincers. Alone in her two-dimensional pandemonium, she seems an ideal candidate for a treehouse. The feathers would be easier to come by, but there wouldn't be as many.

When I say goodbye she answers, as ever, "To God."

I have been entrusted, I know, and I walk back to the treehouse in utter safety, past the garbage drop and a small variety store where I buy the day's needs, my mind still puzzling over Aunt Tasha and her complaint that her phone now keeps ringing off the hook with no one there when she answers. Not even a heavy breather. Nothing obscene. Not even somebody with a loud, ear-rendering whistle human or metallic. Now I know what I went there for: my old boxing gloves, unused (I was a lover, not a fighter), bought in part-obeisance to an American idea. I got them as if to evoke a childhood I'd never had. Retrospective man's stuff. I walk my purchases back to motherly Aunt Tasha, whose motherliness has a spectrum all the way from belligerent possessiveness, which is rare in her, to sentimental aversion, far more common. She says nothing about the phone when I show up again. She does not even speak, but lets Bloch do it for her as if he were the housedog barking. I take my gloves from the closet she calls Teresienstadt. Imagine, to talk with her, you have to know the terms.

"I need my boxing gloves, to keep my hands warm."

On this occasion she says nothing, but she points. Another time, though, she would have said "Look in Teresienstadt first." Are there pictures of that camp in the closet, then? No. She is more metaphorical that that, at least until one of her gentlemen friends calls on her (they all have beards and briefcases), and she suddenly names it Detsky Mir, for the children's toy store right next door to Lubyanka in Dzerzhinsky Square. Do they, I wonder, go in there are play naked? Have they used my gloves?

Always I have this aversion to presenting myself at a counter, or, even worse, of those glass panels with a hold you talk through. Surely they will ask me for my number, then take me all of them calling me Sir to a small back room where the actual charges are read aloud to you. "Don't worry, comrade," they say. "They'll never stick. They never do. We'll look after you, never fear." So I hate to purchase stamps, go to any bank, even get subway tokens. Is it that I think my head will be sucked into the hole and then some see-through blade will descend on the other side of the glass? On top of this phobia, there is another. Well, not a phobia exactly but a dismal recognition: I see the sidewalk and think millions of feet pounded it before you, millions pound it now who don't know your name, and millions to come will do the same. Isn't that refreshing, that anonymity? This is the place to be nobody, so long as your treehouse doesn't catch their eye.

As I leave the store with my rustling brownpaper bag, I stop dead in my tracks, confronted by the back of the man with the eyepatch, going away from me at speed. The same? How many men in eyepatches can there be in New York? In Manhattan. No more than fifty. So the odds are not that convincing. Having seen one, I now recognize them all. I could put an ad in the paper, asking him to own up. Is he following me? Is he one of *them*? Or, remote but languorous solace, could he be someone appointed by the government here to look after me, to see that nobody sticks a poisoned umbrella into my calf on the subway? My love would know, were she here, with her inductive knack, her sixth sense of when someone is observing us, taking notes or photographs.

Is he for me or against me?

Does somebody pay him to do it?

Has he nine-grammed anybody?

In which camp did he lose his eye? Was it deliberate on their part? I am familiar with what they do in some camps, hell-bent on having two or three worthy men to trample down the snow; usually they get the armless ones to do it, but, if they don't have any armless ones, they have been known to manufacture a couple at the drop of an ax. Surely he must have been a spy. The one-eyed man is right for it; the missing eye does not distract him. So, logic says, he would be better carrying around with him a peephole to spy through. Looking at me in the round, from behind nothing, he gets too much of an eyeful. Such mysteries abound in my life, wherever I go. What I need is help from that mythical Rat Man, who certainly knew how to go about things, although he never got *his* way at the guillotine. There must be thousand of applicants among the bereaved, to slip the blade or hold the basket. Yet he got shot in a Paris street, so he can't have had his wits about him all the time. That makes two of us.

"Vot a day," Bimini says when I arrive and she rather enjoys it when I persuade her to sit in the commode and then fasten her to its frame with surgical tape, just to give her the idea. Now she wants to do the same to me, and I have to explain that, in this regard at any rate, I am not at risk. Then she wants to be freed, but I refuse, eager for her to get accustomed to it. Later on, when I really get to work, she can strap me in, but not until.

"Nights only," I tell her, trying to warm up my smile, haunted as I am by the eyepatch man.

"This isn't night," she says.
"This is a demonstration."
"A what?"

I explain what a demonstration is. She doesn't like the sound of it at all and her twitch begins to accelerate, her face becomes once again that awful arena of gulp and recovery, rictus and flick, I am getting to know and, truth told, rather to treasure, as if immobile faces no longer have appeal. Over her mouth it goes just as she begins to scream. I am binding a soft flower to its stem. That's how it feels. Her scream will carry a mile, not as far as Queens, but far enough. To appease her, I gag myself with tape and savor the delights of dumbness. After a while, looking at each other with our mouths bound up, we begin to try to laugh behind the tape, and that is the end of the exercise, until next time.

"You like to tie folks up," she says, massaging her wrists.

"Only when I have to," I say. "I don't do it for the fun of it."

"The fun of it," she says, "is when you get it off."

She means the tape, off arms and legs and mouth. I offer her the wheel to play with, a squashed planet for the asking, but she disdains it with one of her electric shrugs.

"Then how about some food?" I open a can of salmon and with the care of an old monk illuminating a capital letter stir the liquid into the flesh, spilling not a drop. Of course in doing so I mix air into the fish and make it bulge higher than the can's rim. Still without spilling. Then I make our sandwiches, but the liquid makes them soggy, so we eat them from paper plates with spoons. I know the bones are soft after being boiled, or whatever they do to the salmon in the can, but I offer them to her, and she bolts them down as if craving calcium at any price. "I want you to help me, maybe," I tell her, with one foot on the wheel as if I have just wrestled it to a halt, "in something I want to do to bring us a little money." How I have managed to assimilate her presence so far as to think of an *us*, I have no idea, but I suppose that people who live in trees are open to experience: whoever wafts in is home, just like that. After all, we didn't toss the wheel away and we weren't worrying about smashing somebody's head in, watering his dog forty feet beneath us. We're a team.

25. Ere

Aunt Tasha, of course, is the one leading a so-called normal life. She gets bills as part of some ruinous paper chase, which includes one telephone company hitting her for a hundred dollars monthly just for use of their line (no long-distance calls, hardly any local), while some other outfit proclaims on the envelope "Your bill has a new look," as if announcing a daughter's wedding. This is not my world, I the phoneless, the cableless, the addressless, not even a license to my name, "allowed back into the country" by special fiat of the agency I once worked for, the mood of my return interview being very much that of a supreme court indulging an injudicious scarecrow.

"Was it worth it, White or whoever you are?"

"*Some* information," I suggested.

"Obsolete and stale," they told me. "While you were sucking sludge among the Soviets, the world moved on."

I gulped. "At least I still believe they hid their best aeronautical secrets in plain view, such as perforated wing roots. Some of their keenest research was published in magazines for aeromodelers. It makes perfect sense. I was alone in recognizing this."

"You alone? Pfui."

"You are now detached. Give him his papers and let him go. Is there an address?"

"Address?"

"For tax purposes."

I thought about the downward plunge you took in the Gulag, beyond snow and hewn timber into a dark midden of all the previous prisoners. We were at least spared taxes there.

Central Park, I told them.

"Back among the big bucks already! Have you been selling information to anybody else? The Brits, the French?"

"The big dough," I said vaingloriously, "is to be had in Africa. *You* know."

"The number, then?"

"Rural Free Delivery, gentlemen."

"You look worse than ever."

"Apart from the tan."

"There is that."

I took my leave of the suits, half-fancying that, with a little help, I could hang several of them from my own or someone else's tree, snapping the bone with a short drop. I had been summoned to speak with them. I had finished with my business. They must have prayed that no one else would take after me, whether spies or mere layabouts. I had Nimet to comfort me during the nights, and Bimini during the day. Plus of course my *golúbchik-dushá-dúshenka* second by second. I was a man suckered by illusions, urgently believing in the contemptibles of civilization, the homeless and the betrayed, and for that I would pay for the rest of my days. There was one thing:

each of my cross-questioners, formally garbed in tie and shirt, wore a shirt whose collar had begun to fray, as after too many launderings, too much sweat on the job, too much anxiety, chewing, grinding of the teeth. The agency was fading out, I thought, and I was not the only one to fall.

You can often spot a fading, secretive society in its stamps, which I noticed blown-up into posters in the post offices, not only the rate in cents printed at right angles to the legend, but the price hardly visible at all, as if the future would be all sudden changes, cryptic legends about the feeblest celebs, the great names of American literature dislodged from their places in our modern Parthenons (after whose design even the front grille of the Rolls-Royce car was patterned) to make room for financiers, entertainers, cooks, stand-up comedians, anchormen, wiseacres, and wrestlers. I had come back, via the pools along the Hudson, to what Pound the fascist zealot called an old bitch gone in the teeth. At least he got that right.

Anyone can spend his life accumulating *alas*es, if he has a mind to do so. My own version of that, I remind myself from time to time, is a life that imitates coitus interruptus, with all the attendant collapses, anticlimaxes, undischarged nervous tension, and the awful bone-melting awareness that a gigantic bird has flown away never to be seen again, just as it was set to land. Not that she and I were, apprehended is the word, in the dead center of the act. Our act had already taken place and we were smoking something of poor quality, having long since used up our clandestine supply of American cigarettes. We were musing, reclining, watching the clock, but of course naked, when they burst in upon us, faces working and churning almost like Bimini's. She and I never saw each other again, absentees in the Lubianka. That was part of our reward, to make contact with the other only through indictment and deposition, lie and guess, denied the chance to see again the face, the flesh, that had set the whole thing moving. Interruption was just about all we knew. We were broken apart, with broken hearts: a fancy figure, I admit it, but anything is possible when you have spent the rest of your days pondering that ancient doctrine of symbolism, a movement of the mind toward a world made one again. Those of us who have gone through it should be entitled to wear a *boutonnière* of some kind, *le coeur rompu*, say, *Le Coeur Rompu*, Order of, with it taking the form of not a yin and yang, nor of an actual red heart as of the bloodmobile, but a sliced eye, bloodshot and unfocused. More like that, dearest one. In my lapel, but where are you? We would have to get you something with lapels, of course. What we never understood was that our so-called immorality was not only immoral: it was treasonable too, leeching away at not only his happy life in the double bed, but also his ability to perform in the political arena, to do his duty. Then, of course, as we were made to realize, that political offense of ours was also by simple ascension immoral yet again, and so for being ascendedly immoral it was by yet another simple ascension doubly political. On it went, the two offenses winding around one another like creepers in some terrible crescendo of social indignation. There was no way to stop it from getting worse. We sat in cells while it roamed ever upward, no sooner immoral than political, no sooner political than immoral, until we became two separated, severed, lustful traitors, two diabolical swans fit only for nine grams apiece.

We never got it, but only because Svalocin knew it would hurt us more to have to linger apart, and the demon king within him wanted to express his vengeance thus and not otherwise. So here sits she, wondering if her lover has been shot. She assumes he has not and concludes there is yet therefore hope of their being together again one day even if only as geriatric patients. There is no hope of even that. So she assumes he has been shot, after all, and wonders how she will survive that knowledge. There is no difference really, she decides, unless she adds to the puzzle the other element of his wondering, wherever he is, if she herself has been shot, and which is easier for her to bear: either knowing she has not been shot, and may not be, in the act of wondering about a dead him or a live him, or closing her mind to the whole thing and deciding, in some last blaze of reckless love, that indeed she has been as good as shot in the act of wondering about his wondering as he too was shot in the act of it.

All the same.

My capacity to make two self-regarding minds, but no longer interacting except through sheer hypothesis, come together on one of the lower stages of hell has gone. I can no longer reason it through, attending to all the finer shades of reprisal casuistry. I can no longer add it up. I was truly the living death to which we had been condemned, and they knew that she, certainly, would not survive, not with the skin coming off her hands in the first week. He must have gloated about that as the skin that had fondled mine came away like wet confetti in the Siberian wind, blown away so fast to Thebes or any other mythic place it was not itself the instant it tore free.

That was his fun too, imagining how our minds tortured themselves, wondering if a sweetheart dead were a less painful thing to harp upon than a sweetheart fading away from cold, slave labor, and malnutrition. In some orders of being, such as punishment and crime, there is no essential difference between conditions named in different words. The dead death and the living death are much the same, at least after the hope in the latter has quite gone out, like a fleck of hot paper up the chimney, up and wafted away to settle on the snow, flash frozen on its journey down. This means, of course, that truth and lies are the same thing, having the same effect. They tell you she's dead and they tell you she's alive, but to be shot tomorrow. They tell you she is to be shot next week instead, but that she has already been told you were done away with weeks ago, at which she asked to be shot sooner, if they please would. This is where the words break down, and all you have left, if you are unlucky, is emotion, but mostly emotions about having any emotion left. You have become only a twig, a quiver, an exploitable ghost whom, if they are in that mood, they tell about in the cage with syphilitics.

Of course they can't tell you too many tales or the tales would have no effect. They would cancel out. But one a month that already feels like a year is quite enough, just right, giving you only a bit more desire to live than to die, until the next tale, when you reverse the ratio. A guard is in the role of fiction maker, reminding you in his crass and grievous way that fiction does not imitate nature, oh no, but simply the creative habits of nature itself. A good guard can make of you a seedling, an egg, a spore, whereas, unless you are lucky, you have no control over him whatever unless you choose to antagonize him, which is a poor sort of control to begin with. It always ends in his developing an even greater degree of control over you, and even yours. How does that dialogue from hello go?

He's misbehaving again. Tell him to stop.

At her wannest she says: *I never see him.*

Tell him anyway. You have nothing but time.

She collapses at this point, but they go on insisting:

You'll think of something, your highness. If he does it again, he'll be shot.

She pleads. They tell her to concentrate. She faints. End of dialogue.

Thus they flay you alive with varying degrees of the impossible, forcing the still rational mind into leapfrog acts of random insanity, turning your entire world into nothing but ideas, and so forcing you to loathe both ideas and yourself. With a mother they are even crueler because they know the bond is fraught with guilt and pathos, has nothing to do with choice, and so is more absolute. Mothers and sons crack more easily than lovers do, believe it or not, as do mothers and daughters. It's the blood that makes it easy, whereas lovers have within them somewhere vestiges of the apartness they killed by coming together. In captivity, among the lucky, that apartness soon arises again and each realizes all over again the separateness of their two beings. Twins (not many cases) they find hard to vanquish, because so long as one twin lives he or she thinks he or she is the other. So there are really three. Or is it four? Other combinations come to mind, but that should suffice for a general survey of how the courts and the camps deal creatively with those brought forward for punishment. It is, dearest, as if the Sun were put in charge of skin grafts on newborn babies, or a thunderstorm in charge of birthday cards. So long as there is commotion, violence, and a more or less oblivious response to human feeling (cf. so called Acts of God), the procedures prove acceptable. It is the epic form of behavior, with humans given solar or planetary power over others, and I suppose the sensation is almost godlike at times because they are working with the rawest of material, which is far from home, out of breath, at its wits' end, down on its luck, and not long for this world. They might as well experiment while body and soul huddle together.

That's how it was, how it will always be because of the human desire, ineradicable as smell from cheese, to do unto folks as the universe does to them. Can it be as simple as that, dearest? Were we the victims of an equation as simple and soluble as that? Had we known, would we have even smiled at each other? Even once?

Perhaps because I bound and gagged her, Bimini is becoming more straightfoward than ever. Her stomach, flat enough to have an airline schedule laid upon it with no part of it not touching skin, contains a pouch full of boy and girl kangaroos. So she says. She speaks about herself in the guise of the girl kangaroos: "The girl kangaroos don't like to be tied up. They don't want to have that tape over their mouses." Sometimes she speaks for the boys, or as the boys, but much less often, keeping to what she knows best. So I am getting used to her using the first person pronoun less and less and making, more and more, allusions to a distant-sounding zoo in which there are kangaroos only. It's more than just her way of not saying "I," it's some kind of homage to the natural world, to beings that might take her on trust, give her the benefit of whatever doubt. Not that humans treat her badly, at least not those she meets casually on the street, or, indeed, up in the trees. No, she seems to have distributed who she is across a wider spectrum of being than most of us do, heeding the kangaroo in herself and, just maybe, the bit in her that's dinosaur, prairie dog, or leopard. Maybe we should do the same, no longer insisting on our human nature but spotting what links it has with other species. She likes the 'roos because they live in pouches, cozy and custommade, and I wonder who told her about them. Not the reading kind, she might have gleaned it from her mother or a nurse, hardly from a friend, but you never know. Watching her the other night by torchlight, I saw her do something, just before going to sleep reaching into her pocket for a pair of somewhat less than mint condition earplugs and rolling each into a taper before tapping them into place. Hours later I watched as she retrieved one that had fallen out, with an unerring paw lifting it up from beneath her chin, where it had ceased to roll, and then, instead of somehow ramming it back into her ear untapered, putting it in her mouth as if it were a nipple. And that is how she slept the rest of the night. Tempted to go get it before she choked on it, I waited and waited, checking her from time to time with the muted red of my lamp. When at last I went over to her and tried to remove it, I found she had it firm between her teeth, and I wondered what on earth she would have done if her mouth had been taped up. Would she have slid it up her nose or back into whichever ear it belonged in?

Something uncanny in that event heartens me. She must be tuned in exquisitely to the light tensions of her sleeping body, and her unconscious guides her in the tenderest way. Whatever peace she gets, she pays for it in daylight twitches, of course, although for someone with so stressful a face she achieves an extraordinary peace of demeanor. If she were to wake and see me doing what I do while she sleeps, she might be less serene, although she might enjoy it no end as I dab away at my arm with the double blade of the razor, drawing blood and making weals, first this way, then that, until I have a piece of me ready to take flight, held down by only one little hinge of skin, like a stamp in a collector's album. I am my own to play with, I am my own to mutilate if need be, I am surely entitled to do to myself what, both mentally and physically, my guards did to me for over fifteen years. In a twisted sense I am taking charge of my own destiny, doodling with the flesh (I am not cutting at my navel after all: the kind of objection *she*'d raise, if any). It hurts a bit in a dim and distant way, no worse than squeezing a minor boil, and the self-satisfaction is much greater. So far I have left all the little flesh hinges in place, tamping the bit back into place and holding it there until it takes, a matter of half a minute only. It could be worse. In time the inside of my left arm is going to look a mess, covered with hives or pebbles, but nonetheless an exhibit. Look: I've made something of myself after all. I am a translator who has gone beyond his métier, regretful only that he did not rip the living flesh out with his own teeth rather than with this double layer of the extra sharp. You cannot cut yourself deep with such a thing, certainly not to the quick, for which you need a blade of the old kind. It's best at scarifying, taking the skin off flake by flake, but if you gouge deep with a slashing motion you can do bigger and better: easier with Wagner pouring from WQXR, or swoony old Richard Strauss the henpecked, rather than De-

The Ice Lens

bussy or Bach. There's good cutting music and there's bad.

A wiser man that I would have his antiseptic pain spray by him, ready to squirt, but the risk and the discomfort are part of the gesture. You want to seem to be taking the world on, life and limb, and all that, even if it turns out to be nothing more than a more bloodthirsty fashion of always talking to an absent sweetheart. No more darlings and dearhearts and beloveds, but instead a going steady with the constant drip, the sting that comes and goes between wrist and elbow. I'd rather that pain than the pain of wondering if they gave her nine grams of lead or not. I'd rather that than the pain of always trying to conjure her up, by name, out of the shades, as if endearments were some kind of electricity. Build up the voltage and the light goes on, all the way from Siberia. She has heard. She is trying to answer, her bulb blinking on and off. If her arms weren't stiff she'd do semaphore too.

So: I am trying to see if the blood and the cuts can call up her shade for one last conversation. *Ere.* I like that ancient word. Ere we part for *aye.* There's another. When you have sunk this low, the monosyllable with dust on it will do. O my love, the afterlife cannot disappoint: if it exists, *it exists,* and one knows. If it does not, then one does not know. How seemly. It is just a stop in another country, in a country other than the country of origin.

That's what we used to say, and now we have to prove it somehow, from the evidence at hand. To be on the safe side, I take from my pocket an outsize paperclip and, scoring with it until the blood comes, lengthen my left-hand lifeline a good inch and a half, right down to the beginning of the wrist. All done by the light of the flashlight in my mouth. I call it a torch because I am carrying a torch, not twisted straw dipped in wax, as in olden days, but ruddy so as not to wake the sleeper opposite whose eyes behold this carnival without so much as a blink, a word, a movement.

She sees and is willing to watch.

She thinks I haven't seen her open her eyes.

What if she bares her belly, to have either kangaroos or even her ovaries removed?

The best I have, I was saving it for later, is a modeling knife: razor blade locked into a handle, but it cuts carpets like butter, it slides through wood, and it has built into it a tiny lens, although you can't look through it while actually making a cut. You can sight through it and then examine the work: pre-post-erous, meaning both before and after. Imagine the fate of the self-mutilator being locked up into one word sibilant as a wet sail. Blade in hand, I motion her to close her eyes and go back to sleep. She does. She closes them, with a faint stertorous protest, and gradually her overactive face settles into sleep. All of a sudden she is no longer a presence to be reckoned with. Now is the time for all other presences to show themselves, but not a one does. I am alone with the tree, Nimet, Buxtehude, dried blood and the sting in my arm, plus of course the wheel, the inflatable bath, the commode, our provisions, the memory of one gaudy parade, the colossal hubbub of big-band jazz, and the face of the one-eyed watcher. Is it telegamy when you keep speaking to a far-distant dear one? She never answers, she never hears. Above where she is buried, if buried she is, they are still hauling corpses on boards to which they have fastened a length of rope, and I see one poor devil in particular, who had once hung his scarf around the neck of a Lenin bust, his body covered with pimples the size and hue of blackberries, being bumped and slithered back from where he could work no longer. He died en route, so he had a right to be on the board for only half the journey. He had committed one of the few unpunishable offenses. I can still hear them blasting away with explosive to make crude graves which, come summer, would have to be deepened by hand because of the stench. She must have died lugging heavy wet timber around, her shoulders sharp as epaulets, her skin folded over upon itself for lack of flesh to contain, her kneecaps bulbous as bedpost knobs. This was what they wanted to make of her. This was what they wanted me to imagine as having happened to her. Yet, if I could imagine it, why should they need to do it, since I never asked for corroboration? He divorced her long before she had developed the spurious suntanned look of pellagra, before her voice had dried up into that of a fishwife. He had a perfect right by law (no fee either) to divorce her on the grounds of being where she was. Her sexual offense was not the issue, having been settled long ago by the sentence handed down. He never heard her pure cold soprano again, a singing voice so immaculate it made her its own instrument. Perhaps in the early days of her imprisonment she used it, making it figure chastely against the damp-socks air of the jail, raising her soul on a skein of vocal light, lofting herself free on an almost inhumanly denuded sound more abstract than music itself. Until they half throttled her to shut her up, so as not to work up the other women, some of them jailed by mistresses, conniving wives. Informing was just one of the ways to lubricated your sex life, as we knew. Informing was just another of the many ways in which one could use the system. Informing was an art, a science, a mystique.

    If only it had worked in reverse: you inform the authorities that you have absolutely nothing to report against so-and-so, which should surely win them bonus points to be used against eventual denunciation. It never worked thus. As my interrogator, a bookish-looking man with big dirt-seamed hands that belied his looks, informed me as we stood in the early days looking out of the window at the street below.

"Look," he said, "just look at *them*. They have no idea who or what they are."

"Those are the free," I gauchely said. "I envy them."

"You really are a snot eater," he said. "Look again. *They* are the accused. *You* are the condemned. That's the difference." Then I remembered that Sinyavsky-Tertz had said something such before they put paid to him for the last time. Everything seemed skewed. Falling in love was wonderful because it was the prelude to a thoroughgoing patriotic act: informing on the loved one, once you had tired of them and wanted them off the premises unless, oh joy, they had beaten you to the punch. All this made for premature informing, right after the first kiss or coupling, so as not to be left in the lurch by someone in whom ecstasy fought a constant war with self-preservation. There was informing in the very midst of bliss. And vice versa. I don't know how they kept up with it at head office where, once, they considered making love an offense against the state until they realized, of course, that love would only yield to hate, and hate had already filled the jails. What was needed, comrades, was non-possessive lust, or a lust in which there could be no boredom, and some phantom bureaucrat long ago exiled had the brainwave of an entire nation entering sex cooperatives, all by number, if even that. It would be like going to the toilet. After all, almost all of the nation was toilet-trained, so they might be trained in this way too, blindfolded and masked in their brothels, confessing their sperm anonymously like members of the Catholic church. In this way a man might even have a chance of doing his mother, no questions asked. The possibilities were limitless. Nobody would ever recognize the person he or she had been to bed with. It was amazing, and poignant, to watch them as they sniffed one another in stores or at the ballet, wondering was it him, was it her? In this way the amount of ravishing mystery in each life would raise itself to exponential maximum, as if a god had wandered through their midst, dropping here and there a flake of golden leaf. If only, they said, it could have administered itself. The trouble was that someone had to be in charge. When somebody is in charge, nothing works. Things have to be run by remote control from heaven, that's all.

Don't they beloved? Look what kind of life I have without you. It goes from day to day, stumping on its kneecaps, licking the sidewalk, feeding on music and privacy, now and then making a grand sortie to the lucid blue pools of the idle bourgeoisie.

Come back, for a hello.

For one of those mutual smiles as two lovers walk toward each other from some distance, the one's smile altering as the other's does, each thinking how hard it is to sustain the smile through the intervening space, as if the other might feel slighted by the merest variation, as if smiles were meant to be static like birds' nests. We would forgive each other our variations, then embark on the most suffocating kiss known to mankind.

Come and try it once, won't you?

If our lips are chapped, we'll be gentle. If cracked, we'll hardly kiss at all, but, like two hummingbirds, hover, billing each other with imperceptible finesse.

Want to try? Want to give it a try?

The Siberian winds within my head blow that entreaty away, as all else; but, just perhaps, if I do something so awful, so contrary to all we had between us, she will fling herself back through the steaming moat of time to stop me.

See how my wrist is scored. She allowed that. So it was trivial. Look at the inside of my arm. Less trivial. It still did not fetch her back. Were I to cut my throat, would she arrive posthaste, her curls flying, her limbs retracted for flight?

Dearheart, I say aloud, what shall I do? How can you be got?

"Wait one moment," says Nimet, "and you will hear the strains of Handel's *Messiah*, so cherished at this season."

I switch off the radio, note the fading batteries, eye the upward-pouring dawn with a night-person's aversion, and finger the crusts on my arm and wrist, thinking only: I got through another one, like a bird in a bird house. Only another eleven thousand to go, give or take a year or two.

Bimini stirs, opens her eyes, closes them again, and in her sleep coughs so loud I think she'll alert the whole park. I apply the tape again. She hardly stirs. Then I apply it to myself, same place, and we are two dummies on a November morning in the trees, waiting for truer converts to civilization than we to come and get us, install us in the kinds of spaces reserved for the likes of us: padded or steel, sentry-box or hydrotherapeutic tank. Now I know I will need bandages and antiseptic spray, cord and some rubber hoses. Life is going to be even more of a challenge from now on. I have a helpmate, so I am going to use her. Lucky Rat Man of Paris had something to shove against, I suppose: the presence or the supposed presence of his enemy, whereas all I have is an arsenal of ghosts more real to me than anyone in Manhattan or even Central Park. I must have developed a knack for it, this calling up of the dead and gone. It takes flair, plus an ability to change the mind into something like magnesium ribbon or spun glass. Be delicate as a brainwave, I tell myself, and you will pass muster among the shades, the vibrant lights of the might-have-been. The thing to do is to make a strong appeal, to set up a focus of intensity, something so resonant and sharp that no one, never mind how long dead, can resist it. They'll come flocking in. Down the tree I go, to the nearest phone, but first securing Bimini with more tape where she lolls, her mouth a white hyphen in the gaining light.

26. Camps Become Colonies

As the "bad" camps gave way to the "good," at least on the bureaucratic level (name-changes to begin with), I discovered in myself a tendency to personalize what after all had begun as a personal matter: a crime against morality, and common sense as well. The usual tendency would have been to accept the misdeed as the bureaucrats defined it: a political crime tinctured with shameless malice. My own response was to think about the envelope in which I had first secreted locks of my own hair, anticipating, I supposed, the onset of baldness, a catastrophe already visible on the head of Svalocin the commissar. That way I did not wish to go. So, while at liberty anyway, I barbered my own hair, as one might in a foreign country, being a bit sheepish about the chair, the willfulness of Russian haircutters (too many crew cuts by "accident"), and the general drift of barbershop chatter (soccer, about which I did not know). The main reason was personal. Then the Gulag, which enforced the crew cut anyway, then freedom again, enabling me to resume my private hair-cutting ways. The envelope grew bigger, though not at the same speed; the curls gathered together like sheep in a thunderstorm even as, after a whole series of dispensations, *Gulag* became *Guitk* (Chief Administration of Corrective Labor Colonies) instead of Chief

The Ice Lens

Administration of Corrective Labor Camps. Camps had become colonies, a savage innovation, if you pardon my sarcasm. I was reminded of the French saying: the more things change, the more they remain the same.

Truth told, my casual auscultation of the Soviet aircraft industry had fast become a thematic biography of Tupolev, the father and guiding spirit of Russian aviation, perhaps inspired by my seeing a crude piece of film in which he conducted a design class in the open air, amid the wind and snow. Here strideth a noble man, I thought. Aside from that respectable, consuming chore, I wondered and wondered when a *camp* would become a *colony*, and by means of what clerkly finesse, not to mention a greater degree of civilized behavior by the guards: the dis-NKVDing of the NKVD. Oh yes, *we* would become the warders, they the prisoners. This would hardly affect my *dúshenka* since she was being held for special, private reasons unknown to modern man. Indeed, she might end up worse than before, graced with a more satanic stroke of humiliation while the party muck-a-mucks shuffled labels and definitions--after all, in 1934 the OGPU had become the NKVD! Who knew what came next? Someone idly toying with a commissar's mistress in a luxurious dacha would no doubt clinch the whole matter, perhaps converting "colony" to "tent," thus baffling everyone. The same old emphasis on rock-splitting and timber-hauling would endure. One's muscles would go on atrophying, one's heart continue to give way under the same strain of harmlessly renewed "Corrective Labor." We would always be reborn in the same captivity.

Andropov and Chernenko proved it, forever vacillating. Without the Gulag or the Guitk, the political system they personified could not exist. Without the punitive, there can be no virtue. And where there's a will there's a way. The hydra head springs always anew. Abolish the political prisoner and he springs forth as a common criminal; he always did. Yes, we have no politicals; nobody wears such a label. As for Special camps, with their few privileges, she was never sent to one of those (no numbering, no locks or bars, choose your own hairstyle, argue with the camp commander), and so, because we have no politicals, must be dubbed a common criminal, in other words, an adulterer.

Imagine that bit of fundamentalism! And no sly cracks about it. She failed to keep her vagina clean, destined for the exclusive use of one Svalocin, who appears out of the pink mists of history clutching a scrubbing brush and a bar of disinfectant soap, whereas it is well known that women were designed to admit the greatest number of suitors for the sake of mere productivity.

27. The Kohlui Box

When I get back from my shopping expedition, I feed Bimini lunch, I having no appetite, and tell her we are going to the movies again. She smiles, relieved to have the tape off her mouth, her arms, her legs. Into our garbage bags we go, getting comfy, but I don't like things this slippery, unless it's raining, but it won't do that until tomorrow. At least it keeps the drafts out until we seat ourselves, again near the back, and peer at the Rat Man doing his peculiar things. Before he first shows up, you hear him coming even if you don't know it's him. Garbage cans crash and cardboard boxes give off that sullen, hollow note as he kicks them on his way through. You hear a lot of cursing too as he gets nearer, but not curse words, just a sustained baritone mutter as he comes, although other voices seem to be chiding him for this or that. There follows a light skitter of tin cans as he heaves into view, tripping over this or that lump of refuse, on his way back to the horizontally opening door that lets him into his hovel.

Under the battered hat he has this weird smile, like something nailed to him, not a bad smile, really, except that it has too much stoicism in it for anything human. A flash-frozen smile I'd call it, and he has a tan, won from endless days on the boulevards in the sun. I look on. No rat in sight, but he's clasping something to his chest inside his coat, so you can guess what's there all right. He grunts, then sighs, leans over a groin-high doll's house and seems to disgorge the contents of his chest into its unroofed top, all in one lunge, one heave. I saw the rat flash downward and scurry into one of the tiny rooms, only to vanish behind some miniature couch. If I were his rat I'd be shy too.

"The girl kangaroos are getting upset," Bimini says. "Put your hand on them."

"Don't worry, they'll settle down."

"They *don't like it*."

I give her my hand, but she doesn't set it where the girl kangaroos are supposed to be, but lower, much lower, right upon the humped-up bird's nest of her thatch. She sighs like a queen recrowned.

I tell her I am watching the movie, and watching it carefully. Keep still. "Watch the movie, like me."

For a minute she quietens, then at the top of her voice yells "I'm skurd." Now, as before, people turn to rebuke us, with glares, fingers wagged in the half light, and finally with reluctantly raised voices. Now Bimini, once launched, makes the noise she calls the barking cockroach, scapegoat for flatulence, and it is time to go. One of these days I will see this movie through, nothing missed. For now, it is time to find Bimini something to do, to help with, to keep her calm. Out we go in our seagreen plastic like two waves waiting to break, her hand in mine, her mind on the rat, mine on the brick in the velvet bag they used to beat me senseless with.

So it will have to be, what, the twelfth or thirteenth cup of coffee with her, taken on the run in smoky greasy spoons while others sup beer only yards away from us and the waiter wants us to move on, to make room for those who sat as well as drank. I point to the outside world, the sky mainly, and say one of my party-pieces: "No thunderbolts, and just a few rainbows. I'll take it." This impresses her not at all, as her lopsided shrug says. To her, fancy words, far from what matters, such as getting and keeping her chocklits and getting the sticky tape off her mouth. All in all she is not a moviegoer, I can tell that, and I wonder if the flatness of the screen has something to do with her aversion. Now comes her twitch, all over her face, and I get this appalling urge to lean over her and kiss it away, from place to place, not so much quelling it with sheer affection—although that is beginning to enter into it—as hounding it until, having no place to settle, it heads off into her shoulder, gets buried in her shrug. I make no move, however, apart from giving her a cheek pat, which she seems not to heed; maybe she'd had too many. At times her voice is as gruff as that of an old alcoholic, or an opera singer with polyps on the cords:

strained, coarse, dry, yet almost as if at some point undreamed of in *Genesis* she will erupt into golden song, the only thing her voice was born for.

It's as if the huskiness is the voice's manger, drab until the spruced-up, disembodied voice soars forth, the thin sharp gold color of Strega. No, that was another woman, and Bimini's uncleared throat has so far been only itself, making her seem gruff even when she's playful.

Her legs, though, don't seem to match the gruffness. They're lithe and springy. Her walk is more of a lope, as if there is too much space between her legs, and what she touches with the soles of her boots half-electrifies her, sends her feet bouncing upward again at twice the usual speed. Spring-heeled, that's what she is, maybe from her legs being on the thin side, not to mention the pudding-hot mystery clamped between them, to which she thinks I don't attend enough, whereas really I do. The memory is old, but it cuts all the ice I've ever seen. Eating sardines, I smell the smell of my penis, the decomposing of recent ejaculate: tiny proteins going off, which in their turn remind me of sardines. She whiffs of the same. Perhaps we are not as clean as we should be. November out of doors isn't exactly conducive to coldwater baths in the inflatable, but we try, dabbing and rinsing. I guess you need an avalanche of scalding water to blot out the smell of the sea we all slithered out of, to the eventual tender mercies of homo sapiens on the constant rampage. It puts you off, like, in days of old, Svalocin's habit of blocking the toilet every morning with the sheer weight and bulk of his high-residue diet. The wonder of it is that my ideal woman, my idyll, turned to another man at all, instead of a donkey, a sewing machine, a garden she could domineer in chamois-leather gloves. Svalocin was not only repulsive; he worked at being so, aware that any woman he fancied was his, not the prolapses, pellagra-ed, fleshless, breastless, hoarsely gasping paragon my dearheart became, but something flashy with a perfumed pelvis and nails painted the color of our national flag. He never did stray, though, not even as a skunk ambles through a winter orchard; he wanted his own for himself, what he'd paid for. Come to think of it, he drank so much vodka he could have floated her in a thousand-gallon tank, like a pet seal or dolphin. It was he who, if I did not start this legend myself, made sure that the shepherd who'd cursed a cow, calling it a Soviet slut, got five years for his pains, instead of having him pumped so full of milk he burst like a fungus.

"You look as if," Bimini says, giving me a chance to finish the comparison, "as if—"

"I know I do."

"What then?"

"Never mind."

She wants to talk, out of the blue, just as I begin to sink into the morass of the fatidic: based on what I've gone through, I know what is to come.

"Well," she rebegins, "no thunderbolts so far, and there are no rainbows either. You were telling a whopper."

Sometimes I have to, and it's time she knew it. Tell her I will not; isn't she supposed to glean such things from my manner, the air I have, the way I sniffle in the cold?

"Real whoppers," she persists.

"There's nothing else," I say. We had to dig goldmine shafts to a depth four times our heights. Next, I'd think, they might make us dig upward, into the air, and then club us hourly for not producing results. *Where's the shaft? We can see nothing at all and you have been digging for hours.* They punished us by declaring that our bread ration was at the far end of the mineshaft. When we had dug to the requisite depth upward, we would find our bread, and not until. Then they made us remove the boards that flanked the fabric of our communal tent, the boards that kept it rigid and above zero, and it became a tent again. It was as if they had been firing their tommyguns into the long line of us as we returned from twelve hours "on" to twelve hours "off," a lark really because out of the latter twelve they kept us on the go for at least eight. So we slept for four.

And, I have no evidence to the contrary, so did she. My angel of the Arctic.

"Guilt," I say aloud, to Bimini because she happens to be there, troughing on a chocolate soda. Like a prisoner, she receives no mail and sends none, but she is not in handcuffs, not yet, palms outward, behind her back. All she would have to do is live in another country than the country of origin, and they would wallop her with a five-year stint, easy as falling off your stool during interrogation. Her offense: leering (i.e. twitching) incessantly at an official of high rank. Oh, they'd have a field day with her up near the White Sea, showing her the heads of escaped prisoners, brought back in a laundry bag as it was too much trouble to bring back the whole of the captured's corpse.

We are waiting for dark, that's all, and it comes an hour sooner thanks to the clocks having been pushed back. It seems as if, on the brink of winter, the whole nation insists on being in the thick of it. I hate cold. I should go live in the warmth like Rat Man himself, doing the pools where they never have to close them, where heaven is permanent not seasonal. Once I have taken care of certain things this winter, I'll be moving on, treehouse or no treehouse. Down in the Everglades I'll build again, my cherub of the *taiga*, where dogs full of horsemeat chase men empty of bread.

"Come on," I say to her, as she finished her third chocolate malted. I have to go and get ready.

"Arfamoe," she seems to say, going island on me again. "Vnotfinished."

When we go, she takes my arm, creating for those who care to see an odd effect of one garbage bag enamored of another, the white arm snaking out and butting a hole in the bag of her fiancé. No rain, but an enormous piercing dankness has come over the city, even without the wind to give it zip. I have all I need: not much, really, and most of all I have myself, the body of the survivor, the lover, the emigrant, the graft.

Ossa Negra they call the place, vaguely familiar to me from some other town (up the river?). A youth is lying on a cement-stained board, maybe an old door, and various helpers are heaping fresh offal on his naked loins, so that he seems to have been disemboweled in a slovenly way. All through, he smokes a long thin cigarillo, for about fifteen minutes while the taped music achieves crescendo, not unlike the swazz I heard live. Then, it has to be, someone with a briefcase walks up on to the low stage, sets the briefcase down, and beats a hasty-looking retreat. I see that face, the eyepatch, the contained erudite grin as of a clever boy doing something crassly adult. Bang goes the firework in the briefcase. The naked man slithers his way off the board. Bimini hisses something predictable about chocklits and seapud-time, but I ignore her, watching as the cow's liver, the heart, the bladder, the sweatbreads et cetera go into a bucket, and the bloodstained youth goes to (I hope) hose down offstage. I think: Nazi stuff. It surely isn't Russian in here, thank the Tsar. Behold Mister Eyepatch giving a jovial interview, explaining what has just gone on, and I catch the one word, said with sibilant slowness: *GaszimmerDrückeberger*, or something like it, which has to mean *gaschamber-shirker*, a word we hoped we would never need and, even if we needed it, would never have. They are all laughing, and I can only conclude that something radiantly transcendental has taken place, defusing horror by making it silly. Eyepatch seems to know all about it, so perhaps he staged the whole thing, scripted it in his mind's eye. Or his eye's mind. Then, surely, he knows what is to come, what the next few acts will be, the component scenes, with me at the end of the procession, with my paltry props, my threadbare ideas, my yearning to perform.

Bimini has no idea what is going on. She does not recognize the insides of a cow. Oh, it could have been a sow. Or a human. Beyond a certain point, organs become much of a muchness; they do not register pain as a face does, which explains, I suppose, why they ship us to the camps pretty much as we are, and not inside out. They want to see the results on our pain-meters. Clearly, however, I am in the right environment, and I wonder about Eyepatch. I ask. Oh, they say, we're staging some episodes from his new opera. Then the voice comes through more clearly. "The aim is to gross us out. We are supposed to resist. At least until we can't stand it any more." Any person throwing up, or having to leave, has to pay for a copy of the thing from the stack of some twenty I see over by the stage. Surely, there, they'll get splashed, or would a stain or two somehow beef up its appeal? I check my props, hand them to Bimini, who shows no interest in them and hands them back. Clearly I am on my own tonight. The three girls who run this place come and greet us in their perfunctory way: the short blonde with the flawless hourglass, the lisp, the slightly in-bitten lower lip; the sharp-featured, samite-skinned Irish owner, Belle, whose trim hands belie the pool-table splendor of her legs. The third, petite with teeth braces has an inward look, walks with a preoccupied waddle, has hands too big to go into her jeans pockets.

These are Eyepatch's Eumenides.

They minister to his every need. They look up horrors for him to turn into cabaret. I do not believe in coincidence, therefore I conclude that he has been eyeing me all along as a likely participant, no doubt tipped off by Belle, who knew about my part in the subway demo. How discreetly dressed he is, as if ready to lead a seminar on torts or leaseback, but he handles himself with blasé confidence. You can tell he has never had to dig the shaft of a goldmine in either earth or air. I see him talking now into a tiny tape recorder, but looking to his front at some invisible partner. He smiles, he scowls, he begins to talk loudly into the little grille, then fast as if someone is urging him along. But no, it is only the next act coming forth: a buxom girl, nude, swathed in electronic tape.

It seems beside the point that they now begin to spray her all over with a fire extinguisher. She almost vanished in the fan of spray. I am wearing cheap eyeglasses all over again, bought cheap at the five and dime, and when I look up from what I'm reading the whole world quivers and goes vague because I haven't taken them off. I am still looking through them as if I were reading the world itself. You can go and try on a hundred pairs until you find one that suits, far better than having some doctor meddle with your face and brain: you never know when they are going to inject something atrocious into your system to bring you groveling down, to send you finally up, a lunatic leaping at the ceiling of his padded cell.

So: I am to be act five. There are two to go before me. Where they get these things I have no idea, but a beautiful nude woman now lies alongside an eviscerated pig. They shower them both with straw, the woman lights up a cigarette. A more sardonic person than I might have preferred things the other way around. The finale begins. Bimini stares in mingled delight and bewilderment, holding my hand tight. They rig up a plank to make a slide. What about splinters, I think. They slide the woman down the plank, which is greased but not enough, so they have to tug her a little and tilt the plank to a sharper angle. Down she goes, between the legs of a naked man, into the chair set just beyond the plank's end. A good way to get bruised, I'd think. The pig remains where it was, as forgotten as the nineteenth century, while the participants slap one another on the back and laugh. Some triumph, however nebulous, has come about. Over what? Over flesh? Over piggishness? I will never know. I have come here to lose whatever dignity I had while doing my fifteen years, half-hoping for nine grams. The general tone appears to be one of prevailing over odds, or disgust, but the whole things looks forced. What they need is something right out of Siberia to triumph over: having a wad of bread kicked out of your mouth while you lie on the railroad track, or having soon after you escape (as some did) to drink blood straight from the gashes you've cut in the horse you've killed. Surely that is more like true opera, if opera is what these people are trying to stage. They give

The Ice Lens

you twenty dollars and tell you to get on with it.

"What did they do?" Bimini has seen it but doesn't quite fathom it. The happening. The stunt.

"They were having fun with a slide."

"Are they going to eat the pig?"

"Not raw. You get worms that way."

"Will they give us some?" I hear her, but I see the pig lying on the Russian snow, upon which we have built a fire. We do not cook it, there is no time for that: we burn it almost black and devour the black rind, the pink rawness still within. It will all convert to calories, we think, and half of us have tumors of the gut to begin with, treated mostly with kicks and punches. They are trying, these actors or performers, to tap some vein of grief and indignation they have heard about only vaguely. I am the only one here, I suspect, who really knows what they have in mind. Their antic needs my background, that's all, although what happens next is, again, too German for my Slavic tastes, as a man in an ancient and therefore messable-up business suit lies flat as a naked rather emaciated girl crouches over his mouth, the long string of a tampon dangling. Her buttocks and his bald head are towards us. Eyepatch is taking Polaroid pictures at the crouch, slightly to one side, with a serious look on his face; he must be researching something. Or getting ready to place a firework between the pair of them, between string and teeth. No, the bald man tugs the string, the tampon slides out and falls, not bloody at all, which might be a cause of relief to him, onto his closed mouth. The assembled two or three dozen devotees yell at him to open his mouth and take it in, but he clamps his teeth tight, unwilling to throw good money after bad. Slowly the woman sinks onto his face, sits on his face, to consummate her act as well as to ease her legs, and Bimini turns to me, her face flushed red, unable to ask just one specific question, but suffused with incredulous query. Why? What? Who *are* they? Both actors light up the obligatory cigarette and stumble off-stage. Now it is Kiwi's turn, with Bimini to help, and I hope she remembers what to do. The lights are blinding, the gentle surf of chatter is unnerving. They are waiting. So am I. But I am not allowed to wait for me. I am due to perform right now. Eyepatch waves me on, cheerful and dominant, camera still in hand, reminding me of those affable interrogators who reassure you and urge you to sign your confession so as not to bring upon yourself, like a ton of coal, one of his less affable colleagues, kept in reserve in a red room, for the awkward customers. Now Belle tugs at my sleeve, urging me to get on with it, to get ready, so I head for the stage, into the lights, waving Bimini along behind me, as if going to execution. I have to do it, I know, but I hardly know why. The drive is strong, not for twenty dollars, though I wouldn't turn it down, but my knees feel weak. We are still dressed in plastic, so we strip off to our T-shirts and jeans, demotic uniform for the dispossessed, and get our things out of the battered old flight bag, stained with grease and toothpaste, the one outside, the other in.

I sit on the stool provided, Bimini on the wheel in a chair that seats her a little lower as if, I suppose, she were the pupil and I the teacher. Maybe I am. The music begins, then dwindles to a whisper, booms again, and I start. The stomach is first. I dry shave the hair, blond stuff that soon clings to itself and falls away in tiny tumbleweeds. Now I splash aftershave on the oddly cool skin and make the first cut with my balsa cutter: half an inch, which bleeds quite readily, while Bimini dabs the blood with her fingers and smears it on her face. When the flow stops, she is quite crimson and has a wild look to go with it, in her eyes I mean, although to me the eyes of everyone have no expression at all. The expression comes from the surroundings and remains there even though we attribute all sorts of feelings to the eyes: cold, soft, gentle, crazy, and so forth. It's in the mouth more. Eyepatch already has his close-ups of my stomach and Bimini's face. The renegade thought arrives that all this must be against some kind of law. His face comes close, almost too close to be seen, and for a crazy moment I think he is going to kiss and hug me, perhaps to ease the pain. Actually the pain is minor, but not when I get to the next stage, which requires the actual removal of a piece of skin, half the size of an ordinary postage stamp: four little right angles like one of my drawings, many years ago, of the streets in a strange city. Neat and oblong, invisible beneath the blood. The cut that hurts, though, is the one that lifts the sample free, untidy blurred thing that it is. They give me cognac, which scalds my throat into a coughing fit. My eyes stream. Bimini again daubs her face with blood, of which there is a copious supply by now, and Eyepatch with Belle helping press the little patch of skin against the bridge of my nose. The idea is not to push it back in the manner of certain emergency surgeons replacing arms and hands, but to let it wither in the arm and hand it over to the highest bidder. There is only one: Eyepatch, whose real name sounds, from what's been said around us, as the music gets louder and louder, Doctor Veen. It sounds wrong until I realize that his name is Wehn.

"Doctor Wehn" collects skin as other men collect postage stamps. Where does he keep his specimens? I am too weak to ask, and I bolt back another cognac, weeping at my own pain now. Slicing the flange of skin free from its bits of adhering flesh, was like being branded with a red-hot iron, over and over again. All the flesh of my stomach felt molten. Gurgling along, it pouring toward that tiny slot, never to return. I was astonished that so much pain could come from so small a site, but my mind was in another place, hearing not my beloved snow queen, but a voice quite different, conceivably that of someone such as Meta Zeinermayer, diva of the Twenties or Thirties, her voice coming clear across the decades as a meticulous keening, heard as on an old acoustic record with lots of scratch and chafing, yet her nonetheless, doing her most dignified dismal tones. If only Nimet could see me now, I thought, coming back to the present with a wincing flick. Does Meta Zeinermeyer, dead at thirty-five, see me now? Are we in tune? Is this the kind of thing that made her so miserable?

"You've stopped," Bimini says. At first I think she means my heart, but she means the blood. Wehn has all the shots he wants, the skin as well. Belle hands me the bandaid, then applies it herself, having seen how confused and unhandy I look. I have made a start, although expecting to hear through out the act, or now and then at least, the lost voice of my gone beloved, not that of Fräulein Zeinermeyer, whose lissome throat had housed the dominant voice of her time. Was she to be the muse of bloodletting, the siren of skin? Instead of my precious one? Instead of Bimini or Nimet? Perhaps, because all music-lovers have a dimension in common—something unearthly and abstract—

it doesn't matter who comes along into my mind's ear, just so long as someone does and I am not alone during the cutting while Doctor Wehn's learned eye appraises my technique.

His voice is higher than I'd thought it would be. His manner is gravely gentle. Yes, he is a voluptuary, he says, he also writes plays, is interested in happenings, "even if," he says, "I'm a dozen years behind the times. I adore the moment when life slithers off into opera, or vice versa when we can't tell them apart. I'm not asking about Kiwi, but is it really *White*? Your name." It is, I tell him, but he looks puzzled.

"Here," he says. "Had you forgotten?" He hands me the resplendently lacquered Kholui box, which has a faint papery rattle. "It's in there," he says. I look, and there is my little flap together with my drawings of all the pools I've tended: plans, that is, seen from above. Just the outline, with no detail. "You get *you* back," he says. "Did you think I was going to keep it?"

"You paid for it."

"No, that was only a rumor. A sales pitch." He eyes Bimini and then appears to debate the wisdom of asking me about her. "*Protégé*?" he asks. He says it as French.

"I," I hear myself saying, "couldn't protect an aphid."

He laughs and so does Bimini as if she has understood. Her face attracts his gaze, his camera, his imagination, I presume. She is the handmaiden at the gibbet, the blood-wreathed maenad at the human sacrifice. At this very moment I wish I were in my childhood home again with my toys laid out on the rug in the nursery instead of being what I have become: my own whore. I am getting something out of my system, to be sure, but is this going to go on and on? When will I be sure? My system is such that it will kill anything left within it for very long. I corrode things fast. Did I once intercept lightning and thereafter never look back?

"Of course you can," Wehn says, answering a question of what seems ages ago. "You just happen to have unusual needs, which interest me profoundly." He has an antic accent. "Whatever people do that's extreme appeals to me. I don't necessarily write about it, but I do take a developed interested. Not morbid, oh no. Just that nothing human is alien."

"That old Greek," I say, forgetting exactly which one.

"Yes, him. Now, how about a cognac? One for your friend?"

28. Certain Adverbs

It is no surprise to me, and no one else cares, when I revert to my old pool-cleaning habits to cheer me up, or at least stabilize me when I'm in the dumps. I might be cleaning out the Augean stables, which I remember from that tattered old humanistic education—I recall the cleansing, but not Augea. Where was Augea? Simpler, always, to collect up the surface trash, mainly insects, and then swipe them far enough with a catapult action of the pole. Now they fly again, ungainly and smashed, protein for ants and spiders. Even when the surface of the water is immaculate, I cant the scoop at forty-five degrees and in a gentle sweep pick up the tiniest bits of fluff, pine needles already bleached white and the occasional human hair. Unrolled condoms appear once a week, their prospects rinsed away into the blue, while the lozenges made by the sun jostle one another on the bottom like primeval tectonic molecules bucking for dominance. It is an almost complete world, a paradise of ripple and rocking, the one motion stirred by the invisible ceaseless pump, the other by the crosswinds of midsummer. Sometimes, with permission, I perform my labors within the pool itself, sluicing my privates within the stiff sailcloth of my shorts.

The Ice Lens

All this was best done alone. It was no use with reposing, sated swimmers watching me, or even sunbathers who would never have dreamed of dipping a limb. When I was truly alone, say at a house temporarily unoccupied but with open pool against the occupants' return from Key West, I would get that cool-spined, ransomed feeling and slow all my motions out of torrid imagining. I was the last human left in the world, only to half-detect through the rear window of a cab parked thirty yards away what looked like a human head on the move. Not alone after all. It was that kind of flawed autonomy, in which I was master of all pools and all water, all pumps and heaters, all water-spiders and sombre, drowned mice. And, naturally enough, I was the only swimmer left, free to shout obscenities at the picture windows and the eaves, at withered geraniums in their tasteful tubs, and un-nourished espaliers hugging the walls like fugitives. The sun shone on most of this, giving me what I called that old Egyptian feeling, like a well-baked loaf to be installed in the royal tomb.

I never cleaned pools before the Gulag, after which of course I had that abiding horror of not knowing how or where she was. Cleaning pools was an attempt to deflect and calm my agitated mind; there was always worry behind it, gnawing and spewing. Was it then that I first allowed myself to fudge up what I called my calm sea and prosperous voyage stage of thought? It was a deliberate attempt to have wholesome thoughts, to lull and smooth myself during even the worst moments, when it was not enough to shout "Speedo!" and crack off into some jolly fit. A deep breath, the deliberate misuse of certain adverbs (radiantly, mellowly, uniquely, rewardingly) and the donning of rose glasses: that began it, and the rest of it amounted to a translation from the offensive or the baleful into the pacific. Imagine how such a practitioner fared at the Gulag, having begun as a man seeking to cheer himself up, now graduated into put-upon tadpole in a sink of putrid horrors. Sleight of hand gives way to a benign terrorism practiced upon oneself in the interests of staying sane. The combination of joyous elements and callous third-degree mixed us all up, enabling me to recall meadows, but full of blood, warm drinks at bedside (Horlicks or Ovaltine), but poisoned, and so on. Now and then, less the man I was, I recall trapping yellow-jackets under the mesh of the scoop, and forcing them lower and lower into the water, watching them panic toward the rim and climb over, at which I turned the mesh upside down, trapping them again. They soon stopped panicking and did a few barrel rolls, after which they lay inert on the mesh. I never felt so godlike as then.

29. Last Night's Wound

In no time at all, Bimini and I are half smashed, although Wehn himself doesn't drink, watching us wobble around and grin slack-jawed. He asks about the wheel, which fascinates him: the way it just fell on us, the way we took it into our lives in the treehouse, almost babying it to begin with. After some pleasantries he asks about my flesh-cutting career, only just begun, wondering if I am going to go on with it, and why. I hear the impresario in his tone although you would think that he'd be able to invent the rest from what he's seen. What's going on in actual lives draws him every bit as much as what he thinks up. Or so I presume, I with the smarting tummy, the bit of me now cached in a lacquered box, the twenty safe in my jeans pocket. Go on? Why? Not go on? Why not? I don't tell him all about it, of course, neither the sense I have that I am some kind of expendable specimen who, having done his stint in the camps, can survive just about anything, nor the other sense I have that—how mystical it feels—I can somehow reach my long-lost archangel by putting myself through all the maneuvers of pain. The one side of me is pure vainglory, pure conceit, whereas the other must be madness: if I couldn't get through during the camps, why should I be able to get through now? The answer just may be that I *was* getting through: it was an act of faith. And so is this: the more painfully I abuse myself, the more intense the message becomes that touches the exquisite filament of her traveling soul with a white-hot needle, saying: I'm here, I haven't gone off the edge of the Earth, I'm still perched on its rind with my heart aimed backward, my razor toward the future. Do you remember how you used to mispronounce Debussy's name? You called him *Cloud.* We lived to a sharp poignant sound from Mexican trumpets playing in unison. Isn't there going, you'd say, to be *a little bit snow*? This in February.

If Wehn can imagine such things, then fine. If not, he will have to do without them. Surely Bimini and I are enough raw material to keep him going for years. He too has seen the Rat Man movie; indeed, he has read the book it was made from. "Is the author's life," I ask him, "at all like the Rat Man's, then?"

"Not altogether dissimilar," he says. "I think he lives in an old caboose, with a stovepipe, up in the Finger Lakes somewhere, not that far from here, you know, and he invents all this stuff in the very thick of winter, when the snow is piled high outside the caboose's unmoving windows and the trees are frozen still. I know about no rat, though. I think he may have a fox fur hidden somewhere, like Rat Man himself. He does like toys. Skis. Hiking. Vivaldi."

Playing at being in the camps, I think. What he needs is a dose of the real thing. I bet his caboose has central heating. The newspapers get delivered to his very door. His woman no doubt cooks him eggs and ham for breakfast before he puts on his smoking jacket and begins to type. That sort of person. Living, as they say, in and for his imagination, whereas we old stagers of the grisly archipelago, we have to start from scratch: going in with nothing of our own, obliged to eat off and with whatever's provided, and then afterwards having to start afresh yet again as if we have just arrived on the planet from the middle of outer space. My stomach stings. The cognac has somehow widened and amplified the pain; I feel as if I have just given birth or had a hysterectomy, but I am going to persist in my own cosmic version of bush telegraph.

What do they say? A smile wins a smile. When you smile at someone, they mostly smile back. It's a reflex, even when they haven't intended to smile. All I need is one smile back, from my dear heart, across the eons or the light years, whatever unit of whatever separates the living from the dead. After a while, as you get older, you tend not to separate the tissue of livingness into this or that person, but to think of it in the round, as a process, with them and you embedded in it, like pixies in a porridge. Have I reached that stage already? Years ago, probably.

"You're pensive," says Wehn, patting Bimini's arm, but he means me, not Bimini.

"It happens," I say. "Have you ever cut a piece of your belly off and then had a good think about it?"

"You'll be here next week," he says.

"A regular," I say. "Yes, but don't count on it."

"Your companion is unusual," he says, as if commenting on a pet parakeet's plumage.

It is time to go, before he reloads his camera and starts taking notes. We have exposed ourselves enough. I have sent my wire of celestial pain, with all my sensitivity pushed toward that one point where the blade sank in, then sent packing in retreat as the blood began. I feel tuned up in spite of the cognac, as if I have swum for an hour and managed to find the swimmer's bliss. I wanted to come alive in every nerve and every pore, to be focused, made keen. Then everything blurred, diffused; I was nobody, just a partly extruded hunk of tissue expelled from the fully blossomed matrix. In a word, I was being very Russian, very Slav. A true Schwarzkogler.

In the subway she goes to sleep on my arm, her head hot as August. The garbage bags make you heat up. Your body cannot breathe, and you soon become slithery from all the sweat and condensation. Home, I exchange Meta Zeinermeyer for a night's intimately ministering Nimet, who seems to have a slight cold that makes her voice a little huskier than usual, and I wonder, if I were to race over to Forty-Second Street with elderberry syrup, a flannel compress soaking in hot olive oil, and a spoon of butter topped with eucalyptus, would I be welcome? Would I even get in? The thing to do, so long as I phoned first, is to arrive as the right type: a fan, a devotee, a booster. Forty-*Third*, I correct myself. Fancy taking your cold remedies to the wrong place.

Into the blow-up bath goes Bimini, no tape across her mouth. The cognac has knocked her out, but by now it has woken me up into one of my first night fidgets, in which the dragons get close behind me and breathe hard and the devils hang from my neck like wattles. Monteverdi doesn't help me much, nor what she plays next: Brahms. I need something finer, more implacable, excruciated. Down the tree I go. I call with shivering lips. A switchboard operator takes the plea for Shostakovich, Messiaen, or Berg. I almost said a switch*blade* operator. I have lived too much. I am like the man who, having flown all his life, has accumulated more bonus mileage miles than he can ever take advantage of, plus he can't eat the food, drink the drink, or use the elongated slumberette blue-riband excelsior flying carper couchette because he has to sleep in the sitting position with his shoulders hunched, as in economy. Will Nimet hear my plea? Why isn't she Nimette? Do they ever heed requests? Are they there at all? Or is the whole thing taped while the lady sleeps? As with my dearest one, who slept or died, I knew not which, while I lived on, nibbling carp.

The air waves are full of female voices, sirens, bringing us the music we crave, some of them mellow and mature, some with voices brighter than usual, some with voices full of gusty bravura that tips you off to their being black. Some ingratiate, some whisper, some come across as neutral and subdued. Nimet is the only one who sounds as if she's advertising a posh girls' school at the same time as playing the music: very upper snooty, with delicacy galore. Surely she will oblige, if not tonight then another time. She doesn't work the day, thank goodness, or I'd have to change my hours. I suppose someone calls her honey, collects up her laundry, tucks her in at dawn, even—well, I want her kept ethereal, the nightingale of the buttered ear. A bit flirtatious she surely is, but what kind of woman flirts with a hundred thousand invisible souls? Maybe a million, maybe sixty million, as many listening now as died in Mother Russia's biggest circus. I'd get giddy myself, a bit, if I stayed up all night doing what she does. Paid to flutter, to coax, to chide, to smooth us out, she is almost too well-bred to lower the needle to the groove herself. Of course. They don't do it that way anyhow. They have needlemen. Is it even a needle? It's a tape, surely. Unless. I don't really know or care, just so long as the music of true seriousness comes feathering out, saying all hell has broken loose, but there is harmony still, the broken pieces of the shattered world will join up again once the music starts. That's what I like: the way music stays inaccessible, invulnerable, alive in the air but incapable of being sent to jail. Or in your head, where it belongs, flowering, floating, giving you something to steer by, even if only upward until out of sight.

Sing to me then, my archangel.

Meta Zeinermeyer gives me her high, honed warble, as if I have asked for it. Now, who are those other muses of the ether, not singing, but at least purring and inciting as they read off their rehearsed announcements? From all over they come in, if you have a good enough antenna. One was called something like Janice Oolonka, her bright good nature raised to exponential maximum: a cooperative, tolerant voice, mothering us through whatever needs drive us to music in the first place. Now, where did she hail from? Somewhere in New York State, brought to me by some freak in the Heaviside layer, otherwise known as the E layer. That's musical. There they go above us, wafting and trailing away, voices poised above digesting meals, coming out of mouths that only hours ago were—well, not to get too Slavic about it—otherwise engaged. I see how pliable the lips are, how the tops of the pantyhose chafe from all that sitting, how the bladder fills and the breath goes slowly stale in the very teeth of the microphone. They mother us, these women, they breastfeed us with whispers.

Oh my golly, when the needle sticks and you begin to wonder, my dearest archangel, if it mightn't be the latest in musical minimums, but they most often catch it after a minute or two and you know you haven't just heard, on a theme, variations so subtle as to be identical. They never apologize, though, even after the piece is played, and of course they never interrupt. So it's as if the glitch has never been. They come running in from coffee, the toilet, the hallway schmoozing, and flip the point back into the groove, maybe with a chocolatey hand, you never know. And, to the needle, the next minute or so is like touring through the mud-slick trenches of a long-forgotten war. I lean back and at once the signal scrambles itself. My body has blurred it into a noise of inaccurate frying. I sit forward again even as Nimet purrs and Bimini sighs, babbling something I cannot make out, but mouthed with stevedore-like emphasis.

"Music of Roy Harris," says Nimet, and I hear again those oddly clanking sounds, as if the whole thing begins in the corral of a ranch somewhere, and there are blacksmiths too, wranglers and ranch hands gathering for deep-fried eggs and sausages. Early morning in his Third Symphony, by the man who, as Virgil

Thomson says in his guide to American music, was in youth squarely a charmer, in middle age a business man, later prone to anger, at all ages clearly a star. I wonder what happened, and why I remember that, of all things.

When somebody says that about about you, it's then that you feel real: when they hurt you or snub you, get you on the raw. Is it just as true when you feel happy? Is that as real as when you feel degraded? I doubt it, because happiness is a kind of disembodiment whereas pain is being forced deep down into the tissue of things. Roy Harris probably felt more real, which is to say least a phantom, when Thomson said that thing about him, than when his wonderful Third Symphony began to be played worldwide on the radio. I can't get away from the notion that happiness is a mode of escape, even though I know that ecstasy is when you feel thrown out of yourself. Just so: pain, on the other hand, is when you're rammed deep in upon yourself, in upon the fragility you share with the dandelion, the mussel, the lark. When you hurt, you know exactly where you end and the world begins. Your boundary is clear. Happy, though, you are porous, you are part of a big soaring wave like those in the paintings of Hiroshige and Hokusai. How well the Japanese handle pain and humiliation. How ill at ease they are with happiness. They like to be precise, that's all. They cut themselves open in the same place, century after century, although I have heard it said that the latest mode of *seppuku* is done with a very sharp new camera. All I did to myself was a little nick, but it's a beginning, and I have never felt so alive—so aimed at a point, so related to one enterprise, as then, during that instant of pain. You know, in spades, that at least one part of you really belongs to you, in the ephemeral sense at least. We all of us belong in toto to something else that spews us up and takes us back: the fountain of foison. Is this the appeal of giving birth? You love your baby because it hurt so much when it arrived. Perhaps, then, this grateful sense of pain belongs to women only. That must be why I have decided to send her news of myself along with nerve network that shimmers between the living and the dead: haunting her, making her feel agony by proxy, urging her to come from the beyond and, as before, speak all the foreign languages with adroit, gentle twistings of her pliant lips. No use to say: my loveliest archangel of old, we were so happy together. She won't stir herself for that, but she will for Kiwi White in extremis when he moans and bleeds, pops yet another bit of himself into his fancy box and limps home, sheathed in see-through sea-hue plastic, wincing within his bandaid at each step.

That much is clear, then.

And when she comes she will come to inflict on me the most painful thing in the world: absence during presence, the wraith without buttocks.

That kind of thing.

Diminuendo.

Until there is nothing left.

Of what once was.

Hence, in my head and ears, the invigilating chorus of mild-voiced sirens, announcing this or that piece of music, whispering in almost feathery foreplay the opus or Köchel numbers, relentlessly stroking us until the onset of the work: guiding us to the portal, ushering us to the very brink of contrapuntal transport. I am theirs between midnight and dawn, as irrevocably laid out as any Aztec sacrificial boy on the slab with the stone knife poised over him. These are your stand-ins, invisibly vocal and quite stripped of the commonplace chic they have when seen. Better never seen then. Better than they should never see me or they would alter their tone, change their tune. The essence of their company is remoteness; a certain distantness in their intimate manner tunes me up for one unradiatingly far away. And a small vertical piece of my brain does for itself a narrow litany from which any but the simplest or the most poignant words are banned. My Icicle, I call it,

Once I drank light
by yawning skyward,
Once I was all feisty

uplift solos
with saw teeth.
I no sooner found
life's wellspring
than I was done for.
What was it I had
unloseably
worth envying?

She knew the answer to that, younger than I and so entitled, I'd have thought, to see me end my days. So much for justice. The meaning of the word is not what the dictionary says but the changes its utterance brings about. For all I know, Bimini is some avenging angel who has only to manage to stay awake longer than I, or to wake up in the small hours when I have begun to doze, and smash my head with the God-sent wheel. Her presence in the treehouse, my tree of life, can mean this only: she was sent, she was ordered to make the hit. The Russians are still after me, never mind how corny their methods. Can I really see Bimini as my assassin? Why not? She certainly has me off-guard, which must be the yield of her Kremlin training, so the only question remaining is exactly how is she going to do it? She cannot fail. She's not allowed to fail.

I almost cross the platform to wake her and ask.

Instead, I just assume it's so.

The Ice Lens

I could push her over now while she is full of cognac, breathing like someone under anesthesia.

Some she does in with needles, others with gas; some she talks to death. Others she suffocates. Never. I do not mind lying, but I hate being believed. I rattle my lacquered box of maps and trophies. I turn up my radio, unplugging the earphones. I left Nimet, introducing (I just catch the last few words, the repetition at the end of her preamble) the Tenth Symphony of William Schuman, all brass braying.

"Let's get it over with," I say to the huddled heavy-looking form with the long floppy legs. "You hear?"

She stirs with a stuffed nose and mutters something vaguely Bermudian, either an insult or an entreaty. It matters little which. She isn't going to kill me tonight. Her masters and overseers thousands of miles away have as much faith in her as in nine grams of lead. Sooner or later, one-eyed Joe Greens notwithstanding, she will get to it, whether or not she's tied to the commode with her mouth taped. The wrath of Svalocin knows no frontiers, that's obvious, especially in view of his disappointment: he tried to get me a quarter, as we oldsters joshingly call twenty-five years, but even he couldn't manage that. Enough was enough, they told him, "Look at you, happily remarried to a woman of solid worth and ample girth, still hanging on to a cinder. Let him go, let him be.

One of them is weak, the main culprit. Let that be a lesson to you. Lock your doors. A man in your position owes it to himself not to waste more than ten years on mere vengeance as distinct from the public good."

But he came back to the boil, wanting us both kaput, wanting some symmetry in his chamber of horrors. So Bimini, then, exquisitely trained in the finest mental homes in Queens comes on as part nymphomaniac, part mental defective, with Doctor Wehn manager, her contact man, and nothing between me and the end save a fleck of poison on a razor blade in a balsa cutter. Svalocin could hardly come and do me in himself, but he has emissaries by the score, deviant louts and batty ideologues born in Kansas. It's easy, comrade.

Yes: easy as if it were a knife speaking, or cancer, stroke, lightning or flood. I never had this lethal sense when I was a prisoner, though if I'd had my wits about me I'd have realized my danger. The camp routine made you feel safe in a crazy kind of way, as if nothing could disrupt the even tenor of your fifteen; but of course it could, whether a bout of random firing at a column of us shuffling home or some superhuman lifting chore beyond any of us. We were always on the brink, but the brink felt comfy just because we were used to it. We were used to nothing else. A razor's edge felt like home sweet home. By the same token, to be at large in Russia again, or to be in Manhattan, felt like the end of the world. There was danger everywhere, with agents and assassins lurking, death by jovial kidnap always a probability, and, within the head, that awful sense of being unprotected, which is to say: I no longer had the cold comfort every hour of some homicidal guard whose violence only a whim kept still.

Bimini thinks I should go back to the club, *boîte*, or whatever it is, and start again: tonight. "You got to get your hand in," she says, "like a baseball pitcher." She may be right, but the prospect daunts me. At least the pain does. At the same time, something appeals to me: the vision of regular employment, a steady routine akin to that of opening and closing swimming pools. They would hardly be likely to turn me down. I'm a draw, better than dead pigs, better than nudes festooned with electronic tapes. And, each night if you consider the spectacle from the spectator's point of view, there is the additional lure of last night's wound, last week's scars. It's tempting, as if the chance that, if I go through with it every night, I may actually get through to my archangel that much sooner, sending one entranced message after another along the ethereal pathways from live to dead, from moribund to immortal. I wonder. One call does it, just as if I am calling WQXR, offering to be the Nimet show. Maybe I could get them to play WQXR when I perform, starting at midnight of course, so that with the hard corner of the blade within my flesh I'd hear cheery Nimet announcing a Brahms, a Poulenc, a Vivaldi. Music to cut by. Not what the customers would prefer, but useful for half and hour or so while I perform. I can see the headlines now: KIWI WHITE: JACK THE RIPPER TO HIMSELF. Or: KIWI WHITE THE LONGHAIR SLASHER, THE DARLING OF THE BEETHOVEN SET. Something as crude as that, bound to be said, bound to be printed. But we'll keep the plastic bags for sheer style.

I call and ask Belle, who doesn't sound awake, but in her brogue she says of course. Wehn himself had been hoping, she says, for just such a turn of events. I ask for twenty-five a night, but she parries that and offers 130 for a six-day week. It's money. I accept. I will end up, as never before, looking forward to Sunday, and before long Bimini will be arriving in mink, I'll have a vicuna to wrap me in. It will be the golden age after the end of the world. Wehn will get a whole opera out of it, no doubt linking me (without meaning to) with the humiliated professor in *The Blue Angel*, crowing like a rooster while somebody smashes eggs on his head. I'm better than that and much more dangerous. A career offers, a living presents itself. I am going to go down in history after all, after the long anonymous wait in the eternal snow. They will never know that what I'm up to, deep down, is something like voodoo: trying to raise the dead to stop me from cutting myself into smaller and smaller pieces. Who'd believe it? Maybe the novelist would, perched there high above the Bowery, with his door triple-locked and his pistol sitting on his thesaurus. I can see it now as he invents me from real life, embellishes my presence in distinctly sordid ways, and then converts Bimini into some Cleopatra figure who, until the age of sixteen, grew as a mandrake tree in Central Park, planted by her disappointed parents, but then developed uncanny skill in walking and so ran into Kiwi White, the Treehouse Poolside Clipper. What's to stop him? Does he really spend his life like that? Lurking around the sleaziest of clubs, hoping for some garish act to give him raw material. Raw all right, I'll give him raw.

Not only that. What if Bimini turns out to be an agent after all, eager to sink the knife in spite of everything? It could provide him with a new twist, so to speak, one he hadn't bargained for, amid the Victoria Falls of his inspiration. I long. I yearn. I crave. Oh I really do. But is it fame I crave or just some irrevocable sense of having lived more keenly than anyone ever? Not quiet desperation for a lifetime, but an instant of noisy ecstasy. And Bimini will be gone before they know what I've done, if she doesn't do me in up in the treehouse by day. The thrills are gathering. It is not going to be dull for the next month or so. I rapidly multiply 130 by four, then by three, supposing I could last that long, and the sum is so dreamlike, so unappreciable, that I have begun counting from one to fifty, then from fifty-one to a hundred, and keep going like that to savor in full the yield. I'll be the first cut-up to buy a car.

So it is night again. I'm back on stage.

Here he comes, I hear them say. He's ready.

"In the true tradition," Wehn is saying to someone with a beard and a hearing aid, "from Rudolf Schwarzkogler, the pioneer in the mode. I think he was quite right to reject the pain spray as being, well, somehow contrary. Inconsistent. The pain is part of the metaphor."

"Which is?"

Wehn smiles, taps his head, and points to me. "*Ask* him."

As if I knew anything about his blithering metaphor. I do the cut, I leave the fancy talk to experts. This time it's on the other side of my stomach, making me almost symmetrical. It hurts less. They do play WQXR and I hear what sounds like Delius's "On Hearing the First Cuckoo in Spring," but no Nimet's voice, what with the uproar in the club and the general seething in my ears as the pain begins and my message goes out past Alpha Centauri to wherever. It is at Alpha Centauri that they check all the incoming transmissions to make sure of rerouting them correctly, most of all those messages headed for beyond the Galaxy. Now I don't ever need to go to Harvard, lunch in the White House, climb Everest. Things are underway. Ads have gone out. Critics and existentialist reporters will arrive with pads and cameras. That is the common, vulgar side of it, but the other one is graver by far, having to do with blood supply, pain threshold, and the enticing mysterious chance of my not knowing when to stop, so that, at some unthinkable point, someone in the overflow audience asks "How will he manage now? He cut his left hand off with his right. He cut his right hand off with a razor held between his teeth. How will he cut his mouth away?" Every civilization has such pedants, tuned in to events before anything happens, jumping the life to come. They will have to wait and see.

Goodness, think how much an eyelid will cost, not to mention a nipple, a curl of lip. The Jews will pack the place the night I announce my self-circumcision, but I am joking; it will be years before I get to that. Maybe it will be my last act of all, done by a legless armless monster crouching over himself with bris between his teeth. Maybe, however, long before then my archangelic dearest one will have come to get me, telling where to head for, launched starward from my treehouse, past Alpha Centauri, our third brightest in the sky (only Canopus and Sirius outshining it). And, to anyone who might object that, even if I were to start out for the star in the time of Abraham the patriarch, going at a plausible comfortable speed of 110 miles a second, I would be only halfway there, even now. I wouldn't be going at starship speed, that's all. I'd be going at long-lost-lover speed, the fastest under the sun.

Hereos we call it: the illness caused by love.

"Whatever you want," says Wehn, tugging his eyepatch a quarter of an inch away from whatever is underneath. "I am so glad you changed from weekly to daily."

"I won't last as long."

"But you'll be easier to follow, dear chap. It won't be like reading a serial, it'll be like an avalanche, the first thing of its kind in Manhattan, just like the old days in Vienna." His name is Wehn, but he calls the place Vienna, and that is what I call him, mostly *Doctor*, though, conning myself with the illusion that he could be of help during a hemorrhage, say, or a fit of sheer funk on my part (he would feed me tranquilizers on my stool).

The third night, a Wednesday, I make a cut right over my sternum, theorizing that my belly and chest alone ought to get me through a month or two. Leave the legs and face alone, I tell myself. Save them for a rainy day. Don't head south or north until your front is like a beef. At least it'll stop Bimini from lolling her head against my chest, as I shriek and recoil. I am not to be bumped in the street; she has to go before me like a cowcatcher, or ringing a bell like one warning of an approaching leper.

Yes, I can hear them now. "He's coming again. Did you see him last night? Took an hour to stanch the blood."

Here he comes again, his chest a cuirass of bloodstained cotton. Am I dreaming or do the other acts really rush through their moves? Even the other acts can't wait to see what I am going to do next. All of a sudden I see what is going on. I am like some medieval knight stripping off his armor. My skin and flesh are the armor of my chest. I am a human coming clean in full view: a rarity, a prodigy, a freak. I see their faces as I begin, fearful that I won't go on, that I will chicken out at the last minute, and then they would have to find something else to amuse themselves with. I am not going to last for ever anyway, although in days to come they will say I set the pace, devised the style, got the mode accepted.

30. Smiling's Cousin

If there are indeed memories of a knife, they begin with that idle, sketchy touch akin to scratching of the back. There is something optional about it, being as it feels an elongated love tap. Beyond, there lurks the deeper thrust, into the meat of you, changing the direction of a certain part, sending an immediate local message to neighbor viands. We all know this, and act accordingly even if we are not working on a spectrum between a shaving nick and the Chinese ordeal of a thousand cuts. But, if you are doing the cuts yourself, not having them inflicted upon you, there is in even the shaving nick a hint of something cutting deeper than you expect it to, a foretaste of death perhaps, and the experience of that tiny slice is twofold: a faint, almost pleasurable scratch merging into something starker that speaks at once to us of intrusion and electric spike. Going farther than usual, in my own fusion of pain and operatics, I was hardly putting education to the test, but extending my Gulag diploma even farther, consummating it and living beyond my usual scope. Absent the Gulag, I would never have gone this far, I supposed, but my experience of both privation and deprivation had, as it were, conducted me past myself into a region almost impersonal and inhuman. I was fodder for the blade.

That there was a living to be made at this hardly surprised me, Schwarzkoglerian as it was. If I was looking for sympathy or admiration, even after my years of Gulag, I wasn't aware of it. No, I was hardy old Earth being bombarded by meteorites, living up to a slogan from World War II, when one candidate for Hitler's hangman told the others "We have to endure like flowers and plants. Those who come this far have no choice, and certainly not a human one according to the old placebo of it hurts me, please desist." Thus Helmuth von Moltke, aristocratic warrior-diplomat of an ancient clan, recommending an almost botanical death, or the crushed or severed celandine, or perhaps of the cut worm.

Cutting yourself affords you the chance of placing similar cuts in one unique box, allowing you to tell yourself: This is the same as Friday's cut; the sensation is familiar, has already been dispossessed of itself. But a zig-zag after a whole range of short, straight cuts becomes rather more than one can bear. So: subsequent, virtually identical cuts have an almost benign quality, but the first in a new series, say of zig-zags or chevrons, is nightmarish, to be prepared for only with liquor and analgesics. The main thing is to keep smiling or, if you cannot rise to that, achieving the rictus of the mouth that is smiling's camera-shy cousin.

Then I discovered, after quite a few apprentice cuts, a new way of lulling the senses, distracting the mind: an old approach, really, that began casually enough with memories of agents in suits, whose American jackets went convex between neck and shoulder, as if muscles were bulging, while the British version was concave in the same place, as if muscles had fallen away, whose hollowed-out line the cloth straightly followed. From this it was easy enough to shift gears to my sometime work on Tupolev, to his aerosleds, the gigantic hoops he erected in hangars to build wind tunnels upon, parachutists sliding rearward off the huge corrugated wings he loved, how some of his designs looked American-derived, how at his wife's funeral he had snow-shoed around with twenty-four thank you letters to be handed over in person. Once lost in this melody, I managed to cut myself before I knew what I was doing, and I wondered if ever those observing could read my mind.

31. Mutilé de...

Each dawn begins with a rattle of skin and maps in a lacquered box. I shake it, gently touch my chest, and try to sleep. At first I make the maps and pool plans cushion the bits of me cut off, but after a while I like to hear nothing from the box save the sound of what once was me. Slowly the bits dry out, make a crisper noise, as if my proxies have gained in personality.

Each night, to the strains of the world's most august music, I dismantle myself, egged on by Belle, swabbed by Bimini, watched admiringly by Doctor Wehn (whose first name, Ulrich, has Americanized itself into Rich), and peered at by a paying crowd whose bloodlust remains soft-spoken. They pay twice as much as they used to pay for tampon-divers and offal tableaux. Now and then, depending on her schedule of recordings, I hear Nimet gently coaxing us to share this or that masterpiece with her, to tune out the noise of the city and be gracious of ear. It is when she speaks that I sink the blade-corner deeper, pull it farther than I'd intended across the surface of my skin. In those gentle tones I hear the tenderness of things to come from beyond the grave. Once my archangel is ready, she will be in touch, and all my surrogates can go. Wehn seems more than happy, with his free-flying necktie (no clip), his heavy jovial chin, his confident assertive rather square mouth, and the forelock drooping brilliantined to the line of his eyepatch's elastic tape. Surely he has more than enough of me now, but he watches Bimini as well. He never asks questions, seeming intent upon only what happens on stage, or in the club, although surely he works us both up into quite different creatures in the cellar of his imagination. He never answers when I ask him how it's going; he just nods and pats me gently on the back, urging me to do it ever more slowly. Twice the cameras have been, so twice they must have filmed Bimini as well. We have been on TV, which means her parents can't be far behind, if of course they can associate this red-faced ghoul in a plastic bag with the daughter they have lost. Surely it can't be long before someone looks and knows, and the whole act gets closed down as a health hazard, a scandal to taste, and a bad ad for the Big Apple. We are wealthy, though, within our rather narrow limits. I no longer need to go and borrow from my "mother," and every now and then, after an especially harrowing session in the course of which there has been more blood or pain than usual, Wehn chips in with an extra ten, always however asking me for a receipt. It is he who stanches the excess blood, it is Bimini who deals with the usual flow.

"Has the pain," Wehn asks, "become pleasure yet? Have the two things merged?"

The Ice Lens

He clearly has no idea that this happened some twenty years ago, when my entire being garbled itself once and for all. When, at any moment, you can get nine grams, the agony in your joints and your back tells you you are alive. The agony's preferable, I tell him. Death is no alternative to anything. Death is nothing, *mein Herr*, I tell him, getting formal. "Death," I tell him, "is total banality."

"It never needs a helping hand," he says. "What you are demonstrating here night after night, to your infinite cost and our delight, is that self-control is paramount. Than *it*, there is nothing finer."

I'm sure he knows, though from what terrible experience I have no idea; maybe the loss of his eye. From me, however, he has wheedled most of my life story and will no doubt advance to print with each and every detail garbled to fit some notion of a plot. Never mind, he's on the ball in some matters, having already explained to me that he thinks Kiwi is just another version of "Hiwi," the German term for Russians who volunteered to fight against Russia in the Second World War.

"*Hilfswillige*," he says. "Willing to help."

I tell him how right he is. "Of course the Germans lost."

"Nothing to worry about," he says. "After what you've done over the past few days, you belong to the international community anyway. You should talk Esperanto."

"With each cut," I tell him, "I think of someone who perished in the camps." He misinterprets this, thinking I mean a different person every time, and not just one.

Impressed that Bimini rather likes what is going on, he wonders aloud if she too might wish to have a blade to nick herself with. "Cello and kazoo," he says. "Anything to ripen things up."

"Leave her out of it," I say.

"Left," he says. "I agree. So long as you...."

"I've months to go," I tell him. "You surely don't think I'm going to do it wholesale. No, bit by bit, until the lacquer box is full, and then retirement. Rapallo, perhaps, or Bimini's Bermuda."

Busy writing, he says nothing, and I get on with the night's work, this time (the twelfth night) removing a bit of my kneecap flesh, which means I am going to have a stiff leg tomorrow. Doing it gives me the oddest sensations in a peculiar order. To begin with, it doesn't feel like me. There's the twinge, yes, but I soon go into what I have come to know as firewalker's anesthesia. The blood comes from some spigot rigged up behind me. The uncoordinated mutter of the crowd comes from far away, say a distant bullfight or soccer game. All the same, I come here primed with painkillers, at least to take the edge off it. Or, rather, to subdue the mildest pain and throw the worst of it into suitable relief. In the Kholui

The Ice Lens

box I now keep a little chart of my body on which the various sites appear marked in red. For symmetry, but also, I suppose, out of pride. When I look back on all this, I want to feel that I acted with a modicum of dignity. When I sink the blade, they sigh and almost gasp, whereas when I poise it beforehand they do not stir or even seem to breathe. After it has bitten home, they soon relax, and the blood that dribbles and spurts persuades them they aren't dreaming, a fact they find encouraging. As I busy myself with the four corners and the straight lines, they begin to do sharp, sizzling intakes of breath as if I am sinking the edge into *them*. Applause comes only when I hold up the new-clipped bit of me and let it fall into the box that Bimini holds. I rarely go among the crowd afterwards for fear of being jostled and made to bleed, but I hover on the edge, answering questions with questions, letting Bimini shove away those who want to touch, to feel. I never quite feel safe until, vagrant-like, I have climbed back into my plastic bag and sashed it softly around my waist. Then I feel quite monastic but climbing back to the treehouse later on is a chore of increasing difficulty. Now Bimini goes up first and hauls me as best she can. It is not weakness that does me in, but pain, always worse after I have left—what would one call it—the arena, the ring, the tourney. As a *mutilé de* something, not war, not peace, I qualify for special treatment of some kind, but only in treehouses, only in the Ossa Negra *boîte*. The money ought to go into the lacquered box, but there is no room for it, so it goes into the little toilet bag in which I carry the tools of my trade: the blades, the styptic pencil, the swabs and the bandaids, the magnifying glass with which I can loyally inspect both wounds and scars, the pain spray and the bottle of rubbing alcohol. I am almost like a barber who has gotten somewhat above himself. Life has become routine, although with always that bloody ritual to end the day. Sundays (I relive my second one) make me nervous because there is nothing climactic soon after midnight and I can hear my nightingale chirping to me, telling me this is Saint-Saens, and that is Chabrier. How easily we lose habits. I miss the sting, the seepage, the applause, the thrust of the dollars into my hand, into my heart. One bout of blood poisoning would end it all, of course, but so far I have been lucky. Is it much worse, after all, than having a blood test? The scars are big, with lots of bruising around them, but the booty in the box is real, and I can already see it in the Smithsonian for twenty-first century connoisseurs to gape at.

"You gonna last for ever," says Bimini, her finger stuck up into some part of her lower anatomy. "There's lots of you still to go, Kwee." To her, Wehn is Richie, which amuses him no end, and Belle is Bill. No matter. In this domain of dwindling duty, names are the merest shades; the real thing is what you're willing to do to yourself for twenty dollars or so.

It begins as a faint whispering among the leaves as if some infinitely patient animal is making its move, but the animal is sleet, early since it is only November, but something to be reckoned with. Maybe now is the time to head for the Plaza Hotel and live big for one night in a suite. Foolish thought: there will have to be many performances at the Ossa Negra before we get to the point of spending more time in the Plaza than not. Of course there is always a whole range of cheaper hotels, but why bother? We have a roof. The sleet is a rather cozy sound, like what a wound hears from its own blood close up. Oh, crisp-shuffling sleet, are you a friend? Have you come to cool us off? Are you going to sheathe us in silver for a night or two? Who knows, tonight may be our last one: half the kinky magazines in town have been to see me ("Kiwi White the Cut-Me Man"), and people even know me by my disguise as I scuttle around in plastic bag and felt hat with the brim pulled down as far as it will go, through all 360 degrees. Sunday night at the club is slow, they say. They want me for my disregard of flesh. They want me in the next parade, slashing at my stomach with a kitchen knife. They want me for my abiding metaphysical skill about which they know nothing although they discern its impact on my performance: the voices I hear, the voice I want to hear. "You tuck up warm tonight," I tell Bimini. "It's like proper winter."

"You tuck up warm yourself, night owl," she says. "You got to grow fresh blood for Monday."

You got to grow fresh blood for Monday. Do I hear in this some faint echo of a medieval chivalry, some parody of an ancient noble motto? Will I know when I have gone too far? Does a white-hot eagle fly into your face and scratch its message on your tongue? When I have had enough of the *Voice*, the *Times*, the *Post*, the abracadabra letters of the TV stations, when I have had the ultimate accolade of a special request played by Nimet to coincide with one of my shows, what will I do? Is Doctor Wehn the future? Will he next want to accompany me on my pool opening trek during April, May, and June?

"How much longer?" he says.

"How much longer what?"

Cutting, he says. "The act."

Until April, I think, but I'll never be able to bare my chest again to the sun. Children will run screaming from me as from a burn victim. He goes to everything. He sees everybody. He agrees with everybody. He has read everything. He seems a personification of sunlit learning, but I think he is beginning to tire of my act. He wants beheadings and castrations, to round out the picture, and he knows I am not going to oblige. But, just maybe, he will stick around for the recapture of Bimini Engstrom, her return to Queens in a straitjacket, and Kiwi White's first hearing for molestation. *No molestar*, as it says on the door cards in some hotels. Well, *Mole-star? no.* Leave me be. His ghost bows and wafts off into the night. We sleep. Sundays, I am too weary even to stay up for Nimet, never mind the dead and gone, my long lost archangel. He who cuts himself away slice by slice/Must get his beauty sleep and wake up nice.

In her sleep, as exposed by the dim red of my flashlight, Bimini's hands make clawing or dragging motions across her abdomen, almost in parody of what I do nightly, I Kiwi White, Man of a thousand cuts, the Lon Chaney of the blade, already padded all across his front and beginning to look as if I have gained a dozen pounds, not that the green plastic of the garbage bag cares. One good thing about the bag. When I'm cut to death and done for, I'll no doubt be in the very thing I'll belong in, easily disposed of, unwantably drab. Cut to ribbons. Bled White. There's a name for you, for me. And Bimini will have forgotten about the poor itinerant transplant ghost she found up in a tree, yearning heartsick for what, on the few occasions it has happened, has been the source of an extravagant death-defying religion. Archangels do nobody's bidding, do not have schedules, or power over their own movements. They have to be willed into action by the chronic pain of a loved one on the other side of the great divide.

My back is going to come through unscathed. That much is plain, at least as plain that my Sundays are going to be my nights proper, when I sleep, and that proves Bimini is no assassin because I'm still on the premises. Prompted, she will no doubt go to work on my back for me, docking me of bits here and there, but (I hope) never getting carried away to the extent of skinning me down. No, I prefer her in front of me, alongside, where someone if not I can keep an eye on her. She has energy that could lead her into any kind of impetuous thing. I like her tied, even if not gagged. At least she hasn't yet begun to cut *herself* up, although the look that comes upon her, of severely compassionate envy, makes me nervous. Once she started she would never stop.

At this rate I am soon going to look pocked all over, a stippled man like one of those American Indian fire devils who cavort in red and yellow spots. In no time at all it will be convenient to enter the club swathed in cotton, wearing some kind of cotton jerkin that rests gently against the cuts of old. It may come, I hope, to my being escorted in by the sirens of radio, conscripted for special duty, no longer sitting on their soft wet nests and with thin or thick lips flawlessly enunciating the names of foreign composers, but press-ganged or volunteered. But that will not happen until, how shall I put it, I have cut away more of me than there is left. Something like that. If I weigh one hundred and sixty, then, say, I'll only be sixty and the other hundred will be drying out in a bigger lacquer box than I presently have. The objective, surely, if we are logical about it, is to be enough myself to carry the box containing most of what once was. Occam, my patron saint, might have approved of me, in that at any rate. Most of all when I reach the tricky point of the cut that shifts the balance and ratio: in a word when there is too little of me left to life the rest of me up.

Imagine, I say to myself. You have redone the equation of your being. Or you soon will. The intention is there along with the resolve. Thousands will copy you, but none will achieve your special degree of self-denial, lodging you somewhere between a Joseph's coat and a side of bacon. You will have satisfied thousands on some barbaric plane that calls out not so much for blood as for saintly girding of the loins, for an attitude that shows how perishable and vulnerable we are. How much like balsa wood. They go away gladder than ever to be intact. They do not mind as much their next blood test, the removal of the next mole or wart, the little slit that enables the surgeon to install a new pacemaker battery. That, briefly, is the rationale of the Gulag, isn't it, my archangel? When those not, shall we say, *encamped*, see how it is with those who are, they are glad to be alive, even though by latest reckoning it has taken sixty million souls perished to make the point. A successful society or policy must always have some given fraction of its folks at hard labor for a span of years exceeding that which marks either adolescence (15) or the coming of age (21). That must have been the planning behind it all. The rest of the population goes jubilantly about its business, easy meat for optimists, although, in my own version, there comes a time when it is preferable to have the entire population encamped or jailed. Then the instructive comparison has to be made with a country notorious for letting most of its criminals walk free, such as the United States, where the patron saints are gangsters. Perhaps only the interned Japanese of 1941 would understand, abruptly converted as they were into onlookers, not participants. That harsh kind of contrast is what pulls the thrill-hunting audience into the Ossa Negra nightly, ten dollars a head. Belle is growing rich on old Russian folklore, did she but know it. Each and every spectator knows that he or she is not among those who cut themselves to bits for philosophical reasons. The idea has not occurred to them before. It will come to them again, long after I have ceased to be an attraction, or even an acceptable-looking human being. It will come to them in the dead of night and they will be glad to be whole. Actually, what is uppermost in my wandering head is the notion that I, Kiwi White, am doing this to myself. I have pre-empted all jailers, torturers, and interrogators; my self-inflicted pain is the emblem of my American freedom. Or at least it is until they come and close the club, cart me off to Bellevue for observation, and restore Bimini to her queendom in Queens. What is that phrase from Ravel, the title of a short Hispanic-flavored piece? *Alborada del gracioso*: the morning song of the jester, though I like to think of it more vaguely as the aubade of a gracious mind. Well, what I am doing is the serenade of a mind ungracious in the extreme. I have had the graciousness knocked out of me by experts, and what remains—like the rags of a jaunty flag—is at perpetual half mast. Not a flag of truce. Not a surrender. But a duet for skin and balsa cutter. Always, ladies and gentlemen, buy new blades on Saturday, so as to be ready. Wipe off the oil or the dust and soak them in alcohol all day Sunday, and then you will be ready to perform. It helps, as in a hospital. It gives you that little bit of extra confidence when making the first incision.

"Don't you ever sleep?" Bimini says.

"Just Sundays, honey."

"Well, I couldn't do that."

"Bimini," I tell her with gentle finality, "this is the Sunday of life. Not just a day like others. It's the death of the week, see. You are quite safe to go to sleep on Sundays, whereas the other days are much trickier. They belong to people, but Sunday belongs to death."

She laughs and laughs. Death to her is having her ovaries torn out. Then she would want the lacquered box to keep them in like two bountiful retired prunes, and what a rattle they would eventually make, softened with spit at night to keep them from flaking. She goes along with what I do, but she doesn't understand, and there is hope in that. She will never hear it from me. She deserves to live on in her fugitive's paradise. Clearly, her parents have not been looking too hard at their newspapers, or even their TV, or they would have snatched her back by now, and it occurs to me that they wouldn't really want her back anyway. Mightn't is more like it. In which case she will inherit one treehouse and all it contains. Not bad. A beginning. Then to the Ossa Negra for a new career, branching out where I lopped off. If only, for her, there were a climax such as the one I have not yet attempted, with good reason. Clitoridectomy is hardly the slambang feat that castration is. Where are the movies in which the Mafia hit man, after gelding with his ritual knife a villain who lay with a don's wife, goes after the wife with the same zeal? Not as dramatic, nowhere near so blatant. Men are much more obvious, and this my audience knows, hoping I will, wanting to wish I won't.

Hoping I will, wanting to wish I won't: wasn't that the frame of mind of the well-clad

The Ice Lens

guard with the Tommy gun waiting for me to go too near the inner wire? How I longed for just ten minutes in one of those buff-colored overcoats with a collar you could tug erect and bring around your head like a funnel of felt. How I longed for one of those hats that unsnapped and came down on four sides to meet the upcoming collar of the coat. When collar met hat there was no human head in sight and the guard fired, if he did, by peering through a slit that would have served Isaac Newton well when he was splitting light. Something creamy in the texture of the cloth gave those guards an oddly mellow look, a touch of prosperity, or the self-made man; you almost looked for his convertible. Surely someone that well-upholstered would never shoot anyone in cold blood, but they did, they weren't forbidden to, so you ended up, as if at the other end of a tropical world, hoping he wouldn't, wanting to wish he would.

    Now I can afford one, I should have one. I tell Bimini to ready herself. It is almost noon. Off we go to one of those small stores off Central Park South, tucked in between greasy spoons, and treat ourselves for fifty dollars to two military-style overcoats, hers a Coast Guard type of thing with anchor buttons, mine with epaulets, when the store man tells me is a cast-off "British warm," fawn with fleecy linings in the pockets to keep your hands toasty. This is November, my archangel, and we mustn't come to a frozen halt. Not yet at any rate. Now Bimini and I, having shed our garbage bags (which I nonetheless roll up for future use), can walk abroad like a couple of millionaires, secure in the conversion of flesh to brass, the going rate being something like 21.6 recurring dollars per quarter inch. A rather more cumbersome calculation translates my surface area, give or take a square foot or two here and there on the face and the groin, three hundred and seventy-three thousand, two hundred and forty-eight dollars. The immediate problem is that Belle has nothing like that. Maybe she doesn't often have the 248. I have more skin than she can afford. Maybe I need a wealthier sponsor, but who else would put on a show like mine? I ache in many places, but we tuck into the best cheeseburgers and fried fish, and we are highstrung from caffeine. The ideal, impossible but enduring, is to do my show in the treehouse itself, not for actual spectators in the flesh, but before carefully adjusted cameras, maybe twice a week for one of those weirdo cable outlets that transmit opposite Nimet in the skin and music phase of the nightless day.

    Tonight, I decide, I'll ask Wehn to make the calls. He's bound to know somebody who can help. The only snag is that, once known, never mind famous, the treehouse will have to go the way of all the others. But, wouldn't a warm studio be better? Not a news item, but a regular, that's what I'd like to be: Nimet is Nimet, and I'd be Vesalius the Second.

"Coming up in the world," he says with a smirk, that night. "Welcome to commercial success. Now, darlings, is the time to make the pieces smaller."

"Now's the time, darlings," I answer, "to boost the price. Not *here*." I tell him, and he nods, shakes his head. He thinks there's a chance. "You can see most anything on those channels," he says. "Why not have a Vesalius Hour after all? Where Caligula's apple pie, who's to say that the self-skinned man can't be kind? I'll phone around a bit."

So I go to my night's feat with grand expectations, removing a bigger flange that usual, this from my chin, the first facial cut, maybe the last, but something visible after all, like wearing the Légion d'Honneur in my buttonhole: the tiny red thread that says Special. Why, oh why, do not we survivors of the Gulag sport a baby rose like that? White, preferably with a tiny off-center fleck of real blood *to remind*? Of guts in the snow, curdling fast into ivory roots and big bland vein-traceried stones. This is the aphrodisiac of survivorship.

Our blood is a stained glass window.
Our bones are pianos.
Our heads resemble ambushed pianos.
Our families are frogspawn on the wind.
Our relationships are spun silk under the bulldozer.

Our hearts are broken gourds.

"A bit much, isn't it?" Wehn says, examining my chin.

"My hand slipped," I lie.

"You'll never need to shave that bit again."

I have a weak chin anyway, I tell him with a wincing leer. My mind is on the TV prospect, but what I don't want is to have to be filmed at the Ossa Negra, of which I've had enough. They still do other acts although they rush them through, and half the crowd is smashed or high. To my mind, something such as what I do demands an almost ecclesiastical calm, serious contemplative music, a few acolytes in robes, maybe, and cameras not handheld. I am getting choosy with what's left.

"Don't worry, I'll ask around," he says.

I have put him on his mettle, and his connections too. Alas, he will want to be part of the act. Fire Bimini and plant him in her place? Not likely. Let him be impresario, barker, and recording angel all in one. How calm I am, or so I think, accustomed now to ranks of faces peering at me with that odd mix of bloodlust and hypnotic loathing. Do I see the sun coming up? I see a face like a burnished coin. A familiar face. Good heavens: an old survivor come to slum a bit? Not a survivor, but someone from that era, and not so much looking at me as peering clean through me with well-adjusted impersonality. Then gone, a mind's-eye mote, one of those *muscae volitantes* that

The Ice Lens

glide over the surface of the eye like a puck on ice or, as the phrase itself says, a fly in the act of flying. Gone, with not even the back of the head visible now. Nor the profile. Nothing. The crowd has closed ranks like a pond. No ripple either. I am just wondering if hate and pain, mixed at the right temperature, can elicit from the atmosphere images such as, otherwise, only holographic lasers make. Perhaps the heat in here, that makes you sweat too much to make an accurate cut with the palm so wet and the body skin slick, makes faces boil and some of their features recombine. No, it was (I can hardly formulate so dread a thought) a waned, thinned, aged, altogether less substantial looking Svalocin I saw, hardly a fan but a perfectionist come abroad to roost, to gloat, to take his time, before finishing the job with all the resources of an Embassy. I should have lain low. How easy for him to be posted here on some quasi-diplomatic mission trumped up during a hard night's vodka. How easy for me now to walk away, to go bury me and Bimini in rural Tennessee, say, never again to cut, to perform, to make *this* kind of living. How hard to turn one's back on something coming to the boil, even if you're haunted by grandeur, hoping eventually to act with it here or elsewhere. I am the eye of a storm that has come at last to me.

32. Flatlander

Once, in the Gulag, they assembled a crew of us to lift a leaky water heater of some eight hundred pounds, telling us not to worry, boys, only a plumber can understand this. We heaved and strained, shoved plants and poles beneath, but were hardly able even to shift it along the frozen ground. We were too weak, too undernourished, for such stevedore work. At length, we stood back and watched a team of guards remove it inch by inch, only to reveal, squashed flat beneath, as if a tank had rolled over, a two-dimensional zek who had squirted and squealed in vain as he tried to make some last-minute adjustments. Then it sat on him, leveling him with earth. He had been a plumber, they said, a zek, yes, but also slow to maneuver, and a great truster of those who lifted. Sobered by such an apparition, we retreated to our huts to await the next compulsory detail, amazed that, as the story went when spread, no one had asked for him or remembered him, the theory having been that someone so badly squashed was not worth recovering, of no further use either as a prisoner or as a workman. And someone extra to bury, though the grave would have been shallow. So he had endured all these years in flattened obscurity, giving new resonance to the term flatlander that

The Ice Lens

some of us knew from our rudimentary astronomy.

Actually, we were surrounded by graveyards. These camps dated back to the early Thirties, and many zeks died during imprisonment, even some guards, as I said. Was there any difference between the northern and southern camps then, between Kolyma and Chukotka, and, much farther south, Frunze and the evilly named Samarkand? So it was said by those who knew nothing, while those who knew were not heard from, not even after they were let go. A big map would have helped us find and bewail ourselves, a fate for which the University of Arizona had ill-prepared the likes of me. How many camps were there? Dozens, more of them than of extermination camps in Nazi-occupied Europe. They were places in which, if unlucky, you shrank with advancing years as your penis retracted into your body to escape the cold, and your body finally gave up on its vain hunt for hormones. Such was the stone-ache paradise of the frozen toy, with just a few hearty cocksmen whose genitalia had been designed by the aviation industry, picking their bunny-honeys as if their lives depended on it. This was one of the ways you could be broken, allowing your mind to peruse erotic tableaux culled from a misspent young manhood while unable to locate the nerves and capillaries that led "down there," and worrying with sometimes half a brain about the future and the fate of eununchs retrieving a soggy mouse from a sparkling pool.

33. Leiothrix, Omaos, Elepaios

A wiser man than I would go off to the Embassy or Consulate or whatever it is and camp out, hidden in a laundry truck, just to be sure that Svalocin was around. Yet how, if I talk of a man wiser than I, do I not behave like him? If I know anything about him, this wiser man, then surely I know enough to pick his brains. If I know what a wiser man would do, then why don't *I* do it? The answer must be that I'm too lazy. Imagine being the dolt who did the 1937 statute called *Worker and Woman Collective Farmer*, seventy-five tons in all, yet knowing what a wiser man—Donatello, Michelangelo, Rodin—would do, without ever doing it. No, it depends on the talent available. That's what I tell myself. You can't have everything. So stop giving yourself a hard time. Knowing what to do isn't necessarily doing it. Ease up. I do. Or I would if, right on top of the smarts and pain in my abdomen, chin, and upper arms, I didn't seem to have developed something else: pains in the toes, not from cutting, of course, but maybe from walking too much. I can hardly set a foot down without wincing. On each foot the middle toe feels out of joint, and the pain is electrifying. I wear a foam snood on each, then pad the area beneath it with lamb's wool, which I thought was plastic too until I asked. *The real thing*, they told me. And I thought of little lambs with their hides ripped away in the Gulag; but, of course, they *shear* them. It's painless. Now I tread on floats of air, but my toes still ache, and I am going to have them X-rayed soon. I promise myself that. If I could only walk around in carpet slippers, it would help. Shoes hurt, as do boots, and barefoot would be best. Imagine that: walking barefoot through Manhattan all winter, for no fee.

Toes apart, and wounds or scars, I'm not doing too badly. I'm feeling quite affectionate in fact, as if having more money than usual—and more attention—has warmed the chambers of my heart, so much so that we now spend the days up in the treehouse playing tapes of birdsongs to drive the local birds insane, and, just maybe, to thicken up the sound of spring-in-fall for the passers underneath, not that they realize they're hearing, among other birds, mynahs, the Himalayan white-crested thrush, the Chinese leiothrix, omaos and elepaios both from Hawaii, and many others, I having put a dozen dollars down for a Messiaen tape of bird- and Utah music. Nights of cut and thrust. Days of warble. It could be worse, as it would be having to sit inside a blind outside the Soviet Consulate (yes, the Embassy's in DC, as I at first thought), listening to exotic birds while waiting for Svalocin to show his pock-marked face, the plump carrots of his legs when he does his stout but fussy walk out of what is technically Russian terrain.

Was it really he at the club?

Without meaning to say anything I tell Bimini "They'll end up coming for me too, soon." Apropos of nothing.

"Can't have you," she says. "Belong to me."

"No, I don't. I don't belong to anybody."

"Well, you're mine, anyway. All the way from cuddle to fuck."

"Steady on," I say. "That's too much."

"You're not *going*," she commands. "Are you?"

I avoid the question, making the birdsong louder; and the real birds around us, whetted or piqued, get louder too. I half believe these recorded birds have sipped the blood from my wounds. I am half Christ, half St. Sebastian, and half St. Valentine. Half a mo—I'll take the two saints and jettison the messiah.

"You're not *going*," Bimini says. "I'll die of cold. Not going to go. The kangies will freeze to death."

"Where was it," I say, "where I was going to go in the first place?"

"When they come to get you." Twitch-twitch-twitch.

"Oh, that," I say airily, "that was just a bad dream. A face seen in a crowd. An asshole with a face painted in red on it."

"Well," she says, "I can tell you don't want to go."

And, I add, they are not going to come for me either. *He* is not. What, then, is he doing in the country? He could be here on business having nothing to do with me at all. My toes hurt. My carcass stings. Isn't that enough for one solitary wanderer whose dearheart lies under indiscriminate snows in a small trench somewhere between Murmansk and Tashkent? I need to talk with her more to distract my head from a possibility too awful to host.

"I thought I saw an old enemy."

"What's that?"

"You know. Somebody that hates you and is out to get you."

"Going to cut the chocklits out of your insides."

"Sort of," I say.

"I'll kill 'em," she says. "You got enough troubles at night nowadays, champ. You could give them the bits, if they wanting you that bad."

"Not the bits," I say. "All the rest."

"Stay in the tree for ever," she says.

There is no staying in the tree. I belong to the world now, I belong to showbiz; I'm a hit. Now, who ever heard of a celeb shutting himself away in a treehouse? Scores have done it, though, unable to bear the searchlight. No, the limelight. You hear about it all the time. They head off for remote islands. They equip damp lighthouses with a hundred TV sets to drown out the unrecognizing sea. They shave their heads and go begging their way across the Deccan of India. Now, where did I hear all that? For once, with an unanswering darling at the other end of my question, I haven't the heart to call on her, to plead to her among the shades. I talk to Bimini instead, a human with so narrow a basis in ordinary humanity as to have almost alien standing.

"Nobody can live in a tree. It's too late for that."

"Oh," she wails, "but if you warm and dry, and have all the food you need. I'm quite practical, you know."

"More than I am," I tell her. "There must be something wrong with someone who, to make a living, cuts himself away bit by bit. Whittles himself. By the time he has enough to support the body he once had, he only weighs an ounce or two. There's nothing left. The moral's obvious, Bimini: you have to cut it short at exactly the right point—when there's enough of you left to make the most of what you've made by cutting the rest of you away. Imagine just the heart in the rib cage, the liver, the kidneys, connected up to the brain. And nothing else. Why, they'd say, this that was once a man is nothing but his internal organs now, like a clock with only the pendulum left."

This leaves her standing, as my most erratic sallies do, and instead of answering she conducts an orchestra of birds. Do people actually pause, halt, and stare underneath us, wondering at the profusion of birds in so bleak a season? We shall soon be swamped by teenagers with guns, nets, and tape recorders. Anyone out on a so-called nature walk through Central Park is going to get some priceless material, as if we have abandoned the whole idea of a United Nations and delegated its doings to the birds, to a parliament of fowls.

I keep a small plan of where I've cut, just to keep straight. After all, you can't check anything that's wadded in bandage.

"Now you're such a mess," she says, "he'd look away."

"He'd come after me, but look away when he saw me?"

"He'd not bother," she says vaguely.

"He'd have to see me first," I say. "Otherwise he'd never know I wasn't worth it."

"Somebody might tell him A little dicky bird might tell him."

"*You* would, you mean."

She waves that one away and fixes on the birds again, arms outraised as if she is going to embrace somebody. Not me. She keeps her distance now. I wince too much.

"Oh well," she says, "fuck him then. I was just chopsin' anyway. The girl kangies are just a bit upset."

"You're a lot of help."

She waves that one away too. Odd: she senses the affection I feel for her, zany that she is, but it's given her the confidence to be more independent. She doesn't cling as she used to, when she wanted me.

"I'm not here to help," she says. "I'm here for safe keeping. Me and my kangaroos."

"Maybe an earlobe tonight," I say. "A bit of one."

"What's that?"

I show her. Some words she doesn't have and she never guesses. She scowls at the idea, as at anything close to the face. She prefers the arms, the legs.

"Or," I say, "maybe we'll cut a bit off you tonight just to vary things a bit, give my old carcass a rest. How would you like that? There's plenty of you to go at."

She giggles. She understands that all right. She can giggle about her outside, but what's inside her doesn't make her giggle at all, not when they threaten to Kiwi-White it.

"You'll end up killing me," she says.

"A man," I say in my more philosophical vein, has only one chance to kill you. A city has a thousand." I'm not sure what I mean, but, there, I've said it, and it's not going to lead her astray.

"Poop to you," she says. "I thought you kind of liked me. You like doing naughty things to me, anyway." Her twitch erupts.

I am going to protest it was the other way around, but I let it go. I wonder who'll get to us first: the Russians or the parents. She has a winning smile for such a loser, or so I think until I realize that, compared to me, she's an outright winner. She's someone with, if not much future, at least a whole lot of present in front of her, whereas even my present is used up. Thirty-five is half way for a man, I tell myself. Forty if you're a perfect specimen.

I try to bend to treat my feet, at last peeling off the socks and then the snoods, the pads, which always snag together, the one's fibers into the other's, but the cuts on my chest and stomach feel scalded and bring tears. Observant, she crosses the platform and begins to do it for me, asking what's really wrong with my feet. "Ataleet's foot?"

"Anyone less an athlete—"

"Then chilblains."

Now, there is a word from the traveler's phrase book. I never heard anyone say it before. They must have a lot of them out in Bermuda, where the onions grow. That's the link: bunions, which are not what's wrong with me "Maybe," I tell her, "It's a hammer toe forming. Two."

She shakes her head as I rewind the Messiaen tape and launch it again at the greenwood tree, wondering how long we are going to manage it before some public busybody sniffs the artificial among the natural and comes to saw my house down. I need a Nimet of the daytime. Instead of the dead sweetheart I appeal to, I need a live one to answer me from the cold, insensate lap of Mamma Russia. I dread the night's ordeal. My lacquer box rattles mightily, more each day as the cut bits hard-en. Bimini has become an accomplice, an ally, a helpmate, but she doesn't know enough about my other life. Having tried to explain it to her, more than once, I give up. She sees no vice in adultery or whatever I called it when I told her. She sees no vice in anything at all.

After crouching to my feet, getting them free to the air, I lean far, far back to get the muscles back to true, and for half a minute when I sit back up the world is that much redder. Then the blood settles back again into the rest of me, and I prefer things that way: less of a silent inferno.

Odd, when my feet are bare, the toes hurt not at all. It's the shoe that hurts, even with the padding in place around my toes. Perhaps something primitive is taking me over. Until I began to carve myself up, I wasn't that primitive, but now I've become a self-notcher I'm supposed to go barefoot as well. At this rate I'll soon be on all fours, licking the droppings of the primitive trudging ahead of me.

"I don't feel like it, tonight," I say. "I'll skip it."

"Next night it will be even harder," she says, so wise.

I know what she is telling me. Where I heard it first I have no idea, but I have long known that old philanderer's maxim: he who leaves it in all night awakens with a song on his lips. Whereas—well. Something about staying on the job makes a motion in my head somewhere and I know that I have to go and do it, not to prove my courage or to perk my curiosity again, but because I don't have enough money to skip a night and risk a long break in the series. One step back equals a dozen. If you have ever cut yourself apart in this particular fashion, you know. We do it the next night only to see if it might hurt a little less the umpteenth time around.

Anyway, Kiwi White has made the news.

So has his accompanist, which sounds as if Bimini plays the piano during my act; but no, she's just the muse who holds my hand.

Snow flurries upon us, all of a sudden, mop shakings from on high, and I begin to wonder about the winter, in which one can hibernate. But two? With someone else running around you, can you hibernate at all? The process calls for stealth, economy, the deliberate and untwitchy mastication of time. The wind from the East River has corpses in it and the taint of frozen snowplows. Not knowing what to do next, mainly because I am not accustomed to fending for two, not in this country anyway, I decide to go on with the show tonight since I would probably head in that direction anyway, not for thrills, but on the off chance of seeing Svalocin in the crowd or of seeing Wehn himself, either in full cry after me. Sometimes, if one does not cooperate with one's doom, there is no possible chance of enjoying it.

"We'll go, after all," I say.

The Ice Lens

"Who needs me," Bimini says in a ruminative meander of syllables.

"Just going through the motions," I say. "Nothing much tonight." I'll wear the boxing gloves to save my hands.

"That's what you always say, champ," Bimini tells me. I have a sudden sense that she is three fates rolled into one: Clotho, Lachesis, Atropos, a spinner or weaver, a measurer, and one who snips. From the way she talks, you can tell pretty well which one she is just now. That was the measurer talking, I think.

I am wadded and padded like some naval gun, a man of flinches and feints, ready to go through it time and again, but perhaps only because I know that, having cut from a certain place, I will never cut from it again, what with life being short (even without the nine grams into the skull). I am hunting some finality that is not death.

What I do next I do only because my mind is on something else, on an invitation from several of the pool owners to come back in late October and mulch their roses for them, heaving bales of moss about and shaping big pyramids of it around each root, either barehanded or with a trowel. Gasping out in the frosty air, finding always the silver lining behind every last gasp, and wondering where it all blows away to during the winter. Too late to go and do any such thing, but my hands crave the moss, my knees the half-frozen turf evocative of old tundra. Then the hot bouillon or the coffee as I murmur endearments into the steam and ask: Shall I mulch the outdoor hibiscus too, it has a trunk on it an elephant would envy. There follows that easy laughter of the middle class while I heft another bag over the little white fence and dump moss all over the root. Heaven, I think, is compulsory gardening.

I am brooding publically as I apply the cutter to my skin and begin to sink the point: the first cut always up, the second to my right, the third to my left, the fourth always down. The worst part is when I have to slice the little quadrilateral away, which is when the blood comes fastest. This time, though, I cut one from each side of me, then swap the bits and press them home as grafts. Each bit of me has migrated a couple of feet. After bandaids, I try to relax, but the symmetrical pain gives me no peace, and the crowd is wondering why I've changed my act, why I didn't pop the two tiny bits into my lacquered box.

Wehn looks delighted, so maybe the old act was beginning to bore him. Hard graft, I think, it isn't worth the money. Every time it hurts more and more. I am not getting used to it. I'm getting worse at it.

"So?" He seems to think that is question enough.

"A novelty," I say. "A switch."
"For once."
"Looks like a good idea to me," Bimini says in her most high-handed voice, fruity and disdainful. "He's going to last longer if he does."

Wehn nods, but his mind is on some score, you can see that. Or on some ancient penis-in-the-mouth trick: the long tongue of cock-in-gob.

"Somebody was asking for you," he says. "Some Russkie."

All the blood stops seeping from my wounds and begins to huddle deep inside me, ready to congeal.

"Somebody was asking," Bimini says, "who won't get to see him. Not if you ask me."

"No interviews," I gasp.

"No, a friend," Wehn says.

"Some fucking friend," Bimini says, all twitching urgency.

"Where is he," I say. "Who?"

Wehn can't find him.

"They don't have to ask," I tell him. "I'm here and in full view. They can come right up to me and shoot me in the head if they want. They don't need an appointment."

"It's a free country," she says. "Not like where he fucking came from."

"Hush," I tell her. "Language."

"She's quite a mouth," Wehn says, "I'll end up working her into something I'm doing. She's the real thing."

All I can think is the name Svalocin. Twice he's come and twice he's gone. Next time he'll stay and finish the job—unless. Police? Hardly. A guard? Bimini? Stay in the treehouse, then, and let him comb the parks for me. Then his feet will hurt worse than mine.

"Well-dressed," Wehn is saying. "Sort of a bulldog chin. Shiny boots. A coarse face only faintly ennobled by what it so patiently has suffered. English good with a burr. Eyes dead as old hooks. Bad breath—oranges and grease. He must like fried orange peel. That's how he smelled. Cointreau from a fish and chip shop."

"Don't tell me," I say, "you'll end up working him into something you're doing, and by the time you finish it we'll be dead, Bimini and me, and he'll be off back to home and beauty with his hands washed and his conscience clear. He's come to get me. If he is who I think he is, he's come to get me. And, if seeing's close to doing, then I'm a goner already."

"A groupie more like," Wehn says. "You're famous."

"He's famous," Bimini says, echolaliac to the end.

"If I am," I say, "then call the FBI, the Secret Service. I need protection. He's only practicing, but next time he'll do things right. You'll need another act, then, no mistake."

Wehn asks and, briefly, I tell, and he thinks we should phone the consulate and ask for him by name. We do. They hang up, politely saying the visa office is closed for the day. Please to call back. At this very moment they are issuing him with the cyanide needle, the death spray, the silencer. He won't do it in public, of course not. He'll be outside, lurking, and follow us home all the way to our tree. No need. He can do it in the pitchdark street, giggling at his method's certainty. His version of the neutron bomb eliminates me and leaves all the bystanders intact. Then Wehn will take over Bimini and my mother who isn't my mother will marry Wehn. All end happily.

No more roses to mulch.

No more pools to clean and close.

No more frogs.

What would Rat Man do, that old pump of the sidewalks? He'd march the streets with his baby carriage, his drum and his balloon, denouncing the Russkie with a big blow-up of his face. That's because he isn't turned in upon himself. He has more resources, and his woman isn't a Bimini. The Biminis of the world are loyal and forthright, but planning or scheming isn't exactly their strong suit. She'll have to improvise something as good as something planned, if she's going to be any use to me, whose treehouse she barged into uninvited after all, let's face it. *Up* into, then. Up and at 'em, boys. Lead with the bayonet, after the artillery guns. Pound them, Charlie, pound them. Now, whose famous words were those? Famous last.

"Is it pain?" Wehn has my hands in his.

"The pain?"

"You're crying."

"Then I'm a crying kiwi, like a whooping crane." I realize I have been crying all along.

"It's not the pain," Bimini says. "They're coming to get his chocklits off him. There was somebody before he had me. She's dead. That's what makes him cry."

"I know the story," Wehn says. "In outline."

"You'll flesh it out," I say, "once I'm dead and gone."

"Hush," he says, as if I were Bimini.

"I just wish," I tell them both, "I'd started this caper earlier and had cut away so much there wasn't enough left for *him* to come after. Only a piece so small you couldn't get a bullet through it without, well, I mean so's it would leave a *bullet hole*. There'd be no *me*. It's like going through hell and then getting an expense-paid trip to heaven, except the first thing they do to me in heaven is put me on the defensive and say: You're not an actor, so you can't declare yourself *as* Romeo or whatever. You have to be you. There is no *as* for you, never mind how far you've come, never mind how much you've been through. You play yourself. Rat Man was Rat Man and no other. You are not even Mouse Man or Roach Man. This is not the movies. This is the paradise of eligible souls. You are not eligible by some fif-

The Ice Lens

teen years. Apply again later, but first read the small print. Homunculi match minuscules."

"Good line," Wehn says. "Honestly, I don't think there's any problem. I didn't tell him anything at all."

"How would you know?"

'Besides," he says, not listening, "he looked quite safe. Not a madman. Not a freak."

"No," I murmur, "just one of your better-dressed fanatics, trained to be civil when doing his damndest. They show up at your doorstep and ask to sell you some life insurance and, the instant you turn away, they have you from behind and ram the long needle into your eye socket. I know."

He doesn't like the bit about the eye.

"No offense," I say. "None meant."

"Well, in that case."

"He can't stay here all night," Bimini says. "He needs his beauty sleep."

"She's right."

"I'll see you out," Wehn says. "The coast will have to be clear or you'll come home with me. We have some Hell's Angels in the vicinity, just the guys to help us out."

I like the sound of that. "How many?"

"Countless," he says. "Where I live, we never have any trouble."

"Where," I say, "were they twenty years ago, when I needed them as much as I do now?"

He does not answer, but Bimini nods at the question as if she's understood. "They was babies, then," she says, all sage abundance. I can feel it now: in her lethal, hamfisted way, she is going to take care of me. It will hurt, but nobody will ever get near me again. The last incisions will be hers, the last flakes lifted will be hers for the lifting. She will sit on the wheel, balsa-cutter in hand, telling Wehn the story of my last days, making me behave as a character should, and blowing bubblegum bubbles at him while telling him she doesn't know diddly about any other woman in my life. By then the treehouse will be an exhibit on a guided tour and my lacquer box of skin flakes will sit on top of Wehn's two-volume set of *Remembrance of Things Past*. Never again will I, as a child, go running around in the woods pretending to be all sorts of other people from Eugene Onegin to Raskolnikov. No more pretend. We go by taxi to the St. Moritz, then run.

Home, I almost collapse, but Bimini smothers me with hugs. I hug back. Birdsong. Hibachi. Two flashlights. Nimet after midnight. I begin to get going again, even though I hear some alien hands on the bark of the tree, think I feel some deadly hand tugging at the rope, testing it before the murderous ascent.

"Howya fixed now, champ?" She has learned to murmur.

I answer in mumbles.

Cocoa and cookies is the remedy for my shivers. My sides ache as if I have been lanced. The headache is worse, like a thawing out of a deep-frozen brain. Read to me, I tell her, handing her the biggest flashlight and three books. She begins, but she doesn't go on. "*In*," she says, then begins to tremble. The twitch speeds up.

"Read me the bit, right here," I say, pointing to the top of page xv in the paperback one-volume abridgement of *The Gulag Archipelago*, one of my fifteen books. "The part about the ice lens that was really a frozen stream." I know it by heart, but I want to be read to. "They end up eating the fish," I say to her, "and the fish are scores of thousands of years old. Why do they eat these specimens instead of saving them in the ice for museums? Because *they are prisoners*. They have not eaten fish in years." Still she does not read to me, but she says "*In*" again."

"In 1949," I prompt her, hoping she will do more than a paragraph, a mere page, but read to me all night to lull me while Nimet purrs her intros.

Now Bimini tries again and, as I can see over her shoulder, reads aloud the words she knows, from a ten-line paragraph at last culling *in, and, I, in, a, of, if, it,* and another *in*. No good. She can't read, although she is a scandalous talker when the mood's upon her. So we close all books and settle for idioms more abstract, such as sighs and music, hugs and hums. If only we had a crackling fire and, not too far away, the snow swooning down between the skyscrapers. But tonight it is cold only. The snow is taking a breather, saving up for a blizzard: an idea I put to her to see if she understands, and she does.

I am the centipede, I never fall down. My treasures are around me. Olivier Messiaen, Pied Piper of birds, peers at me from a dust jacket, his white hair blowing like a crop, his purple and orange scarf cowling his chest and shoulders, his thick-rimmed glasses almost leaping out of the photograph at me. In my lacquer box, the bits of me cut off may be singing uncanny songs, inaudible but sincere. It must excite them to be next to so much wood. Why I do it I don't know, but I take one out at random and taste it, like moldy bacon. I bite and chew and swallow. I have just come full circle and I wonder if a man dying of hunger might manage to eat himself, bit by bit, just in time, saving himself repeatedly.

Now I know. Monumental self-infliction is worth a thousand things imposed on you. Biting your thumb is worth ten grams any day. Biting and *eating it* too, I mean. You get to keep your thumb, but in a different place. There are wonders undreamed of, dearest dearheart. One only has to hope with almost demented intensity, and one's teeth pour gold. When I at last go, I'll be wandering in my thoughts. When I at last nod off my perch, I'll be a game goner. If not a bucket to kick up here (and one we do have, let's say it's full)

The Ice Lens

then I'll raise my leg, kick the sweetest zone of empty air and sail off the parapet like an angel shot down. No holds barred. No offense taken. No time like the present. No sweat. Only the next morn to come the unseen one, meaning unseen by me, at last the one, the morn not mine. And I will rush into your arms, cleaving, cleaving, my breath like scrimshaw icicles, my heart a red hotwater bottle, made in Russia, my feet perforated as crochet work, my eyes two big balls of bloated dew. Come home to you, at last, I say. Pardon my dirty boots. Police sirens like big Vee-shaped squadrons of geese flying over. Alone at last in the cement. Lightly now. Mind the scars. The bulges are the bits put back in the wrong place like books at the public library. They tell you to leave them out on the tables and not to shove them back any old how. At least this marks the end of praying. Maybe it's the beginning of nonstop thanks to all, from Nimet to Bimini, from Wehn to Svalocin. After a while, if those who've come to get you don't get on with it, you feel crossly stranded in vestigial happiness. Don't we precious? Don't we lay it on thick? As if we were the only two people on the hide of the planet. Come one, come all. Combine a has-been and a have not and you get a forget me not. I think so. I could be wrong. Vaguer than I am gifted. Ask at the turnstile, they say, as you enter. I do. Which way to my dearheart, sir? On down, he says, nearer the boiler room. You were both very naughty. We are going to sweat the badness out of you both. You can hold hands, as in the olden days, if you can take bone on bone. You'll soon get the hang of it, sir. There's millions do. You'll see. On the left, sir, just past the snowfire damper, on the red-hot shelf saying sorry.

34. My Own Chain of Lovely Islands

Now the brain's rallentando blurs all whim.

Can that mauve dream of mine really have been?

Did I, at Rizzoli's, before they crashed, buy my fifteen, one for each year, clad in two garbage bags?

1. The *Gulag Archipelago* (to us as *The Compleat Angler* is to fishermen)

2. Paul Griffiths, *Olivier Messiaen and the Music of Our Time* (I wanted to *read* about his Canyons and his Stars)

3. *Schwann 1* (December 1974): *Record and Tape Guide* (After many a summer dies the Schwann)

4. *Composers on Music,* edited by I can't remember

5. *Boulez: Composer, Conductor, Enigma,* by ?

6. Milton Cross, *Encyclopedia of the Great Composers and their Music,* Volume I (No Henry Cowell, no Busoni)

7. Cross, Volume II (No Rubbra, no Ruggles, no Riegger)

8. *Dmitri Shostakovich* by D. Rabinovich (printed in Russia)

9. Virgil Thomson, *American Music since 1910* (spiky)

And so on. I finger them, stroke them, ask them which of my years each of them would like to represent. This is my own chain of lovely islands, not because I like them as books so much, but because they are books about music, afloat up here like a spaceship assembled in space, on a narrow homemade shelf with screwed ends rather than dovetail joints. For each new book, I vowed, I'd throw one old one away. I haven't ever bought any since '74. There is no need. They know me better than I them. The composers in them know me better than I them. It goes to show how prophetic their intuition can be.

But those who can't replace their books can treat themselves now and then to a new suit of clothes, in our case new garbage bags. Not that we can't afford real clothes; it's just that the bags have a certain honorable status. Handling them when they're new is almost like handling liquid. Two bags is all: hole for the neck and two holes for the arms in the one, two leg holes in the other, and the outfit is complete. I myself prefer a chain with a hook, but Bimini has an actual belt lifted from who knows where. Her old clothes are hung up neatly in the corner of our treehouse arbor. We are both in uniform, although we vary it, some days boots, other days sneakers, some days with a third bag on our heads drawn together gently with an elastic band at the neck. Over mine I sometimes wear a navy blue baseball cap with scrambled egg on the peak to give the right paramilitary effect, although nowadays there should be some streaks of vermillion among the yellow as if the eggs have begun to quicken into life. The one word CAPTAIN gleams gold above the scrambled egg, and, as far as I'm concerned, it refers me to my fate or my house among the trees. Salutes I never get, but then I am no one else's captain, except perhaps those filmy, gauzy folk I think I see among us whenever I remove the lamb's wool from my feet and set it by me on the boards. The little coils of fleece, so light and fluffy to begin with, have firmed up under the onslaught of my toes and assumed semi-human shapes. I see heads, shoulders, paunches, buttocks; loungers and lollers and kneelers and crouchers, all hard at work on something I'll never know about. I sometimes even take off the snood, smooth it out and pick off balls of sock fluff, and then set it as a hat on one or other of the little stunted forms: a tarboosh with no tassel, a sweating cap. It's as human as they'll ever get, but I admire the way the wool springs back to life after being pounded and squeezed all day in the darkness of my boot or sneaker. Nothing in this world compares to the first day with a whole new clump of lamb's wool under my toes. I sink in, I settle, I bounce, but by the end of the day the wool has assumed the contours of my undertoes and has to be fitted back into it exactly the next day. That first day my toes feel as if they are being reborn and I wish my entire body could be laid to rest in a bath full of such thistledown, my chest especially.

That does it. I decide, from now on, to pad my whole chest, and whatever I have cut, with lamb's wool left in the package, in case of bumps. Costly, but worth it to any self-lacerator worth his salt, worthy of the salt within his own blood. The four back-up packs will serve me tomorrow. Then I'll have to buy more: one for my maltreated chin. I show Bimini how and she likes the idea, maybe thinking I'm going to turn into a soft fluffy rabbit before her eyes, a blademan no longer but cuddly stuff, easy to manage, easy to love, easy to get to sleep. Mellow, gentle, and haunting as a wordless song by Villa Lobos. That side of me she likes. The heroic side of me she puts up with, but I can tell she finds it far too masculine, too close to whoever would like to snip her ovaries out. She listens to my incisions behind their surgical plasters, as if auscultating the horror; she hums and coos to them; then she pats them ever so gently, putting them to sleep with an open-mouthed kiss, almost as if my cuts were newborn babies. Well, they are, but the babies proper are in the lacquered box, a pouch nothing so soft and mucously tender as the pouch she pretends is in her tummy, where the boy and girl kangaroos take it out on each other for lack of anything better to do. Her belly isn't Australia after all; or so I reason, further reasoning that, if I buy

The Ice Lens

her premise, at least there won't be any sharks to get the kangaroos whenever they venture into the ocean.

Given long enough, this unreading twitching obscene and elfin thing will spawn pumas from her armpits and starfish from between her toes. It's only a matter of time, waiting her out until her magic has reached boiling point, here in the park, among the tree tops, in the November wind, among the sirens and the rubber-heeled shuffle of traffic.

For a moment I cease to worry, then it all comes back with force renewed. Is that really Svalocin dogging my steps? Is he in league with Wehn himself? Who has been calling Aunt Tasha and hanging up? Seriously, if he wanted to do no more than upset me, he'd only have to follow us home and then phone the police. So he wants more than that. He would. I toy briefly with the notion that he's repented, has found my beloved alive in a coal mine, and has her stashed in the Plaza Hotel, awaiting our reunion. Something wrong with that, I think: all he'd have to do, if that were true, would be to get a message to me in her hand, sensuous cuneiform I adored always, saying: "Dearest: Room 1717. Come and get. It's been so long." I'd fly.

Nothing so lovely taints the offing, though. No other man ever looked so much like Svalocin as he who's show himself twice, not blatantly, but not altogether on the perimeter either, as if indeed he were the wholly unseen assassin, voluptuously biding his time, giving you one second more of your life after another, and then another, like Atropos reversing herself until he can stand it no more. It's as if he's giving you seconds from his own life after all, when clearly he's not, but he takes that for gospel and sedately screws the silencer on to the gun barrel, squirts the little geyser of the hypodermic up against the light.

If I knew where to find him, I'd put paid to him for keeps, I really would. Then *I* should follow *him*, or ask Wehn to do it for me. And I'd have to kill him outside the gates of the consulate, not right outside, but somewhere dark, in the political penumbra.

"You," he'd say.

"Not quite," I'd say.

"Then who?"

"Take this." Like that. Cutting his tongue out to feed to poodles on Fifth Avenue. Or it would go like this.

"At last," I'd say.

"Who on earth?" He'd say, going down.

"Don't you remember us?"

"I," he'd be saying through the death rattle, "am not who you think." Was it he phoning Aunt Tasha?

Better without words at all, it needs no script and only thirty seconds of improvisation in a dark alley. That's the way, I tell Bimini. We'll follow him. She has no idea what I mean, and I am loath to make her think Svalocin is another ovary-cutter. Yet who will tend to her while I tend my long-neglected business? Wehn is hardly the type, so well-adjusted he wouldn't notice she'd gone. No, she comes along. She has to be an accessory, provided anything gets done.

We need some flowers up here, though they'd die off fast. Something to make our imaginations genial. Our boogeymen are taking our lives over from dawn to dark. Only in sleek bags are we suitably camouflaged, the uniform of the also-rans, the regalia of the spoiled. I would love to go out wearing a crown in a satin robe closed by a gold chain at the neck, but I can manage one thing at least, part vaudeville, part honor. I spray the name KIWI on the front of my chest, maybe denaturing the plastic as I do, then I spray the same on hers. In a moment it is dry. We are branded, twinned, ready to sandwich him between us and choke him to death with a plastic bag rammed over his face, his wrists tied before we sling him up on a hat peg in a cloakroom somewhere and watch him pant, the plastic condensing up and clinging like something come alive.

Ah, those were good days when I had the energy to go through with such a thing. When she and I, my dearheart and I, were lovers, we should have arranged an untimely electrocution for him on a house wire and had done with it. Then.

Not now, when, just perhaps, he has come all the way to Manhattan for me to notice him and give him the finish he craves. He has come here to be killed, for all the horrors, the lies, the ever-ripening sadism. Guilt at last, eh, Comrade Svalocin? Remorse from old blood and guts after all?

Well, I am too weak. I spend my nights in the deliberate act of weakening myself, blade in hand, eyes on each millimeter of gash. So: he has come to be cut. That must be it. He bares the throat, the penis, the wrist. Cut them all tonight. He won't be there. He knows how I think. He knows I think. He knows I would rather do anything but think. Bimini has wet herself again, almost as if, poor reading as my thoughts are, she has riffled through them and found them chocklitless.

All goes well. The crowd applauds as I enter the club. They revel in the cuts I make on each kneecap, the rattle of the bits in the lacquer box, the way Bimini sends the wheel rolling fast among them as if they were skittles. "Are you," someone asks, "connected with the boot polish called *Kiwi*? Are you a New Zealander?" "No, he's a citizen of the world," Wehn says at his most majestic. But no Svalocin, maybe already wafting home on Aeroflot, having seen all he needed: Kiwi White not only down and out but making love to his own demise. That would send him home with the same smile on his face as the man who's held on to it all night long.

I do an encore, out of spite at myself, this time cutting my cheek, which bleeds as if connected to a tank. We apply ice and pressure, but not before the sensation-hunters have had their fill, yelling *olés* and combining on a big vocal crescendo as I lift the blade and bear down on my cheek with it, at which they roar as if I've scored a goal. A man in the act of beheading himself would not win from them a much louder *Ah* of shocked gratification. Time to go home.

Not quite yet. I do a third act for them, as if to summon Svalocin up from their very midst as they roar and point. Not the tongue, although I feint at it, to their delight, or an eye, although that too I skim with the point, or an ear lobe although they half-expect it when I twirl the blade an inch from my right hand ear. Instead (how's this for sudden thinking at the last minute), I reach down into my shorts and make a quick slash, bend over howling, spit my gum into my hand, wad it neatly into a little oblong, and rise in agony with it between my lips, as if I have bitten it free from the shank of all that makes a man of me.

A colossal gasp follows, followed by laughter. It is known as light relief, but they will sooner or later want the real thing now they have the idea. They are as simple as that, as conscience-ridden as apricots. With more blood I might have succeeded in conning them.

I have no time to think any more about it as Bimini, blade in hand, flashes it toward her pouchful of kangaroos, grazing the skin, but seeming to threaten to do it unless I stop overdoing my act. I adore her for her sense of measure, not to mention good taste; but then it wasn't she who'd hoped for Svalocin tonight, hoping to track him down and leave him yearning for the harshest camp in the whole history of Siberia.

"Cover up," I tell her.

"Did," she says. Bored and getting restive.

"For one minute," Belle begins.

"I *thought* she wouldn't," Wehn says. "You never quite know, though. I'd keep an eye on her."

"You would, would you?" I say. "Just do it. I can hardly keep one on her and one on me, can I now?" Nimet, thank goodness, is still broadcasting, talking; I hear a mention of Richard Strauss's *Alpine Symphony* and brace myself for something lofty and august: avalanche-sized emotions from the hen-pecked Hun. I am loaded down with unworthy memberships. Yet I belong to nothing. Even my old lethal but unbawling grief sustains me no more as I embark on this new adventure of blood and flesh, for all the world as if I, Kiwi White, have just discovered pain, as one man discovered China and another penicillin.

"He's not been here all night," Wehn says. "I'll keep an eye out for him, but I wouldn't worry if I were you. Tend your friend. She's going to run amok. Too much light, noise, and blood. By the way, does Belle pay you on time?"

Bimini has center stage, both bags off, flaunting her ripe untutored figure to the mob, and yammering at them about kangaroos, ovaries, and chocklits. They have no idea what she's saying, but they love the spectacle. They want her festooned with electronic tape and pig's intestines whereas I all of a sudden, with heartbroken remorse, want to see her installed for safety's sake in the Hall of the North West Indian in the Museum of Natural History. Anywhere but here. I go get her, slipping her two bags in opposite directions to conceal her, and urging her off the low stage, into the back somewhere, out of the light. We have had enough living theater for one night; I am in terrible pain; I feel as if everything that has a fixed place within me has begun to move along like thawing ice. I am churning into a flux, disappointed and aggrieved, wondering petulantly why Wehn did not produce the man. As if he could. A taxi speeds us home to the St. Moritz in silence, our eyes wet with it all.

35. The Great Velvet Negative of Sleep

I go to sleep, aided by three pain-killing pills, half-dreaming as a good Russian sometimes will, of cutting off his nose and finding it the next day embedded in a loaf of bread. Bimini tucks me in as best she can: there isn't much to tuck me into, or with, but she makes a tender job of it, and I feel nursed, tended, like someone repatriated from a war zone. Now she knows how to tune in Nimet, even though it isn't her kind of music.

So the great velvet negative of sleep comes down from wherever it roosts, wanting me, taking me on, as it has not for days. All I know next is that it lets me go, after how long I have no idea, and for one of those stranded instants I am nowhere, aloft and nameless, as if I am sleep only, and what actually slept does not exist. At first glance I see Bimini throwing out into the void a fisherman's net for the first catch of the day. Then she seems to be airing out the laundry with upflings and downflaps of her arms, but there is no laundry, just as there is no sea or lake, no catch. With vision less blurred I see more clearly what she is doing, with the wheel in both hands, battering something at the crouch. Then I see the hulk of the body on the boards, the head, the darkened face. I try to call to her, but my throat is too dry for that. When I do manage it she doesn't hear or heed me, going on at a gentle rhythm with her outsize motions, which their object does not resist. It cannot be he. Surely he cannot have climbed up the trunk using the rope; indeed, finding the rope would be a feat in itself since the lower end is a branch you have to pull, dislodging the rope from its shipshape coils above. He must have, though, having lurked, loitered, all through our arrival and the going-to-sleep process. Then up toward us with not a sound, not even a Russian curseword, little knowing that my keeper had an eye on him from the first, could have kicked him right back down, but let him come nearer. No, he must have been on the platform before she knew. Maybe she was examining a book by flashlight, wondering what marvels it contained. Up she looked and there was a bear in a tree, a troll, not Kiwi White sleepwalking, but our first intruder getting his bearings with difficulty, and wondering where the platform ended, where space began. At this rate there will soon be nothing left of his head except a pulp long longed-for.

At last I feel free to move, but she needs no help from the half-paralyzed. Detecting my move, she pauses and shoots a glance my way, of tense abstractedness, as if interrupted during severe thought, and I manage to mutter something she doesn't answer. She pounds away again and, by flashlight, I can just about make out where the bulky Tartar features must have been: the red broad nose, the mouth made from too much flesh, the uneven-textured mustache. I tell her to stop, but she wants to make sure he won't rear up at her in the night again as a bear or whatever. Thank heaven for the wheel, for wheels. Thank heaven for Bimini, whose aim is sure, whose force is great. Could I have felled him myself? Would I have even seen him? At first he was making a noise, but now the noise is more subdued, what she's pounding softer to the touch, so to speak. Now I restrain her gently, wondering if I'll get a wheel in the head for my pains. But a shush does it. She understands that, now more than ever, we will have to be quiet as field mice, and, above all, not seen. New rules for new emergencies, I think. He is either dead or deeply unconscious, and I find time to marvel that this is really he, all the way from the land of snow. He will be missed. Maybe he told them where to look if he didn't show. No, he would hardly know which tree to tell them about, and, in any event, this was not one of those things he would be telling about. Private vengeance, his. Where, I ask myself, is the first place they would look? Scores present themselves and I give up. Where, then, would the last place be? That's easy: high up a tree, at sixty or seventy feet, and at once I know what to do with him. Gag him first, just in case; but I have trouble finding the mouth, or anything resembling one, even while Bimini sits there

The Ice Lens

breathing hard. Into it I ram one of our cast-off garbage bags, all rolled up into a glossy sausage.

How well he did, getting this far, only a yard or two short of his objective when he had traveled thousands of miles. Imagine his first getting the appointment to the consulate, maneuvering that, and then the listening around, the nonstop asking in Manhattan. He might have been here for months, from long before I even got back. Perhaps he was here, prowling and researching while I was still closing pools and hurling frogs high into the trees. How many folks he must have cheered or irritated with his questions, vaguer than vague; but it must have been the nightclub act that tipped him off.

It is almost as if, without knowing what I was doing, I had come up with the very bait to bring him to me, even from Russia, could he have known. No, he was here when he heard. Countries do not exchange nightclub data, not even for tourists. And here he is, a prize lump of pork if I ever saw one, like one of those Russian boars you can order (saddle, legs, boned shoulder, saddle with leg) from D'Artagnan in Jersey City. How did the prices go? Twelve-fifty per pound for a twenty-pound saddle comes to two hundred and fifty for only a piece of him. We would make a thousand if we cut him up right. It won't come to that, of course, not with, as now, the voice of my dearheart at long last coming through, no longer disguised as Meta Zeinermeyer, conjured back into being by the downfall of our chiefest foe. It does not bring her back to life, though: just the thin wavering voice of her coming among the treetops like a thrown skein of the vocal. She sounds gorgeous, but you cannot hug a voice, you cannot clutch at syllables. I hug Bimini instead and note how grossly she is shaking from the effort of it all, the sudden terror, the violent remedy.

We squat down by him and rest, both breathing hard. It is about four in the morning and, for once, I do not need Nimet. Thinking, I tell myself, has to be done without delay. Whatever is to be done with him has to be done at night. No pulse, in the wrist or the neck. No breath. Bimini puts the little rectangular mirror back on its shelf. If he is not a goner, than a goner I have never seen, and all he needs really, to look quite normal, is a bier of snow, someone to hack his head off and bag it back for reference purposes, as in the good old days.

It is going to be quite simple really. What we have to do with him will occupy three stages. First, bind him tight. Second, camouflage him. Third, hoist him up to his reward. They will never look in the trees, not for years, if we handle it right. Off come the boots, the thick trews, the even thicker outdoor laborer's shirt. For one who made such fuss, his privates do not have that big a heft. Surely this was not

The Ice Lens

the gear that tunneled into her long before, when I could not bear to think about it? Nor will I think now, with her radiant falsetto urging me on to thorough action: not revenge but tidiness, plugging his anus with leaves. What a God-sent chance, I think; but for Bimini, no such thing. Now he is nude, not so hefty to look at, but still warm, and not smelling too well. Ropes make him rigid, with his arms along his sides, his feet tight together, his head lashed tightly to his armpits, with several loops compressing the glossy gag within his jaw. Rigor mortis will do the rest, as for so many of us denied warmth, boots, sleep, and our ration off dried fish. All this, I have to keep telling myself, takes place in the context of Bimini's alertness, her forthright nature, and just perhaps her fondness for a way of life that, hardly gracious or traditional, has endeared itself to me, I who have lived the wrong way for too many seasons. I am no longer that fussy. So: he is still enough and no part of him, however bedraggled, will come toppling down. Worried by the very thought, I make sure that each arm, each leg, is tied to the trunk. What we really need up here is a strait jacket, or even two. But small-hour planners can't have everything, can they? They have to make do and, every now and then, if still on the premises, inspect their guest. All the pain from my latest incisions has gone, annulled by crisis, I suppose, and no doubt due to return once we're done with Svalocin.

"That's better," I say to her.

"He was a real mess before," she says. Her twitch is monumental now, but her face is set, her mouth is closed.

Now begins the work of making him invisible. First we spray him with green and brown matte finish, making more or less wavy lines, all over his skin and the ropes, and then I stipple him with paler green to mimic leaves, and then a copper brown to mimic fall. Already he looks less than human: more like a bunker of foliage, a keg of grass. Somebody must have loved him once, even my dearheart for as long as he fooled her with gifts and fancy phrases. He looks hardly worth it now, but who would after being Biminied with a wheel? If anything, he's heavier than I ever saw him, and I wonder how he got up the tree. How silly he used to look in one of those Soviet peaked caps with too big a diameter, designed (if designed at all) to make the face look small.

Now he's rigid and painted. All we have to do now is the final act, rigging the winch and hauling him up high for the birds to celebrate. Not tonight, of course, but soon after dawn, I'd expect, especially if we play the Messiaen tape to egg them on. I have to climb, but that's my skill. Up I go, like some fugitive from the Royal Navy with Captain Bligh on my tail, the rope around my neck and chest, my cuts not hurting at all, such is the commotion. High enough, I look down, but can see nothing much when I hoist the rope over a thigh-thick branch and oil the part of the bark over which the rope will pass. Both ends go down with not a sound from Bimini. Down, I tie one end firmly to him, round and round since rope we have aplenty, and then we both begin to haul. Slow work, this, taking almost an hour, but go up he does in little fits of three or four inches as the rope catches, then skids loose. Soon he is dangling above our balcony but beginning to skew over until he's above the main roof. Out of sight, alas, but I can imagine how he looks. By craning out and over, I can see him as he arrives and nestles firm against the bough, a starched papoose gone home to his reward. There is something delicate and grave in what we have done. If I was ever Bimini's accomplice in her escape, she is mine now, and I am hers. We belong together under so many umbrellas of criminality I dare not begin to count. Yet the world is cleansed. We defended ourselves, that's all. Left to ourselves, we'd never have gone after him to kill him off. It was he came after us, unable as ever to let things alone, unable to let some poor wretch consummate his *via dolorosa* without giving him a last spinal tap or whatever other drumtap of finesse occurred to him. Now he floats, his other end tied fast to the entire treehouse. Only cruel bad luck will bring him down, although from time to time he will have to be inspected for wear and tear. The hue and cry will reach its peak in a week or two, and then it will have to die down. Some poor American will have to stay in Russia right on the brink of repatriation, and he will probably have to remain there a long time; Svalocin himself will soon be in no shape to be used as human currency.

What did we forget?

"A prayer," Bimini says, who's entitled to say something like that. I have no prayer, but I listen to Nimet introducing Bach, which is almost as good, and I aim up into the branches, through the roof, a look of persevering dismay. If he'd only stayed in Russia. If only he'd long ago adopted some other career such as draughtsman, conductor, plumber; but no, a commissar, deputy kind, he had to be, and that's how history gets made. Once upon a time he charged at us in his fury, bouncing against the walls. Another time he managed to split us up and send us off to different destinations, never to see each other again. Now he rides high and lonely, trussed up under the stars: a star parcel, a goner sent back to nature. It is appropriate, I think, to give him this Indian form of burial. We have not exactly sewn him up in a canvas shroud or equipped him with emblems for the other life, but we have made him harmonize with nature: leaves, twigs, boughs, among which he will have to take his luck: chance of falling to the ground, one in several hundred, if I keep an eye on him. Chance of coming back to life, none. Chance of being spotted from the air by a police helicopter, nil; he's nowhere near the top, and, even in the dead of winter, he won't show. In a month or two come Christmas, I'll spray him brown all over and he will look like a squirrel's dray or a broken drooping bough. And, by the time they find him, if ever, we'll be gone. In fact, before we take our leave, we'll bring him down and settle him in, put him at ease on the floor as if all along he's been the real treehouse holder, the founder and user, the hermit of Central Park.

"Well," Bimini says, "who was that?"

"An old friend."

"You got any other friends like him?"

"No," I tell her, "nobody has any friend like him. Ask him, though, when he was alive, and he'd say he'd been a friend of thousands."

"Will they come and get me for it?"

"Nobody will come. I'll save you."

She is unconvinced. "Will he smell?"

She knows how the dead go off. "Not for long. If all the people he's befriended were to come to Central Park this very night and each agree to eat a bit the size of a bouillon cube, he'd be gone in half an hour or less."

She doesn't fathom this at all, but she doesn't seem to care. I wish she didn't hold on to the wheel as if it were the planet of her being. Surely my own head isn't next. No, an unworthy thought, it has to go.

Now she leans against me, having wet herself for perhaps the first time in an hour, murmuring "Hold me, hold me," and I do, even as my cuts begin to sting, even as I marvel at the notion of a sadistic official who, having got his revenge, seeks to renew it, fulfilling it beyond even the letter of an insane law, journeying all the way to the Big Apple as if he were Adam in a frenzy, vowing to incinerate the garden and all within it. Yet his death has quenched *her* voice, that diligent ornate soprano from Outre Tombe, and all I am left with is Bimini, untutored and raw, whom he could just as easily, had she been born Russian, have put down in one of his unspeakable camps, for saying "seapud" or "chocklits." He didn't reckon with the likes of her, who did not scream or melt, who didn't call out for help (unless I never heard her) or leap off the platform, but dealt with him in his own terms. What perplexes me, as dawn begins, she having fallen into a mumbling, jerky slumber, is that he did not seem to have a weapon with him: no knife, no gun, no needle, no spray, not even a sentence for me to sign, handing out an extra ten years. Was he just coming to talk? To make up, to apologize? Hardly within his nature, these things bloom and appall me. A change of heart would surely not have sent him across an ocean in search of a man easily presumed dead. Then what? A fluke: he was more surprised to see me at the club than I to see him, and he tracked me down to talk, wanting to see how I lived now, thinking I wasn't yet home, or was out lurking by the consulate. Well, he's as safe as any *zek* now. Was he, perhaps, bringing me a copy of Galler's and Marquess's *Soviet Prison Camp Speech: A Survivor's Glossary*? I have one already, sir, tucked there like a little pansy plant in the corner of my bookshelf. I do not need it. I do not read it.

In the headphones I hear devotional music of such fervid intensity I half persuade myself that my dearheart is singing to me again and to no one else. The high soprano, supposedly doing something of Charpentier's, a setting of concise lamentations by Jeremiah, achieves a tone both needle sharp and oblivious while the male voices in the background seem to be groaning in pain, but this headlong, alert soprano, lolling at the top of the register yet evoking sounds beyond those singable, seems to purge itself of human concern, trilling and immaculately chirping words I cannot understand, unless they are Latin, and I chafe at so many blithe halleluias. No, this is not my dearheart but some abstruse find of Nimet's, who will soon be going off the air, not in the least aware of yet another drama enacted to the accompaniment of her luscious tunes.

Now begins the first of our dawns with Svalocin above us. Nothing has changed, yet nothing will ever be the same. A cold wind reaches the bone marrow, and I busy myself with hibachi and powdered soup, anxious to bring the color back to Bimini's cheeks. Eyes half open, she follows my movements as from a drugged dream, clutching her wheel like Judith her head. Nothing invites us less than winter in the trees, but, in an awkwardly irresistible way, the presence of Svalocin seems to demand attention: someone on the spot, even if we never look at him.

When the rational part of me surfaces again it will tell me to move house, build anew, get out from under the corpse. Go far away. Proximity will be everything if we are ever caught, whereas if we are even only a hundred yards away that will count for a hundred yards. One should always build in conifers, but once the deciduous trees have shed the conifer stands out, to be admired, revered. And that is that. So we will build or just go, and if we go we go south. The wheel has already gone into the garbage at the other side of the park, over Bimini's sullen protests, and now I know it won't mash my head during sleep. All very well to think of leaving the park, which is one thing, whereas leaving Manhattan is quite another, like having surgery. Quite simple, I tell myself. We have our blood money to spend. All we have to do is head for the Port Authority Bus

Terminal and say goodbye, easy as boarding a river tram on the Moskva River.

"You need some extra attention now," I say.

"I didn't do anyting," she says.

"No you didn't."

"Well then. He flew away."

"Who flew?"

"Mister Nobody, that's who, that's who."

"Mister Nobody," I tell her, "never came. Once a nobody, always one."

This was the man who rang Aunt Tasha's phone and never spoke, who hovered in front of me at the Ossa Negra but never came up to me, who cut me and my dearheart in two as if each were giving birth to the other. Up there they breakfast on him. No need, as in Scandinavia or Scotland, to lash a big herring to his head to make sure the dive-bombing skuas get the idea. Those crows are connoisseurs. They are not going to look a gift commissar in the mouth, except when troughing on his tongue. I am not even glad. A nullity has replaced the nullity he made me feel. Nothing comes back because he is dead, nothing revives. For that minus there is no repreiving plus. It is almost worth yanking him down to have a good full-blooded gloat, just to make sure, just to embed his broken image in my brain. I sometimes—no, I never—no, I cannot join myself to any form of time. I have gone out and beyond it, cancelled one life as fast as blinking, without the faintest thought of how to start another.

And now, as the moralists say, I have added responsibilities: a changeling for a dearheart. I exclaim silently at the line of causation linking this to that old Russian love affair of ours, after which even her plight and fifteen years for me was not enough for him. He had to project the line, if not to infinity, at least to the edge of doom, making his beeline across the Atlantic to the dire cluster of consulate, night club, and tree. It will eventually be asked what he was doing up a tree in Central Park, at whose invitation, at whose order. As if he were some truant schoolboy in patriotic quest of a better view, even from here, of the Kremlin's domes, white and gold against the severe clear blue of a tourist sky.

I foresee an end to music. No more Nimet. No more atmospheric nights al fresco. More nightclub, yes, and more cuts, more blood, more money too, provided we can go away from here and somehow live a standard life without becoming too easy to pin down. Unless track is the verb. If, in six months, he is still here, then it may be safe to move back into the treehouse, unless they'd leave him and it alone as bait. By then the leaves would be back in force. It would be time to leave again, to open pools and sling the frogs. What would the point be, given all the other options? It is no use asking Bimini, essentially a passenger in this transit of Mars; if she was a hostage to fortune before, now she's its parasite. As fate's perspective narrowed like a wake behind us, she was at the other end of it, in the pinpoint on the far horizon's curve. This would be a good time to leave it all behind me, but there is no cutting free, not now. Best climb into some good old suburb-haunting clothes and wrap up all the evidence of our being—the chair, the bath, the nightclub leaflets—in the garbage bags we used to wear. Lower it all to the ground by rope and cart it away. I feel like someone planning the invasion of Russia. We will never do anything bad again. There is no one else wants us, apart from the Engstrom family, apart eventually from the entire Soviet diplomatic mission, unless they'll be glad to be rid of him, never having sent for him in the first place, but putting up with him, humoring him lest he get up to his old tricks all over again and have them sample his Siberia.

I don't explain. She can tell from my motions what we are about to do. Is this night or day? I suddenly find myself unable to interpret brightness. Can it be that I am once again capable, like any Russian, of lining up in the zero cold to buy an ice cream cone? Is it all coming back to me? What would they make of her there? Were there a grave to go to, I might just try, but there never was, not even a fake one. My dearheart turned into motes wafted about on the headless winds. Wehn will come get us at the St. Moritz. He says he will. Says he will help us without writing our opera. We will have to trust him rather than Aunt Tasha, who is likely to blab all to anyone happening by, most of all one of her gentlemen friends. From our outpost in the Bowery, where Wehn lives, we will continue at the Ossa Negra for half a year at least, and *that* story he will write, at least until there is less of me to cut at than there is to do the cutting, which is when Key West will call us. I see us on one of those narrow parapets over the pastelly green ocean, fishing for our supper on a long line, then the walk back to the tiny intermediate Key on which small deer roam and rub shoulders with our tent. That will be then, a time of intolerably tender remorse, less harsh than now. I tend to think of now as a harvesting of hell, a razing of the ground. It is already too late to look up Engstrom in the Queens telephone book and ask if anyone is missing whom they would now like back. It is just as well that nobody seems to be writing it down, except for Wehn who will spin us out for as long as he needs songs. Then he will speed us on our way, paying our air fare if he has to, but he will never go and bare his breast in the Ossa Negra, there to wield the balsa cutter. For now, a quiet mouth and a contained tongue shall be my lot other than saying once, in an act of dedication unique in this torrent, the beloved name denied till now: Vera Lydia Pugachev.

36. The Sweetness of Epicurus

You would think a teeming brain was just the place for a brilliant plan of action to take shape in, but the teeming is topsy-turvy. Because someone is missing does not mean he cannot be found. Not everyone, even among those in the know, think he has really gone on leave, never mind what messages he has left behind, to be passed on or otherwise delivered. Who knows what has or has not changed him in the last dozen years? Perhaps he is here to fulfill a lifelong dream of watching movies at the Thalia. In the midst of his mental commotion, yours truly fumbles his motives, makes wrong assumptions, puts on his bravest face, and decides to risk never coming back. The bizarre thought of Bimini up a tree with a corpse she does not take seriously does not occur— nor that of the police destined to run me down sooner or later, treed or at the Ossa Negra, or even at Aunt Tasha's. I have decided to be vainglorious, befitting my longlost membership in the agency. Whatever comes, I say, it will be mine. I have a good hunch about something. A new era has begun. I hardly realize that the demise of Svalocin, the unlikeliest of unlikely events, has whetted my appetite for further action, which cannot be far off. Character-shaping happenings are like camels in the night, lurching past, and worth going without sleep for. I stare into the darkness, watching the trees move.

When you have been ushered into a room by an underling, an underling who knows his own power but stores it up against a desperate day, you feel nervy when there is no need to, not even after you decide the chandelier is ponderously baroque and quite unnecessary in a room that is a blaze of light. This is only a consulate, not an embassy. The aroma of this chamber, to be polite when I should say stink of a dump, is of onions and ammoniac disinfectant as if corpses were stacked up behind the unread-looking books. Someone else is here, lurking with revolver or hypodermic, waiting his chance, or S. has given orders to have me strangled in the lavatory, a job they could have left to the solemn young guards in the Gulag. Or is this the standard treatment in 1976 of the newly released, American style? Let him go, but don't forget to slice his cock off at the consulate. When you call him or contact him, tell him nothing.

It is a wonder I've shown up then, a golem of fresh gashes. Except that I am hoping for news of *her*. I have left Bimini guarding our tree. I sit. I stand. I have not the faintest idea what I am doing, but I do spurn the leaflets left on the seedy banquette for some caller to find, not necessarily me. They left a note at the Ossa Negra, nice of them, unless they have a bullet ready for me.

The Ice Lens

Enter another flunkey, determined to spend as little time on me as possible, making a meal of his own haste after delivering the few words of his script. It is as if he's said "Eugene Onegin" or "sudden death." *What* did he say before decamping? "She. Has. Been. Released." I did a nominal faint, as when you topple forward while you are falling backward. Imagine how that random series of phonemes shocks the ear braced for something worse. "*Golúbchik!*" I exclaim to the microphones awaiting me in that sullen chamber. "*Moyá dúshenka!*" There is no one to hold on to, no fawning commissar now appointed paramilitary attaché or something even sleazier; not even the flunkey assigned to fainting relatives. A void. I see where cigars have been crushed out by a heel in the anemic rug. I freeze. I do not ride to the rescue. At first I do not pick up the brown envelope he left among the pamphlets.

Two much-thumbed tickets on Aeroflot fall out as I slowly heave the concept from one part of my brain to another, seeking an outlet, but wholly unable to voice the tweet of triumph, knowing better, awaiting the bullet from some secret spyhole among the flags. What did the backs of the bomb-armers at the air force base say? "I am a bomb armer. If you see me running, try to catch up."

"Oh," I say aloud after a long pause of at least an afternoon, "the sweetness of Epicurus," little knowing where that phrase has come from. Ushered out of my trance by yet another flunkey, surely the stiff-faced executioner at last, I shuffle back, limping with both legs, into the entrance hallway and pocket the tickets, chattering to myself the gibberish of zeal. Svalocin must have repented, that vile cuckold, not wishing to have too foul a name in America, no doubt with his masochistic dumpling of a new wife. Dazed by clumping euphoria, I shove along against the tide of New Yorkers returning from lunch not in the trees, I bum-like, ecstatically addressing randomly chosen strangers with "She's out," and "It's over." "Change of heart," I tell them. Oh, but she must live in the neighboring town, not far from the Gulag, and receive no visitors. *Bastard*. I must put my maltreated body on a Russian stage and not be box-office poison.

Change of heart? Change of mind? If I am brilliance injured, as the *I Ching* says, I must go. I point myself at southern Central Park, and fly.

On looking back, as we tend to do overmuch, we find it hard to overestimate the shock of going to a strange culture, then returning to our own, or, as in my own case, going to a strange culture mysteriously equipped with estrogen designed to be spread on Stalin's carrots, then being deported to an even stranger subculture, then returned home, after which off to Russia again. At its own slow speed, the head twirls. Surely, I argued with myself, it would be just as easy to poison as to feminize him. Still, the agency always had secrets that its agents never knew. You enter a cluttered office, and wonder how to keep mind straight amidst all this, but that is the triumph, surely. You enter an uncluttered office and ask yourself How, with so little of the external world in view, think in a worldly fashion in here? But that is the triumph too. It is the random details that occupy the brain after the massif of memory has let you down: the Gulag survivor who, as Head Slavic Bibliographer, haunted several Ivy League campuses dressed in black and Wellington boots, murmuring about the so-called Gulag canapé, consisting on a worm-eaten rye wafer plastered with the mingled smegma of uncircumcised prisoners. It was offered to the guards as a delicacy, like Brie with a hint of Camembert. He was found self-hanged, still in his oilskins and boots, on each of the campuses he haunted.

Ah, memory, the temptation to call the treehouse Ann Arbor! Resisted. The effort and expense to procure Bimini a passport. The constant worry about the tree surgeons of December, and then April: abolishers of home sweet home. The high palmy days back in Moscow, making money for the eventually permitted trip to see her at long last, *dúshenka*, with me cutting littler and littler snippets off my naked body in front of seething Muscovites long denied the uncouth theatrical (no overcoats in the auditorium, please, except in the cinema; all those *dezhurnayas*, keepers of the hotel keys; what a hidebound society). I was box-office ambrosia, but not allowed into circuses to frighten the children; for me, the late-night *boîte*, the zone of *noir*, with the new Moscow drunks bellowing for blood and flesh. Would we ever go back? Will we? Where will we be safer? For the time being, we play it by ear. Bimini, our treasured war criminal, is gradually picking up Russian and adores the contortions of her face when she looks in a mirror and tries to say *zdrastvuytye*. It is like living with a dolphin. I have heard it said the agency will come to our aid, but no approach has been made so far, and we prefer to keep clear of all investigative folk. I am back to translating, from the gossipiest of America's aviation magazines. My body heals. We eat well.

Grit keeps forming in the caruncles of both eyes. Is this sand from the sandman persecuting one who has overslept, willing the years to pass? Or is it the detritus of someone overaccustomed to cold, who never worried much about it even in Central Park in December. Out it comes on my fingertips, a narcoleptic's pepper; save it over the years and, after ten, you have a baby pea of it. I miss my old job just enough to want no return to it, although I relish pondering the foul-up when, because we had all kinds of wrong data about the MIG "Foxbat" (the 25) and its successor the "Alcohol

Container" (the 31), that we devised the F-15 to surpass it. How come, with such bright and inventive spirits as me squirreled away in the Soviet Union, we never found out the 31 was ultra-heavy, flew fast only in a straight line, and—I forget the rest. *Fubar*, I say, meaning fucked up beyond all recognition.

37. Russia, 1982

Sometimes, I tell myself, I have the steeped graciousness of a god in training. I write this in a foreign country, not my favorite but the one I have had most to do with, hence the self-glorification going on. One has to do something to impress the natives.

I'm not, by any stretch of the mind, mechanical, as now, prone on the fluffy prayer rug as I dub it in front of the Kalingrad-made "Diefenbaker Televizor" that's gone wrong with a big smut in its celestial eye. I know how to "reboot" it by unplugging for a few minutes and then plugging in again with the electrons all straightened out. I envision this box of stained rosewood with its oblate porthole as a shrine of sorts and would love to bring the divinity down to haunt it. Dream on, I tell myself; it must sometimes weary of being a mere conduit for electrons and pixels and so goes on strike. To my dismay: I do not want the ruptured tone, the scrambled jigsaw puzzle of Russian gone wrong, smudged or smeared. I want perfection without having to think about it.

And thereby hangs a tale. Call me Kiwi (or Kiji), name I try not to associate with a bird. I'd rather the TV screen were a pool of water, with Narcissus regarding his own chops, marveling that the reflection of the bookcase behind me enters the scene on the screen, layering a bookish veneer on scenes of lust and execution, especially during daylight.

In the never-ending debate I stage with myself, I claim to be a modern man, last century or this, attuned to the foibles of electricity, radio waves, and the Gorki Street post office. It's just that I don't own a computer, obsolete before it was born and a mare's nest of inconvenience thereafter. Nor do I drive. I have learned the jargon through (mouse, spam, and burn; lay rubber, hang a right, and pedal to the medal). I rate among my proudest moments my sang-froid stroll as I tootle from one imaginary computer to another, twirling my keys all the way across the parking lot. Watch me approaching just about any vehicle in sight at the sidewalk, insouciantly waggling my key. I could drive them all if I chose to. I yearn to belong, to the universe especially, like some old pharaoh, but instead I anxiously quiz airport staff about the availability of the Concord sky lounge of old.

A phoney, then? Like the Canadians who now own the hotels. No, not quite. If I had the money I would ape that Frog, Roussel or Russell, who used to sail away to see India or Malaysia, actually glimpse the coast from several miles away, then about-ship and sail home. He, Roussel or Russel, saw many countries in this way, actually making the trip but vouchsafing the fabled coast just a peek, on which he could dine out for months, populating the unseen lands with creatures from his fervent imagination. In the same way, he would squint through telescopes and conjure up extraordinary Martians.

A visionary then?

A seer's more likely.

I mean someone prey to the faint importunings of untutored eloquence, rather too fancy for this world, in which he nonetheless leads a rather primitive existence, eating fruit from cans with a steak knife, heaping fried potatoes into his sandwiches. Obliged to be here, rather than India or Mars, he is afraid to weigh down the world with his thumbprint, relieved only not to have such a long name as Mister Kurfurstendam or Mynheer Theodopolostoukos.

A silkworm gossips to me what others would not know: The silence in our lives we carry with us from place to place, oasis to wen, wen to oasis, like a golden eggshell in whose recesses we catch the faint bruit of peristalsis, the timeworn snuffle of the heart, the vexed creak of muscle. Whether we have gasped at some swivel in a bullfight, or ducked a wave during *La Mer*, we retain and cherish the silence of a winter snow when all shovelers have ceased. This is Russia after all. A provincial town famous for coal and a slave-built railroad to Moscow, population easily one hundred thousand, all short of entertainment, gross or prim.

All this renews me, telling me there exists some thing not yet revealed to human kind, some eternal object already a plaything of the gods, just maybe on the verge of entering among us. Sometimes I call this thing that leans over us, and impends, a caustic shadow, at other times a hesitation tremor, as if the gods could not make up their minds. They doodle, we worry. They twiddle their thumbs and we worry ourselves to death. I just want to warn you that, now and then, like camels gliding past your tent in the desert night, certain things will come sneaking up out of nowhere, unauthorized but defiant, demanding attention yet fitting no class: the loin-shaped cloud, the two-stroke tiger, the thorny bicycle. You are in for a ride. You are in it for the ride. As when, absently cupping your elbow, you find that two fingers splayed fit exactly into grooves that flank the elbow itself, as if there since the year dot, the purpose unknown, but perhaps that is how we were once folded in the womb, or led one another over the savannas, spliced at the elbow, or, groping in the roaring nights, found courage in the little notch, before the heart-spoon became all the rage.

Thanks to a fluttery tendency in my fingers and, in my soul, huge swells of emotion, I have always thought I was meant to be a pianist, which I guess is a sentimental, shallow view of that art. In that way, I conclude, I would have been able to bring into the world the things that keep hovering on the brink, somewhere near what I call the Invisible Riviera of the Visible World. No such luck, though. I never learned to read music, even, but, hurrah for me, did not flounce away and found my own Nazi part in revenge. The desire to produce the goods never left me, though, and no doubt never will. It is something related to music, I know that much, and possibly mathematics, although I can no more count than I can tickle the ivories. Perhaps it is a music that will teach us how to want to die. But perhaps I will only, after all my various employments at the level of well-read menial, discover that in Ancient Rome public toilets had a sponge fastened to the end of a stick that sat in a bucket of brine. Wealthy Romans used wool and rosewater. *We* live in couch-potato squalor here, as the law requires.

Well, you're just about ready for it now. You'll notice I address an absent lady in affectionate terms, a Gulag trick I learned that sweetened all ordeals, almost medieval in its succulent gush. If she is or is not there, you'll find out; she's used to gentle handling, so be careful. Be blithe with us both, and any others on the way. Kiwi White out. More from Russia follows.

38. Why So Large a Vagina?

I am best, I have discovered, when I have something to do, something that has been assigned, preferably for money. Then I can fend off those tangents and ricochets that blight my daily life around the recognition that I am not leading the right life, but what on earth would that be? I feel perniciously scattered, having mustered and wasted all my powers of concentration back in the Gulag, gnawing on grass soup, if you *can* gnaw on a soup. When my mind wanders, I find out what I prefer, if given half a chance. For instance, I own (inasmuch as I own anything much) a tinny, decrepit radio smaller than my hand, which will play only one station, the classical music; from long abuse, it has frozen internally and cannot be redeemed. I find that I have no interest in fine-tuning anything else, am perfectly willing to listen to whatever they dish out, mostly golden oldies. The batteries give out every month, but I like the radio best when it's failing and the sound begins to blur and get ragged, distorting the music, as if an entire civilization is running down, which it is. Those rumbling, grating noises-off please me no end, especially when the music seems to be coming uncertainly from Mars. You see, I have renegade tastes; I *want* things that go wrong.

A near parallel, altogether more intimate than a mere radio, but on a related theme, is the hand-held CD player, like a scallop shell, akin I always think to the diaphragm case to be found in the purses of most women. Why so large a vagina, Ma'am? I wonder, have you been measured? My experience of sex with humans is woefully limited, and no better with animals, but I do have a lingering sense of proportion, and the remains of a once-acute spatial sense. I know these things are too big for the zone they serve, or the impedimenta they house; but in my mind, alongside the waning, limited radio, they have a garish cartoon existence. Only a shred of me inhabits the so-called real world; I have too vivid a recall of a world made of sand, ice, corrugated iron, sacking, pocked enamel, barbed wire, and acrid soup. So, you might say, he has no real footing in history, except of a specialized kind.

Scratchy music.

Elephantine diaphragms.

What a basis for life!

And there is more of course as the undeployed man lives from day to day, assimilating a scrap of this, a relic of that, maybe in hope of cobbling together a real world from it, but mostly enduring on the periphery. Spoiled Chopin as we tup. Vagina needs widening like certain throats. A new radio and a normal-sized woman would help, but it's all beyond me. I accept what I have.

The Ice Lens

Let me add one more thing. (How could you stop me, anyway?) At home, or rather at hovel, bibbing syrup from a can of sliced pears, I have to be careful not to slice my face on the vestigially attached lid with its sawteeth edge. By all means winkle out the slices with a fork or pointed knife, but to tilt the can to pour the syrup brings a severed lid close to your eyes. One slip and you have only one eye to gamble with. So this adds a frisson of danger to the eating act, which can also be had from cans of red salmon or asparagus. My own technique is to bend the lid all the way backwards until it meets the body of the can, well out of sight, a flimsily attached flange. Slashes up by the eyes rarely heal well, not that I have been so unlucky. One day I will make the grand conversion to bowls and plates; what holds me back is a sense of hunting: wrestling with the can reclaims, for me anyway, the old sense of adventure—picking the fruit live, fighting bears for sprightly red salmon. That kind of thing. One could, I suppose, cut one's upper face to ribbons, then pass the scars off as fending trophies from an earlier, more Germanic era. Items for further thought, these, saved-up cravings from the Gulag time (no cans), then put into practice later as if civilization had only just begun, long before twist-offs with a key or peel-offs with a loop.

As you see, I am not much of a soul to send anywhere to do much of a job: kidnap, whack, steal, clean up, bring home the bacon of one kind or another. Sending me out on any such errand (go and occupy Burma) would be like sending a widow woman to slap Jack Dempsey. But show me where to stand or kneel, and I'm a pip, I really am. I have the smarts, but not the ferocious zeal of the Skorzenys, say, he who sallied forth and captured Mussolini way back when.

    I respond to these events as if they were yesterday's. Nothing fades or withers. Everything done remains in the present, if you see my drift. Let us envision an ant crushed in a wad of Kleenex, then the wad used to soak up a spill or asparagus liquid. Is this the only way the ant has of testing its waterworks, just like a human? As you know, the faster the asparagus perfume, beloved of Proust, comes through, the more effective your kidneys are supposed to be. Now *that* is information right up my alley as I stand or squat in the sun, leaning against my skimmer, my mind asleep on how rubber bands, dried by summer then sapped and snapped by winter's bony fingers, abandon all constraint and greet your fingers with dry strings and little attached squares of sticky rubber. One day I hope to bring together all the quiddities of a single instant's perception, after which there will be nothing to say.

39. So

I am to meet her at long last not at the gate or in the street, but at a squalid-looking little beer stand, as if we were teenagers somehow disguising a first date. I almost hiccup as I realize that is what it will be. She is late, fifteen minutes or so, but so what? One moment there is a dumpy couple buying beer, this in early winter with a nip in the air, then, like some newly arrived ghost, there is a woman in drab clothes badly affixed to her frame, leaning against the wall of the little hut. I never saw her arrive and take station. Rather than a body she has a wooden frame, all straight lines and corners, an unbecoming tan suggesting jaundice, in her hand a crumpled handkerchief squashed into a white rose; mere struts for legs, on her feet clodhoppers that might have doubled as sabots. I recognize none of her, even though she manages a feeble wave that consists of one arm drooping. I do not move or wave. This phantom, I instruct myself, has not of late, like the other prisoners in special detention (you will ultimately get all the news when living in a camp's town) had cottage cheese, milk, walks, scissors, thread, flowers, use of the formal personal pronoun, all of which at the time caused me much relief. She has not been treated that well at all, thanks to Svalocin, vindictive to the end.

I nonetheless lumber toward her. She straightens. We aim at each other, step sideways into each other in that motion for which we do not have a name, recover and stammer something, after too many years.

"Well!" She is all gristle.

"Here I am," she says in Russian, with trapped breath.

It is a hopeless conversation as we stare around us to see who might be watching, just to pull us back behind the razor wire. No one. A hug forms itself, each looking past the other. Full, I take it, of feelings about coming full circle, we seem paralyzed by history. Later, I will rate myself according to the old Egyptian custom of pelting with pebbles the man who has cut the corpse's belly open; he runs away, part of the ritual. What dreadful thing have I done to bring her to this? A gaunt, leathery, almost dwarfed crone confronts me to echoes of my *golúbchik, dúsha, dúshenka.* Even if I were to take refuge in the whole of music and literature for the rest of my days, I would never get over this apparition. These endearments are the words she is babbling through her tears, and how long has she saved *those* up? We will never attempt endearments again, never mind how holy they seemed in the vacuum of apartness.

Like the puffed-out hair breath of horses in cartoons, the stuffing of our couch bulges out as we three sit to our nightly chore: I in one corner, my *dúshenka* lying full length on her back, Bimini crouched on the floor, eyeing naked feet, black and scaly. We have soaped and scrubbed and scraped, soaked the ravished skin in Gardener's Delight (from Saskatoon, Saskatchewan where the feet need it), mopped and massaged, until some vestige of life returned. Now she can wriggle her toes. Bimini takes all this in her stride, so much so that she will not complain until we head back to Leningrad or Moscow, where I will resume my travesty of a thousand cuts. Here we are podiatrists. Our client says nothing, just lies back and sighs in catatonic relief. First the rough file, then the smooth, dusting away the calluses. We have already clipped and trimmed the nails. A bottle of *Frosty Murmansk Corral* (misspelled) waits, like pink typing fluid, brush and all. We say nothing about years. It takes eons to talk about them. Now she purrs as I shift to the super-smooth file, making not dust but heat. No matter how many times we wash and tend her feet, they will never quite perform again; how could she ever have survived in Central Park? She says they creak and tingle, as they would, and we are addressing them only, with selective tenderness, her hands next.

After all that abrading and cleansing, scrubbing and honing, with her feet coming back into the region of dankest white, something else comes to light in a deeply incised wrinkle behind her left big toe, impossible to identify unless you have made a study of it: hunched or humped, actually stirring into motion after years of immobility. Some of these tardigrades, so-called, stand inert for a hundred years, awaiting the conjurer's touch of moisture to twitch back to life. Infinitesimal, less than a millimeter in length, this creature has lodged in the crack in her toe skin and stayed put for much of her twenty-year sentence, undergoing everything with her, though better equipped than she with its staghorn coral head, its claws on all eight feet, the severe shell on its back. Through the tiny magnifying glass built into the cap of my fountain pen (a Russian "Boatman"), I peer at its ragged morphology, its elephantine folds of chitinous stuff, and wonder at the finds the Gulags can create. It is almost as if the human were sentenced for harboring so dead-seeming a creature, which for so long has resisted all touches of water until this final immersion. Otherwise known to some as the slow-step or, how Russian, the water bear.

"A great writer."
—Hector Bianciotti, front page, *Le Monde*

"One of the most consistently brilliant lyrical writers in America... [West is] possibly our finest living stylist in English."
—*The Chicago Tribune*

"West has been for several decades one of the most consistently brilliant writers in America. His aim seems to be the rendition of an American odyssey analogous to Joyce's union of mythic elements in which earth-mother, shaper-father and offspring, as well as the living and the dead, all achieve communion. The language is Paul West at his best.... shows perfect pitch."
—Frederick Busch, *Chicago Tribune*

"West, prolific novelist and critic, is a literary high-wire artist, performing awe-inspiring aerial feats with language while the rest of us gape up at him in dumb amazement."
—*The Boston Globe*

"Out on those risky ledges where language is continually fought for and renewed—that's where Paul West breathes the thin, necessary air."
—Sven Birkerts, *American Energies*

"A rich, often astonishing meditation upon how a particular human culture can represent a source of 'otherness'—imagination itself—that persists even in a world that other modes of thought and desire have made almost uninhabitable."
—Thomas R. Edwards, *The New York Times Book Review*

"Paul West's epic touches upon the most powerful human themes—the meaning of home, the desecration of war, the quest for a curative past out of spiritual exile."
—Bradford Morrow, *Trinity Fields*

"West's enormous pastiche of yarn-spinning, meditation and sheer wordplay is precisely the sort of work that can help us understand the ways in which we approach and avoid the realities of being human.... Paul West is a worthy custodian of a time-honored tradition."
—Alida Becker, *The Philadelphia Inquirer*

"West's astonishing new novel, which maps the lives of Indians in the American Southwest, reveals a Joycean genius in its exuberant play of language, and its epic and mythic resonances.... West's prose, dazzling in its fecundity, affirms the erotic nature of the literary act."
—*Publisher's Weekly*

"Intoxicated by the novel's unparalleled capacity to connect life and ideas in an unholy mix, he likes fireworks in his fiction, the blow-torch of art that brings reality to the boiling point.... Thorough, passionate, opinionated—West never lets his judgments interfere with his considerable ability to evoke the texture and character of the work under review."
—*Washington Post Book World*

"A writer of distinction and originality."
—The Los Angeles Times

"West is an original and daring writer...he has never written anything so risky and triumphant."
—Richard Eder, *Los Angeles Time Book Review*

"No contemporary American prose writer can touch him for sustained rhapsodic invention—he creates a hyperbolic hymn to joy, a swashbuckling swirl of sentences. West stands as an authentic voice in the wilderness, a visionary who plugs the ghosts of history and morality into his textural dream machines."
—*Boston Phoenix*

"In his many works of fiction, memoir, and criticism, West proves himself to be a writer blessed with a cheerfully mordant wit, an acrobatic way with words, ebullient learnedness, and a deep if wry perception of the human

condition. Each previous *Sheer Fiction* volume has offered pleasure, revelation, and provocation, and now, in West's fourth collection of biting literary essays, he again covers a remarkable breadth and complexity of terrain."
—A.L.A. *Booklist*

"West argues passionately for a literature that reveals brilliant minds at work shaping it, that incorporates the world we know today—quantum physics, computer technology.... [His] argument is likely to provoke much disagreement, especially from the academic community... Yet his argument needs to be heard. ...*Sheer Fiction* demands the attention of any reader seriously interested in the purposes of fiction."
—*Wilson Library Bulletin*

"This kind of infectious enthusiasm is rare to the point of non-existence among modern critics. ...Sheer pleasure."
—*Kirkus Reviews*

"The inimitable, brilliant Paul West never ceases to amaze. *Love's Mansion,* orchestrated with Proustian care, offers unforgettable episodes of familial dark and light, bittersweet recollections activated by empathy and sexual awareness. A revelatory book of extraordinary power."
—Walter Abish

"*The Tent of Orange Mist* is a bold, shocking book, filled with cynical brilliance and sensual power."
—*The Boston Review*

"Paul West is one of American literature's most serious and penetrating historical novelists. *The Tent of Orange Mist* is a gorgeous assertion of human life."
—*The San Francisco Chronicle*

"If there are no 'men of letters' any more, there are innumerable figures writing now…who move easily among the fictional, the confessional, the polemical, and the critical. If Paul West is not the most conspicuous of such a group, he is the most stylish and intelligent."
—*Journal of Modern Literature*

"A towering astonishing creation."
—Irving Malin, *Pynchon and Mason & Dixon*

"Paul West's book is transformative. West's immense narrative gift has transformed a traumatic historical event into art. He has re-imagined experience and made literature from it. His book will live."
—Hugh Nissenson, *The Song of the Earth*

"It takes a writer like Paul West to explore the deep psychic lacerations occasioned by [9.11]… Anyone who thinks he or she knows

anything about that harrowing moment should read this novel; it will change their perceptions forever."
—David W. Madden, *Understanding Paul West*

"West's phenomenal command of language and the flux of consciousness, and his epic sense of the significance of 9.11 are staggering in their verve, astuteness, and resonance."
—Donna Seaman, *Booklist magazine*

"Not since Proust's *Albertine disparue* has a novel explored the subject of anguish and loss with such unflinching persistency and such annihilating force. This book will have you on tenterhooks and will break your heart."
—Mark Seinfelt, *Final Drafts*

"Paul West, among our more formidable literary intelligences, is not afraid to take risks. His ability to give original expression to complicated ideas about culture and personality is gargantuan. *The Place In Flowers Where Pollen Rests* presents a stunning, hyperbolic vision of men between cultures, between darkness and light, groping for authenticity."
—Dan Cryer, *Newsday*

"Extraordinary in its scope, inventiveness, and prose.... spectacular writing."
—Gail Pool, *Cleveland Plain Dealer*

"An exciting and evocative tale of love and treason."
—Andrew Ervin, *The Philadelphia Inquirer*

"While this biting, scatological tour de force will appeal mostly to West fans and more experimental poetry readers (many of whom are already West fans), it deserves a prominent place in poetry collections."
—Rochelle Ratner, *Library Journal*

"An exhilarating collection.... West's genuine excitement for this fiction is contagious and his own language is as splendid."
—*Review of Contemporary Fiction*

"[This novel] thrusts us into a rich domestic situation that reflects the complexities of our century like a prism. *Love's Mansion* is the late 20th century's contribution to the great, classical love novels of history."
—Elena Castedo

"[*The Tent of Orange Mist*] is both a terror and a joy to read."
—Kathryn Harrison

"The rest of us will despair of ever being able to write prose so immaculate as that of Paul West."
—Jonathan Yardley

"Most intriguing is the overarching narration told by Osiris, god of the Nile, who comments on this swarm of events with hilarious and humane authority. Profound and entertaining, *Cheops: A Cupboard for the Sun* is perhaps Paul West's greatest novel yet."
—J. M. Adams

"West, a writer of finesse, amplitude, and wit...describes his father in startlingly tactile detail as he recounts the wrenching war stories his father told him.... West's sensitivity to the vagaries of temperament is exquisite, his tenderness deeply moving. Writing of wars past in a time of war, West creates a portrait of his father that has all the richness of Rembrandt as it evokes the endless suffering wars precipitate."
—Donna Seaman, *Booklist*

"For beautiful sentences fed on brainpower, there is perhaps no other contemporary writer who can match him."
—Albert Mobilio, *Salon.com, Reader's Guide to Contemporary Authors*

CPSIA information can be obtained at www.ICGtesting.com
Printed in the USA
LVOW06s0721070814

397824LV00004B/7/P